"The world seemed to change that night, as though we'd become different people."

"Yes, that's true. I no longer really know what to think about anything."

"Is that why you refuse to marry me?"

"I haven't actually refused. I just can't take it for granted the way you did. I don't like being given orders."

"That's not what I did."

"But it is. You just assumed I'd jump at the chance to marry you. How arrogant is that?" She gave a brief laugh. "I once looked up your name and found that Leonizio means 'lionlike.' That says it all about you. The lion rules the plains, and Leonizio thinks he can rule wherever he likes."

Briefly she wondered if she was wise to risk offending him, but his smile contained only wry amusement.

"Except for the lioness," he said. "She could stand up to him better than anyone else."

She nodded. "As long as he understands that."

EXPECTING THE FELLANI HEIR

BY

LUCY GORDON

MILLS & BOON

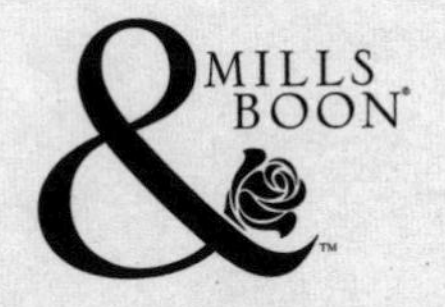

First Published in Great Britain 2016
By Mills & Boon, an imprint of HarperCollins*Publishers*
1 London Bridge Street, London, SE1 9GF

ISBN: 978-0-263-91994-3

23-0616

Our policy is to use papers that are natural, renewable and recyclable products and made from wood grown in sustainable forests. The logging and manufacturing processes conform to the legal environmental regulations of the country of origin.

Printed and bound in Spain
by CPI, Barcelona

Lucy Gordon cut her writing teeth on magazine journalism, interviewing many of the world's most interesting men. She's had many unusual experiences, which have often provided the background for her books. Once, while staying in Venice, she met a Venetian who proposed in two days and they've been married ever since. Naturally this has affected her writing, in which romantic Italian men tend to feature strongly. Two of her books have won a Romance Writers of America RITA® Award. You can visit her website at www.lucy-gordon.com.

CHAPTER ONE

Afterwards Ellie always remembered the day when things really started to happen, when the sky glowed, the universe trembled to its foundations and nothing was ever the same again.

It began gloomily, a cold February morning with the traffic in a jam, delaying her as she drove to work. Drumming her fingers against the steering wheel, she drew in sharp breaths of exasperation.

The world would call her a successful woman, a highly qualified lawyer employed by one of London's most notable legal practices. To be late for work should have been beneath her. But it was happening.

When she finally arrived, Rita, her young secretary, greeted her with agitation.

'The boss has been asking about you every minute.'

The boss was Alex Dallon, founder and head of Dallon Ltd. He was an efficient, demanding man, and it was no small achievement that Ellie had earned his favour.

'Is he annoyed because I'm late?' Ellie asked.

'A bit. Signor Fellani called to say he was coming in this morning and Mr Dallon doesn't have time to see him.'

'I wasn't aware that Signor Fellani had an appointment.'

'No, but you know him. He just announces he's coming.'

'And we all have to jump to it,' Ellie groaned.

'I wouldn't mind jumping for him,' Rita declared longingly. 'He's gorgeous!'

'That's not the point,' Ellie told her, severely but kindly. 'Looks aren't everything.'

'His are,' Rita sighed.

'No man's are,' Ellie said firmly.

Rita's response was a cynical look that Ellie understood. She knew exactly how she appeared to her secretary. Rita was a pretty, vivacious young woman with an eager interest in finding 'the one'. Ellie was a successful, efficient woman in her late thirties, with no husband or lover. Rita would clearly see that as a fate to avoid. To her, a man as attractive as Leonizio Fellani was not merely a client, but a dream to sigh over.

Ellie could understand how naïve Rita could fall for him. He was a man nobody could overlook, in his early thirties, with black hair and dark eyes that drew instant attention. He had a tall, athletic build and moved with a masculine grace that drew many eyes towards him. His face, she conceded, was handsome, although too often marred by tension.

Just once she had seen him smile, and there had been a glimpse of the kinder man he might have been. But it was over in a moment as the unyielding side of his nature took over again.

She herself ignored male attractions. There had been moments in her past when she had weakened, which was how she thought of it. But things hadn't worked out and she'd gathered her defences again.

Her appearance disappointed her. Her face was pleasant but not strikingly pretty. She possessed only one outstanding feature. Her hair. If she wore it long it could appear lush and wildly wavy. But she chose to scrape it back, tying the length into a bun at the back.

Businesslike, she often thought, regarding herself sadly in the mirror. *Nobody is going to sigh over those looks.*

She tended to judge herself severely. Many women would have envied her slender figure, but she considered herself too thin and overly angular. It was her nature to be realistic about her own lack of conventional attractions. Unlike Rita, she would never sigh over a handsome man like Signor Fellani.

He was an important client, wealthy, Italian, strong-minded. Curiosity had inspired Ellie to look up his name and she'd discovered that Leonizio meant 'lion-like'. It suited his commanding ways, she reckoned.

He had made a fortune manufacturing shoes. His luxurious, elegant products sold all over the world, especially in the UK. Just across the road from Ellie's office was a large store that sold them in great numbers.

His base was in Rome, but he employed this London firm to handle the divorce from his English wife. Alex Dallon liked Ellie to deal with this client often because her grandmother had been Italian and she had a basic knowledge of the language. Not that she ever needed to use it. Signor Fellani's command of English was like everything else about him: precise and efficient.

'Has there been any more mail from his wife's lawyers?' Ellie asked. 'The last I heard was that she was refusing to budge about custody of their baby.'

'But since she's left him and the child hasn't been born yet, she's bound to get custody,' Rita pointed out.

'I'm not looking forward to telling him that. Anything significant in the mail?'

'Not that I've seen so far, but I haven't opened them all yet. I'll check.'

She vanished and Ellie went to her desk. Taking out the Fellani file, she glanced quickly through the papers, reminding herself of the details.

Three years earlier, Signor Fellani had made a whirlwind marriage with Harriet Barker, an Englishwoman he'd met while she was on holiday in his native city, Rome. But after the initial excitement died the marriage had suffered. When Harriet finally discovered that she was pregnant she had left him, coming back to England.

He'd followed her, insisting that she return to him, and, when she refused, he'd demanded joint custody of the unborn child. This she also refused.

Harriet must be a woman of great courage, Ellie thought. Leonizio was an autocrat, a man who demanded obedience and knew how to get it. In their few meetings he had treated her with cool courtesy, but she had always sensed an underlying steeliness. To the wife who was defying him he might be terrifying, but perhaps that was why she was so determined to escape him.

Rita appeared in the doorway, holding out a letter.

'He's going to create merry hell when he reads this,' she said.

Ellie read it with mounting dismay. It was from Harriet's lawyers.

Your client must understand that he has no rights over this child, because it is not his. His wife left him because she had found another partner and become pregnant. Now a DNA test has proved that the child she is carrying is not her husband's.

She is anxious to conclude the divorce as soon as possible so that she can marry the child's father before the birth.

Please persuade Signor Fellani to see sense.

A copy of the paperwork for the DNA test was enclosed. There was no doubt that the baby had been fathered by the other man.

'Oh, heavens!' she sighed. 'What a dreadful thing to have to tell him.'

'Especially today,' Rita said.

'Why, what's different about today?'

'It's Valentine's Day. The day for lovers, when they celebrate the joy of their love.'

'Oh, no!' Ellie groaned. 'I'd forgotten the date. You're right. But he's Italian. Perhaps they don't celebrate Valentine's Day in Italy. I hope not because that would really rub it in.'

A noise from outside made her glance through the window. She saw a taxi draw up, and Signor Fellani get out. She went to wait for him in her office, longing for this soon to be over.

A few moments later he appeared at her door, his face stern and purposeful.

'I'm sorry to spring this meeting on you without warning,' he said, 'but something has happened that changes everything.'

Did that mean he already knew?

'I went to see Harriet yesterday evening,' he continued. 'I believed we could talk things over properly; find a way to make a future together for the sake of our child. But she wasn't there. She's gone, and not left an address. Why? Why pick this moment to run away from me?'

So he didn't know, Ellie realised, her heart sinking. The next few minutes were going to be terrible.

'She obviously doesn't feel able to talk,' she said. 'Perhaps you should just accept that it's over.'

'Over between her and me, but not between me and my child,' he retorted swiftly.

She hesitated, dismayed at the disaster that was heading their way. Sensing her unease, he spoke more quietly.

'You probably think I'm being unreasonable about this; pursuing a woman who doesn't want me. Why don't I just let her go? But it's not that simple. I can let *her* go, but not the baby. There's a connection there that nothing can break, and if she thinks she's going to make me a stranger to my own child, she's wrong. I'll never let that happen.'

Ellie wanted to cry out, to make him stop at all costs. Never before had this hard man revealed his feelings so frankly, and her heart ached at the thought of how she was about to hurt him.

'I need you to find her,' he said. 'Her lawyers won't tell me where she is but you can get it out of them.'

'I'm afraid it wouldn't help,' she said heavily.

'Of course it would help. They tell you, you tell me, and I go to see her and make her stop this nonsense.'

'No!' Ellie clenched her fists. 'It isn't nonsense. I'm sorry, I hate to tell you this, but I have to.'

'Tell me what?'

She took a deep breath and forced herself to say, 'The baby isn't yours.'

Silence. She wondered if he'd actually heard her.

'What did you say?' he asked at last.

'She's carrying another man's child. I only found out myself just now. It's all in this letter.'

She handed him the letter from his wife's lawyer, and tried to read his expression as he read it. But his face was blank. At last he gave a snort.

'So this is her latest trick. Does she think to fool me?'

'It's not a trick. She had a DNA test done and that proves it.'

'A DNA test? But surely they can't be done before the child is born? It's too dangerous.'

'That was true once. But recently new techniques have been developed, and it can be done safely while a baby is still in the womb.'

'But they'd have needed to compare the child's DNA with mine. I haven't given a sample so they can't have.'

'They got a sample from the other man in her life and compared it with that,' Ellie said. 'The result was positive. I'm afraid there's no doubt he's the father. You'll find it here.'

He took the paper she held out. Ellie tensed, waiting for the storm to break. This man couldn't tolerate being defied, and the discovery of his soon-to-be ex-wife's treachery would provoke an explosion of temper.

But nothing happened. A terrible stillness had descended on him as he stared at the message that meant devastation to all his hopes. The colour drained from his face, leaving it with a greyish pallor that might have belonged to a dead man.

At last he spoke in a toneless voice. 'Can I believe the test?'

'I know the lab that did it,' she said. 'They are completely reliable. I'm afraid it's true.'

Suddenly he turned away and slammed his fist down on the desk.

'Fool!' he raged. *'Fool!'*

Her temper rose. 'So you think I'm a fool for telling you what you don't want to know?'

'Not you,' he snapped. '*Me!* To be taken in by that woman and her cheap tricks—I must be the biggest fool in creation.'

Her anger faded. His self-blame took her by surprise.

His back was still turned to her, but the angle of the window caught his face. It was only a faint reflection, but she managed to see that he had closed his eyes.

He was more easily hurt than she'd suspected. And his way of coping was to retreat deep inside himself.

But perhaps a little sympathy could still reach him. Gently she touched his arm.

'I know this is hard for you,' she began.

'Nothing I can't cope with,' he said firmly, drawing

away from her. 'It's time I was going. You know where I'm staying?'

'Yes.' She named the hotel.

'Send my bill there and I'll go as soon as it's paid. Sorry to have troubled you.'

He gave her a brief nod and departed, leaving her feeling snubbed. One brief expression of sympathy had been enough to make him flee her. But then, she reflected, he hadn't become a successful businessman by allowing people to get close. For his wife he'd made an exception, and it had been a shattering mistake.

Ellie got back to work, setting out his bill then working out a response to the lawyer's letter. It took her a few minutes to write a conventional reply, but when she read it through she couldn't be satisfied. Something told her that Signor Fellani would dislike the restrained wording.

Yet is there any way to phrase this that wouldn't annoy him? she wondered. *He seems to spend his whole life on the verge of a furious temper. Still, I suppose I can hardly blame him now.*

She rephrased the letter and considered it critically.

I should have done this while he was here, she mused. *Then I could have got his agreement to it. Perhaps I'd better go and see him now, and get this settled.*

She went to find Rita.

'I have to leave. I need to talk to Signor Fellani again. My goodness! Look at the weather.'

'Snowing fit to bust,' Rita agreed, glancing out of the window. 'I don't envy you driving in that.'

'Nor do I. But it has to be done.'

She hurried outside to where her car was parked, and turned onto the route that led to the hotel. It was about a mile away, and the last hundred yards took her along the River Thames. Driving slowly because of the snow, she glanced at the pavement, and tensed at what she saw.

He was there by the wall, staring out over the river. A pause in the traffic gave her time to study him as he stood, wrapped in some private world, oblivious to his surroundings, unaware of the snow engulfing him.

She found a space to park, then hurried across the road to Leonizio.

'Signore!' she called. 'I was on my way to your hotel. It's lucky I happened to notice you here.'

He regarded her, and she had a strange sensation that he didn't recognise her through the snow.

'It's me,' she said. 'Your lawyer. We have business to discuss. My car's waiting over there.'

'Then we'd better go before you catch your death of cold.'

'Or you catch yours,' she retorted. 'You're soaking.'

'Don't bother about me. Let's go.'

She led him across the road to where two cars were parked, one shabby, one new and clearly expensive. He headed for the shabby one.

'Not that one,' Ellie called, opening the door of the luxury vehicle. 'Over here.'

'This?' he demanded in disbelief. 'This is yours?'

Obviously he felt that the decrepit little wreck was more her style, she thought, trying not to be offended.

'I like to own a nice car,' she said coolly. 'Get in.'

He did so, and sat in silence while she took the wheel and drove to the hotel. As she pulled into the car park he said, 'You're shivering. You got wet.'

'I'll be all right when I get home. But first I must come in and show you the letter I wrote to your wife's lawyer.'

The Handrin Hotel was famed for its luxury, and as she entered it she could understand why. The man who could afford to stay here was hugely successful.

They took the elevator up to his opulent suite on the top

floor. Now she could see him more clearly and was even more dismayed by his condition.

'I'm not the only one who's wet,' she said. 'You were standing too long in that snow. Your hair's soaking. Better dry it at once, and change your clothes.'

'Giving me orders?' he asked wryly.

'Protecting your interests, which is what I'm employed to do. Now get going.'

He vanished, reappearing ten minutes later in dry clothes. He handed her a towel and with relief she undid her hair, letting it fall about her shoulders so that she could dry it. When he joined her on the sofa she handed him the bill, and the letter she planned to write to his wife's lawyer.

'I suppose I'll have to agree to it,' he said at last. 'It doesn't say what I really think, but it might be better not to say that too frankly.'

'You'd really like to commit murder, wouldn't you?' she said.

He regarded her with wry appreciation.

'A woman who understands me. You're perfectly right, but don't worry. I'm not going to do anything stupid. You won't have to defend me in court.'

His grin contained a rare glimpse of real humour which she gladly returned, enjoying the sensation of suddenly connecting with him in both thoughts and feelings.

'I'm glad,' she said. 'I'm not sure I'd be up to that task.'

'Oh, I think you'd be up to anything you set your mind to. Can I offer you a drink?'

Ellie knew she should refuse; she should get this meeting over and done with as quickly as possible. But she still had to get his agreement to send the letter. And she was freezing. A hot drink would be very welcome.

'I'd love a cup of tea, please.'

He called Room Service and placed an order. While

they waited she watched while he read through the papers again.

'How do you feel about the answer I planned to send to your wife's lawyer?' she said.

'It's a damned sight too polite. But you haven't sent it yet?'

'No. I thought we should talk first.'

'And what are you going to advise me to do?'

'Go ahead with the divorce as quickly as possible.'

'So that she can marry the father and make the child legitimate? Her lawyer said that in his letter, didn't he? And he told you to persuade me to 'see sense'.

'I wish he hadn't said that—'

'But that's how lawyers think,' he said bitterly. 'Let my treacherous wife have her way, no matter what it does to me. That's seeing sense, isn't it?'

'Don't be unfair. I don't see everything like that.'

'I think you do. After all, you're a lawyer.'

'Yours, not hers. If things were different we could try to make *her* see sense, but she's pregnant by another man and there's nothing to be done about it. The best advice I can offer you is to put her into the past and move on with your life.'

Before he could answer, the doorbell rang and he went to collect the delivery of tea and cakes. He laid the tray on a table near the sofa, sat down beside her and poured tea for her.

'Thank you,' she said. 'I needed this.'

She sipped the hot tea, feeling better at once.

'How come you were standing by the river?' she asked. 'Did the taxi drop you there?'

'I didn't take a taxi. I walked all the way. And don't say it.'

'Say what?'

'*In this weather? Are you mad?* That's what you're thinking. It's written all over your face.'

'Then I don't need to say it. But you've had a terrible shock. You were bound to go a bit crazy.'

'Like I said before, I was a fool.'

'Don't blame yourself,' she said gently. 'You loved her—'

'Which makes me an even bigger fool,' he growled.

'Perhaps. But it's easy to believe someone if your heart longs to trust them.'

He looked at her with sudden curiosity. 'You talk as though you really know.'

She shrugged. 'I've had my share of relationship traumas.'

'Tell me,' he said quietly.

Her disastrous emotional life wasn't something she usually talked about, but with this man everything was different. The blow that had struck him down meant that he would understand her as nobody else understood. It was strange to realise that, but everything in the world was becoming different.

'Romance hasn't been a large part of my life,' she said.

'I guess your career comes first. Your car tells me that.'

It was true. The purchase of the glamorous vehicle had been one of her most delightful experiences.

'But there has been something, hasn't there?' he said. 'The path I'm treading is one you've travelled yourself.'

'Yes. There was a time when I thought things were going to be different. I allowed myself to have feelings for him and I thought he—well, it just didn't work out.'

'Didn't he love you?'

'I thought so. We seemed good together, but then he met this other woman—she was a great beauty. Long blonde hair, voluptuous figure—I didn't stand a chance.'

'And that was all he cared about? Looks?'

'So it seemed. Isn't that what all men care about?'

'Some. Not all.' He gave a brief cynical laugh. 'Some of us can see beyond looks to the person beneath: cold and self-centred or warm and kindly. Didn't this man see your warmer side? I can see it.'

'He didn't think it mattered, unless he could make use of it.'

She made a wry face. 'You said I'd travelled this road before you, and you were right. I don't normally talk about it, but at least now you know that this isn't just a lawyer "seeing sense". I really do have some idea of what you're going through. I know what it's like to be lied to, and to wonder afterwards how I could have been so naïve as not to see through it. But if you don't want to see through it—' She sighed.

'Yes,' he said heavily. 'If you don't want to face the truth, there's a great temptation to ignore it. You have to beware of that in business, and I suppose it's true of life as well.'

It was the last thing she had expected him to admit, but something about him had changed. He was speaking with a self-awareness that made him seem more pleasant. It was almost like talking to a different man, a kindly one who felt for her own pain as well as his own.

'I know this is all very hard for you,' she said.

He shrugged. 'I'll get through it.' But suddenly his voice changed, became weary. 'Oh, hell, who am I kidding? Can I call this managing? What she's done has destroyed the world. I wanted to be a father, to have someone who was really mine. My parents died when I was a child. I was adopted by an uncle and aunt who treated me properly but—well, we were never really close. I believed my wife and I were close, but that proved to be an illusion.

'Now I realise she was already sleeping with another man, but I never thought of it. Then, suddenly she was gone, demanding a divorce on the grounds that we were incompatible. I found out afterwards that she'd set spies on me to see if I had other women. But I hadn't. I'd been boringly faithful, which must really have disappointed her.'

'It certainly weakened her case,' Ellie agreed.

He gave a grunt of mirthless laughter.

'And she dumps this news on me on Valentine's Day. She could hardly have timed it more cynically.'

'Do you celebrate Valentine's Day in Italy?'

'A little. Not as much as you do in England, but enough to make me see the irony. The great day for lovers, except that it's smothered in snow, both physically and—well, there's more than one kind of snow.'

'Yes, it couldn't have worked out worse, could it?' she said sadly. 'I don't suppose she thought of that—'

'Of course not. She never thinks of anything except what suits her. But her pregnancy made it all different. The world changed. For the first time ever there was somebody who would be mine, connected to me in a way that nothing and nobody could deny. I told her that I couldn't let her go. She made a dash for it and came to England because she must have thought divorce would be easier, since we married over here.

'I followed her, determined to keep her, and if not her then at least my child. But now I learn that the baby's not even mine—'

'And I'm afraid it isn't,' Ellie murmured.

A tremor went through him. 'Then I have nothing.'

The way he said 'nothing' made her want to reach out to him.

'You think that now,' she said gently, 'but you'll come through it. There's always something else in life.'

'Only if you want something else. What I want is my child. Mine and only mine.'

He spoke like a man used to bending the world to his

will. But there was a blank despair in his face, as though even he knew that he couldn't control this situation.

She guessed that such helplessness was alien to him, and he was finding it frustrating. He was used to giving orders, demanding total subservience, which was why this left him at a loss. Ironically, the strength he was used to wielding had undermined him now. She felt a surge of pity for him.

'There are other things to care about,' she urged. 'You'll find them.'

But he shook his head. 'Nothing,' he said softly. 'Nothing.'

She gingerly placed a comforting hand on his shoulder. 'What will you do now?' she asked.

He sighed.

'Accept reality in a way I've never had to before.' He frowned. 'I'm good at arranging things the way I want, or at least persuading myself that I've done so.' He made a wry face. 'Meet the biggest self-deceiver in the world.'

'No, you're strong. And you'll be strong now.'

'Why are you so sure? You don't know me.'

'Do you know yourself?'

'I guess not,' he sighed. 'Oh, heavens!'

He dropped his head into his hands. Touched, Ellie drew him closer, enfolding him in both arms, her instinct to offer comfort to him overwhelming. He raised his head so that their eyes met, hers gentle and tender, his full of confusion and despair.

'That must be how it seems now,' she said gently. 'But your life isn't over. You'll meet someone who'll love you and give you a child. And the two of you will be united in that child for ever.'

'You make it sound so easy,' he whispered.

'When the time comes it will be easy,' she promised.

'For other men perhaps. Not for me. I said I didn't know

myself, but I do know a few things. I know I can come across as overbearing, so that even if I like a woman she recoils from me.'

His words caused a pain in her heart. Driven by an impulse she barely understood, she took his face in her hands.

'I'm not afraid of you,' she said softly. 'Life is treating you cruelly, not the other way around.'

'How do I stand up to life and fight it back? And if I win, how will I know?'

'You might never know. Sometimes the fight goes on for ever. But you don't give in. There's always something to fight for.'

A new look came into his eyes and he leaned forward until his mouth almost met hers.

'Yes, there's always something to fight for,' he whispered.

The soft touch of his lips sent a tremor through her, then another, with such power and intensity that she had no choice but to return the caress. And then again, responding helplessly to the sweet excitement of the feeling.

'Ellie,' he murmured.

'Yes—yes—'

She could not have explained what she was saying 'yes' to. She only knew that the desire to continue doing this had taken possession of her.

She felt his arms going around her tentatively, as though leaving the next move up to her. She returned the embrace, moving her mouth softly against his.

'Yes,' she repeated. 'Yes.'

Then his arms became stronger, his embrace more desperate, and she felt herself drawn into a new world.

CHAPTER TWO

THE FLIGHT FROM London to Rome took two and a half hours. Ellie spent the time gazing out of the window, trying to escape the thoughts that haunted her. But in her heart she knew there was no escape.

She had thought of herself as sensible, controlled and disciplined. These were the characteristics that had enabled her to keep command of her life. Years of watching the aching unhappiness that had destroyed her parents' marriage had made her overcautious. Feelings were dangerous things to be kept to herself.

Yet Leonizio had destroyed her caution without even knowing he was doing it. He was a hard man, protected from the world. That was how she saw him, how he preferred to be seen. But suddenly there had been a crack in his armour, giving her a glimpse of the pain concealed within.

Even more surprising had been the sympathy he'd shown for her own troubles. It was the last thing she'd expected from him, and it had softened her heart, making her reach out to him even more intensely.

The result had been devastating. She had meant only to offer him comfort. Yet the touch of his lips had sent desire and emotion blazing through her, destroying common sense, destroying caution, destroying everything but the need to travel this road to the end.

Night after night the memories returned as she lay alone. The sudden cool air on her skin as he'd stripped away her clothes and laid his lips against her breasts; the fierce yearning for him to touch her more—then more—and more. Finally the great moment when he had taken her completely, and everything in her had rejoiced.

It was something she would never forget: the fierce pleasure, unlike anything she had ever known before, the blazing satisfaction as they both climaxed. The feeling of empty desolation as they'd parted, each avoiding the other's eyes.

When her mind cleared she was shocked at herself for having given in to her feelings without caution. But how could she have thought about it in advance when it had sprung on her out of nowhere, like a storm from a calamitous sky?

And if I'd seen it coming I wouldn't have let it happen, she mused. *Would that have been better?*

She found that a hard question to answer. Would it really have been better not to discover the fierce pleasure of his lovemaking?

And could she have turned away from Leonizio when everything in her had flamed with need of him?

When it was over there had been the dizzying sensation of seeing her own reflection, her locks cascading about her shoulders. It was like meeting another person and trying to believe that it was herself.

Silently she'd addressed the woman in the mirror.

I guess you're my other self. A different me, and yet the same me. I've never met you before, and I'm not sure I want you to hang around. You've already got me into trouble.

To make certain of it, she pulled her hair back again, fixing it tightly as before.

Now stay away, she told her other self, now fading into the mists.

If Leonizio noticed that she had changed selves he didn't mention it. He'd paid his bill and they bade each other a polite farewell.

He'd soon returned to Italy and after that they had communicated only formally. He had abandoned his claim on his wife's child and the divorce was moving to a speedy conclusion. That was the end, she told herself. Leonizio no longer needed her professional services and each could forget that the other existed,

Eight weeks had passed since she'd last seen him. She'd spent the intervening time telling herself that it had been a fantasy. Nothing had really happened.

But, with shattering impact, she had discovered that she was wrong. She'd been reckless to sleep with him, but they had used protection. Only it must have failed. It had to have failed. She was carrying his child.

To make her troubles worse, she desperately needed someone with whom she could share the news. But she was alone. Both her parents had died several years before, and there were no other family members that she was close enough to confide in.

Suddenly her life had become a desert. She was thirty-eight, and pregnant by a man four years younger than herself. Who else could she tell but her baby's father? However hard it would be to manage, they must have one more meeting so that she could reveal the news that changed the world.

By good luck some papers arrived that required his signature.

'Best not entrust these to the post,' she'd said to Dallon. 'I'll hand deliver them.'

'There's no need for you to go all the way to Italy to be

a messenger,' he'd protested. 'There's a firm I can use to deliver this stuff.'

'I think it would help if I was with him when he signs, in case he raises any problems.'

'Fair enough.' He'd given her a friendly grin. 'You weren't planning on doing some sightseeing in Rome as well?'

'Well, it's my grandmother's city and I've always longed to see it.'

'Ah, I see. Get a sneaky holiday under the guise of duty. Very clever.'

He'd winked kindly. 'All right, I'll fall for it. You're due for a break.'

She'd smiled and let the matter go. Anything was better than having him suspect her real reason for going to Rome.

She'd emailed Leonizio that she would bring the papers and set off at once, without waiting for his reply. There was a flight due to leave that same day.

She landed in Rome in the evening, too late to go to his office, so she made for the Piazza Navona.

It was among the most prosperous places in the great city. Here, Leonizio's business centre was located, with his apartment two streets away. Checking into a nearby hotel, Ellie asked herself for the hundredth time whether she was doing the right thing in coming here. But these days most of her own actions confused her.

I was mad to come, she mused. *I should have sent someone else. I was also mad to go into his arms, but it all happened so fast I couldn't think. I have to see him. I have to tell him everything myself.*

Briefly, she considered letting her hair hang loose, but all her defensive instincts rose against it for fear that he would get the wrong idea.

'I don't want him thinking that other me is still around. He must have no doubt who he's dealing with now.'

From their correspondence she knew his private address. As the light faded she slipped out of the hotel and made her way to the nearby street where he lived. There was an elegant block of apartments, with lights in almost every window. She looked up, wondering if she might see him.

Several minutes passed while she tried to pluck up the courage to ring the bell. But she couldn't manage it, and had almost decided to retreat when the sight of him at a window made her draw in a sharp breath. He pushed it open, leaning out, while she stood, tense and undecided. She was just beginning to back into the shadows when he looked down.

His face was in shadow but there was no mistaking the shock that pervaded his whole body.

'Ellie? *Ellie?*'

'Yes, it's me,' she called back.

'Wait there.'

He was with her in a moment, ushering her inside and towards the elevator, which took them up to the second floor. Once they were inside his apartment she walked ahead a few steps, then turned and saw him standing by the door, regarding her curiously.

'I couldn't believe it was really you down there,' he said.

He approached and put his hands on her shoulders.

'Let me look at you,' he said. 'It *is* you, isn't it?'

'Can you doubt it?'

'Maybe. You look like a woman I once knew—just for a short time.'

A very short time, she thought. *And we didn't know each other, except in one particular sense.*

Aloud, she said, 'Nobody stays the same for ever.'

'That's true. So tell me, has the divorce hit a new problem at the last minute?'

'No, you have nothing to worry about. Harriet has

signed all the papers so far, and we've fixed a date for her to sign the rest. There are some more forms for you to sign, and then it will be pretty much over. I've brought a few of them with me.'

'Instead of just putting them in the mail? Thank you so much.'

'Things can get lost in the mail,' she said. She was prevaricating as the crucial moment neared, but she knew she must soon summon up her courage.

'Here they are,' she said, drawing out the papers.

He seized them eagerly. Watching his face, she saw it flooded with relief tinged by a hint of sadness.

'It's nearly over,' he murmured. 'I'll soon be free of her. But I'll also be free of the child who should have been mine, and that's a freedom I never wanted.'

'But soon you'll have the final documents, and then you can make a new life.'

'That's what I tell myself, but I keep thinking of that little boy. Even though he isn't born yet, I loved him so much. But the love must stop.'

'And now you think you have nobody to love,' she said gently.

'That's one way of putting it.'

'But it isn't true. I came to see you because—' She paused. Now that the moment had arrived she was suddenly nervous.

'I needed to see you,' she said slowly. 'There's something I have to tell you.' She took a deep breath. 'I'm pregnant.'

She wasn't sure what reaction she'd expected, but not the total silence that greeted her. At last he managed to speak in a voice so low that it was almost inaudible.

'What—did you say?'

'I'm pregnant. That night we were together—there was a consequence.'

He drew in a sharp breath. 'Are you telling me that—?'

'That I'm carrying your baby.'

'But we used protection. How can that be? You're sure? Quite certain?'

'I promise I'm not trying to trick you. You're the father. It has to be you because there's nobody else it could be. I don't know how but the condom must have become damaged. I swear I didn't plan this…'

'I wasn't accusing you of—I only meant—are you sure you're pregnant?'

'There's no doubt of it. I did a test. It was positive.'

Suddenly the tension drained from his face. Now there was only a blazing smile.

'Yes!' he cried. *'Yes!'*

He tightened his grip and drew her forward against him in a hug so fierce that she gasped.

'Sorry,' he said, loosening his clasp. 'I must be careful of you now.'

'It's all right,' she said. 'I'm not delicate.'

'Yes, you are. You're frail and vulnerable and I must do everything to look after you and our child.'

He led her to the sofa and nudged her gently until she sat down.

'How long have you been sure?' he asked.

'A couple of weeks.'

'And you waited this long to tell me?'

'I've been trying to get my head around it.'

'Is that all?' he asked quietly.

She felt she understood his true meaning and said, 'Look, I told you, you're the father. There are simply no other candidates. There's nobody else. You have to believe me.'

'I do believe you. You told me before that your relationships tended to be unsuccessful. It sounds like a lonely life.'

'Yes,' she said thoughtfully. 'It has been.'

'But not any more. When we're married you'll have me to care for you.'

'Wait!' She stopped him. 'Did you say "married"?'

'Of course. Why do you look so surprised? Did you think I wouldn't want to marry you?'

'To be honest, I never even considered it.'

'But you must have been thinking of the future when you came here to tell me. What did you expect would happen?'

'I thought you'd be pleased. You want a child. I can give you one.'

'And I can give you a lot—a good life with everything you want.'

'But I'd lose my career, which I enjoy. I'd lose my country. We barely know each other but you expect me to move into a new world with you—'

'And our child.'

'Our child will live with me in England. But I'll put your name on the birth certificate and you can see him or her whenever you like.'

It was sad to see how the eagerness drained from his face, replaced by something that might have been despair. He dropped his head into his hands, staying there for a long moment while she thought she saw a tremor go through him.

'It's too soon to make a decision,' he said at last.

Tact prevented her from pointing out that she'd already made her decision. Clearly he didn't regard it as final until it suited him.

'I'm going back to the hotel,' she said.

'I'll drive you.'

'No need. It's only a couple of streets away. Just a short walk.'

'But you must be careful about getting tired now. My car's just below.'

'Signor Fellani—'

'Don't you think you could call me Leonizio—under the circumstances?'

'Yes, I suppose so.'

'Let's go.'

He put his arm protectively around her. She gave in, letting him take her downstairs, into the car and back to the hotel, where he escorted her up to her room.

'I'll collect you tomorrow morning,' he said. 'We have a lot to talk about.' He grew tense suddenly. 'You will be here, won't you?'

'I've arranged to have several days off, so I don't have to dash back.'

'Fine. I'll collect you tomorrow morning.'

For a moment she thought he might kiss her, but something made him back off, bid her farewell with a nod and retreat down the corridor until he was out of sight. With any other man she would have felt that he'd fled for safety, but with Leonizio that was impossible.

Wasn't it?

After the traumatic events of the day it was good to be alone. She needed to think. Or perhaps just to feel. She went to bed early, hoping to sleep at once, but sleep wouldn't come.

She had a strange feeling of being transported back to the past, when she had been a child, watching the misery of her parents' life together. They had married only because Janet, her mother, was pregnant. Ellie recalled an atmosphere of hostility between two people who didn't belong together, even with a shared child.

'I should have known it could never work,' Janet had once told her bitterly. 'But our families were thrilled at the thought of a grandchild, and determined to make sure of it. So they pressured us into marriage.'

'Didn't you love Dad?' Ellie had once asked. 'I thought that sometimes there seemed to be love—'

'Oh, yes, sometimes. He was a handsome man and all the girls were wild for him. They envied me being his wife, but he only married me because he was backed into a corner. After a while I started to have feelings for him, and I thought I could make him return them. But it didn't work. Why should he bother to court me when he already had me there to do his bidding? You have to keep a man wanting, and if you can't do that he'll take advantage of it.'

Thinking back now, Ellie remembered that the only happiness had come from her grandmother, Lelia, who was Italian. She had married an Englishman, given up her country to live with him in England, and been left stranded by his death. When her son, Ellie's father, married she'd moved in with him and his wife.

Ellie had been close to her grandmother. Lelia had enjoyed nothing better than regaling her with tales of Italy, and teaching her some of the language. It had been a severe loss when she died.

Without her kindly presence Ellie's parents had grown more hostile to each other, until their inevitable divorce.

'Will you be all right on your own?' Ellie had ventured to ask her mother.

'I won't be on my own. I've got you.'

'But—you know what I mean.'

'You mean without a husband? I'll actually be better off without him. Better no man at all than the wrong man. Better no relationship than a bad one.'

Life was hard. Her father paid them as little as he could get away with, and Janet took a job with low wages. Determined to have a successful career, Ellie had buried herself in schoolwork, coming top of the class. In this she was encouraged by her mother, who told her time and again that independence was the surest road to freedom.

'Have your own career, your own life,' she'd urged. 'Never be completely dependent on a man.'

Ellie had heeded the lesson, took a law degree at university and qualified as a solicitor with flying colours. Alex Dallon was eager to employ her. She was a success.

The firm specialised in divorce cases. In the years she had worked there she'd witnessed every kind of break-up for every kind of reason. She'd soon realised that wretchedly unhappy marriages were more common than she'd thought. Men and women swore eternal love and fidelity, then turned on each other in a miasma of hate and mistrust. She wondered if love was ever successful.

Her own experiences gave her no cause for comfort. There were men attracted by her wit and her lively personality. But the attraction soon died when they were faced with an intelligence often sharper than their own, and an efficiency that tolerated no nonsense.

Finally there had been the man she'd described to Leonizio, briefly interested in her but then leaving her for a woman of more conventional charms.

Besides, how could Leonizio want marriage after the disaster that was his last one? His divorce wasn't even through. He'd be mad to even entertain the idea of getting involved again so soon.

No, whatever the solution was for her situation with Leonizio, it certainly wasn't marriage. They were both adults. She felt sure that they could come up with a solution for sharing their child that would suit them both.

Reassured that her sensible side had returned, she turned over and drifted off to sleep.

Next morning she went downstairs to eat breakfast in the restaurant. Her table was by the window, looking out on the street. After a while she saw a familiar figure appear, heading for the hotel entrance. She hurried out into the lobby, waving to Leonizio, and he followed her back into the restaurant.

'Did you sleep well?' he asked as they sipped coffee.

'Not really. Too much to mull over. You?'

'Same with me. Have you done any more thinking about what we discussed yesterday?'

'We agreed to be good parents, friendly for our child's sake.'

'That isn't what I meant. I proposed marriage. You were going to consider it.'

'I gave you my answer last night.'

He didn't reply at once, seeming sunk in thought. At last he said, 'We're still virtually strangers. It can't work like that. At least let's spend some time getting to know each other. You might find I'm not the monster you think me.'

'Or I might find you're worse,' she said in a teasing voice.

'I'll just have to take that risk. I want you to stay with me. You'll find the spare room very comfortable. My housekeeper will take care of you.'

'But—I'm not sure. It might be better if I stayed in the hotel.'

'The more time we spend together the better it will be.'

'But I don't think—'

She stopped as she saw a young man approaching their table. He handed Leonizio a piece of paper, saying, *'Ecco la ricevuta, signore.'*

Ellie frowned, recognising just one word. *Ricevuta* meant receipt.

'Receipt?' she asked when the man had gone.

'I've paid your bill here. I called them last night and paid over the phone. There's no reason why the cost should fall on you.'

It sounded fine and generous, but something about it made her uneasy.

'Last night?' she queried. 'Why? My bill won't need to be paid until I check out.'

'Actually—you already have.'

'What? You mean you—?'

'I told them you would be leaving this morning.'

'Oh, really? And the little matter of consulting me slipped your mind. So this is your way of showing me that you're not a monster?'

'I just want you to stay with me. Ellie, you're important to me—both of you. I couldn't let you go.'

'You mean you couldn't let me do what I want if it conflicts with what you want.'

'It'll help us get to know each other really well so that we can plan out a future that's good for all of us. Isn't that what we both want?'

Ellie regarded him with her head on one side. 'So that's how you do it.'

'Do what?'

'Conduct your business. Nobody else stands a chance, do they? You get the better of the other guy by doing something outrageous that he can't fight. Then you put on an innocent look and say, "Isn't that what we both want?" And he gives in. Or so you hope. And that way you get everyone so scared of you that they can't fight back.'

'Are you scared of me, Ellie? Strange that I never noticed. You're not afraid of anyone.'

'True. And in my own way I too can be fearsome. I keep my worst side hidden until it leaps out and catches you unprepared. So be very careful.'

'I'll bear your warning in mind. As for persuading you to stay with me—I guess I used the wrong method. Perhaps I should try another way.'

'Such as what?'

'I could beg you.' He assumed a slightly theatrical air. 'Please, Ellie, do this for me. *Please.* Stay with me for the next couple of days, at least until we can agree on the best way to move forward with this situation.'

Ellie had to concede that he had a point. They did need to sort things out. And maybe a venue more private than a busy hotel was a better place to plan their future. 'I will stay with you, but only for a few days. And I won't be sharing your bed.'

He nodded, giving her an unexpectedly warm smile.

'Whatever you want, Ellie. I only want to make this work. When you're ready we'll go up and collect your things.'

'Let's go,' she said.

Be realistic, she told herself. *He changed tactics and got his own way again. And he thinks he always will. But he's got another think coming.*

Upstairs, she packed quickly, then let him carry her bags down to the car. A few minutes and they had reached his home. As they approached the front door, a window opened high above them and a young woman looked out, smiling and waving down to them. Leonizio waved back.

The front door was already open as they approached. The young woman stood there, smiling.

'Mamma indisposta,' she said. *'Non puo venire oggi.'*

Ellie just managed to understand this as, 'Mamma is unwell. She can't come today.'

'Better speak English,' Leonizio said. 'Ellie, this is Corina. Her mother is my housekeeper.'

'But today she has a bad headache,' Corina said. 'So I came instead. I must go now, or my husband will be cross.' She smiled at Ellie. 'But first I show you your room.'

The room was large and luxurious, dominated by a double bed.

'The *signore* left before I arrived,' Corina said, 'but he

left a note saying everything in this room was to be perfect for you.'

'How kind of him,' Ellie said politely.

So he'd left those instructions before she had agreed to come here, she thought. Just as he'd checked her out of the hotel without asking her. Those were his methods, and she would have to be always on her guard.

Corina helped her unpack, then went out to Leonizio, who paid her and showed her out.

'Let's have some coffee,' he said to Ellie.

He made good coffee, and they sat together in the kitchen.

'We can make our arrangements,' he said. 'You can tell me how you want things to be.'

'Is that meant to be a joke? How I want things? After the way you've controlled me today. You ordered the room to be fixed before I'd even agreed to come.' She gave a brief laugh. 'Suppose you hadn't been able to get me here? You'd have looked foolish in front of Corina.'

'It wouldn't have done my dignity any good,' he agreed. 'And you'd have enjoyed that. I'm going to have to beware of you.'

'As long as you realise that.'

Before he could reply the telephone rang. He answered it, spoke tersely in rapid-fire Italian and hung up.

'I've got to go to my office for a couple of hours. Why not come with me and let me show you around?'

'Thank you but there's no need. I won't escape. I promise.'

He made a wry face. 'I wasn't exactly thinking that—oh, hell, yes, I was.'

'I wonder what your employees would think if they saw how easily you get into a panic.'

'Only with you. You're the scariest person I know.'

'Then I'll just have to stick around for the pleasure of scaring you.'

He smiled suddenly, but his smile was quickly replaced by a frown. 'I have to be going. I'll be back as soon as I can.'

He departed quickly, leaving her to lean from the window, watching him until he vanished. She had a good view of the neighbourhood, with its expensive shops and elegant roads.

So many roads, she thought. And no way of seeing where they all led.

CHAPTER THREE

LEFT ALONE, ELLIE explored the luxurious apartment. Her own room was large with a double bed, extensive wardrobes and bulky drawers. Putting her things away, she couldn't help noticing how plain and dull they looked in these glamorous surroundings.

If I was in search of a rich husband I'd jump at his offer, she thought wryly. *But I'm looking for something else in a husband. Something Leonizio can't give me. Not that he'll ever understand that. He's got money and why should a wife ask for anything else? That's how he sees it.*

She switched on the television and sat watching a news channel, discovering that her understanding of Italian was better than she'd thought.

I could do with something to read, she mused after a couple of hours. *That looks like a newsagent just over the road. Let's see if they've got any English papers.*

Hurrying downstairs, she crossed the road to the shop, which turned out to be a delightful place, full of foreign publications. By the time she left she had an armful of papers.

But a shock awaited her when she arrived back at Leonizio's apartment. As she reached the front door she could hear him inside, shouting, 'Where are you? *Where are you?*'

There was something in his voice that hadn't been there

before. It was no longer the cry of a bully demanding obedience, but the misery of a man in despair. She thought she could guess the reason. Once before he had gone home to find his wife vanished, taking with her the unborn child on which he pinned his hopes. Now he was reliving that moment, fearing that he was deserted again, seeing his world collapse and everything he valued snatched from him.

'Where are you?' came the frantic cry again.

Unable to bear it any longer, she opened the door. At the same moment he strode out so quickly that he collided with her, forcing her to cling to him to avoid falling. He tightened his grip and they stood for a moment, locked in each other's arms.

'So there you are,' he snapped.

'Yes, I'm here.'

'Come in,' he said, still holding onto her as he led her inside. His arms about her were tight, as though he feared to release her.

He saw her onto the sofa, then stood back and regarded her uneasily.

'Did I hurt you?' he growled.

'Not at all. But there was no need for you to get worked up. I just slipped out for a moment to buy a few things over the road. I'm here now.'

He sat down beside her.

'You should have left a note saying where you'd gone.' He spoke calmly but his face was tense.

'Yes, perhaps I should have done that,' she said, 'but I knew I'd only be away for a couple of minutes, and I thought I'd be back here before you returned. I'm sorry. I really am.'

She spoke gently, regretting the distress she'd caused him. When he didn't answer she reached out to put a hand on his shoulder.

'Finding the place empty made you think I'd deserted you, taking your baby, as Harriet did.'

His shoulders sagged. 'You're right,' he said heavily.

'But I promised to stay, and I'll keep that promise. So stop worrying, Leonizio. It's not going to happen again. If you need to go out, just go. I'll always be here when you get back. Word of honour.'

He turned, looking her in the eyes as though he couldn't quite believe what he heard.

'Really? You mean that?'

'When I give a promise I keep it. You have to trust me, Leonizio.'

'I do trust you. Completely.'

'But you're still afraid I might betray you as she did.'

'No. You're not like her.'

'Then relax.'

He smiled and squeezed her hand.

'Actually, I need to go out again for a little while,' he said. 'Why don't you rest, and when I return I'll take you out for dinner? We can start to get to know each other.'

'That would be lovely, Leonizio,' she said.

He seemed to relax but she knew the pain and fear she had heard in his voice had been real. It was there in his heart, and she would always remember it.

'Go out,' she said. 'And stop worrying.'

'I'll try.'

He departed, giving her a brief glance before he left.

She was glad to be alone again that afternoon. Since her arrival in Rome, everything that had happened had disconcerted her. Leonizio's reaction had only underlined how little she knew him.

But something else disturbed her even more. It was the memory of their collision in the corridor, the way his arms had enfolded her. She knew he'd been protecting her from a fall, but the sensation of being held against his body had been shattering, recalling another time.

That night still lived in her heart, her mind and her senses. She, who had never before even considered a one-night stand, had gone willingly into this one, letting it tempt her as though it was the most natural and the most desirable thing in the world.

She had come to Rome because Leonizio had the right to know about his child, yet she was still determined to stay in control of herself and the situation. Perhaps it was going to be harder than she had thought, but she was strong. Whatever disagreements they might have, she would be the winner. On that she was determined.

She prepared for the evening ahead with a shower, followed by an inspection of her clothes. She had nothing glamorous, but a simple green dress gave her an air of quiet elegance.

She hesitated briefly over her hair, finally deciding to wear it pulled back, sending a silent message that tonight her controlled self was the one in command.

When she heard Leonizio's key in the lock she positioned herself so that he could see her as soon as he entered, and was rewarded by the look of relief that dawned in his eyes as soon as he saw her.

'Let's go,' he said.

His car was waiting below, with a smartly dressed chauffeur in attendance. He opened a rear door, bowing to Ellie.

'Take us to the Venere,' Leonizio told him.

Ellie gave him a quick startled glance.

'Is that the Venere Hotel, near the Colosseum?' she asked.

'Yes. It's got a fine restaurant. You know it?'

'I've heard of it,' she said.

Lelia, her Italian grandmother, had worked in the

Venere and had described it as one of the most luxurious places in Rome. It would be fascinating to see it now, Ellie thought.

She understood its reputation as soon as they arrived. The building looked as though it had once been a palace. Inside, a waiter greeted them and led them to a table by the window, from which she could see the Colosseum, the huge amphitheatre built nearly two thousand years ago.

'It's eerie,' she mused. 'Once people crowded there for the pleasure of seeing victims fed to the lions. Now the tourists go because it's beautiful and fascinating. And maybe we've all got somebody we'd like to see fed to the lions.'

'You wouldn't be aiming that at me, would you?' he queried.

'I'm not sure,' she said. 'I'll let you know when I've decided.'

'Well, I can't say I haven't been warned.'

'Right. I can be a real pain in the neck. You'll probably be glad to be rid of me.'

'Forget it. There's no way you'll escape.'

She gave him a teasing smile. 'Surely you don't want a woman who's a pestiferous nuisance?'

He returned the smile. 'I might. They can often be the most fun.'

He held out his hand and she shook it. 'As long as we understand each other,' she said.

'Perhaps we always did.'

'No, I don't think we ever did.'

While he was considering this a waiter approached with a menu, which he gave to Ellie.

'Need any help?' Leonizio asked.

'I can manage the Italian but I'll need you to explain the food to me. What's *Coda all Vaccinara?*'

'Stewed oxtail in tomato sauce,' Leonizio told her.

'It sounds nice. I'd like to have some.'

'May I suggest the Frascati wine to go with it, *signorina*?' the waiter said.

'No,' Leonizio said at once. 'Sparkling water for the lady. No alcohol.'

'And for you, *signore*?'

'I'll have the Frascati.'

When the waiter had retired, Leonizio said, 'I know you can't drink wine while you're pregnant.'

She didn't reply and after a moment he demanded, 'Why are you glaring at me?'

'I'm not.'

'Yes, you are. You'd like to thump me.'

'That's very perceptive of you. All right, the way you made that decision without consulting me makes me think a good thump might be satisfying.'

'You do me an injustice. I paid you the compliment of assuming that you would already have made the sensible decision. You're such an efficient, businesslike person that—'

'All right, all right. You can stop there. You always know what to say, don't you?'

He gave her a cheerful grin. 'Luckily for me, yes. With some combatants it's a useful skill.'

'Is that what we are? Combatants?'

'Not all the time. But it's something that's going to crop up now and then.'

'Now and then. I suppose that's true.'

'And while we can have an evening out like this, we can relax together and find a way to solve the problem.'

His tone was friendly, but a man working at a business arrangement might have spoken in just this way, she thought.

'How are you feeling now?' he asked.

'Fine. That rest did me good. Now I'm in the mood to enjoy myself.'

'You're all right after what I put you through?'

'You mean when you got so upset because I wasn't there? I'm sorry for the whole thing. It must have been terrible for you, feeling like you were reliving the past.'

He nodded. 'It was exactly the same. I came home one day and she'd gone. She didn't leave a note. I was left to wonder until an email arrived the next day.

'Yes. Coming back to an empty house is something I don't cope with very well.' He gave a brief self-mocking laugh. 'I remember telling you that we should discover things about each other. Well, that's something you've discovered. Perhaps you should take warning.'

'I've already had plenty to warn me, and there's nothing I can't cope with. Beware. This lioness has claws.'

'Well, I know that. They left a few scratches on me when we were together.'

She drew a sharp breath. His words brought back the memory of the time she had spent in his arms, overcome by a physical excitement she'd never known before. Bereft of all self-control, she had clutched him in a fever of desire that it shocked her to remember now.

'I'm sorry,' she said hastily. 'I didn't mean to hurt you.'

'Don't apologise. It was an accident. The world seemed to change that night, as though we'd become different people.'

'Yes, that's true. I no longer really know what to think about anything.'

'Is that why you refuse to marry me?'

'I haven't actually refused. I just can't take it for granted, the way you did. I don't like being given orders.'

'That's not what I did.'

'But it is. You just assumed I'd jump at the chance to marry you. How arrogant is that?'

She gave a brief laugh. 'I once looked up your name and found that Leonizio means 'lion-like'. That says it all about you. The lion rules the plains, and Leonizio thinks he can rule wherever he likes.'

Briefly she wondered if she was wise to risk offending him, but his smile contained only wry amusement.

'Except for the lioness,' he said. 'She could stand up to him better than anyone else.'

She nodded. 'As long as he understands that.'

'He understands completely. And he knows he'll have to be cleverer than usual to achieve victory.'

'But he doesn't really doubt that he'll be the winner, does he?'

'Tact prevents me answering that.' He raised his glass. 'Here's to victory—for both of us.'

She raised her own glass and they clinked.

'As long as we each understand what victory means,' he said. 'You know what it means to me but—' He paused.

'You just can't understand why I don't jump at the chance to marry you, can you?' she said.

'I'm not the conceited oaf that makes me sound. As a person I may not be likeable. I understand that.'

'Is that what your wife said?'

'She said plenty about me. None of it good, in the end.'

'In my experience, marriage ends badly. My parents divorced. You're about to be divorced. It's par for the course, it seems. Can you blame me for refusing you?'

'Yes, but don't forget that not all marriages need end that way. Ours would be different. We would be entering it with our eyes wide open. What do I have to offer to persuade you?'

'You don't understand. It's what I'd lose. My country, my career, my freedom, my independence. I'm not ready to rush into it.'

'Not even to benefit our child?'

'But does marriage always benefit the child?' she asked. 'My parents were married and the unhappiness filled the air. I need to know—this is going to sound crazy to you—but I need to know that we can be friends.'

'I don't think it's crazy at all. It makes sense.' He gave a contented nod. 'We've got a while to get to know each other, and hopefully like each other.'

'Yes,' she said eagerly. 'That's the luckiest thing that can happen to a child, that its parents can be best friends.'

'You think that's luckier than if the parents love each other?'

'It can be. Friendship doesn't have so many ups and downs, so many dramas and crises. I can remember coming home from school wondering if my parents were speaking to each other today. When I got the lead in the school play they each came to a different performance. It would have been lovely if they'd come together and we'd had an evening as a happy family, but—' she shrugged '—that's how it was.'

Suddenly they were surrounded by applause. A man had appeared, bearing a guitar. He bowed to the guests at the tables who were applauding his entrance, and began to sing. Ellie listened with pleasure as he made his way between the tables, coming close until she could see him clearly. Noticing that she was delighted, Leonizio signalled to the man. He approached them, carolling cheerfully, until Leonizio held out a generous tip. He bowed and departed. When he finished his performance she clapped eagerly.

'That was lovely,' she said. 'It's such a nice, cheeky song.'

'You understood it?' Leonizio asked, astonished. 'But he was singing in Roman dialect. I know you understand some Italian, but dialect?'

'My grandmother used to sing it to me when I was a little girl. She came from Rome; she was born and spent her early years in Trastevere and she told me so much about it that I longed to see it. I loved my grandmother so much. I used to call her Nonna when I knew that was what Italians called their grandmothers. Now I'm here I feel wonderfully close to her.'

'Tell me about her.'

'She's the reason I'd heard of the Venere. Years ago she worked here as a chambermaid.'

'Here? In this very building?'

'Yes. Then she met an Englishman who was a guest, and they fell in love. He took her back to England with him. They married and had a son, my father. Sadly, my grandfather didn't live very long. Nonna mostly brought up my father on her own. When he married my mother she lived with them, looking after me.

'So you're nearly as much Italian as English?'

'In some ways. My mother didn't really like my grandmother very much. She said Nonna was a bad influence on me. She was very cross one day when she found her playing me some music. It was opera and my mother said it was way above my head.'

'And was it?'

'No, I like opera because of its terrific tunes. That's all.'

'So if I want to take you to an opera that would be a mark in my favour?'

'It would be lovely.'

'You're so knowledgeable that I'm sure you know about the Caracalla Baths.'

'They were a kind of spa built by the Emperor Caracalla nearly two thousand years ago. There's very little left standing, but what's left is used as a theatre for open-air performances.'

'Right. They open every summer, but this year they're doing a special run in April. We'll get the programme and you can take your pick.'

'That's lovely. Oh, how I wish I had Nonna here now so that she could see me becoming her real granddaughter after all this time. She died many years ago, and I miss her so much.'

'You're going to enjoy Rome, I promise you.'

Of course he wanted her to enjoy Rome, because it would make it easier for him to persuade her to stay and marry him. A slightly cynical voice whispered this in her mind, but she refused to let it worry her. Leonizio was handsome and attentive and part of her simply wanted to relax and be with him.

A sudden loud noise announced the arrival of a crowd. The waiter dashed around, trying to find room for them all. Ellie closed her eyes, trying to shut out the commotion. These days she tired easily.

'Perhaps we should go,' Leonizio said wryly, looking at her. 'It's time you were getting some rest.'

'Giving me orders again?'

'Yes.' He said it with a smile that made the word humorous.

'In that case I'd better obey,' she chuckled.

A few minutes' drive brought them home. He saw her to her bedroom door.

'Is there anything I can do for you?'

'No, thank you. I have all I need.'

'Go to bed, then.'

For a moment he seemed on the verge of kissing her, but he only opened the door and indicated for her to go in.

'Goodnight,' he said softly. 'Sleep well.'

'And you.'

She slipped inside and closed the door.

Now she could go to bed and try to come to terms with everything that was happening to her. It was hard because so many things in her mind seemed to direct her two ways. Some were troublesome, others suggested the hope of happiness if only she could understand many ideas. Still trying to get clear, she faded into sleep.

Suddenly she found herself in a new place, one where there were no boundaries, no definite positions. Here there was only mist and sensation, leading her forward into an unknown world.

But she realised that it wasn't completely unknown. She had been here once before in another life, another universe, one that was still offering intriguing possibilities. She could feel again the sweetness that had tempted her, the touch so different from anything she had known.

But there was also the apprehension at the way she was losing control. Deep inside her a nervous voice was crying out.

'What am I doing? Do I dare do this? Am I just a little mad? Or am I turning into somebody else—somebody I don't know? I mustn't do this…not now—not this time—'

Even as she spoke, she gasped with the tremor of remembered sensation that possessed her.

Be strong, whispered the warning voice. *Stay in control. You lost control that time and you're paying for it. You know that.*

'Yes, I do. And I mustn't—*no—no*!'

Then everything changed. There was a pounding on her door. The next moment Leonizio was there, leaning over her, taking her in his arms.

'Ellie,' he said hoarsely. 'Ellie! Wake up!'

The sound of his voice startled her awake. Gradually her breathing slowed and the world came back into focus. She found that she was clinging to him.

'Wake up,' he said again.

'It's all right… I'm awake now.'

'You must have had a nightmare.'

Her mind and senses were spinning. 'A nightmare—yes—no—I'm not sure—'

'You sounded as though you were suffering something

terrible. I could hear you right out in the corridor, and I just had to come in and see if I could help.'

'Thank you but I'm all right. It was just a dream.'

The sight of this room was bringing reality back, but the dream was still there. It would always be there, she realised. As long as she lived.

His arms were around her and she could feel his hands stroking her hair, which flowed loose again. It was a sweet sensation and she yielded to the temptation to rest her head on his shoulder, enjoying the soft caresses.

But suddenly the pleasure stopped. He snatched back his hands and rose from the bed. He turned away to the door, but there he stopped, standing with his back to her. She waited for him to turn around but something seemed to be constraining him.

'What is it?' she asked. 'What's wrong?'

'When you were asleep you were crying out, *No—no.* Why was that?'

'I can't remember,' she said evasively.

'Tell me the truth, Ellie. That time we spent together—' a shudder went through him '—I've always thought you enjoyed it as much as I did.'

'I did. It was beautiful.'

'Yes, it was. I can remember when you were in my arms—feeling that I wanted you more than I've ever wanted any—' He paused, full of tension and self-doubt.

'I felt like that too,' she assured him.

He turned back and came closer, though still keeping a slight distance between them.

'But just now,' he said uneasily, 'I heard you crying, *No—no*!'

'I didn't say no that day. If I had you'd have stopped.' She reached up to take his hands, drawing him down to sit on the bed. 'You would have stopped,' she repeated gently. 'You're a good man. Much kinder than you like people to know. But *I* know.'

'I would never have done anything against your will, I swear it. But hearing you cry out tonight scared me—made me wonder—'

'Don't. There's no need to wonder. It was all lovely.'

'Truly? You embraced me of your own free will?'

'Absolutely. I wanted you. Couldn't you feel that?'

'Yes. At the time it felt so wonderful to be together.'

'At the time? But not afterwards?'

'Afterwards you seemed to turn against me. You couldn't get away from me fast enough.'

'That's not how I—' She sighed. 'I guess we misunderstood each other.'

'There's a lot about that day that I didn't understand, but things look different now. I wanted you then and now I want you for always.'

But did he want her, or only the child she carried? If only that thought would go away and leave her in peace.

'I guess we have lots to talk about,' she said. 'You speak of marriage but you know nothing about me except that I'm pregnant.'

'What else do I need to know?'

'I'm thirty-eight.'

'Why should that matter?'

'It makes me four years older than you, and it gives me a slightly greater chance of miscarrying. You might simply find yourself stuck with an older wife who can't give you a child. I could be very bad news for you.'

'Stop it, Ellie. Stop trying to put me off. I want you, and I want you to want me.'

'It's not that simple.'

'Then we'll make it simple.'

'How?'

'Like this,' he said, taking her into his arms.

The kiss he gave her wasn't passionate but gentle and comforting, filling her with happiness.

'We belong together,' he said. 'And one day you'll see that.'

'Perhaps,' she whispered.

'There's no perhaps about it. You're mine.' His words might sound demanding, but his tone was gentle.

'So I'm yours,' she said. 'That's an order, is it?'

He rose and went to the door, pausing to look back at her.

'It could be.' He smiled. 'But I guess I'll have to be patient.'

Then he departed, leaving her full of confusion.

She closed her eyes, trying to make sense of the crowd of impressions and memories that converged on her. But it was impossible. She needed more time to come to terms with Leonizio. The authoritative man she had known at first had seduced her by letting her glimpse his vulnerability.

The discovery that she was pregnant had brought his commandeering side back to the surface. But his other side had been there again in his plea to be reassured that he hadn't behaved badly.

He has good qualities, she mused. A woman who wasn't careful could even be tricked into falling in love with him.

But I'm going to be careful, she promised herself. *Oh, yes, I am.*

CHAPTER FOUR

NEXT MORNING LEONIZIO waited for Ellie to join him at breakfast, but time passed with no sign of her. At last he knocked on her door. When this produced no response he opened it quietly and went inside.

She lay still and silent in her bed, her luscious hair spread over the pillow. Her head was turned in his direction, enabling him to see her gentle, relaxed expression. Last night she had been wretchedly agitated by whatever she had dreamed, but now peace seemed to have come over her, as though she had slipped into a kinder world.

How long would she stay in that world? And was he the demon who would destroy her peace? He was reluctant to think so.

He left the room quietly and breakfasted alone, trying to come to terms with the different signals coming from every direction.

She was a woman to confuse any man. From the first moment of knowing her he'd felt at ease with her serious mind, her businesslike efficiency, so appropriate in a lawyer.

But that had changed in a few stunning hours. Her understanding of his pain over his lost child, the sympathy he had sensed in her, these had drawn from him a reaction that had surprised even himself. He was a man who allowed few people to see inside his mind, and even fewer inside his heart. Life was safer with defences in position.

But she had seen beyond the defences, reaching out to touch him in a place where he badly needed to be touched.

The instinct to draw her closer had overcome him without warning. His arms had tightened, and their lovemaking had been just what he'd longed for.

But afterwards she'd seemed reluctant to meet his gaze, and their parting had been inevitable.

Memories of their lovemaking were still vivid. She had brought him wonderful news, but somehow she seemed to be the lawyer again. Instinctively, he had assumed that she wanted marriage, but the cool way she'd discounted it had told him much that he didn't want to know. Already she had planned the future she wanted: a life in England, her career, his place in their child's life limited to occasional visits.

As they'd dined together her manner had been pleasant but behind it he sensed her laying down the law in a way that aroused his opposition. Years of wealth and success had accustomed him to women seeking his attention and goodwill. A woman who rejected all he had to offer despite carrying his child was a new, stunning discovery.

By the end of the evening he understood how fiercely determined she was to do things her way, and summoned in himself an equal determination not to let her get away with it.

She was right. They were combatants. He would do whatever he could to win her to his point of view, but he would always be wary of her.

But there was another surprise for him: her nightmare, the way she had clung to him, his stab of pleasure at comforting her. These had knocked him back, weakening his resolve. And the sight of her sleeping this morning had touched his heart, weakening him further.

He checked the clock. Her office would be opening about now, and it was time to get everything sorted. Ellie must marry him. On that he was determined. He picked up the phone and dialled the number of her office.

Ellie awoke to find the room already light. For a few moments she allowed herself to stretch out and relish her comfortable surroundings. At last she slipped out of bed and opened the bedroom door a crack, looking out into the corridor. On the far side was another open door, from behind which she could hear Leonizio's voice.

'I want no more delays. Get the divorce papers ready… Yes, I know it's not what I said before but I've considered the matter. Get it done, fast.'

There was the sound of a telephone being slammed down.

She closed the door and stood quietly considering what she had heard. Leonizio was intent on finalising his divorce quickly. Last night she'd told him he was close, but that wasn't enough for him. He wanted to be free to marry her and secure his child as soon as possible.

She showered, dressed and went out to meet him, expecting to find him in the grim mood suggested by his phone call. But he gave her a friendly smile.

'Did you sleep well? How do you feel this morning?'

'Fine, thank you.' She touched her stomach. 'We're both in good health.'

'Sit down while I get you some breakfast. Then we can make our plans. Today you're a tourist and I'm your guide.' He poured her coffee. 'That is, if you want to do that.'

'Oh, yes, I've always been fascinated by Rome. All that power—emperors who are famous even today. Tiberius, Caligula, Julius Caesar, Augustus, Nero, all conquering their neighbours.'

'Including your country,' Leonizio observed lightly.

'Right. You invaded Britain and ruled us for nearly four hundred years. But then we got rid of you and that was that.' She raised the coffee cup in comical salute. 'Here's to telling the Romans to push off.'

He raised his own cup. 'Here's to pushing off for a while but coming back later.'

'If we let you,' she teased.

'Yes, we'll have to see who wins that one.'

They shared a laugh and clinked cups.

'Your emperors didn't just go to war,' she mused. 'They used to murder each other. But actually—oh, thank you.'

She broke off as he set a dish before her.

'There's more right next to you,' he said. 'Yes, I think you'll enjoy the grandeur of Rome.'

She had been about to say that she was equally fascinated by another part of the city: Trastevere, the impoverished part where her grandmother had lived. But perhaps that could wait.

'Anywhere you want to start?' he asked.

'Yes, the Trevi Fountain. I've always thought it looked lovely.'

'We'll go as soon as you've finished breakfast,' Leonizio said.

When they were ready to leave, his driver was waiting. A few minutes brought them to the Trevi district, where a building almost as big as a palace rose up. In front of it was a huge pool into which water flowed, and standing just above the pool was the statue of Neptune, the Roman god of fresh water and the sea. Splendid, handsome and nearly naked, he seemed to symbolise power and authority.

Crowds had gathered around the edge of the water, including a few market stalls. One elderly woman, selling flowers, waved some of them hopefully. Leonizio purchased a small bouquet and gave it to Ellie, who received it with pleasure. It was lovely to be treated like this, even if she did know that his behaviour was calculated to win her over and gain his own way.

At the edge of the water she paused, reached into her bag for coins, and flung them into the air.

'Not like that,' Leonizio said. 'The proper way is to stand with your back to the fountain and toss the coin over your right shoulder.'

'But it might not go in properly.'

'Then you must toss another coin, to be sure. And perhaps a third.'

'Here we go.' She tossed three coins over her shoulder, but Leonizio shook his head.

'Not all together. One at a time. Do it again.'

'All right. One—two—three.'

From behind them came a cackle. Turning, Ellie saw the flower seller, convulsed with laughter.

'Never trust a man,' she said. 'He tells you to throw coins but he doesn't tell you the secret code.'

'What secret code?' Ellie asked.

'It's the legend of Trevi. One coin will bring you back to Rome. Two coins will make you fall in love with a Roman man. Three coins will make you marry him.' She cackled again. 'But perhaps you're already in love with him, and scheming to fix the wedding.'

'No such thing,' Ellie announced. 'I've never been in love in my life, and I hope I never will be. As for scheming to marry—not a chance.'

The old woman sent a crow of amusement up to the heavens.

'But he fooled you!' she cried.

A naughty imp seemed to take over Ellie's mind, making her say teasingly, 'He fools everybody. That's how he's got so many wives. They toss three coins and they all have to marry him.'

Cheers and laughter from the crowd. Leonizio regarded

her wryly, partly amused, partly disconcerted at having the joke turned back on him.

'I think we should go,' he said, drawing her away.

She let him lead her to a small café in a side street.

'Very clever,' he said when they were seated. 'But did you really have to make a fool of me?'

'What about the fool you made of me? Tricking me like that.'

'Well, I've got to get you to marry me somehow, haven't I?' he said cheerfully. 'And if I have to invoke Neptune's help—that's what I'll do.'

She laughed. 'That's your code of life, isn't it? Get your own way at all costs, no matter what you have to do.'

'Are you saying your code isn't the same?'

She considered a moment before admitting, 'Exactly the same. Of course, I don't have a lot of practice—'

'You astonish me.'

'But I'm learning from you.'

'Yes, you got your revenge today, didn't you?'

'I made sure of it. Besides, where's the harm in a bit of fun?'

'No harm at all, especially if you take the other guy by surprise.'

'And it did take you by surprise, didn't it? You're not used to people fighting back.'

'I'm getting used to it with you. You obviously relished every moment.'

'I do enjoy a laugh.'

'So you think our marriage is just a joke.'

'What marriage? We're not married and who knows if we ever will be? I think it's a joke that you thought you only had to snap your fingers and I'd jump to obey. And you didn't tell me about the danger of tossing three coins.'

'Seriously, do you think I really believe that mad legend?'

'I'm not sure what I really think. This city is so different to everywhere else that I could believe impossible things. Besides which—' she regarded him ironically '—some people have a gift for making things happen. You have to be wary of them.'

'You do me an injustice. If I had anything like the power you seem to think, you would already have my ring on your finger. But I have no power at all, which is why you can keep me dancing to your tune.'

'You?' she echoed, astonished. 'You, dancing to my tune? Never.'

'I want you, Ellie, but you act like that is a crime.'

No, she thought, laying her hand gently over her stomach. *It's not me you want. If you did, everything would be different.*

'Have you really decided against me so completely?' he said. 'What have I done that offends you? Or is it that?' He indicated her stomach. 'Was that unforgivable of me?'

'Don't be melodramatic. I just haven't decided and I don't like you trying to make my decisions for me.'

'No, you like to be the one telling me what to do. Does it occur to you how alike we are? That could make a very happy marriage.'

'What, with each of us giving orders?' she demanded. 'That's not a happy marriage, it's a recipe for disaster.'

'Is that what went wrong with your parents' marriage?'

'That was a big part of it. But they didn't have the best start. They only married because they were expecting me. It wasn't what either wanted but they went ahead with it to please their parents, and were miserable together for years as a result. So, believe me, I know that isn't a good reason.'

'But wasn't there any affection between them?'

'If there was it didn't last. The air was always sharp and hostile. They made their mistakes. I'm not about to repeat them.'

Ellie stopped suddenly, her skin paling visibly as she gasped and clutched her stomach.

'What is it?' he asked urgently.

'Nothing— I just feel a bit—ooh—'

'You're nauseous, aren't you? Keep still and take deep breaths. Does it happen often?'

'Too often. I hate it. I thought pregnancy sickness only happened in the mornings.'

'It can happen any time, and it's actually something to be glad of.'

'You're kidding me.'

'No, it means that you have a lot of pregnancy hormones, and that's good news. They nourish the baby until your placenta has grown big enough to take over the job.'

She stared. 'You sound like a doctor. Have you studied medicine?'

'No, I've just trodden this path before.'

Of course he had, with his wife. Ellie could have cursed herself for her momentary forgetfulness.

'Did Harriet have a lot of sickness?' she asked.

'Plenty. She really suffered. I went to the doctor with her because I wanted to understand what she was going through, so that I could help her with the pregnancy.' He gave a wry grunt. 'There's a laugh if ever there was one.'

'It means you were a kind, considerate husband. That's not at all funny.'

'It is if I was helping her care for another man's child,' he said with a touch of wry bitterness. 'That's the biggest laugh of all time. But enough of this. You're the one who matters now.'

You mean my baby is the one that matters, she mused silently. But she suppressed the thought. Leonizio's concern was pleasant, whatever his motives.

'Let's go home,' he said. 'You need to rest.'

Taking out his cell phone, he called his driver, to summon him. A few minutes later they were on the road.

'Deep breaths,' he reminded her. 'We'll be there soon.'

In a few minutes they had reached his home. He supported her into her room, easing her down onto the bed.

'What can I get you?'

'Just a little water,' she gasped.

She drank the water he brought her, then lay down and drifted into a contented sleep. Dreams seemed to come and go. Once she had the sensation of opening her eyes to find Leonizio looking down at her anxiously. But then the mist descended again, and he vanished.

When she finally awoke the sickness had gone and she felt much better. She rose and left the room, finding him in the kitchen, cooking.

'Better?' he asked.

'Everything's fine.'

'Then you need a good meal. It'll be ready in a moment.'

She guessed this was what he had done for Harriet, caring for her when she felt poorly, feeding her to ensure she recovered properly. But he'd acted out of love for his wife, which meant Harriet had been fortunate.

How could she have betrayed a man who so loved and protected her? Ellie wondered.

But she knew the answer. It was because she hadn't returned his love.

How could she not return it? How could any woman be indifferent to such adoration?

'Are you all right?' Leonizio's voice broke into her consciousness.

'I—what did you say?'

'You had a strange look on your face—as though you were lost in a lovely dream. Or perhaps a troublesome dream.'

'A little bit of both,' she murmured.

'Care to tell me?'

'It wouldn't interest you,' she said hastily. 'You're right about supper. I'm hungry.'

She would have said anything to get him off the subject.

'Let's eat.' He led her to the table.

The light meal was delicious. As she tucked in he handed her a newspaper.

'Look at this. It lists the opera performances at the Caracalla Baths. Take your choice.'

'Lovely.'

Eagerly she scanned the paper and found one of her favourite operas being shown the following evening.

'The Barber of Seville,' she said.

'Let's hope it isn't sold out.'

He took out his mobile phone, embarked on a short conversation and gave her the thumbs-up sign.

'We're in luck,' he said. 'I think we got the last two tickets going.'

'Lovely. I'm looking forward to this.'

'There is one thing. They were very expensive seats, so you'll have to dress up to the nines. Give it everything you've got. Your most luxurious dress, your best jewellery.'

'But I haven't got anything like that with me,' she said, alarmed. 'I just came out for a quick visit with casual clothes.'

'Then we'll have to get you something suitable. There's a shop just around the corner where they sell very nice dresses. We'll go there tomorrow.'

'How much do I owe you for my ticket?'

He gave her a wry, teasing look. 'Never ask me anything like that again. It insults me, and I take terrible revenge.'

'I'll just have to risk that. You can't pay for my ticket.'

'I can if I say so. Now, be quiet, finish eating and go to bed.'

She gave a comical salute. 'Yes, sir.'

He saw her into bed, pulled the duvet up over her and kissed her cheek.

'Goodnight,' he said.

'Goodnight.'

She was glad to be alone to brood over the day's events, and the confusion they inspired in her. They had the advantage of a shared sense of humour, which enabled them to fight their battles without bitterness. Thus far, things looked hopeful, if only she could keep her feelings under control. His feelings were for the baby, not herself, and the worst thing that could happen to her would be to fall in love with him. That was something she would never allow to happen.

Finally feeling safe and content, she fell asleep.

The next morning Leonizio took her to the shop, whose window featured a dress more luxurious than she had ever dreamed of wearing. It was made of deep red satin, tight-fitting to emphasise her perfect figure. She tried it on and was left breathless with delight at the sight of herself.

'Like it?' Leonizio asked in a casual tone that suggested no real interest.

'Yes, I love it. Will it make me look suitable?'

'Hmm.' He seemed to consider the matter. 'I guess it will.'

'Then I'll— *What?*'

The exclamation of horror was torn from her as she saw the price tag.

'Oh, I've been so stupid!' she cried. 'I should have checked that sooner. I can't afford that much.'

'You don't have to,' Leonizio said. 'I've already paid for it.'

'But—you can't have.'

Leonizio inclined his head towards a staff member standing nearby. The young woman held up her hand, revealing that it was full of notes.

'You've already paid?' Ellie said, aghast. 'But suppose I hadn't liked it?'

'Then you could have chosen something else.'

Except that he had already made his own choice, she thought. It looked like an act of generosity but actually she was being steered to do his bidding.

'Leonizio, I can't let you buy my clothes. We're not—'

'It's too soon to say what we are and what we're not. Just now you look perfect in that dress, and it's what you ought to wear.'

'Thank you,' she said in a voice that gave nothing away.

They were still playing a game, she thought. He was charming, yet she knew it was chiefly a way of overcoming her refusal.

But I can play as cunning a game as you, she thought. *Beware.*

When they returned to the apartment she donned the dress again, studying herself with satisfaction as she thought of the evening ahead. When it was time to leave, he came to find her.

'You look splendid,' he said. 'You'll do me credit.'

'And that's what matters, of course,' she said lightly.

'It matters more than you think. My business is well known in Rome, and so am I. I have a reputation to keep up.'

'And a woman who looked too ordinary would take you down a peg?'

'Exactly. I can't be seen with a lady who doesn't wear glamorous clothes and expensive jewels.'

'Then you'll have to ditch me. I have no expensive jewels.'

'Luckily, I anticipated that and took precautions.' He reached into his pocket. 'Turn around.'

She did so, and gasped as he came close behind her, raising his hands to fit a glittering diamond necklace about her neck. Ignorant as she was about jewellery, she could tell that it was worth a fortune.

'Whatever is that?' she asked breathlessly.

'My proof to the world that they needn't have doubts about me,' he said cheerfully.

She turned and saw him laughing in a way that made her heart leap.

'You're right,' she said. 'We'll flaunt it tonight and tomorrow you can take it back to the shop.'

'Hey, you're up to every trick,' he said admiringly.

'Sure I am. I could probably teach you a few.'

'Here's another one. We won't be taking this necklace back. Once I've given it you, it's yours.'

'But—'

'No buts. It's yours. My gift to you.'

'But I can't let you give me something like this.'

'Let me? Did I ask your permission?'

'You never ask my permission for any of your crazy ideas.'

'Certainly not,' he said cheerfully. 'You'd refuse, just for the pleasure of being difficult.'

'Of course. Because that's the kind of maddening woman I am.' She challenged him humorously, 'And you actually want to marry me? Are you out of your mind?'

'Probably. I've always enjoyed a challenge. And something tells me you're the biggest challenge I've ever faced. Now, stop arguing. Take the necklace and wear it for the sake of my reputation.'

She wasn't fooled. Behind his talk of reputation he'd performed a cunning manoeuvre to make her accept a luxurious gift. It was beautiful and generous. It was also a way of asserting ownership.

He stood beside her, facing the mirror.

'Will we look good together?' he asked.

Anyone would look good with such a handsome man, she thought. But she only shrugged and said lightly, 'I guess we'll pass.'

'That's all it takes. Let's go.'

CHAPTER FIVE

THE CARACALLA BATHS were unlike any other opera house in the world. The ruins of the original building provided the open-air stage, with sides marked by two vast columns. Facing it was a huge array of seats, climbing high.

'I can hardly get my head round this,' Ellie laughed as she looked around. 'Here we are to enjoy ourselves, but I looked up the Emperor Caracalla and apparently he was one of the most horrifying men who ever ruled Rome. He murdered his brother, murdered his wife and daughter, murdered anyone else who got in his way.'

'It's what emperors did two thousand years ago,' Leonizio said with a grin. 'But in the end someone murdered him.'

'Oh, that's all right then,' she chuckled. 'Fair's fair.'

She soon realised what Leonizio had meant about needing to maintain a reputation. Heads turned at the sight of him, and as he led her towards the seats nearest the stage they were greeted many times, sometimes eagerly, always respectfully. Leonizio introduced Ellie as 'a friend visiting from England'.

'Aha! Doing business in England now?' teased one man.

'But of course,' Ellie said. 'Why else would I be here?'

'It might be something to do with his weakness for a pretty face,' joked another man.

'No, no,' she assured him. 'Strictly business.'

Cheers and laughter. The murmur went around that Leonizio's latest 'friend' was shrewd and funny.

'You're a success,' Leonizio told her as he showed her to her seat. 'Strictly business, eh? Who knows?'

'Nobody. It's too soon to know.'

When everyone in the audience was settled the conductor appeared, bowed and raised his hands to conduct the overture and for the next couple of hours there was no need to talk as both Ellie and Leonizio were swept up with the drama and romance unfolding on stage—their own drama temporarily forgotten.

The performance came to a triumphant end. Smiling, the cast bowed, the audience rose and began to leave.

'Let's have a snack before we go,' he suggested.

She agreed and they headed to the theatre's bar.

'An interesting evening,' he said ironically. 'Even after watching that performance, are you still determined that you are against marriage?'

'I don't believe it's a guarantee of a happy ending.'

'True. If a couple are dazzled by unrealistic dreams they're asking for trouble. But if they're not—if their eyes are open and their thoughts realistic, they can be a success.'

'But what kind of success?'

'You said it yourself when you told my associate that we were strictly business.'

For a moment she was too taken aback to speak. Then she said, 'You think we could have a successful business relationship?'

'We each have something to offer. We arrange the terms, shake hands, and if we trust each other to keep our word it can be a successful arrangement.'

'And just what are the terms?'

'I want our child. You are carrying our baby. In return

I'll provide you with a life of comfort. Whatever you want will be yours.'

'Including your fidelity?'

'If you include that in the terms.'

She considered her answer for a moment before saying casually, 'I might include a certain level of affection in the terms. But I don't think you could manage that.'

'On the contrary. My gratitude for what you have given me would ensure my warmth of feeling.'

But that's not the kind of feeling I would want, she thought. *And no life of comfort would console me for the loss.*

But there was no way she could speak such thoughts to this cool, detached man.

Assuming her most businesslike tone, she said, 'Now let me declare my terms. You can take your proper place as the child's father. Your name will be on the birth certificate, you may visit us whenever you like and establish a relationship. I promise I'll never try to shut you out, but there will be no marriage and we will not live together.'

'Meaning that we'll live in separate countries,' he declared. 'What kind of an arrangement is that?'

'The only kind I will agree to.'

He leaned back and regarded her shrewdly.

'You're a very astute businesswoman. You know you've got the power on your side and you don't concede a single point.'

'But I've conceded a lot. You'll be a real father, part of our child's life.'

'At a distance. If only you knew how much I—' He checked himself and said quickly, 'Time we were going.'

'No, finish what you were saying. If I knew how much you—?'

'It's late. You're tired. Let's go.'

She understood. He'd been on the verge of revealing

the depth of his inner feelings, and he wasn't a man who did that easily. Now he wanted to escape her.

She was beginning to feel sleepy and it was pleasant to let him escort her home and to her door.

'Goodnight,' he said. 'Tomorrow we'll have another chance to talk.'

'Yes,' she murmured. 'There's still a lot to say. And we never know what may happen next.'

He placed his hands gently on her shoulders. 'Sleep well,' he said. 'And if you need anything, call me.'

He backed out, closing the door firmly. He felt a sudden need to be free of her, and the unsettling effect she could have on him.

There was a mysterious quality in Ellie that tempted him to venture into dangerous territory. He'd discovered that on the day they'd first got to know each other, when something about her had lured him out of his protective shell, to make love.

Since then there had been other moments when his defensiveness had faded, alerting him to danger. Tonight he'd hovered on the brink of telling her how much pain he suffered from the feeling of being excluded.

It had been something he'd known all his life, first with the family that reared him, then with the wife who had cheated on him. With the hope of a child he'd cherished a new dream: someone who belonged to him in a way that couldn't be denied. The disillusion had been an experience that made him think of hell.

He confided in nobody. That was weakness, and weakness was something he despised. But with Ellie he was tempted to yield and it alarmed him.

He stood for a while, gazing at the door that he had shut between them. Then he went back to the main room, opened the drinks cabinet and poured himself a large whisky.

* * *

He was up before her next morning, greeting her politely, making the coffee.

'You must tell me where you want to go today,' he said. 'The Colosseum, the Pantheon, more fountains?'

'It sounds wonderful. Rome is so beautiful, so grand and glorious…' Ellie paused.

'But it's not enough for you,' Leonizio ventured.

'No, if anything it's too much for me. I was hoping to see the other Rome—not the one where the emperors ruled, but where the poorer people lived.'

'Of course; you told me that your grandmother came from Trastevere. Is that where you want to see?'

'I'd love to. But I'm not sure that you'd enjoy it.'

'You mean I'd stick out like a sore thumb?'

'No, of course not.'

He gave a wry smile. 'I think you do. When your grandmother lived in Trastevere it was a much poorer district. But now the tourists have discovered it, it's not really poor. Just lively and colourful.'

'Yes, I remember her saying that was beginning to happen.'

'Let's go to the car and we can head there first.'

'Oh, no,' she said quickly. 'I'd like to walk. We're not that far away. Trastevere is just the other side of the river, and we can get there over a footbridge.'

'The Ponte Sisto,' Leonizio murmured.

'Yes, Nonna used to say it was the loveliest way to cross the river. And the bridge isn't far from here.'

He regarded her curiously. 'You've really studied Rome, haven't you?'

'One part of it, because that's the part I've always heard about. It felt like another home, and I always promised myself I'd come here one day. I promised Nonna too, and it makes me sad that she isn't with me.'

'We'll make a good day of it,' he assured her.

'Look,' she said uneasily, 'you really don't need to come. I've studied the route. I can find my way.'

'You think you can but you'd get lost and who knows what would happen to you? The fact is you're afraid I'll spoil it, just by being there. Don't worry. I know when to back off.'

She didn't try to argue further. He was right. She was afraid that his presence would spoil everything. How could this wealthy man, so used to luxury, ever appreciate the special pleasures of Trastevere?

But she understood that he wouldn't let her out of his sight, lest some harm come to the unborn child around whom his world now revolved.

A few minutes' walk brought them to the footbridge that would take them over the Tiber River. Walking across it slowly, Ellie was able to enjoy the sight of a great hill on one side and St Peter's Basilica on the other. But at last she saw something that drove everything else out of her mind. There ahead were the tightly woven cobbled streets of Trastevere.

Soon they had left the bridge and were walking through the streets. With cobblestones underfoot and laundry hanging overhead, it was so different from the neighbourhood they had left that it might have been a new world.

Ellie walked slowly, stopping to look inside a shop or glance upwards at the flowers that seemed to decorate every balcony. Leonizio waited for her patiently, content to let her take her pleasure in her own way. He thought wryly of other women he had entertained in Rome, flaunting the glamorous city to impress them.

But Ellie was different. He had the strange sensation that very little impressed her.

Suddenly she paused, alerted by something she had seen attached to a wall.

'What is it?' Leonizio asked.

'There—just there. The name—I can barely read it—'

He leaned close and read the name of the street.

'That's it?' she gasped. 'That's really it?'

'Yes. Does it mean something?'

'It's where Nonna used to live.'

'In one of these tiny little houses?'

'Yes. And the café must be at the end of the street. Oh, I do hope it's still there.'

'What's its name?'

'I don't know. But it was something to do with clowns.'

'Let's go.'

He took her hand and led her until they came to a place where the narrow road expanded into a square, full of shops and cafés. Although it was still before noon the place was full of life. The shops were open, the cafés had tables out on the pavements. Music and laughter floated through the air.

'Oh, it's lovely,' Ellie breathed. 'But can you see any clowns?'

'I think so,' Leonizio said. 'Over there.' He pointed to a café on the corner with a notice that read, 'Casa dei Pagliacci'.

'Is your Italian good enough for that?'

'Oh, yes!' she cried in delight. 'It means Home of the Clowns.'

He took her hand. 'Let's go.'

As soon as they entered she knew she was going to love this place. Clowns were everywhere. Pictures of them covered the walls, and the waiters were all colourfully dressed as clowns.

The place was crowded, with just one unoccupied table, which they approached quickly. A waiter danced up to them, showed them a menu and bounced away.

'It's like nowhere I've ever been before,' she breathed.

They were just enjoying a light lunch when suddenly there was the sound of cheering. A musician dressed as a clown appeared, bearing a guitar, and began to play. He was joined by another clown, who did a little dance and sang a cheeky ballad. The crowd applauded and he bowed theatrically, travelling around the tables, gesturing to everyone and accepting their gifts.

The first clown went on singing, bowing elaborately when the crowd applauded. Ellie clapped excitedly and the clown approached her, performing theatrically, evidently enjoying her contribution. When they had finished everyone applauded and the clown gazed at her.

'Do you know this song?' he asked.

'My grandmother used to sing it,' Ellie said. 'She came from here.'

'From here? From Trastevere?'

'She lived nearby and she knew this very café. She had friends here.'

'What was her name?'

'Lelia Basini.'

The clown stared in amazement. 'Lelia? You are Lelia's granddaughter? Oh, yes, you must be. Your face is so like hers.'

Now she could see him more closely, and realised that beneath the clown's make-up he was an old man.

'Sit down and talk to us,' Leonizio invited. 'What is your name?'

'I am called Marco. And it is a pleasure to meet Lelia's granddaughter. Is Lelia still alive?'

'Sadly no. It's a long time since she was here,' Ellie said. 'Did you really know her?'

'Oh, yes. I was a waiter here in those days. There were many young men who courted her, and she flirted with us all, but not seriously. She fell in love with another man and went to England. We had only the pictures she left us as memories.'

'Pictures?'

'We all had our photographs taken with her, so that we could keep and treasure them.'

'You have photographs of her?' Ellie breathed. 'Are any of them here? Can I see them?'

'I'll go and find out.'

He returned a few minutes later with a large folder that he laid on the table before Ellie.

'These pictures belong to my great friend, Paolo. He also knew your grandmother well,' he said. 'He doesn't keep them at home in case his wife finds them.'

'After so many years?' Leonizio queried.

'Yes, indeed,' Marco agreed. 'He was very much under Lelia's spell.'

'I can see why,' Leonizio observed.

The girl in the pictures was no beauty but she had a charm and personality that glowed even through the old black-and-white photographs. She laughed, she met the eyes of the men she was with. She was an enchantress.

'Do you recognise her?' Leonizio asked.

'I remember her as a lot older, but yes, it's the same face. And something about her smile never changed over the years.'

'And you are very like her,' Marco said. He addressed Leonizio. '*Signore*, you are a lucky man.'

'Believe me, I know it.'

'Was she happy in England?' Marco asked.

'Oh, yes, my grandparents were happily married.'

'I'm glad she was happy,' Marco said, adding theatrically, 'No man here was happy without her. Ah, but I must leave you.'

He made as if to gather up the pictures, but Ellie fended him off.

'Let me look at them a little longer,' she begged.

When he'd gone she went through the pictures again, entranced by this new view of Lelia.

'I don't believe this is happening,' she said in a daze.

'We were right to come here,' Leonizio said. 'You're a different person in these surroundings.'

'Different? How?'

'You're more relaxed, as though you felt at home here in a way you haven't before.'

'I hoped it would be a nice day,' she said happily, 'but I couldn't have hoped for anything like this. I have the strangest feeling that Nonna is here somewhere; like a ghost haunting me.'

'Not a ghost,' Leonizio said gently. 'She really is with you, here—' he touched her forehead '—and here.' He laid his hand over her breast. 'She's still in your mind and your heart, and I think she always will be.'

It was true, she realised. But what surprised her most was that Leonizio had been able to see it.

She realised that her knowledge of him was limited. His mind and his feelings went deeper than she had understood.

'Just a moment,' he said. 'I've thought of something.'

He rose and left her, heading for the door through which Marco had disappeared. Ellie barely noticed him go. She had found one picture that seemed to speak to her more than any other.

In it Lelia sat alone, smiling at the camera, her gaze full of a kind of cheeky charm that Ellie remembered well from her childhood.

'Oh, how I miss you,' she murmured. 'We understood each other. If only—'

She stopped as she saw Leonizio approaching her with Marco.

'He says you can have any of the pictures you like,' Leonizio said. 'Just take your pick.'

'You mean—?'

'Whatever you want,' Marco said.

Her heart leapt with happiness. 'Can I take this one?' she said, holding up the picture that had entranced her.

Marco nodded. 'You are welcome to keep it,' he said.

He backed away, but not before Ellie had noticed him reaching out to take something from Leonizio's hand. She couldn't see exactly what passed between them, but she reckoned she knew. Astonished, she looked up at Leonizio as Marco left them.

'Did you pay him?' she gasped.

'Just a little. I could see what those pictures meant to you. I thought you should have at least one.' He added wryly, 'Of course I did it without consulting you, which doubtless condemns me as a bully. You might want to take some revenge.'

'And how would I do that?' she said, smiling.

'It's up to you. I suppose you could thump me.'

'Mmm. I'm sure I could think of something more interesting. In the meantime, I'll just say thank you. It's a lovely thing to have.'

She gazed at the photograph, eyes shining with pleasure. Leonizio regarded her, fascinated. He thought of something else he'd given her, the luxurious diamond necklace. He'd offered costly gifts to women before and they had seized on them as the natural spoils from a rich man. But this woman cared nothing for expensive jewels. She had even tried to reject the diamonds. It was a memento of her grandmother that made her happy.

This was his chance to get closer to her, Leonizio realised. Ellie had let her guard down around him for the first time since arriving in Italy. When they got home they could talk more freely than before, and everything would be different. By the end of the day she might even have agreed to marry him.

'Perhaps we should go home now,' he said. 'You're looking tired.'

'Yes, let's go.'

'And this time we're taking a taxi. No arguments.'

'All right. Whatever you say.'

He grinned. 'Now you've got me really worried. When you speak in that submissive way I wonder what you're planning. I guess I'll have to wait and see.'

She chuckled but made no reply in words. He paid the bill, adding a substantial tip to reflect his pleasure in the way the lunch had turned out, and led her out.

In the taxi she leaned back, sighing with pleasure. 'That was lovely,' she said.

'Yes, wasn't it? But the day doesn't have to end now. We could go somewhere else this evening.'

'Actually, Leonizio, I'm rather worn out. If you don't mind, I would like to rest up this afternoon and evening. And I should really check in with the office. I'm sure that my work is really piling up back in London. But thank you for taking me there.'

Back at his apartment, she touched his arm gently and went into her room, leaving him standing there, reflecting on how wrong he'd been to think they could have an affectionate talk.

It was true, he thought wryly, that the day had aroused her warmer feelings.

But not for him.

CHAPTER SIX

THE NEXT MORNING Leonizio was already up, making the coffee. He greeted Ellie with a smile when she wandered into the kitchen.

'Did you have a good night?'

'A lovely night. I felt Nonna and I were back together, talking as we used to.'

'Did she say anything interesting?'

'Oh, yes. She's so wise. She helps me see everything differently. I want to remember seeing her street, the house she once lived in and going to that café. It was such a happy day. Did it seem that way to you? Or isn't Trastevere your kind of place?'

'What makes you think that? Why shouldn't it be?'

'Well, since you made your fortune don't you live a more high society life?'

'You think I'm too lofty? You couldn't be more wrong. Trastevere is very much my kind of place, and I know it well. My uncle owned a little shop there, and he made such a success of it that he managed to buy another shop. I used to earn pocket money being his messenger boy.' He grinned. 'And not just him. A lot of the other shops used me to run errands—for a price. Those were good times. I had a lot of friends there.

'In fact I still have friends who live there. Taking you

there yesterday made me realise how long it's been since I've seen some of them. In fact I quite fancy looking up some of my old friends.' A thought seemed to strike him. 'Do you fancy coming with me?'

'Oh, yes, I'd love to.'

'We'll go tonight then. Do you want to do some more exploring this afternoon?'

'I'd like to see the Pantheon.'

'That's where we'll go.'

After the Pantheon they took a stroll through the streets. Ellie found Rome so beautiful that just wandering about was a pleasure. Escorting her, Leonizio was alert for anything that might interest her.

'Over there you'll see— Ellie? Ellie—where are you?'

Looking around, he saw that he had completely lost her attention. She had moved away and was gazing ecstatically into a shop window at a collection of shoes.

'I've heard that Italian shoes are lovely,' she said. 'And these really are. Especially those.' She indicated a pair in the centre of the display. 'I'm going in to try them on. Hey, let me go.'

Leonizio had put his arm about her waist, holding her back.

'Don't move,' he said, smiling. 'You're not going in there.'

'Why? Is something wrong with those shoes?'

'No, the pair you're looking at are Fellani shoes.'

'Fellani? Yours? Really?'

'From our latest range. Come to the factory and see.'

She agreed, eager to see the factory, which she felt would tell her so much about him.

In half an hour they had reached a large building near the edge of the city. Looking at the windows, Ellie saw faces which lit up at the sight of him.

Inside, there were machines everywhere, making buzzing noises. A young man came to meet them.

'My assistant, Francesco,' Leonizio said.

He introduced them, explaining that Ellie was a lawyer, and a friend. On his instructions, Francesco fetched a collection of shoes, which Leonizio proceeded to fit on her feet. The ones she liked best were the ones she had seen in the shop, but they were too small.

'I'm afraid we don't have a larger size here at the moment,' Francesco said.

'Then we'll make a pair specially,' Leonizio said.

They proceeded to examine Ellie's feet.

'I hadn't expected this,' she said when Francesco had left them. 'How much do I owe you?'

'Owe me? You surely don't think I'm going to charge you? You're a special guest.'

'But the shoes look expensive and I sort of forced this on you,' she said, embarrassed.

'Do you really think you could force anything on me against my will?'

'Well, if you put it that way—I guess I couldn't. But I'm honoured. A pair made especially for me. Wow!'

'You're not just an ordinary customer.'

His voice was warm and she wondered if she'd only imagined that his glance fell on her stomach.

But of course, she thought. It was her pregnancy that made her special. He had never pretended otherwise. But still his care of her was heart-warming.

When it was settled that the shoes would be delivered next day they left to finish the journey to Trastevere.

As they went through the streets Ellie recognised some of the places they had passed the day before. Leonizio stopped outside a little shop.

'This was the first one my uncle owned,' he said. 'He made a success out of it but it took all his energy.'

The shop was tiny and narrow, selling everything at low prices.

'Did you ever work for him in here?' she asked.

'Yes, for hours. And I promised myself I'd escape and make a different life.'

'You certainly did that,' she laughed. 'Is there anyone who hasn't heard of the powerful Leonizio Fellani?'

He grinned. 'I hope not. Of course, some of them disapprove of me.'

'Naturally. If you've got the better of them they'll curse you, but that just means you're a success.'

'Ellie, you have the soul of a true businesswoman.'

'So I should hope,' she said cheerfully. 'Life's more fun that way.'

'Hey, Leonizio!'

The cry made Ellie look round at the man waving and making his way towards them.

'Ottimo per vedere di nuovo.'

Ellie just recognised the words as 'Great to see you again.' Leonizio greeted him, introduced her and said, 'Speak English for my friend. Ellie, this is Nico.'

'It is a pleasure to meet you,' Nico said, taking her hand. 'In fact it's always a pleasure to meet one of Leonizio's lovely ladies.'

'Be careful,' Leonizio warned.

'Don't worry,' Ellie said. 'I doubt he could tell me anything I haven't already worked out. And I am only your lawyer.' She faced him, smiling. 'Aren't I?'

Leonizio's face betrayed his confusion. 'Whatever you say.'

'Ah, then all is well!' Nico exclaimed in relief. 'Now let me take you for a coffee.'

'I don't think—' Leonizio began.

'That's a lovely idea,' Ellie said. 'I could just do with a coffee.'

As they left the shop Leonizio whispered in her ear, 'You're enjoying this, aren't you?'

'More than you'll ever imagine,' she agreed.

There was a small café next door. When they were settled, Nico ordered for them before saying, 'Hey, look who's over there!'

Another man was waving to them from the far side of the room. He too seemed familiar with Leonizio, signalling him to come over.

'Go and say hello,' Nico said. 'After all, you owe them.'

Leonizio glowered at him but went across to the couple, both of whom embraced him heartily.

'He owes them?' Ellie queried.

'Yes, but not money,' Nico chuckled. 'A favour. Something to do with a young lady. It was several years ago. In those days Leonizio was a *libertino*, a rather wild young man.'

'You mean wild where women are concerned?' Ellie queried. 'Libertine is an English word too.'

'Ah, yes. He often created trouble for himself, and they gave him an alibi for—well, I don't know the details. It was before he got married and became middle-aged.'

'Middle-aged? He's only thirty-four.'

'On the outside. Inside, he's grim and ferocious and years older than he actually is.'

'I see what you mean. So he has quite a history?'

'They say he had his pick of all the girls in Rome, and sometimes he seemed to pick them all. And they picked him. But then he fell in love with this English lady and became a different man—at least for a while. I heard a rumour that he was divorcing her for infidelity.'

'That's true.'

'Then he must have turned into a different man again. Who can say who he is now?'

She nodded, but did not reply. Nico had struck a nerve.

Who could say who Leonizio was now? Perhaps he didn't even know himself.

'Have you known him long?' she asked.

'I used to work in the shop when his uncle owned it. I hated that man. So did most people. Cold, hard, indifferent to everyone but himself. When Leonizio inherited it I worked for him, which was much more pleasant. He's a hard man but a generous employer. Then I managed to raise the money to buy it. Ah, here he is.'

Leonizio returned and now they were able to settle down together for the evening. Ellie was fascinated. She was seeing new sides to Leonizio and he intrigued her more every moment.

As they left the building he said in a cheerful voice, 'I guess I don't have any reputation left.'

'Why should you think that?'

'I overheard some of what Nico said, especially *libertino*.'

She laughed. 'Well, you never pretended to be a man of strict virtue. Actually, Nico said some very nice things about you. According to him, you're better than your uncle, who was cold, hard, indifferent to everyone but himself.'

'True enough. Growing up with him and my aunt was like growing up without any family. I used to envy the other kids who had parents who visited their school, got involved, came to see them in the school play.'

'They didn't come to see you in the—?'

'Why should they bother? They cared nothing for me.'

'But if you were your uncle's heir, mustn't he have had some feelings for you to make such a will?'

'He didn't make a will. My aunt died before him and his possessions came to me as his closest living relative. I was grateful for the lucky stroke of fate, but—well—' He shrugged.

But there had been no emotional comfort in his inheritance, she realised.

'Never mind.' He put his arm around her. 'I have a family now.'

'Yes,' she said. 'Yes, you do.'

'And it means more than money ever could.'

'As long as it makes you happy.'

'Happy? There are no words for how happy I am. I didn't believe it was possible.'

She looked down at her still flat stomach, caressing it gently.

'Do you hear that?' she asked their unseen companion. 'Your daddy is already crazy about you. Aren't you lucky?'

'I'm the one who's lucky,' Leonizio said. He addressed her belly. 'Are you listening? I'll always come to your school play. That's a promise.'

Ellie laughed and hugged him. In the taxi on the way home she leaned her head on his shoulder, wondering when she had ever felt such a sense of peaceful contentment.

Several pairs of shoes were delivered next morning. She tried them all on, enchanted by their beauty and comfort.

'They're lovely,' she said.

'Glad you like them.' Leonizio grinned. 'Now I know that our customers will like them.'

'Oh, I see. I'm a marketing experiment.'

'You don't mind, do you?'

'Not at all. I hope I'm a success.'

They both laughed, and he said, 'We'll drop by the factory and let them see you wearing them. They'll love it.'

He was right. The workers cheered when she arrived. Francesco took a load of photographs of her feet.

'They'll make great advertisements,' he said.

'You might end up with a modelling fee,' Leonizio teased her.

She stayed at the factory the rest of the morning and had lunch with him in the works canteen.

'Oh, I'm loving this,' she sighed. 'I don't know when I've enjoyed a holiday so much.'

'Is that what I am to you?' he asked ironically. 'A holiday?'

'No, I didn't mean— It was just—'

Words failed her. There was no way to express what they both knew, that they were getting to know each other to see how the future would work out. The more she enjoyed Rome, the more confused she became. Her life was settled, and how much Leonizio would be a part of it was something she still couldn't decide.

But she'd be wise to remember one thing. Leonizio was taking wonderful care of her, but chiefly because he wanted something. And she was hovering dangerously on the edge of being fooled.

It was time to escape.

'I really must leave Rome and get back to work,' she said uneasily.

'So soon? Can't you stay a little longer?'

'No, there are things I have to do—I can't just neglect my job. This has been lovely but—'

He shrugged. 'All right, let it go. I know what you're really telling me. We'll both go to England. I want to be there to see my divorce become final as soon as possible, and sign anything I need to sign.'

'Yes, it will all be simpler if you're there.'

'I must stay here for a few hours now and fix things so that they can manage without me while I'm away.'

'I'll get out of your way. I can go home and watch the news on television, and see if my Italian is good enough to follow it.'

'Fine. I'll see you this evening. I'll send for the car.'

'No need. I can walk back. It's not far, and I like to explore.'

She enjoyed the stroll through the streets. At home she put her feet up and watched the television, then took up a newspaper that had been delivered and began to read it. She found that she understood more than she had expected.

Perhaps I should try reading a book, she thought. *Let's see.*

She began to browse, remembering seeing Leonizio glancing through a large volume about Rome, which he had finally put away on a tall shelf. Searching, she found it easily and reached up to take it down. But her movements dislodged other books on either side. She grabbed them quickly, but one fell to the floor. She dropped down beside it, suddenly tense at what she could see. The book had fallen open at a page that contained a photograph of a man and a woman, dressed for a wedding.

Only half believing what her eyes told her, Ellie studied the man's face and realised that it was Leonizio. He was looking at his bride—this must be Harriet—with an expression of love. She looked up at him, not with love but with a teasing expression.

Had there really been so much difference between them? Ellie wondered. She could easily believe it. The story of their marriage and Harriet's deception suggested that she had seen him as a man she could use.

There were more pictures in the album. Absorbed, Ellie went through it, watching the couple enjoying each other's company in many different ways. One picture of them relaxing on a beach showed Leonizio in a pair of swim shorts that showed off his shape: slim but muscular, perfectly proportioned.

Could any woman look at that body without wanting to take it to bed? Ellie wondered. The memories it revived in her were achingly beautiful.

There was a brief letter enclosed, from the friend who had taken the pictures.

Thought you'd like to see how they came out. Nice to see you and Harriet so happy. Here's to your future.

Browsing through the rest of the album, Ellie grew very still when she came to another picture. The couple were sitting together with his hand on her stomach. Again he wore a look of adoration, but this time it was clearly for the baby, and the happiness he was sure would soon be his.

The sight of his face hurt her. It was so vulnerable in his belief that his dreams had come true. Ellie had always known that the truth had hurt him, but now she could sense how brutally his heart had been broken.

And so he now clung to her, she mused. Because in her he sensed a chance to revive his hopes. She couldn't blame him, despite the ache of regret that this was the only reason he valued her.

At last something in the silence made her look up to find Leonizio standing there, his eyes fixed on her.

'I'm sorry,' she said hastily. 'I didn't mean to pry. I just came across this accidentally.'

'Don't worry,' he said. 'I guess you know about that part of my life.'

'Yes, and I'm glad to understand you a little better.'

'How do you mean?'

'I've heard you talk about Harriet with something like hate in your voice. I hadn't realised how deeply you once felt about her.'

'You don't think love can turn into hate? On the contrary. The deeper the love, the deeper the hate.'

He spoke quietly but there was a violence of feeling in his eyes. This was a man who had not merely felt a mild affection. He had loved with an intensity that had put his life on the line.

She wondered how it would feel to inspire such feelings.

'What about you?' he asked. 'Don't you know how it feels to hate?'

'No. Nobody has ever mattered that much.'

'What about the guy you told me about, who left you for another woman?'

'I put him behind me. When I decided that he no longer existed—that's when he ceased to exist.'

'You make it sound so easy.'

'It can be, if you really want it to be.'

As she watched, the intensity vanished from his face, leaving it blank.

'It will happen to you one day,' he said quietly. 'Someone will become your life to such an extent that when they betray you there's nothing left.'

She shivered. He had driven all feeling out, leaving only emptiness inside himself, and somehow he troubled her more this way.

'Nothing?' she asked.

'Nothing.'

Suddenly she heard her cell phone ringing from another room. She headed out but turned in the doorway, meaning to speak to him. But what she saw held her silent.

Leonizio was looking at a picture of Harriet, and Ellie thought she had never seen so much sadness in anyone's face. He didn't move, but sat with his eyes fixed on the woman who had illuminated his life, then destroyed it. Only a moment ago his face had been blank and empty. Now it was haunted by despair.

She hesitated, longing to speak to him but fearful lest any word from her would be ill-chosen. While she tried to decide, the telephone shrilled again and she hurried away to her room.

It was her boss on the phone.

'OK,' he said. 'We've got the final papers.'

She drew a sharp breath. 'Everything?'

'Everything. Best get back here fast, both of you.'

'Yes. I'll call you back when I've spoken to him.' She hung up.

Leonizio appeared in the doorway.

'Has something happened?' he asked tensely.

'That was Alex. You were right about coming to England. We're in the final stage.'

'Great. Let's be on our way.'

'I'll check some good London hotels, although I'm sure you already know the best.'

'Hotels?' he said. 'That's a very unkind suggestion. I'd hoped you were going to invite me to stay with you.' He gave a brief laugh. 'If you could see your face! I guess I know what you think of that suggestion.'

'It's only that my place is small. I don't have another bed.'

'Do you have a sofa?'

'Well, yes, but—'

'Then I'll sleep on the sofa. And I'll do my share of tidying up. Don't argue. It's settled.'

A combination of exasperation and amusement made her say, 'There's really no getting rid of you, is there?'

'That depends how much you want to get rid of me.'

She gave him a teasing look. 'Perhaps I haven't quite made up my mind.'

'Let me help you.'

Dropping his hands on her shoulders, he drew her close enough to lay his mouth against hers. It wasn't a passionate kiss, but a gentle assertion of possession, lasting just long enough to make his point.

'Does that make it any easier?' he asked.

She considered. 'Not really. Some things are hard to decide.'

'I could try again—with your permission, of course.'

Oh, he was a cunning so-and-so, she reckoned: putting the decision on her.

'All right,' she said, 'but try to do better this time.'

That would provoke him, she thought. His next kiss would be fiercer, more determined.

But his lips only brushed her mouth even more softly than before.

'Get rid of me later,' he murmured. 'For the moment I'm coming with you to England.'

Without waiting for her reply, he turned away to the telephone and called the airport.

Ellie clenched her fists, alarmed at her own reaction. She'd been ready for the second kiss to be passionate, and its restraint had left her heart beating fiercely with disappointment.

She stepped back, annoyed with him for disappointing her, but even more annoyed with herself for caring.

'The plane leaves this afternoon at four o'clock,' Leonizio said, hanging up. 'I've bought us tickets.'

'How much do I owe you?'

'Nothing. I'll pay for your ticket.'

'Thank you, but no. I pay for my own ticket. I don't ask you to support me.'

He seemed about to argue, but changed his mind, muttering, 'I'll go and pack.'

'Me too.'

She left him quickly, lest he see how disturbed she was. The touch of his lips had aroused an eagerness for another, deeper kiss. She had resisted it, but was dismayed at herself for feeling it at all.

And why had he picked that particular moment to kiss her? Just a few minutes ago Harriet had intruded on his consciousness, reviving thoughts and feelings that disturbed him. Had he turned to her in genuine desire? Or was it an act of defiance against the past, against Harriet?

Whatever the answer, she must struggle harder to be in control of the situation. She had promised herself that control. But it wasn't working as she'd planned.

Was there any way of coping with this infuriating man?

There was no chance to brood further. Now the time was taken up with practical matters: packing, getting to the airport, boarding the plane.

'The flight will be two and a half hours,' he said, 'and it will be late by the time we reach your place. So let's eat plenty on the plane.'

He was right. By the time they landed and left the airport the light was fading. It took another hour for the taxi to reach London and start the journey to her home. At first they travelled through the expensive part of town, but gradually the streets grew shabbier.

At last they pulled up near a five-storey block of flats. Leonizio looked up high.

'You live there?'

'Yes, I'm in one of the top apartments.'

Inside, they headed for the elevator, but got no further. A notice announced that it was out of order.

'Oh, no!' Ellie groaned. 'It was supposed to be mended by now. Oh, well, up we go.'

She headed for the stairs, followed by Leonizio, who took her suitcase as well as his own.

'You can't carry them both,' she protested. 'They'll be much too heavy.'

He grinned. 'Nonsense. Superman can carry any weight. Lead on.'

She began to climb the stairs, going slowly. About halfway up she paused, taking deep breaths.

'You shouldn't be doing a climb like this,' he said. 'It's taking too much out of you.'

'Nonsense, I'm Superwoman.'

'But Superwoman needs Superman.'

They had reached a corner where the stairs flattened out into a wide ledge. Leonizio dumped the suitcases and reached out to her.

'Come here,' he said. And the next moment she was lifted high in his arms.

'Direct me,' he demanded.

'Two more flights and then we're at my front door.'

He mastered the two flights quickly, setting her down by the door while he went back for the cases. She hurried inside, wondering what would happen now.

The way he'd lifted her without checking her feelings left her in two minds.

Chivalrous? she mused. Or controlling? Or perhaps they were two halves of the same.

But she had to admit she didn't mind being saved the effort of climbing the last stairs.

He appeared with the cases and looked around. She wondered how he would regard her plain little apartment after the glamorous luxury of his own home. He'd chosen to sleep on the sofa, but that was before he'd seen how narrow and hard it was.

'You'd really better go to a hotel,' she said. 'You can't sleep on that sofa.'

'I'll be fine. I'm staying here. No arguments. My mind is made up.'

'All right, I'll get you some blankets.'

She did her best to make him comfortable, fetching some blankets and a pillow, then arranging them on the sofa.

'Can I have that?' he asked, pointing to a small table. 'And a lamp? I like to read at night.'

She put the table where he indicated, near his head, and set a small metal lamp on it.

'So what's the next step?' he asked. 'When do I sign the papers?'

'I'll call my boss. Luckily, I've got his home number.'

Alex Dallon answered the phone at once.

'We're here,' she said.

'You don't mean you actually managed to make Fellani see sense? Well done, Ellie. You've got a great career in front of you.'

Leonizio glanced up and she realised with dismay that Dallon's voice was loud and sharp enough to carry beyond the phone.

'Shut up!' she said desperately.

'Get him in here tomorrow,' Dallon continued. 'Drag him if you have to.'

'Goodnight,' she said desperately and hung up before he could say more.

To her relief, Leonizio was grinning.

'You won't have to drag me,' he assured her.

'I'm sorry. He had no right to speak of you like that.'

'Especially when I'm near enough to overhear him. Don't worry, it's not your fault. And in a way he was right. You have helped me to see sense about some things.' His tone became ironic. 'You might say there are things I'm trying to get you to see sense about. Except that so far I'm not doing well.'

'I'll ignore that remark,' she said lightly.

'Very wise. We both have to sort out our brains before anything more happens. The problem is that we don't agree what "seeing sense" means.'

'We'll have to wait and discover how things turn out. We don't know each other very well yet.'

'Don't we? Wasn't there one moment when we knew each other very well indeed?'

'No,' she said softly. 'We thought we did, but—well—it was…'

'An illusion,' he sighed.

'I think so.'

'The trouble is, there are some illusions you want to cling to.'

'But it isn't always a good idea,' she said.

'True. Or it can be a wonderful idea.'

'But if it's only an illusion—'

'Then we could work to make it reality. What is an illusion, what is reality? Is there really a difference?'

It could be so tempting to follow him along this path, she thought. But it was a temptation she must resist, and it would be better to escape him now.

'Can I get you anything before you settle for the night?' she asked politely.

'No, thank you. Just don't vanish without warning.'

'Promise.'

She left him and hurried to her own room. It felt like taking refuge, so troublesome did she find him these days. There she could enjoy the sensation of relaxing, free from the world. Poor and shabby her apartment might be, but to her it was home in a way that nowhere else ever had been. She had found it when she went to work for Alex Dallon, knowing that she had defeated four other applicants for the job. It was her independence, her success, her right to be herself, think her own thoughts, travel her own path.

She knew Leonizio had seen only its disadvantages. He would never understand her thoughts or dreams, and perhaps for that reason they would never be truly close.

CHAPTER SEVEN

ELLIE SETTLED CONTENTEDLY in bed and managed to get to sleep quickly, but awoke after a while with the night only partly over.

She wondered how Leonizio was managing next door. She could hear some faint creaking which went on for several minutes, suggesting that he was tossing and turning restlessly. She understood that very well. What was happening to them now was disturbing.

Suddenly there came a loud clatter and the sound of crashing. Hurriedly, she jumped up and dashed into the other room.

Leonizio was lying on the floor, looking stunned. Beside him lay the metal lamp.

'I fell off,' he growled. 'And I knocked your lamp down. Sorry.'

For a moment she couldn't respond. He had removed all clothes but for a pair of boxers. The sight of him almost naked made her draw a sharp breath.

He tried to hoist himself back onto the sofa, but gave up.

'My arm,' he growled. 'I landed on it. Ouch!'

'Let me help you,' she said. 'Put your other arm around me.'

He did so. She wrapped her arms about him and together they managed to lift him the few inches onto the sofa.

'Thanks,' he growled, dropping his head and beginning to rub it.

'Is your head injured?' she asked anxiously.

'No, just a little bump. I'll be all right in a moment.'

'Can I get you something?'

'No, I'll just go back to sleep.'

'Not here. This sofa is too small for you. You must sleep in my bed.'

'You mean—?'

'I'll sleep on the sofa. I'm small enough to fit on there. Come along. Don't argue.'

'Yes, ma'am.'

Leaning on her, he rose to his feet and let her support him into the bedroom and onto the bed, where he stretched out with a sigh of relief.

'I'm supposed to be here looking after you,' he sighed. 'You could say I'm making a mess of it.'

'No, you couldn't. Stop making a drama out of a little accident.'

He regarded her wryly. 'Well, you did warn me the sofa was too small. I should have listened.'

'You? Listen to advice? Don't make me laugh.'

'All right, all right. I give in.'

'That's what I like to hear.' She pulled the covers up over him. 'Now, go to sleep.'

He snuggled down and closed his eyes. After a moment she retreated into the other room. There she lay down on the sofa and tried to go back to sleep.

But sleep eluded her. Her mind was filled with visions she didn't want to see, and thoughts she didn't want to indulge.

She had made love with this man, but until tonight she hadn't seen him nearly naked. His smooth, muscular torso, narrow hips and long elegant legs had come as a shock. Even more stunning had been the sudden urgent desire to wrap her arms about his naked flesh, holding it against her, enjoying the sensation.

But it was a losing battle. The feel of his body had been so thrilling that it haunted her still, inflaming her anger and defiance.

She had vowed to fend off his attempts to take control of her, and she could manage that where it concerned him giving her orders. But there was no protection against the surges of temptation that he could inspire against her will. She could only determine not to let him suspect.

She was up early the next morning, preparing breakfast, wondering how Leonizio would cope with everything that was to happen that day. When he appeared she was shocked at the bruise on his forehead.

'I hit the lamp a bit harder than I thought,' he said, reading her expression. 'But it's all right. Your colleagues will think you've started beating me up already.'

She didn't query 'already', guessing that it was a hint about the marriage he was still trying to talk her into.

'I'll pick my own moment for that,' she said lightly. 'Eat up, then we'll get going.'

When they reached her office Alex Dallon was engaged with another client. While they waited for him, Leonizio stood by the window, gazing out at a row of shops over the road.

'That department store over the street stocks Fellani shoes.'

Ellie looked up at him and smiled. 'Your shoes are very desirable to the UK market.'

He nodded. 'Some of my best sales are in England. It's worth thinking about.'

'Sorry to keep you waiting,' came a voice from behind them.

They turned to see Alex, holding a sheaf of papers.

'I expect Ellie's told you how close we are to the finish,' he said. 'Your wife applied to the court for what's known as a 'quickie divorce' and a few brief formalities will tie up all the loose ends.'

He handed Leonizio the papers, which he sat down to read. Ellie went to sit beside him.

'You'd better go through them for me,' Leonizio said. 'I'm not sure my English is up to it.'

She did her duty, explaining as she went, making sure he knew how completely final this was. Remembering how the picture of Harriet had affected him, Ellie wondered how this would make him feel, but he listened with a blank, unresponsive face.

'And when I sign these papers, that's it?' he said.

'There will be no barriers to divorce,' Alex said. 'And it will be granted in a few days. You'll be completely free.'

'Thank you,' Leonizio said in a toneless voice. 'Now I must go. Send me your bill and I'll pay it at once.'

He headed for the door. Alex indicated for her to follow him and she did so, gladly. Something told her that Leonizio shouldn't be alone just now.

They found a restaurant with tables in a small garden. Leonizio ordered coffee for her and whisky for himself.

'I need a drink,' he said. 'So that's tied up all the ends. Now Harriet has her divorce it leaves her free to marry her lover before they have their child.'

'Don't,' Ellie pleaded. 'I know it's hard for you, but let her go. Let the baby go. Don't grieve for the rest of your life.'

'But what am I supposed to do? Forget grief because it's inconvenient?'

'No, I suppose not,' she sighed.

It hurt her to see his air of defeat. It was as though all life and hope had ended for him.

'That's it,' he said. 'All done. All over.'

'Not over,' she said. 'You haven't lost everything.' She took his hand and laid it on her stomach. 'You still have this.'

'Do I?'

'Yes. This baby is yours and nothing will ever change that.'

'Does that mean you'll marry me now that I'm a free man?'

'It means it doesn't matter whether we marry or not. You'll have a relationship with your child whatever happens. Marriage isn't everything. I can give you a great deal without that.'

He made a wry face and took a sip of whisky.

'I'll be going now,' he said. 'I mustn't keep you from your work. I'll see you at home tonight.'

'You'd better have your key,' she said, reaching into her purse. 'I got you a spare before we left this morning, so you can come and go without me.'

'Thanks. And thank you for—for everything.' He departed so quickly that she sensed he desperately needed to get away.

For the rest of the day she tried to concentrate on work, but it was hard when she couldn't help thinking of Leonizio, wandering alone, brooding bitterly on the feeling that his life was over.

Unless I agree to marry him, she thought. *It would be so easy to say yes, but I just can't. He has no feelings for me. Only for our baby and his other life. Could I bear to live with that?*

No. She couldn't face it. It would be easy to develop

feelings for Leonizio, and that was a reason for not marrying him. It would mean a life of misery and jealousy.

At last the day was over and she could return home.

'I'm here,' she called as she entered.

Silence.

'Hello, Leonizio. I'm home.'

But there was no reply. She wandered through the rooms, seeking him, finding only emptiness, while her heart sank.

Where was he? What was he doing that had taken him so long? Now she recalled that when he had left her in the café he'd had an air of purpose.

But what could his purpose be?

Was it possible that he had gone to seek Harriet, determined to have one more meeting with her?

Was his love for her really as dead as he thought? Had he discovered renewed feelings that made it vital for him to see her again? He had spoken of the link between love and hate. Had his hate taken a new direction?

No, she told herself. That was absurd fantasy. He would return soon.

But an hour passed without any sign of Leonizio. Glancing out of the window, she saw an empty street.

Now she knew she had no choice but to accept the truth. She could only go to bed, not on the sofa, as she had previously decided, but in her own bedroom, since he would not be coming back. There she lay in silent desperation until at last she fell asleep.

She awoke in the early hours to find the apartment still silent. She knew at once that he had not returned. He was out there, making the plans that suited him, ignoring her wishes, thinking only of his own.

And what are his wishes? she wondered. *If I give in and do whatever he wants, what happens then? He doesn't care for me. I'm useful to him, that's all.*

She had sensed a growing warmth between them, but it had all been an illusion. She had deceived herself, ignoring the warning signs that had brought her to the edge of reacting to him with dangerous intensity.

'Fool,' she muttered. 'The truth was always there before you, but you wouldn't see it. Fool!'

She lay motionless for an hour, finally drifting back into sleep. She was awoken suddenly by a noise from next door. Rising quickly, she went out into the main room, switching on the light.

'Have a heart!' said a voice.

He was there on the sofa, covering his eyes against the light.

'I'd only just gone to bed,' he complained. 'And you had to do that.'

'I'm sorry—I didn't know you were here. You weren't here an hour ago.'

'I came in quietly, so as not to wake you. I fell asleep almost instantly. It's been a heavy day.'

'Why? Has something happened?'

'In a way. Things don't always turn out the way we expect. I've had a lot of thinking to do—decisions to make.'

'Hard decisions?' she asked, as lightly as she could manage. It wasn't easy.

'Some of them.' He made a wry face, full of self-mockery. 'I'm not one of the most original thinkers in the world. I can handle business fine, but when it comes to people I tend to make a mess of it.'

'Don't be so hard on yourself. Why must you take such a gloomy view of life?'

'Is that how I seem? Well, maybe—it's just that things don't seem to work out as I hoped. I've had ideas we need to discuss before we—' He checked himself sharply, as though continuing would be a problem. 'You couldn't get me a drink, could you?'

'Tea?'

'I was thinking of something a bit stronger.'

Wine, she thought. Men always chose alcohol when they needed all their courage for a tough conversation.

She could almost hear him saying, *Ellie, I'm leaving you. I still want to see my child, but there's nothing else between us.*

How much wine would he need for that?

She poured him a glass of red, thrust it into his hand and stood waiting, silently preparing herself for the worst.

'All right,' she said at last. 'Let's hear it.'

He hesitated. 'Some things aren't easy to say.'

The words seemed to confirm her worst apprehensions.

'I'm sure you're good at them,' she said, forcing herself to speak casually.

'Sure, I've had some practice at that. More than I'd like. But we need to talk about how things are now.' He waved his hand around the room. 'This isn't working. We're getting on each other's nerves here, so I thought about it and—well—'

'Decided to get out,' she said quietly. Her heart was quivering.

'Yes. That's where I've been this afternoon—looking for somewhere. I think I've found the perfect place.'

'When are you leaving?'

'That's up to you. I'll take you to see it later on today. I think you'll like it, and then we'll move in as soon as possible.'

'*We?* Did you say *we*?'

'Of course. You can't go on living here with those rickety stairs and the lifts that don't always work.'

She stared at him. Now her heart was thundering.

'And that's what this is all about?' she whispered.

'Look, don't be offended that I went searching without you. I wanted to see what was available. I know what you're thinking.'

'I really don't think you do.'

'Yes, I can follow your mind by now. You believe I should have discussed it with you first, that I take too much on myself. But I just wanted to look at some nice places and see if any were likely to appeal to you.'

She had been wrong. He wasn't leaving her. Her relief was so fierce that she almost lost control.

'Ellie, are you all right?'

'I'm fine—fine.'

'You don't look fine. You look as though something has knocked you sideways. I didn't mean to upset you.'

'I'm not upset. Just confused. You've been looking at apartments?'

'I've seen several, and there's one in particular that I think would be right for you. The sooner you see it the better, so why don't we go today?'

'You mean you've already made an appointment?' she guessed.

'Yes, I felt I should. Sorry about not consulting you first but I didn't want it to slip through our fingers, so I've arranged for us to see it.'

'But I have to go to work.'

'Can't you slip out for an hour at lunchtime? I don't want you to miss this.'

She didn't want to miss it either. She was alive with curiosity to see the place he had chosen as right for her.

'All right, I'll come at lunchtime.'

'It's a date. I promise you, this place will make your head spin.'

Her head was already spinning, but in ways he must not be allowed to know.

'I'll see you in the morning,' she said, and left him quickly.

* * *

Alex Dallon was waiting for her when she reached work, full of praise for her skill in looking after a wealthy client.

'I heard what Signor Fellani was saying about his English sales yesterday,' he said. 'It would be good for his business to have a branch over here. And it would certainly be good for our business to handle his profitable stuff. So try to keep him in a cheerful mood.'

'I'm having lunch with him today.'

'Good work. Take as long as you need. Call him now and tell him to collect you early.'

She did so, and was ready when Leonizio arrived at midday. Alex gave her a thumbs-up sign and waved them off.

'You're doing my career a mass of good,' she teased when they were settled in the back of a taxi. 'Alex thinks you're planning to expand into an English branch, and he's tasked me with making sure that you do.'

'Sensible man. So is that why you're with me now?'

'Officially, yes.'

'It's all going to be very interesting. But let's get this apartment sorted first.'

'Yes. I'm really looking forward to seeing it. Is it far?'

He gave her a scrap of paper on which he'd written the address, and her eyebrows rose. It was only a short distance away, which meant it was in the expensive part of town. At last they drew up outside an elegant building, and made their way inside to an apartment on the ground floor.

It was large and well furnished, with three bedrooms, plus a well-equipped bathroom and kitchen. She liked it at once, but she guessed the cost would be beyond her.

'What do you think?' he asked.

'It's lovely but I doubt if I could afford it.'

'You won't have to. I'm paying. Yes, I know what you're

thinking. You reckon this is me being controlling again. But I'm doing it for practical reasons. This place is much nearer your office, so that will be easier for you.' He added wryly, 'Unless you've decided to marry me and just forgotten to mention it.'

'No, I haven't changed my mind about that.'

'So you'll continue working, and living close will be useful. But that's not my real reason for wanting you to live here. You can't stay in that dump where you're living now. You'll have an accident on those stairs any day. Here there are no stairs and you're much safer.'

'I can see that, but—'

He laid his hand on her stomach. 'You wouldn't take risks just for the pleasure of telling me to go to the devil, would you?'

He was right, she knew. Here the baby would be far safer than in her present home.

'I guess I wouldn't,' she admitted with a smile. 'All right. You win.'

He gave a grunt of ironic laughter. 'I can only guess what it cost you to say that. You can thump me if it makes you feel better.'

'I'll save that pleasure for another time. This looks like a nice place but—isn't it really too expensive?'

'You have two options. You tell Alex how successful you've been in persuading me to open a branch here. He's impressed by your skill and gives you a huge rise. Or you could just accept that I'll pay. I'll be spending some time here when I need somewhere to stay.'

'Well—' she paused, seeming to consider '—I guess I'll end up doing it your way, as usual.'

'That's what I like to hear.'

She touched his cheek. 'And you are taking good care of me—of both of us.'

'Yes. We're a family now.'

She wasn't sure how she should answer, but he saved her from having to.

'There are different kinds of families,' he said. 'We'll have to wait and see about us. Now, let's go and make sure you can rent this place.'

'Wait,' she said quickly. 'Isn't it better if you rent it?'

'But it'll be your home.'

'Not yet. Don't hurry me.'

'All right,' he said reluctantly. 'It will be mine—until you say otherwise.'

A short journey brought them to the estate agent's office that handled the arrangements. Leonizio organised everything with his usual stern efficiency and in a short time the key was his.

When they returned to the new apartment she had to admit that it would be a pleasant place to live. Leonizio showed her into the main bedroom, which contained a double bed. But he made no attempt to join her there, retreating into the second bedroom.

Ellie studied everywhere carefully, lingering in the doorway of a third smaller bedroom.

'This is just what I need,' she murmured.

'For the baby, when it's born?'

'No, for the help that I'll have to hire. I want to keep my job, which means I'll have to employ a nanny to live in and care for my child.'

'You mean our child, don't you?' he asked quietly.

'Yes, our child.'

He touched her cheek gently. 'Don't shut me out, Ellie.'

'I didn't mean to. But we won't be living together all the time.'

'We would if you married me.'

'But I can't.'

'Can't or won't?'

'It's just not a step I feel I can take, and I have to make

plans for when you're not here. But I won't shut you out, I promise.'

'You *are* shutting me out.'

'I'm sorry. I wish I could do what you want but it's not so easy. There's something in me that just can't— I guess I'm just awkward.' She gave a brief laugh. 'Just like you. Well, you know that by now. But I'm not spiteful, and I want you to be happy with your child.'

She spoke warmly, and he returned her smile. The moment passed and all seemed well between them, but she could sense the tension that had briefly possessed him. It was a reminder, if she needed it, that only one thing really mattered to him. And it wasn't herself.

'Now tell me,' he said, 'do you like this place?'

'Yes, it's lovely.'

'You're not thinking of me as a controlling fiend any more?'

'I never said that.'

'Not out loud, but admit it, when we arranged to come here you were thinking the worst of me.'

'How do you know that?'

'Because you always think the worst of me. It's your default position.'

'Well, I don't like you paying for everything,' she agreed.

'Too late. You've already agreed to accept it.'

'In a sense, but I must tell you—I'm not going to give up my own apartment.'

'You what? But you don't need that place any more.'

'But I do. Please try to understand—it's mine. When I'm there I'm myself, completely myself. It's like my own little kingdom.'

'But, Ellie, we're a couple now. This will be our home.'

She clenched her hands desperately. 'No, we're not a couple. Maybe one day we will be but there's a lot we still need to know. And it's too soon to call it our home. I still need my own place.'

He gave her a look of wry bitterness. 'So that if I annoy you, you can walk out, tell me to go to blazes and escape into your kingdom. That's letting me know where I stand, isn't it?'

'It's telling you that there are still question marks hanging over us. We need to give it a little time. Please, Leonizio, don't let's argue any more. Let's just wait and see how things work out.'

Reluctantly he shrugged.

'I guess I have no choice. You win.'

'Good.' Having scored a victory, she felt her mood soften. She was going to enjoy the next few moments. 'And now I have some news for you. I'm planning something that will annoy you, but you'll just have to accept it.'

He looked uneasy. 'What's this? You're annoyed with me and you're going to make me suffer?'

She gave him a teasing smile. 'Terribly.'

'You're going to thump me, kick me in the shins, lock me in the cellar?'

'No, that would be boring. I'm planning something that you'll object to a lot more. But you have no choice. I simply won't accept a refusal.'

'You're scaring me.'

'Good. You're going to do what I say without argument.'

'I can't wait to hear this.'

'Tonight we're going out for a celebratory meal. And I shall pay for it, whatever it costs. I want no arguments. However much you dislike it, you'll just have to put up with it. *I'll* pay, not you. Do you understand that?'

His face brightened as he understood her jokey mood.

'Yes, ma'am, no, ma'am. Three bags full, ma'am.'

She burst out laughing and he joined in, wrapping his arms about her and hugging her tightly.

'I mean it,' she cried. 'Don't you dare try to pay. Don't even mention money or my revenge will be terrible. Now, let me finish settling in here, then I'll sort out the details for tonight.'

CHAPTER EIGHT

ELLIE CHOSE THE restaurant carefully. It served Italian food, luxuriously presented, and was one of the best in London. Also one of the most expensive. In this too she was making a point to Leonizio. He might have more money but she had enough to cope, and she would show him that she couldn't be bought and sold.

She called, booked the best table and gave a happy sigh of anticipation. She was really looking forward to this.

When the time came she put on the glamorous dress he'd bought her for the opera.

'Very nice,' he said, nodding approval.

'Is it?' she asked, turning around in front of a floor-length mirror. 'I shan't be able to wear it when I start putting on weight.'

'But just now it's perfect. The only thing you need to change is to let your hair hang loose.'

She let it fall, and at once her other self confronted her from the mirror.

'I'm not sure,' she said, pushing it back a little.

'Let's see.' He took over, brushing his fingers against her face until they became wreathed in hair. 'Like that? No, perhaps this way.' He drew her tresses forward again. 'I like it like this.'

'But drawn back makes me look more sensible. Which I am, although you don't want to believe it.'

'Perish the thought. I prefer the girl who seduced me.'

She gave him a teasing smile. 'Oh, yes? Are you sure who seduced who?'

He grinned. 'Well, I can't quite make up my mind. My partly conceited side tells me I was the seducer. My totally conceited side says it was you who wanted me. My hopeful side says it was mutual.'

He was still smiling as though his words were humorous. But there was something in his eyes that made her heart beat a little faster.

'I guess your hopeful side—is very knowing,' she said, a touch breathlessly.

He nodded. 'I like to think so. After all, you could always have socked me on the jaw.'

'Yes, but it wouldn't have been very polite. And I'm a polite person.'

He kissed her cheek. 'I'm glad of that. Let me get dressed and it'll be time to go.'

He vanished. Not until he was gone did Ellie yield to the temptation to touch her cheek where his lips had brushed it.

When he reappeared, dressed in elegant evening clothes, she had to admit that his conceited side had a point. He was the most attractive man she had ever seen, and his hopeful side was right. Their lovemaking had been mutual.

But she concealed these thoughts beneath an efficient manner, and they set off.

As they reached the restaurant she had the satisfaction of seeing him gape with astonishment at the luxurious place.

'Ellie, you can't mean here. You'll never be able to afford it.'

She met his eyes, her own full of teasing, to reassure him that their battle was light-hearted, although she meant every word.

'You don't know that,' she told him. 'In fact, you don't know the first thing about me, except that I've always given in and let you have your own way. Now I'm asserting myself because it's time for a change.'

'I guess it is.'

'So come along, our table is waiting.'

A waiter greeted them, checked her booking and led them to a table in an alcove by a window. There they studied the menu.

'Great food,' Leonizio observed. 'But did you really think the prices would be so high when you made me this offer?'

'It wasn't an offer, it was a command,' Ellie reminded him.

'But perhaps you'd like to have second thoughts.'

'Don't even mention it. I've made my own choice.'

She indicated two of the most expensive dishes on the menu and he followed her lead, occasionally pausing to give her a questioning glance. She met it with a smile.

'Here's the waiter,' she said. 'You give him the order for the food and wine. And mineral water for me.'

He did so, but he had a surprise for her. When it came to the drink he simply ordered mineral water for both of them.

'Did you do that for the sake of my purse?' she demanded when the waiter had gone.

'No, I did it because we're in this together. Can't you understand that?'

'Yes, I guess I can,' she said, pleased. 'All right, one up to you.'

'One up to me? That makes a change. Normally you enjoy wrong-footing me, don't you?'

'However did you guess?'

'I'm getting used to it. I'm even beginning to enjoy it.' He gave a brief laugh. 'I've got to say this for you; you're never dull.'

'So you'd like a few more threats as entertainm

'Why not? I'm sure you've got plenty up your slee

'You'll find out—gradually. You might find me a ver interesting enemy.'

His face softened. 'Joking apart, you're not my enemy. You're my best friend. And you always will be.'

'Friend?' she echoed, instinctively touching her stomach.

'Yes, I know it sounds a little strange, considering our history. But in a way it's our success. We have a lot of arguments, but we've spent some valuable time trying to get to know each other. You said I don't know the first thing about you, but I think I know the things that matter.'

'I wonder what they are,' she mused, giving him a speculative glance. 'We might have different ideas about that.'

'We know how to make each other laugh. And, let's face it, I also know how to make you good and mad.'

'And that's important?'

'Considering how mad you can make me, I think it's vital. When I think of our future I see some of the most entertaining rows there have ever been.'

'Hmm. I wonder who'll win,' she mused.

'My money's on you. You know more of my weak spots than I know of yours.'

'Weak spots?' she echoed. 'You have weak spots?'

'Don't pretend you don't know by now. It's you who can knock me into a corner.'

'Very tactfully said, but I think it's just about even.'

'We'll have to wait and see.'

At last the meal arrived, everything was set out on the table and all was ready.

'Here's to you,' Leonizio said, raising his glass in salute.

'No, here's to us,' she said, raising her own. 'It's all going well, and we're a great success.'

He clinked glasses with her.

'I'm not sure I can claim to be a great success. You said that you always let me have my own way, but that's not true. I don't see any wedding ring on your finger.'

'Weddings aren't the only things that matter,' she hedged.

'They are if you're having a child. But let's leave it for the moment. In time you may come to feel differently. At least I hope so.' For a moment he paused, seeming to consider, as though trying to make a decision. At last he said heavily, 'I don't want to lose that special feeling you give me. It means more than I can say.'

She could hardly believe her ears. A special feeling. Had he really said that?

'Couldn't you try to say it?' she murmured.

'It's hard because I'm not sure of the right words to describe it.'

But it's called love, whispered a voice in her heart. *Why is it so hard to say?*

If only he would speak of love, then perhaps she might be able to marry him. Somewhere deep inside her was the hint of an emotion that longed to respond to him, but could never do so while he kept his distance.

'The fact is—I want to tell you about how I've felt since that first day we made love,' he said. 'You inspired me with a feeling of—' He paused again.

'A feeling of what?' she asked softly.

'A feeling of—safety.'

'"Safety"?' she echoed, only half believing.

'It goes back to that time we spent together. Do you remember it?'

How could he ask her? she thought desperately. That wonderful hour had lived in her mind ever since, never banished for long, always returning.

'Yes, I remember,' she said quietly.

'So do I. I'll never forget how it felt when we were talking and I looked into your eyes and saw there a sympathy and understanding unlike anything I'd ever known. I knew then that you were different from all other women, with a generosity and kindness that I had to reach out to, hoping it would reach out to me. And you did.

'Since that day nothing has been the same. I don't just mean because of the baby. I mean because of you, because of your strength. You're the one person I've ever met that I know I could trust with my life, and with everything that's in my life. I've been betrayed so often—'

By Harriet, she thought, who had seemed to offer him new hope, then snatched it away, leaving him desolate.

'But you make me feel that there's someone in the world who can be relied on,' he said. 'With you I know I'm safe.'

Suddenly he checked himself and spoke self-consciously. 'Oh, heavens, listen to me. Why am I talking like this? Admitting that I cling to you for safety.'

'Isn't it true?'

'Yes, it's true, but there are some things a man shouldn't admit. It's not exactly macho, is it?'

'Do you have to be macho?' she asked.

'I'm supposed to be. Ask anyone who's done business with me. Hard, cold, grim, unyielding, unforgiving. That's my reputation.'

'And with them you should keep it up. But not with me.'

'No, because I trust you as I thought I'd never trust anyone again.'

He took her hand in his and raised it to his lips.

'Thank you,' he whispered.

'I'm glad if I've given you something.'

'You've given me everything. And when our child is born you'll give me everything again. A future, a reason to live. I even think—'

He stopped suddenly, his face filled with dismay and tension. Following his gaze, Ellie saw a man and a woman entering the restaurant. The woman was young, beautiful and heavily pregnant.

'Oh, goodness…' she breathed. 'Isn't that—?'

'Yes,' Leonizio said softly. 'It's her.'

Ellie could just recognise her as Harriet, the woman in the pictures in his possession. She was filled with shock at suddenly finding her here, and Leonizio's expression told her that he felt the same.

Harriet and her companion had not noticed them, being totally absorbed in each other. Harriet's eyes were fixed adoringly on her lover's face, and his attention was riveted on the swell of her pregnancy.

Leonizio turned his head away sharply, as though unable to bear the sight.

'Is that really her?' Ellie asked.

He turned his gaze on her and she was astounded at the change in him. The gentle affection of a moment ago was gone, replaced by harsh suspicion.

'Yes, it's really her,' he said. 'You knew, didn't you?'

'What?'

'You knew they would be here. That's why you chose this place. How could you?'

She stared at him in outraged disbelief. 'You think I knew she was coming? You actually think I brought you here on purpose? How could I even know that she would be here?'

'You chose this place. Am I supposed to believe that it's coincidence?'

'Yes, because it is. I didn't know. I chose this because it's the best Italian restaurant in London. If I'd known she would be here I'd have found somewhere on the other side of town. Leonizio, you've got to trust me. I would never play such a trick on you. How could you imagine I'd ever be so spiteful?'

'I don't know. But it's enough to make a man believe in a malign fate.'

'Let's hope it teaches you not to make meaningless speeches,' she said bitterly. 'It's only a minute ago you were saying how much you trusted me. I'm telling you I didn't know she would be here, and if you can't bring yourself to believe me then your so-called trust means nothing.'

She braced herself for a vitriolic response but he didn't reply. Instead, his shoulders sagged and he sighed.

'I'm sorry,' he muttered. 'I should have known better than to blame you, but I'm in such a state, I don't know if I'm coming or going.'

'If you ever treat me like that again you'll be going. A long way away. And for ever. I won't have it, do you understand? I deserve better from you than that. Now, let's get out of here.'

'No!' His tone was quiet but forceful. 'I'm not going to run away as though I was scared of her.'

On the last words his voice faded as though something had stunned him. Following his look, Ellie saw that Harriet was holding out her hand for the man to put a ring on it.

'Their engagement,' Leonizio said bitterly. 'Now our divorce is almost finalised she's a free woman, they can marry and acknowledge that her child is his. I've played right into her hands.'

'No,' Ellie said fiercely. 'You've claimed the right to live your own life and to hell with her.' She took his face between her hands and said, 'Forget her. She doesn't exist any more.'

'You're right—you're right—'

'And we are leaving. Waiter, my bill, please.'

Leonizio made no protest, seeming content to follow her lead. In a few moments they were on their way out.

'That was a great meal,' he said. 'Thank you.'

'Yes, it was good to celebrate,' she agreed. 'Now, it's time to go home.'

'Home,' he echoed. 'That sounds nice.'

'Yes, doesn't it?' She took his hand. 'Let's go.'

Outside the restaurant there were several taxis waiting. She hailed one and headed towards it. But suddenly her foot seemed to turn and she felt herself falling. The next moment Leonizio had seized hold of her.

'I've got you,' he said. 'Just hold onto me.'

She did so. 'I'm all right, honestly.'

'Better be on the safe side,' he said, lifting her in his arms and heading for the taxi.

As he turned to set her down she glanced over his shoulder and gasped at what she saw. There was a woman looking out at them through the restaurant's window. Her face was disconcertingly like Harriet's.

Perhaps Harriet *had* noticed Leonizio in the restaurant and tracked them as they left, curious about his companion. Now she was watching them as they clung together.

Surely not, Ellie thought.

She tried to look back again, but the face had vanished from the window. The next moment she was in the taxi.

I'm just imagining things, she thought. *At least I hope I am.* She didn't need any more complications.

They didn't speak again until they reached the apartment.

'Shall we celebrate a fine evening with another drink? Even if it's only a cup of tea?' Leonizio attempted to lift the dark mood that had descended between them.

'Thank you but I'm very tired,' she said quickly. 'I can hardly keep my eyes open.'

'Goodnight then.'

She departed for her own room, undressed and got into bed quickly, feeling a strange need to escape him. The evening's events had left her in a turmoil. Leonizio had spoken with such fervent emotion that she had been sure it was a declaration of love. The truth, when it came, had been startling.

The one time he had made love to her, it had not been out of passion but out of a need to cling to her.

She knew that many women would have entered eagerly into such a marriage, glad of a husband who needed his wife so intensely. She thought of her own mother, shut out of her husband's needs and emotions, devastated by the isolation.

But there's more than one kind of isolation, she thought. Leonizio wanted her, but not in the right way. He didn't love her and that mattered. She wished it didn't, but she couldn't deceive herself. They could never have a happy marriage.

But there was something else that tormented her. How quickly his faith in her had turned to suspicion.

One moment he was saying that he trusted her as he'd thought he would never trust anyone again. The next moment he'd accused her of playing the most appalling, spiteful trick on him.

How bitterly he'd asked, *'How could you?'*

True, he'd recovered himself at once and apologised, but she couldn't forget the burning suspicion in his eyes. Instinct told her that he'd asked her forgiveness with his brain, not his heart.

He didn't really mean that apology, she thought. He just wanted to keep her on side for the sake of their child. But that suspicion would always be there. He might think he trusted her, but at the back of his mind there would always be a doubt. And that doubt would come between them.

She kept her eyes closed, hoping to vanish into the safety of sleep. But was there anywhere that was really safe?

* * *

In his own room, Leonizio stripped off his clothes and lay down, but almost at once he rose to his feet again, knowing that it was useless trying to sleep. Tonight, things had happened that both gladdened and confused him. The moment when he'd suspected Ellie of treachery had burned into him with terrifying pain. If she could not be trusted then nothing and nobody in the world could be trusted.

He'd pulled himself together, fighting off the sensation that the world had collapsed about him. But it had left him weakened and fearful. He needed to explore and understand his feelings, yet something warned him to keep a safe distance, lest exploring only confused him with more mysteries.

For half an hour he managed a kind of restraint, but then he couldn't stand it any more and slipped out of his room, heading for hers, two doors away.

Quietly he entered, going closer to the bed where she lay motionless, her breathing soft and steady. Slowly he dropped to one knee, leaning close to her until he could feel her breath on his face.

'Ellie,' he whispered, 'can you hear me? I hope you can. I so much need to tell you everything I feel. When I said you were my friend, and you made me feel safe, I meant that you're the most important person in the world. I thought you'd know everything I meant because we once talked about friendship and how much it matters in marriage. Do you remember that? I thought we'd understand each other at last.

'I know that's not easy. Sometimes I think we'll never understand each other. At other times I believe we'll find a way. Don't you think so?'

She didn't answer. He waited, holding his breath, while she began to twist restlessly, her arms flailing until one hand brushed his bare chest. But it fell away at once, and he knew she hadn't meant to touch him. She didn't even know he was there.

'You're not awake, are you?' he whispered, drawing back. 'You haven't heard a word I've said.' He gave a sigh. 'But, since everything I say seems to annoy you, perhaps that's just as well.'

He rose, backing out of the room, keeping his gaze on her until the last moment.

Only when she heard the door close did Ellie open her eyes. For a while she lay staring into the darkness while the sounds and sensations whirled in her.

The most important person in the world. He'd said it, but then been glad that she couldn't hear him. Hadn't he? Or had he meant—something else?

He'd said they might never understand each other. Or perhaps they might find a way.

Don't you think so? he'd asked in a voice that sounded like a plea.

But she didn't know what to think. And perhaps she never would.

Rising next morning, Ellie dressed and went out into the main room.

'Are you up?' she called.

Silence.

'Leonizio. Are you there?'

Silence.

Flinging open the door of his room, she found it empty. There was no sign of him anywhere in the apartment, and her heart sank.

He'd gone. The events of last night had disillusioned him. How quickly he'd mistrusted her. How fearful he was of life with her. Even the hope of their child wasn't enough to bring him back. The voice she'd heard in the night had been no more than a dream.

A fantasy, she told herself bitterly. *You heard what you wanted to hear because you need to believe you're growing closer. But the reality is he's gone and left you in a desert.*

But then a sound from the front door made her turn her head to see something she could hardly believe. There was Leonizio, entering with his arms filled with newspapers.

'I went out to the newsagent,' he said. 'I ordered us a delivery every morning, and bought several papers. Ellie? Ellie, are you all right?'

'Yes, I'm fine.'

'Sure? It seems that whenever we meet you look as though you've had a nasty shock. Do I have that effect? Do you want to get rid of me?'

She pulled herself together, managing to say in a teasing voice, 'Suppose I said yes. Would you vanish?'

'I might try to persuade you I'm not as terrible as you think. But I doubt I'd succeed.'

She laughed, almost dizzy with the pleasure of having him back when she'd seemed to lose him for ever.

'I'll leave you to think about that,' she said. 'Time I made the breakfast.'

Over breakfast they scanned the newspapers until she said, 'Aha! Look what I've found.' She showed him a column of text. 'If you really want a factory in England there's a building in this area that might be ideal. Apparently the owners have big financial problems.'

He studied the paper eagerly. 'So I might get it at a knock-down price. Well done! I'll get onto this today. But first I'll call Alex Dallon and tell him what a brilliant job you're doing as my right hand. Then he'll be only too glad to give you the time off.'

'You really know how to move the pieces to your own advantage, don't you?' she laughed.

'Of course. To gain control, that's what you've got to do,' he replied. 'One thing I've learned in business is that power is everything. If you're not in charge you have no control over your fate.'

'Control over fate,' she mused. 'But who in the world has that, ever?'

'We're going to have it if we do things properly.'

'Will we? Or are we hoping for too much?'

'Stop looking on the dark side, Ellie. We're going to make things happen as we want them to.'

'You make it sound so easy.'

'If you're determined enough it can be easy.'

'All right. Let's stop nattering and get out and view that building.'

'That's my girl!'

CHAPTER NINE

LATER THAT MORNING Ellie contacted the estate agent to arrange for them both to look over the building. She was about to call Leonizio when Rita, her secretary, appeared in the doorway.

'There's someone to see you,' she said. She lowered her voice to add, 'It's *her.*'

'Who is *her*?' Ellie queried, but fell silent when she saw Harriet standing behind Rita.

Now she realised that she had always known this would happen. Two women at war with each other were always bound to meet.

'Please come in, Signora Fellani,' Ellie said calmly.

Up closer, Harriet was a beautiful woman, but her face was sharp, her eyes hard.

Her pregnancy was nearing its final moments. Ellie pulled out a chair for her and Harriet edged carefully into it.

'I don't call myself Signora Fellani any more,' she said. 'I stopped being Leonizio Fellani's wife months ago, when I couldn't stand him any longer.'

'Are you saying he ill-treated you?' Ellie said, speaking with difficulty.

'That depends what you call ill-treatment. He didn't knock me about. He didn't have other women. The world would have said he was a good husband, except when you got close to him, tried to look into his heart and found that there was nothing there.'

'I really don't think—' Ellie began carefully.

'You don't think I should be telling you the truth about what a cold, hard man he is because you don't want to know it. Oh, yes, I know all about you and Leonizio. I've heard the rumours but I didn't believe them until last night when I saw you together.'

'You saw a lawyer dining with her client—'

'So I thought until I saw how you were with each other at the table. And then you ended up in his arms.'

'So it was you watching us through the window. But what you saw was an accident. I fell over.'

'Don't try to fool me. You're in love with him. I recognise the signs because I was in love with him once. It was the biggest mistake I ever made. Oh, he's pleasant enough until he gets his own way, but that's all that matters to him. And if he doesn't get it—heaven help you!'

'You didn't love him,' Ellie said passionately. 'If you did, you could never have gone with another man.'

'I found a man who truly valued me, put me first, treated me as though I mattered. You know what Leonizio cares about? His business, his ambitions, his power, *himself.* And people fall for it. They all jump to do his bidding. But you'll learn. He'll break your heart as he broke mine.'

'As you broke his,' Ellie raged.

'He's hurt because of the child, not because of me.' She leaned closer to Ellie. 'I'm really sorry for you. On the outside you're all businesslike efficiency. Who could suspect that you could let emotion get the better of you? But I think you have. You won't admit it to yourself, but it's true. And he'll make you pay for it.'

'Get out,' Ellie said furiously. 'Get out of here *now.*'

A jeering smile illuminated Harriet's face. 'Don't worry, I'm going. You've told me all I need to know.'

In the doorway she paused, looking back. 'I tried to warn you. Never forget that.'

Then she was gone.

For a moment Ellie was too shocked to move. At last she managed to make her way to the door and look out into the corridor. It was empty. There was no sign of Harriet. It was as though she had never been there, except for the legacy of dread and dismay she'd left behind in Ellie.

Businesslike efficiency. That was what Harriet had said, and at this moment she must cling to it, doing her job, refusing to let herself be disturbed by what she had heard.

The phone rang. She snatched it up and heard Leonizio's voice.

'Did you call the estate agent?' he asked.

'Yes. He's expecting you this afternoon.'

'Can you come with me?'

'Yes, I've no appointments.'

As she'd expected, Alex was ready to give her the time off to indulge such a client. It brought back the uneasy memory of Harriet saying that people jumped to do Leonizio's bidding.

Leonizio arrived to find her waiting for him outside her office.

'Are you OK?' he asked. 'You look a bit shaken.'

'No, everything's fine.'

She wondered if she should tell him about Harriet's visit, but just now she couldn't bring herself to do it.

Together they inspected the building. It was a large, bleak-looking place that had been built nearly fifty years ago. As far as Ellie could tell it was in good condition, but she could be sure of little else.

She found it hard to know if Leonizio was pleased with

what he saw. He allowed very little satisfaction to be revealed to their guide.

'It's not quite what I expected,' he observed at last.

'There's more I could show you,' the agent said in a pleading voice.

'No need. I'll take another look around before finally deciding against it. I'll see you before I go.'

When the agent had hurried away Ellie said, 'So you really don't like it?'

'Whatever gave you that idea?'

'You told him—'

'I said what was necessary to knock the price down. In fact it's ideal for me. I can see exactly where I'll put all the machinery. Let me show you.' He led her to a nearby wall. 'The toe-laster will go at this end.'

'Toe-laster?'

'It's the machine that shapes the front point of the shoes. And over there I'd put the heel-attacher, which makes sure the heel is straight with the toe. A little further on there's the perfect place for the finishing room.'

'You've got it all worked out,' she said, dazed. 'However did you do it so fast?'

'It was obvious to me the moment we came in. Not that I said so to the agent. If I'd told him how much I really like this place it would have cost me a fortune.'

'You conniving so-and-so!' she exclaimed.

'I'll take that as a compliment. It's just another name for a good businessman. I do it my way and I won't yield more than I have to.'

She looked at him with interest. 'But you don't just mean that in business, do you? That's how you live as well.'

He seemed to consider.

'Mostly,' he said at last. 'Sometimes I achieve my victory, sometimes I'm defeated.' His tone changed, became more thoughtful. 'But the thing to be really wary of is that occasionally a victory turns out to be meaningless. You think you've won everything you want, but something you hadn't anticipated undermines it. There's no way to predict in advance what it's going to be.'

'That's true,' she said quietly. 'You can make me quite nervous that way.'

He shook his head. 'Let's be clear about one thing. I don't make you anything like as nervous as you make me.'

'Oh, surely—'

'You're the one with all the power, Ellie. We both know that.'

'And you hate it, don't you? It makes you furious with me.'

'It's not that simple.' He hesitated before saying quietly, 'I have angry moments, but there are also other moments when you make me think—'

'Think what?'

'Think all sorts of things that I don't want to think, but I have to because I'm afraid they're true. And think about how I have to change myself to—'

'Hello! Are you there?'

The voice of the agent a few yards away made them both tense. Leonizio checked himself and looked away from her.

'Yes, we're here,' he called back.

Before her eyes he became his other self, confronting the agent with a wry, dismissive manner.

'This place isn't bad,' he said grudgingly. 'But it's not worth the price that's being asked.'

'It's a very fine building,' the agent protested. 'Well built, well designed, and in good condition.'

'So I should hope. But my best offer is—'

The price he named made the other man gulp then attempt an unconvincing laugh.

Ellie regarded the ensuing discussion with fascination. Leonizio had described his business self as hard and unyielding. Now she saw that it was true.

Eventually the agent telephoned the head of the company that owned the building. A sharp conversation followed, after which he hung up and told Leonizio, 'He'll call you tonight.'

'Fine. Tell him not to keep me waiting too long. Now, I'll be going.'

She thought wryly that if he was trying to win her admiration he was succeeding. His ruthless manner might have seemed chilling, but she'd heard enough about the previous owners to know that they had brought their financial problems on themselves by bad management. Leonizio was merely proving his skill.

As they left the building she said, 'Do you think they'll give in?'

'Not a doubt. I recognise the signs.'

Of course he did, she thought. Making the other side give in came naturally to him.

But his other words haunted her. He'd spoken of having to make changes in himself. That suggested a different Leonizio, one who could be self-critical. It was a side of him she hadn't suspected, and which warmed her to him.

On the way home he said, 'I've got some investigating to do before I conclude this. Okay if I use your computer?'

'Go ahead. You need all the backup you can get. Let me know if I can help.'

When they arrived she expected him to head straight for the computer, but he picked up the phone.

'Alex? It's Leonizio. I just want to thank you for letting me have Ellie's services. She's the best. I've found the place I want to buy and she's been a great help. I'll rely on her to handle the purchase, and I hope you'll let her hang around to help me. What's that? You will? Great! You want to talk to her? Here.'

He handed over the phone and vanished.

'Ellie?' Alex sounded full of eagerness. 'Congratulations. You're doing a fantastic job. He wants you to stick with him and I've told him you can. Well done. We won't have many customers rolling in as much money as him. Bye now.'

She found Leonizio sitting at her computer, using the Internet to connect to his firm in Italy, his professional contacts and his bank accounts.

'Great,' he said at last. 'Whatever the price, I can handle it.'

He sent a few messages, then gave the thumbs-up sign. Ellie returned it in a mutual salute.

'What's that noise?' he asked, turning in the direction of the front door.

'Maybe the postman. I think something landed on the carpet.'

She was right. A letter with her name lay there. Opening it, she found a note from a friend who lived in the same building that she had left.

The postman was about to put this through your door. I stopped him so that I could send it on to your new address.

It contained a letter that made Ellie draw a sharp breath of delight. 'They want to set a date for my first pregnancy scan,' she said.

'Great. We'll go together.' He gave her a quick sideways glance. 'Unless you object.'

'Of course I don't. How can you think that?'

'I'm not usually part of your plans.'

'Nonsense. Just because I won't marry you doesn't

mean I'm shutting you out. You're this baby's father, and nothing's going to change that.'

'Thank you,' he said. 'And you're right. Nothing will change that. And I'm going to be there, part of our child's life. Always. Give them a call and set the date for us to go.'

She called the hospital, but received an offer that made her hesitate.

'It could be tomorrow,' she murmured to Leonizio.

'Excellent.'

'But won't you be busy tomorrow, making all the business arrangements? That building is important.'

He shook his head. 'Not as important as this,' he said, pointing to her belly. 'Nothing in the world is as important as this.'

Joyfully, she turned back to the phone and made the arrangements.

'Ten o'clock tomorrow morning,' she told Leonizio.

He nodded, smiling in a way that touched her heart. It had a warmth and eagerness that was unlike anything she had seen in him before. He was happy, she thought. Involvement with the baby gave him a pleasure that nothing else could offer.

That evening he insisted on cooking supper for both of them.

'You shouldn't exert yourself tonight,' he said. 'I'll even do the washing-up, while you have an early night. No arguments.'

'No arguments,' she promised.

It was lovely to be so well looked after, even if she knew that she wasn't really the object of his loving concern.

He was the same next morning when he cooked breakfast and served her carefully. When it was time to leave for the hospital he took her in his arms, drawing her close for a hug.

'Look at me,' he said at last.

She looked up and found him gazing at her tenderly.

'Are you all right?' he asked.

'I'm fine, looking forward to what we're going to find out.'

'Yes, it'll be wonderful.'

He dropped his head and she felt the soft touch of his mouth against her own, lingering for the briefest possible moment.

'We're in this together,' he whispered. 'Now, let's hurry.'

She nodded and backed out of his arms, knowing that she must escape before he sensed the reaction she could barely control. Another second and she would have yielded to the temptation to return his kiss.

Perhaps it was better that she hadn't, she thought. Her own lips might have revealed too much of the reaction she could barely control.

They reached the hospital in good time and were directed to the department where scans took place. There they were greeted by the sonographer.

'It's not a long process,' she said. 'Maybe twenty minutes. I'd like you to lie down on this couch and remove all covering from your stomach.' She smiled at Leonizio. 'Are you staying with us?'

'Definitely,' he replied.

He assisted Ellie in removing some of her clothes and took her to the couch, where she lay down.

'What actually will the scan reveal?' Ellie asked.

'Several things,' the sonographer said. 'It will give us some idea of exactly how far along in the pregnancy you are and when you're likely to give birth. That's why it's called a "dating scan", because it makes it easier to plan dates. Can you remember the date of your last period?'

'Yes, but I can also tell you exactly when the pregnancy started. It was—' She gave the date of their love-making.

'As precise as that?' the sonographer queried.

Ellie met Leonizio's eyes. 'Yes,' she said, smiling. 'That date and no other.'

'You didn't need to tell me that,' he said softly.

'That would mean you're about twelve weeks pregnant,' said the sonographer. 'So the baby should be about five or six centimetres. Let's see.'

She began work, smoothing some gel over Ellie's stomach, then began to move a small handheld device over it. Leonizio sat beside Ellie, taking her hand in a comforting hold. She squeezed and felt him squeeze gently back.

At last a picture began to appear on a screen just above Ellie. Astounded, she saw the shape of a little head, viewed sideways.

'Is that—?' she gasped.

'That's your baby,' the sonographer agreed. 'And it seems to be the right size.'

Ellie felt Leonizio's hand tighten. She looked up, meaning to meet his eyes but his gaze was fixed on the screen. The sonographer continued moving the device over the gel and gradually more details came into view.

'You can even see some features,' Ellie murmured.

'That's a real personality coming out,' Leonizio agreed. 'Our child. *Our child.*'

'And it seems to be a very healthy child,' said the sonographer. 'All the signs are good.'

'Perfect,' Leonizio murmured.

He put his arms around Ellie and drew her close to him, looking down into her face, his eyes shining with delight.

'Thank you,' he whispered. 'Thank you with all my heart.'

'You can get dressed now,' the sonographer said.

She went to the other side of the room, leaving them

alone while she put something into a computer. Tenderly Leonizio supported Ellie as she eased down from the couch, and helped her to dress.

'Do you feel all right?' he asked anxiously. 'Did you suffer at all?'

'No, I'm well. Isn't it wonderful?'

'It's the most wonderful thing that's ever happened,' he said with intensity.

Over his shoulder she saw the sonographer signalling for her to approach, but also making a slight gesture indicating that she was to come alone.

'I'll be back in a moment,' she said, and slipped away.

The sonographer greeted her with a smile, murmuring, 'Are you completely certain when the pregnancy started?'

'Absolutely.'

'And the information from the scan confirms it. So we know when you can expect the birth. Here.' She gave Ellie a printout from the computer. 'This is a report of everything we've discovered today, and it makes cheerful reading for you and your partner.'

'I can't believe that we actually saw our baby,' she said.

'It was an excellent picture, and you can keep it. Here.'

She held up a paper for Ellie to see. It was a printout of the picture that had appeared on the screen.

'Oh, lovely!' Ellie gasped, seizing it. 'Thank you, thank you!'

She tucked it away. Showing it to Leonizio was a treat to be enjoyed later.

As they left the hospital he said, 'Let's find somewhere to celebrate.'

When they were settled in a restaurant he ordered sparkling water for them both.

'But aren't you having champagne?' she asked.

'Are you?'

'No, we agreed I couldn't drink alcohol.'

'And neither will I.'

'Thank you. That's nice of you, but I really don't mind. Have champagne if you want to.'

'But I don't want to.'

The waiter arrived with the sparkling water. Leonizio filled their glasses and raised his to her, saying, as he had often said before, 'We're in this together. Isn't that true?'

'Oh, yes.'

'Here's to our baby. Here's to the future. Here's to the best day of our lives. At least—' he checked himself '—the best day of my life. I hope you feel the same.'

'I feel wonderful but—' she sought for the right words '—I'm cautious, superstitious maybe. Just when things seem most hopeful, that's when they can often go wrong. You told me yourself that a victory can sometimes turn out to be meaningless.'

'And I have reason to know it,' he agreed wryly. 'This isn't the first pregnancy scan I've been to.'

'You went with Harriet?'

'Yes, although she tried to persuade me not to. Idiot that I was, I didn't realise that she might have a suspicious reason. But of course I wasn't part of her life any more.'

'But could she have known for certain that you weren't the father?'

'I suppose not. She must have slept with another man while she was still sleeping with me, so she must have known it was possible but she couldn't be sure. I guess she didn't want to risk me finding out at that moment. It was only later that she decided to leave me.'

'So you went to her scan. What was it like?'

His face became bitter. 'The cruel irony is that it was pretty much like today. A perfectly formed baby, the right size, everything happening as it should. It felt marvellous, both then and subsequently. But it was an illusion, and I should have known it.'

'But how could you have known it at that moment?'

'Because I knew her, the kind of person she was. I knew she told lies when it suited her, but I told myself they were only little lies about unimportant things, so it didn't matter. She'd buy an expensive dress and pretend that it had cost less than it really had, so I just shrugged. In fact, I believed what I wanted to believe.'

'The way people do when they're in love,' Ellie ventured.

'Whatever being in love means,' he grunted.

'It means what you felt about Harriet. You ignored the truth about her because you didn't want to know it.'

'Because I'm a coward who couldn't face it.'

'Love can make people weak,' she mused.

'Is that experience talking?' When she didn't answer he said, 'I can't believe that a woman like you has never been in love.'

'A woman like me?' She gave a little laugh. 'Awkward, stubborn, recklessly stupid, opinionated—'

'Of course. Those are the things I like best about you.'

'That's lucky, because that's the only side of me you'll ever see. It tends to get in the way of the sentimental stuff.'

Without looking directly at her, he poured himself another glass of water.

'But surely there's been some sentimental stuff in your life? What about after your ex-boyfriend left you?'

'What happened with him taught me a lesson about survival, but it doesn't haunt me. Why should it?'

'If it really meant anything to you, it would never completely go away.'

Like Harriet has never really gone away from you, she thought.

Still, Leonizio was curious about her love life. What she had told him on their first night together had made it easier for him to confide in her about his wife. Her warmth and kindness had made him reach out to her, with results that once he would never have expected.

She'd implied that a man had left her because her looks weren't up to standard, and certainly she was no conventional beauty. But she wasn't plain. There was a beauty in her face that had little to do with the shape of her features. It was the light that sometimes shone in her eyes. There was warmth in that light, also a shrewd intelligence that could make a man want to know and understand her better.

She could intrigue him, charm him, but also make him want to fight and overcome her. The one thing she never did was bore him.

He reckoned the man who'd abandoned her because she wasn't pretty enough was a fool.

He glanced up, intending to meet her eyes, but found he'd lost her attention. She was looking around her urgently.

'Is something the matter, Ellie?'

'I'm trying to find the waiter. I'd like a little snack. Ah, there he is, but he's not looking this way. I'll go and talk to him.'

She vanished before Leonizio could protest that this was his job. For a moment he sat brooding about the events of the morning. Then he noticed where she had left the large envelope that contained the details of the scan. Eagerly he reached out to open it. There was the picture of his unborn child. He studied it, remembering the other time that had seemed full of hope, until the hope died. But this hope would not die. He would cling to that belief. He raised his head, closing his eyes, withdrawing into another world where there was only himself and his determination.

On the other side of the restaurant Ellie caught up with the waiter, asked him to attend and turned back to the table.

What she saw made her pause. Leonizio was holding

the baby picture, his face full of an emotion she could not understand. Was it happiness or sad remembrance? Sometimes, when he laughed and joked with her as he often did in their relationship, he seemed like a man who hadn't a care in the world. But for him laughter was a protective shield. Beneath it there was always the sadness and vulnerability that he was determined the world would never discover.

As she watched he raised his head, closing his eyes, seeming to retreat to a place where he was alone.

Ellie had sworn to protect herself against love, but in that moment her heart went out to him. She wanted to console him, reassure him that he wasn't alone, that she was there, that she would do anything for him if only it would bring him joy and confidence.

She returned to him slowly. At first he didn't seem aware of her and she sat opposite him, staying silent until he looked down.

'Are you all right?' she asked.

'I'm fine.'

'You don't look fine.'

'It's just that—when I think I'm managing all right certain thoughts come over me and catch me unprepared.' He made a wry face. 'I don't come out of this well, do I?'

'You come out looking vulnerable, the way people do when their feelings are more than they can cope with.'

He frowned ironically. 'I don't think I can agree with that. I'm a businessman. I don't have feelings.'

'You'd really like to believe that, wouldn't you? Even though you know it's not true.'

He sighed and shrugged. 'I guess you're right. You know, I could get scared at how well you understand me.'

'Nonsense. We're best friends, remember?'

He nodded. 'The best friend I'll ever have in my life.

I've begun to realise that I've never talked to anyone the way I can talk to you.'

'Not even Harriet?'

'I could never be completely frank with her, certainly not about my failings. She'd have used them against me.'

'And you think I won't?'

He gave her a warm smile. 'No, you'll just laugh at them.'

'One of the great pleasures in life,' she said with a soft chuckle. 'A man you can laugh at.'

'Let's hope I don't disappoint you.'

She had a sense of delightful warmth. They were growing closer, drawing her nearer to the moment she longed for.

'I'll let you know if you do,' she said.

'So I needn't kid myself that I'm the boss.'

'Well, I might let you kid yourself, now and then.'

'I'm sure you will. We have a saying in Italy. In any relationship the man is the head. But the woman is the neck, and the neck controls the head.'

'I must remember that. It could be useful.'

'Now you've really got me scared.'

But he smiled as he said it, and again she had the sensation of being engulfed in warmth and pleasure. Every instinct told her she was where she belonged, with the man she belonged to and who belonged to her.

If only he would admit that he did.

Briefly Harriet appeared in her mind, warning her.

But Ellie shooed her away. Harriet had admitted defeat, something she herself would never do.

The waiter appeared, apologising because he could not supply the cakes she had ordered.

'Never mind, I'm happy to go home,' she said. She wanted to be alone with Leonizio.

'Me too,' he agreed. 'It's time you had a rest.'

'I don't think I need one. I'm stronger than you think.'

'Let's not take chances on that. We've already agreed that we don't know what the future holds. Come along. Home.'

CHAPTER TEN

HE TURNED OUT to be right. On the journey home Ellie began to feel a little queasy. She was glad to lie down while Leonizio sat at the computer. She needed to think of many things, for which she needed to be alone.

As she relived the afternoon in her mind certain moments stood out. The way he'd taken her in his arms, holding her close as he might have held a treasure he wanted never to lose. The warmth in his embrace and the even greater warmth in his eyes as they met hers.

We were together, she thought joyfully. *Together as we've never been before, even when we made love. Only it wasn't love that we made. There was passion, but not the feeling that now—*

She stopped, reluctant to face what lay in wait for her, although she knew now that it could no longer be avoided.

Love, she thought. *It's been there all the time but I was afraid to admit it. I want him. I want him in every way, but all he feels for me is kindness and need because of the baby. If Harriet hadn't betrayed him he'd still be with her. That night he saw her in the restaurant with the other man, it hurt him more than he could bear.*

But there was always hope. With every day they were growing closer and surely soon they would reach the moment when he reached out to her as a man to a woman?

She knew from their night together that she could inflame his desire, and perhaps with a little tenderness and encouragement she could make everything else happen.

I can make him realise he's mine, she thought. *Surely I can.*

There was a click as the door opened.

'Are you all right?' he asked. 'I didn't wake you, did I?'

'No, I'm awake.'

He came in and sat on the bed.

'I thought today must have been a strain on you.'

'It was better because you were with me. You make everything better.'

'Do I really? Sometimes I think I just drive you mad.'

She smiled. 'I don't mind being driven mad, as long as it's you.'

'Nice of you.' He laid a gentle hand on her stomach. 'It's too soon to know if we have a son or a daughter.'

'Do you prefer one to the other?'

'Not really. A man wants a son that he can raise in his own way, teach him his own ideals. But if I could have a daughter who was like her mother, with the same wicked sense of humour, the same lovely blue eyes with the hint of something mysterious behind them—I think I might prefer that.'

The emotion in his voice almost made her weep. The moment she longed for was drawing closer. He loved her, he was hers and soon he would declare it.

'You might not like it at all,' she mused. 'A daughter like that can be exasperating. That's what my father used to say.'

'He obviously didn't know how to appreciate such a daughter. But I may manage better. With you to help me.'

Her heart began to beat a little faster as her hope grew. It was happening, everything she longed for.

'Tell me,' she said softly. 'Do you think—?'

But she was interrupted by the sound of his cell phone.

'Damn!' he muttered. 'Why do people always ring at the wrong times?'

He answered the phone with a grunted, '*Sì? Sono* Leonizio.' Then he glanced up at her. 'It's my assistant in Rome. *Ciao*, Francesco.'

As he listened Ellie saw him grow still, frowning with displeasure. She could follow enough of the Italian words to know that there was a problem. Leonizio became annoyed, and he hung up suddenly.

'He's got rocks in his head,' he growled. 'A tiny difficulty with one of our customers, and he's confused. He wants me to go back fast, actually get on the next plane.'

Her heart nearly stopped. 'Oh, no, surely not?' she whispered.

'Of course not. I told him I can't even think of it, not when there are so many things here that matter.'

She knew a leap of pleasure at his refusal to leave her.

'No,' she said softly. 'You can't go back. Not now, when there's so much happening.'

'So much happening,' he repeated. 'And so much that's going to happen that we have to be ready for.'

'But we will be ready,' she said happily.

'Oh, yes, we will. How could they imagine I'd go back to Rome when I have to be here to finish buying the factory?'

'What? The factory? You mean—?'

'There's a mass of things to do, and I'm not leaving until it's all finished.'

Her head was spinning, and she could hardly believe she'd heard correctly.

'Yes, of course. The factory is a big development. We mustn't lose sight of what's important.'

She didn't know how she'd forced herself to speak so casually when her heart was thumping with disappointment. She'd convinced herself that he would stay for her sake, that he was beginning to love her, but it was only a stupid illusion.

Fool, she thought. *He's made his feelings plain enough. Just accept it. You can always marry him.*

But she knew she could never do that. Marriage would mean a life full of the aching desolation that pervaded her at this moment.

'Perhaps you should get back onto the Internet,' she said. 'Send Francesco an email with a lot of information about the business you're engaged in here. That should make him more realistic.'

'You don't know Francesco or you wouldn't talk about him being realistic.'

'No, but I do know that realism is vital,' she whispered.

'You're right. Of course it is. And I'm going to do what you said—get onto the Internet and contact Francesco with things he needs to know. Thanks for that. What would I do without my lawyer friend?'

'Hire another lawyer?' she ventured.

'No, thank you. You've got a terrific brain, and I don't want anyone else. Come on, let's get online.'

'You want me there too?'

'You're part of the firm that's handling the purchase for me. How can I manage without you?'

He led her into the next room and started the computer. Ellie's head was reeling from his words.

You've got a terrific brain. That was his idea of a compliment. She would just have to be satisfied with it.

She performed her duties with rigorous efficiency. He was grateful, hugging her warmly, declaring that he was lucky to have found her.

She managed to follow the emails he sent to Francesco, saying that he must remain in England. She drew comfort from that. He wasn't staying to be with her, as she would have wished, but it would buy her time to draw him closer to her.

She would cling to that hope. It was all she had.

After that she forced her efficient side to take over. Returning to work, she had a good meeting with Alex Dallon, who praised her skill in securing Leonizio and assigned her the task of handling his purchase.

'There's an interesting conference coming up in a few months,' he observed. 'You might like to attend with me.'

'I'm afraid not,' she said. 'I've been meaning to tell you that I'm pregnant, and I'll be on maternity leave by then.'

'Pregnant! I never suspected. Who—?'

'Leonizio.'

'So that's it. Will we be hearing wedding bells soon?'

'No.'

'You mean the wretch won't marry you?'

'Don't blame him,' she said quickly. 'I'm the wretch who won't agree to marry.'

'What? You'd turn down a man with his money? That security? Are you out of your mind?'

'No, but I'm a woman who prefers to live her own life, make her own decisions. We can do that now. This isn't the nineteenth century.'

'But surely—you could gain so much. A rich husband, an established place in the world—'

'There's more than one way to have a place in the world,' she said. 'And marrying a rich man isn't necessarily the way to do it.'

Now her work was even more concerned with Leonizio's business as she handled the purchase of the factory. He was greatly appreciative of her efforts, and often complimented her. Soon, she thought, he would speak some loving words. Just a few. And after that she could tell him that she agreed to marriage.

One night she returned home to find the apartment empty. There was a brief note from Leonizio letting her know that he was visiting some clients.

She had supper, then an early night. But there was no sleep. His unexpected absence had revived the old fears, making her recent hopes seem foolish fantasies. Restlessness grew in her. It was intolerable to be lying here, doing nothing when so much was happening that she longed to control. But the truth was that she had no control. There was the brutal fact she must face. She could do nothing while life whirled past, spinning her in directions she couldn't see or understand.

An ironic memory came back to her: Leonizio saying, 'Power is everything. If you're not in charge you're not in control of your fate.'

He'd been talking about business but she realised his words could apply to anything. From the start they had been engaged in a power game. They smiled, laughed, teased and flirted, but the underlying tension between them had always been a battle, never completely resolved.

Where will it end? she wondered. *How will it end? Or will it ever end?*

She rose and went to the window, gazing down into the street below, which was deserted. The street lamps were out and only the moonlight broke the darkness.

He could have gone anywhere in the dark, she reckoned. What was to stop him seeking the company of a woman who satisfied him more than herself? Restlessly, she paced the floor, but stopped as she saw her door opening.

'I got back half an hour ago,' he said. 'I tried to be quiet so as not to disturb you. Then I heard you moving about. I was worried about you. Are you all right?'

The relief of seeing him there was so great that she gasped. 'Yes, yes, I'm fine.'

He came further in and closed the door. 'Why aren't

you getting the sleep you need? Are you worrying about anything?'

'Worrying? Well, a little. There's a lot to worry about, for both of us.'

'You won't believe this, but when I heard movements coming from in here I got a bit scared,' he said. 'I thought you might have decided to slip away from me in the night, and I could hear you getting ready to go.'

'That's funny,' she said. 'I thought you'd vanished too.'

'Don't be silly. The only thing that bothers me is the thought of losing you. I'd do anything to prevent that.' His voice became gently humorous. 'Lock you up, bolt the door, bar the windows.'

'In other words, keep me a prisoner?' she asked lightly.

'I'll do what I have to.' He wrapped his arms about her. 'Don't forget I'm ruthless in pursuit of my ends.'

She rested her head against him. 'So am I,' she said.

His arms tightened a little. 'You might be shocked to know just how terrible I can be.'

'I could say the same.'

'Are you warning me to beware of you?'

She raised her head to look him in the eye.

'You already know that,' she whispered.

'I guess I do. But it might be interesting to find out the rest.'

He drew her closer, letting his mouth rest on hers in a way that made her heart beat faster. But suddenly he tensed and drew away.

'I'm sorry,' he said. 'I should have more self-restraint.'

'You mean you shouldn't kiss me?'

'If we went any further I couldn't stop at kissing you. I want to make love to you but—well, I know I mustn't. Not now.'

'Leonizio—'

'When our child is born and it's safe again, then we'll

make love urgently. We'll have a wonderful night. But now I could do harm to you and the baby. I'm just concerned for you both.'

No, she thought. *You're concerned for the child. Not me.* Besides, it simply wasn't true that making love would hurt their baby. The medical advice she'd received had reassured her that there was no danger of that at all. But it hurt that Leonizio seemed to be using her pregnancy as an excuse to keep her at arm's length.

She was still tormented by the flood of desire that had risen in her, and which now turned into agonising emotion. She tried to control it but it overcame her and suddenly she began to cry. Tears poured down her face, defeating her efforts to stop.

'Ellie, please—'

'Go away,' she choked.

'I'm sorry I made you cry. I should have remembered that it happens easily in pregnancy. Harriet used to cry over nothing at all.'

'Yes, and you didn't care for her feelings.'

'Don't say that. How could you possibly know?'

'Because she told me what you were like.'

She spoke without thinking, and knew at once that she had done something disastrous. Leonizio's hand on her shoulder grew tense and his voice was harsh.

'What did you say? Have you and Harriet been talking?' His hands gripped her painfully. 'You told me you and she weren't in cahoots, but you were lying, weren't you?'

'No, I wasn't. She turned up in my office the other day. I didn't invite her and I threw her out.'

'But that night in the restaurant—'

'I hadn't met her then. I didn't meet her until she arrived in my office. She saw us together and wanted to come prying. She said things about you that I couldn't bear.'

'What did she say about me? Tell me.'

'I didn't mean to talk to her—'

'Tell me!'

'She said she wanted to warn me that you were a hard man with an empty heart; pleasant enough until you got your own way, but that was all you cared about. She said everyone jumped to do your bidding, and you'd break my heart as you broke hers.'

'And you believed that nonsense?' Leonizio exploded. 'I never broke her heart. If anything, it was the other way round. But you know that. I've told you things I'd die before telling anyone else.' He broke off and a frozen look came over his face. 'Now I'm beginning to wish I'd died before I told you. You swore I could trust you.'

'But you can,' she said desperately. 'I told you I didn't know Harriet was going to be in the restaurant that night and it was true. But she saw us there and came to find me at work. I couldn't stop her, and I told you I threw her out.'

'But not before you'd put your heads together and had a sneering talk about me.'

'Why do you find it so easy to believe the worst of me?' she demanded furiously. 'Or is it just that you believe the worst of everyone?'

'I don't want to. I guess sometimes I can't help it. After all, you might have told me she'd met you before this, but you chose not to. Am I supposed to trust you after that? Sometimes the worst is true.'

'Yes, I suppose it is,' she agreed quietly. 'That's something we have to decide. I think I'll go to bed now. No, don't come with me. I want to be alone.'

He didn't try to dissuade her, but stared blankly until she had left the room. Then he turned and left the apartment, slamming the door violently behind him.

Ellie heard the slam, feeling the sound go through her.

It was like listening to the world end. Whatever she had hoped might happen between them, it wouldn't happen now.

Maybe they never had a chance, right from the start. Perhaps she should have told him about meeting Harriet but she'd thought she was doing the right thing. Sometimes the right thing was the wrong thing. But it had proved that they could never have a life together.

She lay down and tried to sleep. But sleep wouldn't come. There was something she had to do. She got to work.

Leonizio returned hours later to find Ellie sitting at the computer. She rose to confront him.

'Look, we have to talk,' he said.

'I don't think so. Everything's been said and we understand each other.'

'But earlier I said things I didn't mean—'

'I know what you meant. I understand far more than you think. Now, I have something to say to you.'

He was very pale. 'What is it?'

'I've been reading Francesco's emails. I don't understand the Italian perfectly, but I can follow enough to understand that he needs you out there urgently. I think you should go.'

Silence. Leonizio looked at her closely, as though trying to read in her face the things she refused to say.

'I've told him how to handle the situation,' he said. 'If I advise him some more I'm sure he can manage.'

'No, I think you should go back there at once. Francesco obviously feels he needs you.'

'Yes, but—don't you need me to look after you?'

'Thank you but I can look after myself.'

'In some things, yes, but—'

'I don't work too hard, take too much exercise, eat the wrong food.'

'Yes, the practical things, but is everything practical? Haven't there been nights when you awoke from bad dreams and came into my arms for me to comfort you?'

Yes, she thought bitterly. *But that was a mistake, and one I regret.*

'Don't you care about things we share?' he asked.

'I care about a lot of things you never even think of,' she said.

'That's not my fault. I don't know what it's like for you to be pregnant, and what you could be going through. I try to imagine, but I'm sure I get it wrong. You should tell me more about it. Can you feel the baby moving? That sort of thing.'

'No, not yet.'

'But when you do, won't it be a wonderful moment for us to share?'

'Of course, but—there are lots of things we can't predict. It might not happen until you come back from Rome.'

'So you really think I should go?'

'Your business needs you. Don't leave Francesco fumbling on his own.' She managed to put a teasing note in her voice. 'After all, what kind of father lets himself go bankrupt?'

'Well, I suppose if you put it like that—'

'We can stay in touch.'

'Of course. We must.'

'I'll continue handling the factory purchase according to your instructions.'

'Oh, yes—I see.'

His expression showed that he'd finally understood that she was putting a distance between them.

'I guess I'd better go then,' he said.

His voice was blank and emotionless. Try as she might, there was no way she could be sure what he was thinking and feeling. And that was how he wanted it, she realised.

He telephoned Francesco for half an hour, then hung up to say he would leave that afternoon.

'It sounds serious,' he said in a low voice.

'Then you'll be gone for some time.'

'I guess so. I'd better start packing.'

She accompanied him to the airport, waiting in silent patience while he went through the formalities. For the last few minutes they went to a small café.

'Let me know when you arrive safely,' she said.

'Yes. And we must stay in touch. Let me know when you have appointments, and what the doctors tell you.'

'Of course I will.'

'How are you feeling now?'

She pointed down to her stomach.

'All is well,' she said. 'We're fine, both of us.'

He looked closely. 'You're just beginning to show a slight bump.'

'Is it really beginning to show? Oh, good! It makes everything more real, especially now I have that picture.'

'Yes, there's a new person on the way,' he said softly. 'Something to look forward to.'

Before she could reply, the loudspeaker proclaimed the start of boarding.

'Time to say goodbye,' Leonizio said. He laid his hand gently on her bump. 'Goodbye to you too, little one.'

'Goodbye, Daddy,' Ellie said.

He grinned. 'Thanks. That's lovely.' Laying a hand on her shoulder, he drew her forward and laid his lips on hers. It wasn't a passionate kiss, but it was affectionate and she returned it with pleasure.

She went with him as far as the check-in gate.

'Here's to the next meeting,' he said. 'Whenever it is.'

'I guess that's not in our control,' she said. 'We'll just have to hope for a kindly fate.'

He made a wry face. 'Don't count on fate being kind.

It's more likely to be spiteful. The best fate is the one we make for ourselves. I wish—'

He hesitated, as though uncertain what to say next.

'What?' she asked.

'I wish—it's hard to explain, but I wish—if only we—'

Final call for Flight—

The crowd was moving about them, making further talk impossible.

'Goodbye,' she said.

'Goodbye—goodbye.'

She kept her eyes on him until the last moment. She had a feeling that he'd turned back for a last look at her but with so many people milling around him it was hard to be sure.

Then he was gone.

CHAPTER ELEVEN

ELLIE KNEW THAT the sensible thing would be to return home at once, but these days she found it hard to be sensible. Instead she lingered in the airport, seeking a place where she might be able to see his plane begin to move slowly towards the take-off point

As she went out to the taxi rank she heard a sound overhead and looked up to see the plane soaring into the sky. She watched until it vanished into the clouds. Then she turned away and walked back to the taxi rank.

She could sense herself moving like a robot, and even thinking like one. Leonizio was gone. Life was over. Why was she bothering to return home? What was home? Did she have any such place?

At the end of the day he emailed her to say that he'd arrived safely. She already knew, having checked the plane's arrival online. But she was glad to hear from him, even though his tone was efficient and unemotional.

But perhaps that was only to be expected, she thought. She had urged him to leave, making it plain that he was no longer welcome. And now that he had gone there was no indication when she would see him again. Or if she would ever see him again.

She returned to work at the office, seeking comfort in her career, which was reaching a high point. Alex was proud of her, assigned more cases to her care and expressed his pleasure at the way she dealt with them.

Her thoughts of Leonizio grew more confused every day. He had turned against her in a way that seemed to freeze her out. But, to her amazement, she discovered that he had taken practical steps to protect her.

Two days after his departure she received a letter from the bank saying that every month a large sum of money was to be deposited into her account, from Leonizio.

She emailed him.

Why didn't you tell me?

He emailed back.

Why are you surprised? It's my job to look after both of you.

She surveyed the words with bitter irony. In her job she often talked to mothers frantically fending for themselves because the men who'd fathered their children had abandoned them, ignoring their responsibilities.

How those women would have envied her, thinking her lucky to have a man who attended so rigorously to his financial duties.

Lucky, she thought. *That's what they'd say I am. If only they knew.*

As promised, Leonizio stayed in touch. His business dealings were troublesome, but he seemed able to get control. At her end the formalities of the factory purchase were also going well.

In this way time passed. Any hope she might have had that he would seize the first chance to hurry back proved empty. Often she relived the moment at the airport when he had said, 'I wish—it's hard to explain, but I wish—if only we—'

What had he wished? What was the meaning of 'if only'? She longed to understand but she could gain no whisper of hope.

Many times she asked herself why she had not simply taken the easy option of marrying him and enjoying whatever closeness could unite them. But she knew she couldn't have done it. The pain would have been too great. She could never have deceived herself that he loved her. If she'd had any hope his casual acceptance of their parting would have forced her to face the truth.

Gradually the time passed, more time than she had ever imagined when she'd first urged him to go. At last came something she had longed for and dreaded equally: the feeling of her baby moving in the womb.

It was what Leonizio had wanted. 'A wonderful moment for us to share', he'd said. But he wasn't here to share it. And that was her fault, she reflected sadly. She had sent him away.

She emailed him.

The baby's moving. I can feel it.

It took two days for him to reply.

Sorry to be so long but I've had to be away for a few days dealing with someone who's trying to ruin my business. Dealt with him, but got behind with my mail. Wonderful news about the baby moving. Glad everything's going well. Take care of yourself.

She was lucky enough to feel well most of the time; the morning sickness had abated now, and so she was able to bury herself in work. Alex was pleased with her success and she could sense her career climbing as never before. How she was going to combine it with motherhood was something she still hadn't worked out. But she had no doubt it could be done.

Often she would brood over the different choices that faced her. It was hard to sort them out when she didn't know how large a part Leonizio would be playing. But she didn't regret her decision not to marry him. She was her own woman, independent, able to stand alone whatever happened. And she wasn't going to let that change.

Days passed relentlessly. Her pregnancy was now nearly twenty-four weeks along and it was time for another scan. The first one had shown everything was normal, which was likely to be the case with this one. She was in a confident mood as she entered the hospital and headed for the department.

The sonographer was the same one who had scanned her before. She greeted her cheerfully, indicating the couch. Ellie settled herself on it, then pushed down her skirt to her hips and raised her top high up, leaving a bare space for the scan.

They started work. Again the sonographer adjusted the screen in a position where they could both see it easily. She spread gel over Ellie's stomach, then began to move a handheld device over it. As before, the baby appeared on the screen.

Ellie drew in her breath in delight at the picture, larger than before. There was her child. Its head was at a slight angle, but her impression was that it was facing her, sending a silent message of love and need.

If only Leonizio could have been here now to see this new picture. How happy it would have made him. She smiled at the picture, sending back her own message of love.

'Isn't he gorgeous?' she breathed. 'Or she.'

'One moment,' the sonographer said. 'I need another look.'

After a few more tense moments she said, 'I'm afraid we'll have to do another scan soon. The baby is a little smaller than I'd expect at twenty-four weeks. It might not be serious, but we need to discover a little more.'

'Discover what?' Ellie asked in a shaking voice. 'What will you be looking for?'

'It's too soon to say—'

'But what could the worst be? Tell me. I must know.'

'There is the possibility of foetal abnormalities. It's not certain, but there's just a chance that we have to look into.'

'Abnormalities. Oh, heavens.'

The sonographer uttered more comforting words but Ellie barely heard them. The word 'abnormalities' thundered in her head. Filled with confusion, she left the building and made her way home in a daze.

Once safely shut inside, she found a silence that descended on her like thunder. Everything she had believed in, hoped for, was suddenly snatched away, leaving her in a nightmarish desert.

For hours she remained there, sometimes walking about from room to room, sometimes sitting with deadly stillness.

At last she knew what she must do. There was only one person she could tell about this disaster. He had a right to know and he was the only person she could trust to understand. She checked the time. It was late afternoon but she might just catch Leonizio at work. She seized the phone and dialled the number of his office. The call was answered by his secretary, who fortunately spoke English.

'I'm sorry, Signor Fellani is not here,' she said.

'Where is he? I must speak to him. It's desperately important.'

'He isn't in this country. He had to go to Paris to attend a business conference. There is much depending on it.'

'When will he be back?'

'Maybe next week.'

'Oh, heavens!' she whispered through the tears that were beginning to choke her. 'Ask him to call me then. Goodbye.'

She slammed down the phone, then dived into her diary, seeking his cell phone number. Wherever he was, she would find him now. But when she had dialled she received only a recorded message saying that the number was unobtainable. She fired off an email, not giving details but urging him to call her as soon as possible. Surely he would be checking his email, even if he was away from Rome and his office at the factory?

With all her heart she longed to reach out to Leonizio, but now she felt it was hopeless. It was surely not a coincidence that she couldn't reach him. He'd switched off his cell phone and instructed his employees to shut her out.

Bitterly, she reckoned that she had only herself to blame. She had banished him from her life, and he'd accepted her decision. She couldn't hope that he would call her.

He didn't. Hours passed, darkness descended and there was no sound from the phone. She knew she was clinging to false hope. Even if he finally called, would things be any better? He valued her only because of the baby, and would he still value their child when he learned of the disaster that threatened them?

There was no escape from the despair that had descended on her. There was only desert loneliness, and perhaps that was all there would be for the rest of her life.

Suddenly the silence was broken by the sound of the doorbell, ringing urgently. She stumbled out of bed, made her way to the door and pulled it open, too dazed even to put on the light. She could barely even see who was there until she felt herself seized in his arms.

'Ellie—Ellie—'

'Leonizio—it's you?'

But it couldn't be him, said a voice inside her. Dreams didn't come true like that.

'Yes, it's me—I'm here—hold onto me.'

She did so, clinging to him frantically, desperate to believe this was really happening.

'Leonizio! But you're in Paris.'

'I was, but when I got your message I came at once.'

'Your business conference—she said there was much depending on it.'

'To hell with that. Do you think it matters beside you? What's happened?'

'Oh, Leonizio—'

'Ellie, what is it? Why did you call? What's happened?'

Suddenly tears overwhelmed her and she collapsed against him. He lifted her, carried her to the bed and sat down, still holding her.

'Tell me,' he said.

'It's the baby—there's something not right. I had another scan today and there might be abnormalities.'

'What do they mean by that? What kind of abnormalities?'

'They don't know yet. They still have to find out. They say they can't be certain. It might still be all right or…or maybe not.'

His arms tightened about her and she felt him draw her down so that they were both lying on the bed.

'Hold onto me,' he said.

'Oh, thank heavens you're here.'

'I've always been here for you, even if you didn't know it. And I always will be.'

She clutched him, burying her face against his shoulder

while her tears flowed. He held her in silence, letting her weep while she needed to. He waited until she'd calmed down a little before speaking.

'Try to talk. Try to tell me everything that happened today.'

In a shaking voice she described the scan, the results.

'They'll need to do more tests,' she said, 'to find out how bad it is.'

'Of course. I have to see the medical report about the test you had today. So that I can show it to the doctors in Rome when we go over there for the tests.'

'Rome? You mean—?'

'Trust me, Ellie. I'm going to keep you with me all the time. If a disaster happens I'll be there, on the spot, to care for you.

'If you knew what my journey here was like today, terrified what might have happened, whether I'd find you alive…I can't endure another separation, so—' He hesitated before saying with a touch of nervousness, 'You have to come home with me, because I couldn't stand anything else. I'm sorry if you don't want to—'

'Yes—yes—I do want to.'

'You're sure? I know I'm giving you orders and that annoys you but—'

'You can give me all the orders you like. We're a family, all three of us.'

'Are we?' he asked. 'Do you mean that? I've never been sure that you actually felt that way.'

'But I do. You were right. There's nobody I need as much as you. *We're in this together.*'

'Yes,' he breathed joyfully. *'Yes, we are!'*

He lay down beside her. 'Go to sleep,' he whispered. 'We'll worry about the rest tomorrow. Tonight, it only matters that we're together.'

He couldn't have said anything more true. He was here.

He had put her first. It was like a dream come true. She lay in his arms, holding him with love and tenderness, while some of his words echoed in her brain.

He had said, 'You have to come home with me.'

Home. Wherever he was, that was home. And never had it been truer than now.

She awoke in the dawn to find herself still in his arms. He was regarding her tenderly. He looked down at her bulge, now much bigger, and touched it with tentative fingers. His eyes were alight with pride.

'It's about time you two reconnected,' she said. 'It's been a long time.'

'Yes, too long. The way you told me to go—I had a feeling you might be throwing me out for good.'

'I could never do that. But it seemed—we've never really understood each other.'

'That's true. But the time is coming when everything is going to be different.' He looked a little anxious. 'Don't you feel that?'

'Yes, I do. But we don't know how—'

'Hush!' He kissed her forehead. 'We must make it the right way, for the sake of—' He touched her bump. 'Come now. We have much to do.'

He helped her up, and remained at her service while she dressed. Over breakfast he studied the scan report. She watched his face, frowning, troubled, but then smiling as he glanced up at her, as though determined not to worry her.

At last he returned it to her, saying, 'The sooner we're gone the better. I've checked the times of the trains.'

'We're going by train?'

'It's better that way. I know flying in pregnancy is mostly safe, but if there are any fears about the baby it's better not to fly. It'll be a long journey, but I'll make sure you're comfortable all the way.'

He took her to the station and helped her into the first class carriage he'd booked for them both. At last they started the journey from London to the coast, through the tunnel beneath the sea and on their way to Paris. There they had to change trains for the final part of the journey to Rome.

She had an uneasy journey. For much of the way she felt queasy and had a headache. Leonizio cared for her every moment and when night came and she fell asleep she awoke to find him leaning anxiously over her.

'We're nearly there,' he said. 'Did you sleep well?'

'Oh, yes,' she whispered.

She'd had a lovely night, safe and contented in the feeling that she was going home. She reached up to him and they held each other close as the train headed for the last lap to Rome.

Ellie was only vaguely aware of the next few hours. A taxi was waiting for them at the station, and soon they were on their way home.

A doctor called the same evening. He talked to her at length and studied the information from the scans.

'I will make a referral. He's the best obstetrician there is.'

He arranged the appointment for the very next morning. Leonizio accompanied her and sat in tense silence while more tests were made.

'Is the baby really too small?' Ellie asked nervously.

'A little smaller than I'd expect, but it isn't necessarily serious.'

'But when will we know if there are any abnormalities?'

'When we get the test results. Don't assume the worst. Things could still go well.'

'And if they don't?' she wept. 'How badly could our child be hurt?'

'It's much too soon to say.'

'Could it be my fault? Have I done something wrong?'

'Stop it,' Leonizio told her. 'Don't look for reasons to blame yourself.'

'I'm afraid it's what mothers tend to do,' the doctor said. 'But sometimes things just happen for no apparent reason. I'll be in touch as soon as we know more.'

'Don't you have any idea now?' Ellie begged.

'I couldn't possibly speculate.'

His words seemed to threaten the worst. She dropped her head, feeling as though the world was crashing around her. Only the support of Leonizio's arms prevented her from crying out in despair. While he held her she could feel safe.

'Come along,' he murmured. 'Let's go home.'

They were silent on the journey home. When they reached the apartment he made her some coffee and sat beside her, sad and serious.

'I want you to stay here now,' he said. 'I have to look after you. I couldn't bear it any other way.'

'Nor could I,' she said. 'As long as we have you—'

'You do have me. Both of you.'

For the next few days Ellie tried to think as little as possible. She functioned mechanically, fulfilled her domestic duties, and did whatever Leonizio asked. But she kept her brain silent as much as possible. Brooding about what might be about to happen only brought pain.

She sensed that Leonizio was going through exactly the same thing. They didn't talk about it, but his fear was in his eyes. Whenever the phone rang he would answer it tensely, always expecting the crucial news. But it didn't come, and when he'd hung up he would shake his head and pat her on the shoulder.

At last, after three tense, agonising days, it happened.

The phone rang again. Ellie's eyes were fixed on

Leonizio's face as he snatched up the receiver, grating, *'Sì?'* in a harsh voice.

Then he didn't speak for several seconds, while her heart thumped with fear. But suddenly his face brightened, his eyes lit up and he made her a thumbs-up gesture.

'Yes!' he cried. *'Yes, yes!'*

He slammed down the phone and seized her in his arms.

'Good news!' he yelled. 'Everything's fine.'

'You mean the baby—?'

'Our baby is perfectly healthy. The tests say there's nothing wrong.'

'Oh, thank heavens!' She burst into sobs against him and for several moments they clung tightly, as if protecting each other from the world.

She could feel him shaking. Looking up, she saw that his face was as wet as her own, as though he too had been weeping tears of joy.

'I don't dare believe it,' she said. 'Can it really be true?'

'We're going to see them tomorrow,' he said huskily. 'And they'll show us everything. That call was just to alert us in advance.'

They saw the doctor next day and received a mass of communication that eased their minds. Also included was the estimated date of the birth, over three months ahead.

'And until then I strongly advise you to avoid all stress,' the doctor said. 'You've been lucky so far, but you're to take no chances.'

'We're going back to England,' Leonizio said.

'That's all right, as long as you go by train. No stress.'

'She'll be resting from now on,' Leonizio said. 'I'll see to that.'

'That's good to know. It's a relief to be able to leave her in your care.'

When they were alone Leonizio said, 'Aren't you going to say it?'

'Say what?'

'How dare I make decisions without consulting you? How dare I say that I'll make sure you rest when you have a job to go back to?'

She gave him a warm smile. 'I guess I know you too well by now to say any of that. I guess you've made all my decisions.'

He eyed her with a wry smile. 'Am I allowed to make your decisions?'

'I suppose I'll have to give you my permission. So tell me what I'm going to do.'

'We're returning to England because I think you'll feel happier there, and feeling happy will make you safer. You've done a great job buying the new factory, and I'm going to base myself there until our child is born.

'We settle back into our apartment and you stay there, where I can protect you and our baby, because nothing else matters but your safety.' A sudden thought seemed to trouble him. 'You did really give me your permission, didn't you? I didn't imagine that?'

'Don't worry. I'm not going to fight you about this.'

'What will Alex Dallon say when we tell him you're taking a long maternity leave?'

'He'll understand. I know it's what I must do.'

'Then everything's going well and we can stop worrying.'

'Hush, don't talk like that,' she said, urgently putting her fingers over his mouth. 'Never be too sure that things are going well. It's bad luck.'

'All right, I'll be cautious.' He gave a small wry laugh. 'I used to think that we made our own luck, that control was important. But now it's you who makes my luck, and I lost control a while back.'

'Are you saying that I have control?' she teased. 'You

don't really mean that. Tomorrow you'll say just the opposite.'

'You have some control. But our little unborn friend has most of it. Since the day we knew about him he's given the orders and somehow I find myself dancing attendance.'

'He? You want a son?'

'No, I'll be happy with a girl or a boy, as long as it's mine.'

'I've promised you it's yours. Don't you believe me?'

'Yes, I believe you. When I said "mine" I didn't mean like that. I meant that he or she will call me Daddy, ask me questions, tell me what they're thinking and hoping for, give me birthday and Christmas cards. If they get into trouble I want to be the one they send for. I want to know that nothing can ever take me out of their life.'

The emotion in his voice affected her painfully. His child meant everything to him. More than she ever would.

'You can be sure of that,' she said, speaking with difficulty. 'I won't come between you.'

'Does that mean you'll marry me?'

'Don't. I can't talk about that now.'

'But why—?'

'You don't understand. There are so many things we have to—let's talk later. I'm carrying your baby. Can't that be enough for the moment?'

'Except that you could run out on me whenever you like.'

'And you think if I was your wife I'd be your prisoner? Marriage certificates and formalities don't make it work,' she persisted. '*We* have to make it work.'

'And you don't think we can? All right, don't answer that. Your refusal is an answer in itself. Let it go. I promise not to trouble you again.'

So that was it. He'd bowed to her wishes and would no longer annoy her with marriage proposals. She guessed she should feel satisfied and triumphant.

But she only felt sad and defeated.

CHAPTER TWELVE

THE TRAIN JOURNEY back to England was peaceful, and life settled down quietly. As the weeks passed Leonizio behaved perfectly. He cared for Ellie like a dutiful protective father, anticipating her needs, ensuring that she was never under strain. And, true to his promise, he never uttered a word about marriage.

Ellie supposed she should be glad of that. It made her life easier and more relaxed. And if she occasionally had moments of desolation she told herself firmly to ignore them.

Gradually she grew bigger. The time was coming when they would know everything about the future. One night Leonizio helped her undress for bed. As her bump came into view he touched it reverently.

'I'm a lucky man,' he said. 'So much happiness now, and so much more in store for us. I can hardly wait. Do we really have to wait another month?'

'So the doctors say. But it moves so much I get the feeling of a real personality in there, almost as though our child was with us already.'

'In a way it is. Hey there!' he addressed her stomach. 'Be careful of your *mamma*. Don't give her a hard time.'

'I can always hope he or she will listen to you,' Ellie chuckled. 'But I don't think I can count on it.'

'True.' He grinned, saying, 'After all, its mother never listens to me.'

'Well, that might change—ah!' She checked herself with a gasp as a sharp pain attacked her stomach.

'What is it?' Leonizio demanded. 'Ellie, what's the matter?'

'I'm not sure. I just—something happened—' She clasped her bump and gasped again.

'Is it starting?' he asked in an alarmed voice.

'It's too soon for that but—yes, I think it is. Oh, heavens, I can feel such—*ah!*'

Now there could be no mistake. The pain that went through her was fierce and threatening.

'It's happening,' she groaned.

'Happening?' he echoed in alarm. 'You mean the baby—?'

'Yes, but—oh, no—please, this mustn't happen. It's too soon.'

'I'll call the ambulance,' Leonizio said through gritted teeth.

He seized the phone, made a tense call, then gathered her in his arms.

'Hold on to me. It's going to be all right.'

Desperately she clung to him as the pain ripped through her again, warning her of possible tragedy to come. The birth wasn't due for another month, yet now—

'It can't happen yet,' she groaned. 'It can't, it can't.'

But it could. In the despairing depths of her heart she knew that fate could be against them, snatching their child away in the last few moments before life began.

Her heart broke for Leonizio. She had promised him so much, longed so fiercely to make him happy. But in a few cruel minutes it might all be snatched from him again, banishing him back into the same bleak desert from which she had vowed to rescue him.

'They'll be here soon,' he said. 'We'll go to the hospital and they'll make everything right.'

But he sounded too firm, too determined, as though he was trying to convince himself as well as her. Looking at his face, she saw fear as well as hope.

'I'll do everything I can,' she choked. 'Truly—I'll try—I'll try—I don't know why this is happening—'

'It's not your fault,' he said fiercely. 'Don't even think like that.'

They clung together until the sound of the doorbell made him go and look out of the window.

'They're here,' he said, and hurried away.

A few moments later a stretcher was wheeled into the room. Leonizio lifted her in his arms, laying her gently upon it then taking her hand, which he held for the whole journey.

She was only vaguely aware of what was happening around her. There was the hum of the vehicle, and she could hear voices as Leonizio asked fearful questions, but she could understand little. The greater reality was the surge of pain that went through her again and again.

The ambulance stopped. They had reached the hospital. Through her spinning senses she could feel herself being wheeled inside. Faces appeared, full of concern. Hands touched her gently. She heard Leonizio talking to the doctor, explaining what had happened, exactly when the pain had started.

'The baby isn't due for another month,' he said. 'That's what we were told. It can't be coming now, can it?'

'We'll have to see,' the doctor said quietly.

Again pain flooded her, making her scream. 'Leonizio—*Leonizio.*'

Hardly aware of what she was doing, she reached out blindly and felt him take hold of her hands.

'I'm here, *cara,*' he vowed.

'Don't leave me.'

'It's all right if I stay, isn't it?' he demanded of the doctor. 'I can't leave her.'

'If she needs you it may be best for you to stay,' the doctor agreed. 'But please—'

'I won't interfere or get in your way,' Leonizio promised at once.

'Excellent.'

Again Ellie cried out. Now there could be no more doubt. Her body was possessed by contractions that told her things were moving fast. She clung fiercely to Leonizio, looking up so that her eyes met his.

'Soon,' he whispered. 'Soon we will have everything.'

If only, he thought desperately, her suffering could end now. It tortured him to see her terrible pain and know that he couldn't help her bear it.

Useless, he thought. *That's all I am. Useless!*

Time passed slowly. Sometimes she seemed able to relax, but then another contraction would seize her, leaving her seemingly exhausted.

'How long can this go on?' Leonizio asked wretchedly.

'It's coming,' said the doctor. 'Any moment now—'

Then he was reaching forward to help the baby out into the world. Leonizio had a slight vision of a tiny body, but it did not seem to move and he held his breath, silently praying in hope.

Suddenly it happened. The air was split by a wail that grew in vigour until everyone was smiling with relief.

'That's it,' exclaimed the doctor in delight. He examined the baby closely. 'It's a girl. She's a little small and she'll need extra care at first, but the signs are good.'

Leonizio leaned close to Ellie. 'Did you hear that, *carissima*? We have a daughter, and we're a family. Isn't that wonderful?'

But her eyes stayed closed and she only murmured, 'Mmm?'

'Ellie—Ellie—'

'I'm sorry but you'll have to leave now,' the doctor said grimly. 'She's losing a lot of blood and it needs urgent action.'

'Or what?' he demanded. 'If she loses too much blood—what will happen?'

'Then we'll have a tragedy, which we're fighting to prevent. Please, you must go now.'

Leonizio felt like tearing his hair out. He knew he must go but he couldn't bear to leave Ellie. Her eyes were still closed and he didn't know how much she heard. Leaning down, he kissed her forehead, her cheeks, her mouth.

'I'll be back,' he whispered. 'Just promise to be here, waiting for me.'

He went out into the corridor and found a seat just a short distance from the door. From here he could return in a moment if she needed him.

But he couldn't banish the thought that she didn't need him and would never need him again. She was disappearing into another world.

He had the strangest sensation of watching a parade. Everyone he had ever cared about was there, reminding him how little warmth and love there had been in his life and how cruelly it had vanished. The uncle and aunt who had raised him had merely done their duty, without giving him anything he could feel as affection. With Harriet there had been love, or so he'd thought until she'd betrayed him. And the child he'd believed his, who'd inspired his love while still in the womb. That love too had been snatched from him, abandoning him in what would have been a desert but for Ellie.

With Ellie there had finally been hope, but now she too was slipping away, leaving him the baby he wanted so much, but which he now realised could never console him for her loss.

He tensed as the door to the delivery room opened and a nurse emerged pushing a small trolley. She came over to him.

'I'm taking your daughter to the Special Care Unit,' she said. 'She won't have to be there long. Being a month early, she doesn't have full strength, but apart from that she's doing well. Once she's through this she can have a wonderful life.'

He looked at the tiny creature who lay with her eyes closed, clearly unaware of the world she had entered.

'My little girl,' he whispered. 'Mine. And Ellie's.' He leaned closer. 'Your mother and I are going to be so happy with you. She'll be well soon, and she'll hold you in her arms.'

The doctor appeared in the doorway. 'Would you like to come back in now?' he asked.

'Is she—what's happening?'

'She's still losing blood. We're doing our best but it may not be enough.'

'Not enough?' he echoed wildly. 'She can't die—she mustn't—'

'We'll keep her alive if we can,' the doctor assured him.

'But *can* you?'

'I hope so, but I can't give you a promise just now. Please come in.'

He returned to the delivery room. Ellie lay there, still and quiet.

'Ellie,' he whispered. 'Ellie, can you hear me?'

'Yes—yes.'

She hardly made a sound, but the movement of her lips encouraged him.

'It's me, Leonizio. I'm here. I'll always be here for you. And you must always be here for me. I can't lose you. I couldn't bear it. Promise not to leave me. Promise. Promise.'

At last she opened her eyes. He moved his face closer, desperately seeking some sign that she understood him. But she looked at him in confusion.

'Promise me,' he repeated frantically. 'I couldn't endure life without you. I love you.'

'Me?' she whispered. 'Love me?'

'Of course. You must always have known—'

'No—no—'

'But you know now. Tell me that you understand, please? *Please.*'

There was no response. Her eyes had closed again and for a terrifying moment he thought the worst had happened. But then he saw that she was breathing. She was still alive, but she had slipped away into another dimension and he must somehow find the strength to wait patiently for her to return to him.

But perhaps she would never return. She was close to death and he had a despairing feeling that his pleas to her had gone unheard. Perhaps for ever.

He leaned down so that his face was against hers.

'Wherever you are,' he whispered, 'come back to me. Please come back. *Please, Ellie, don't leave me.*'

Ellie had the sensation of wandering through a corridor of shadows. She was in a place where she had never been before, not knowing what lay ahead, able only to hear mysterious voices. One of them sounded like Leonizio's.

'Ellie, can you hear me?'

She whispered, 'Yes,' but she couldn't be really sure what she heard. Leonizio's voice was speaking of love, saying he couldn't live without her.

She opened her eyes, hoping that he was there, but she could see nothing clearly.

'I couldn't endure life without you. I love you.'

'Me?' she whispered in disbelief. 'Love me?'

He spoke again but she couldn't make out the words. She knew now that it was a delusion. She believed in his love because she longed for it, but the mists were swirling her away and unconsciousness was claiming her again.

Now only one sound reached her. A desperate voice, whispering—

Wherever you are, come back to me. Please come back. *Ellie, come back!*

She turned, reaching out with her hands and her heart. But there was only the mist swirling about her until everything else vanished.

She didn't know how long she was unconscious, but when she awoke her mind was clear.

'Ah, good, you're back with us,' said the nurse.

'My baby—?'

'She's fine. A little small but she looks good.'

'She?'

'Yes, you've got a lovely little daughter. Her father's enchanted with her.'

'He's here?'

'He brought you into the hospital.'

'Oh, yes, I think I remember. But it's so confused. I can't be sure of anything.'

'He was with you during the birth. He left to spend a little time with your baby, but he came back a few minutes later. We were getting worried in case you didn't survive, and he just had to be with you. When we told him the danger was past he nearly collapsed. He's with your little girl now, telling her she's lucky to still have a *mamma*.'

'Oh—goodness!'

'Hey, don't cry. Everything's going to be all right.'

Everything all right, she thought wistfully as memories of her dream haunted her.

It had been an impossible fantasy, with Leonizio reaching out to her, declaring love in words she could never hope to hear in real life.

She was vaguely aware that the nurse had gone away, but she wasn't alone. She thought Leonizio stood there, watching her with anxious eyes. She held her breath, fearful that this too was a fantasy.

He came to sit by the bed, leaning close enough to talk softly.

'Thank you,' he said. 'Thank you for coming back to me. I dared to hope you couldn't leave me after I begged you to stay.'

'You—begged me—?'

'Don't you remember?'

'I'm not sure. Did we—talk?'

'Ellie, what do you mean? How can you ask if we talked? We said things we've never said before, perhaps because the moment was never right before. I told you that I loved you. You didn't seem to believe me, but it's the truth. Don't you remember?'

'I was in a strange place. I was walking through a dark mist and heard your voice, calling me.'

He hesitated, then asked quietly, 'Did you know the place you were heading for?'

'No, but I think now—that if you hadn't made me come back—' she trembled '—I would never have returned.'

'That's what I was afraid of,' he said. 'You were so close to—' He paused, unwilling to say the word. 'I couldn't have endured it. How could you go away from me when I love you so?'

'Do you really—love me? Truly?'

'Why can't you believe me? Haven't I begged you to marry me all this time?'

'Only because of the baby. You wanted to love someone who would always be there for you, a child who would return your love because it was yours. After what Harriet did, you needed your own child even more. And I could give you one. That was all I meant to you. I was sure of it.'

'Perhaps that was true once, but the longer we were together the more you came to mean to me. And that scared me.'

'Scared? You?'

'It takes a lot to scare me, but you managed it as nothing else ever could. I think my love for you began our first night together, when I discovered your warmth and kindness, and I was so glad to fall into your arms. It was a sweet feeling but it took me time to realise how it had taken me over. And then I was horrified to realise the love was all on my side.'

'But it wasn't. It isn't. I do love you. I've loved you for a long time.'

'How can you say that when you've always refused to marry me?'

'Because I couldn't bear the thought of an unequal marriage, loving you but knowing that you didn't love me.'

'I did love you, all the time. When you refused to marry me it hurt, and not just because of the baby. I wanted you. Nobody but you. But I thought you despised me, and I must work hard to overcome your scorn.'

'How strange that you should say that,' she murmured.

'Why?'

'Because sometimes I've felt that it was you who felt scorn for me.'

'Ellie, no, you can't have felt that.'

'I've longed for some sign that you cared for me, not

just the baby. It never came. You minded about the baby, but never me.'

'That's not how it was. I minded about you so much I was afraid to face it. But even then—I knew I loved you, but until today I didn't fully understand how deep my love is. When I thought you were dying I couldn't bear to think of what my life would be without you. A blank desert with no hope of any kind.'

'But if that had happened—if I wasn't with you any more—you'd still have our child.'

'And I'd treasure her, for her own sake and in memory of you. I'd have called her Ellie, after you, because I can't survive without an Ellie in my life. Now I'd like to call her Cosima. It means order and beauty, which is what you both mean to me.

'You must promise to stay with me. Nothing and nobody could ever console me for losing you. Please, Ellie, tell me that I can hope. I'll do all I can to win your love, however long it takes.'

'But I've already told you that I love you. Don't you believe me?'

'I'm almost afraid to. If you believe in good news too easily, it can get snatched away. You warned me of that once yourself.'

'It won't be snatched away, I promise you, Leonizio. You are my love, now and for ever.'

'Do you love me enough to marry me?'

'I always have.'

'Say yes,' he begged. 'Just that one word. Let me hear it.'

'Yes. Yes, I'll marry you. Yes.'

For a moment he didn't move. His eyes met hers, full of happiness and adoration. Then he lowered his head, resting it against her breast like a man who'd finally found the way home to a safe haven. It was a feeling that Ellie completely understood because it was her own.

'Yes,' she repeated. 'We took too long to find each other, but now we have and nothing will separate us. We're together—all three of us.'

'All three of us,' he repeated. 'Marry me, and I ask for nothing else.'

He glanced up as the doctor appeared.

'We're going to be married as soon as she's out of here,' he said. 'When will that be?'

'I'm afraid I can't tell you,' the doctor said uneasily. 'The danger isn't over yet.'

'But we thought—when she came round—'

'That was hopeful, but not final.'

'You mean she might still die?' Leonizio was aghast.

'I'm afraid it's possible.'

Leonizio dropped his head, putting a hand over his eyes. Ellie reached out to touch his face.

'Then we must marry now,' she whispered.

'Ellie—'

'If I'm going to die,' she said urgently, 'I want to die as your wife.'

He dropped to his knees beside the bed and she felt his tears against her skin.

She looked up at the doctor. 'Will you arrange it?'

'Yes,' he said, and hurried away.

Ellie stroked Leonizio's face, saying softly, 'If I do die, it's better for you if we're married. You'll find it easier to claim our baby.'

'That's not why I'm marrying you,' he said fiercely. 'I want you. No one but *you*.'

'I'll be there. Even if I'm not alive—I'll always be there with you.'

'And you will be alive. You simply must be because to lose you would break my heart for ever.'

'Together,' she whispered. 'Always together.'

The doctor appeared again.

'It has to be a civil ceremony,' he said. 'That's all we can arrange under these circumstances. Of course you can have a religious ceremony later.'

He didn't add, *if you're alive*, but they both understood.

'How quickly can we do this?' Ellie asked.

'Yes, we've waited too long,' Leonizio said, looking at her.

'I'm sorry,' she whispered. 'I should have understood before—'

'Don't blame yourself,' he said, leaning close. 'It's my fault that you didn't understand—I did everything wrong. But at last we've found the way and can marry now.'

'There are some formalities that have to be gone through first,' said the doctor. 'The law requires us to establish that the patient is in her right mind and acting of her own free will.'

'But I am,' Ellie said urgently. 'I'm doing what I want more than anything in the world. Please, please, sign anything you need, to confirm that.'

Fear was rising in her. Only a few minutes ago she had seemed to be slipping away into the darkness and Leonizio had drawn her back with his love. But, despite the power of her heart, her body was still weak and the darkness beckoned again.

For months she had loved him and longed to be his wife, despite the problems that made her refuse him. Now her moment had come, but perhaps it had come too late. In a few minutes they would have lost each other. When he raised his head and met her eyes she knew that he too understood everything.

The doctor returned with a middle-aged man that he introduced as Mr Dale, an official who could perform the ceremony.

'There are two kinds of vows,' he said. 'First, the traditional ones that everyone speaks. But then there are some more vows that you create for yourselves, that express your own true feelings. Do you think you can manage them?'

'Oh, yes,' Ellie said fervently.

Leonizio nodded. 'Yes,' he said softly.

Mr Dale handed them papers with the official vows, and looked around to check that the doctor and a nurse were present as witnesses. 'Now we can begin,' he said. He uttered the introductory words, then glanced at Leonizio, who took a deep breath as though trying to control his nerves, and began to speak.

'I, Leonizio, take you, Ellie, to be my wedded wife.'

Mr Dale nodded, then looked at Ellie.

She tightened her grasp on Leonizio's hand and said fervently, 'I, Ellie, take you, Leonizio, to be my wedded husband.'

Watching his face, she thought she saw the gleam of tears upon his cheeks, and felt her own tears begin to flow. To her horror, she could feel her strength fading and knew that they had only a little time left to belong to each other.

But she would make the most of that time, for Leonizio's sake. It was the only thing she could do for him before their terrible parting.

'What personal vows do you wish to make?' Mr Dale asked.

Gently Leonizio laid her hand against his lips.

'I promise that nobody in the world will ever matter more to me than you,' he said in a gentle voice. 'I belong to you now and for ever. You are my life, and that is what you will always be. Only promise me the same, and I will have all I'll ever want.'

There was an urgent question in his eyes, fixed on her, pleading.

'I can promise you the same,' she said. 'And I do. I am yours. I have been yours from the first moment, and I will always be yours.'

'Always?' he whispered.

'Always—and for ever.'

She saw joy come into his eyes as she said 'for ever' and hoped that he could see the same joy in her eyes as they committed themselves to each other.

At last came the declaration. *You are now man and wife.*

'We're married,' he whispered. 'You belong to me and I belong to you.'

'Yes. I'm going to stay with you always. Even if I should—'

'Don't say it,' he said urgently. 'That mustn't happen. You've got to live because I can't endure life without you.'

'Then I will,' she said.

'Swear it.'

'I swear by everything I hold sacred.'

She had given her word and she knew she must keep it at all costs. To lose her would devastate him in a way she had never imagined. Feeling sleep overtaking her, she struggled to fight it off.

Watching her, Leonizio was suddenly terrified. 'Ellie—Ellie—'

'It's all right,' the doctor said, feeling her pulse. 'She's stronger already.'

'Already? How can you tell so soon?'

'Because the tide has turned. Something—or someone—has given her the strength to fight for life much more strongly than before.'

Something or someone? Looking down at her in his arms, he wondered if their marriage could really have provided her with a reason for living. Was he hoping for too much?

As the minutes passed he felt the dawn of hope. Holding her in his arms, he murmured, 'Stay with me, Ellie. You promised—you promised—'

Gradually he sensed her breathing grow stronger until at last she opened her eyes again and he could see in them everything he longed for.

'You're better,' he breathed. 'You're going to live. Can't you feel that?'

She smiled. 'Of course I am. I promised. And I'll never break a promise to you for as long as I live.'

Now they were legally married, but when Ellie was released from hospital they both wanted another ceremony to proclaim their love to the world.

On their wedding morning he awoke to find her sitting on the bed beside him, with Cosima in her arms. The sight flooded him with peace and happiness, which was how it would always be, he realised.

They'd travelled to Rome for the ceremony. Many of Leonizio's employees were there, anxious not to miss the sight of the woman who had transformed their employer. Some of her friends, including Alex, came over from England.

When Ellie appeared in her bridal gown there was a murmur of astonishment, for she was carrying little Cosima in her arms. Leonizio's eyes were fixed on them with joy, and a whisper went around that he was marrying both of them.

Then it was time to answer questions. The preacher asked, 'Do you take this woman to be your wedded wife?'

Leonizio's eyes met Ellie's. 'A thousand times over,' he said quietly.

The preacher looked uneasily at the bride. 'That's not the answer you're supposed to give.'

'Don't worry,' Ellie said. 'To me it's the perfect answer.'

A little gulp came from Cosima. Both her parents smiled at her in delight.

'We're agreed,' Leonizio said. 'All three of us.'

'Yes,' Ellie said. 'All three of us.'

And that, they both knew, was how it would always be.

* * * * *

"Would you want to do this the natural way?"

The look on his face when he asked that question was comical. Taylor started to laugh, even though Clint didn't join her. They both had something the other needed, so it truly could be a win-win if they played their hands correctly.

"I'd prefer…" She couldn't believe she was about to say this. "Natural."

She was tired of shots and doctors and scheduling and waiting rooms. She just wanted a man to knock her up the old-fashioned way. Was that too much to ask for?

"Would you have any… objection to that?"

"No." Clint's response was direct. "I wanted to take you to bed the first time I saw you."

HIGH COUNTRY BABY

BY

JOANNA SIMS

First Published in Great Britain 2016
By Mills & Boon, an imprint of HarperCollins*Publishers*
1 London Bridge Street, London, SE1 9GF

ISBN: 978-0-263-91994-3

23-0616

Our policy is to use papers that are natural, renewable and recyclable products and made from wood grown in sustainable forests. The logging and manufacturing processes conform to the legal environmental regulations of the country of origin.

Printed and bound in Spain
by CPI, Barcelona

Joanna Sims lives in Florida with her wonderful husband, Cory, and their three fabulous felines, Sebastian, Chester (aka Tubby) and Ranger. By day, Joanna works as a speech-language pathologist and a clinical educator for a large university. But her nights and weekends are reserved for writing contemporary romance for Mills & Boon. Joanna loves to hear from Mills & Boon readers and invites you to stop by her website for a visit, www.joannasimsromance.com.

Dedicated to my mentor and dear friend

Libby

I love you.

Chapter One

Clint McAllister heard the familiar *click* of a bullet being chambered. He'd slept just like a baby once he'd polished off a fifth of tequila, and he'd awakened with a well-deserved hangover. Groggy, irritated, with a massive headache, he'd stumbled over to the edge of the wooded area just beyond his campsite to relieve himself. The last thing he'd expected was to get caught with his pants unzipped, barefoot and without his revolver. Damn rotten luck.

"Put your hands up and turn around nice and slow." Taylor Brand stood confident in the "ready" stance she had learned during concealed-weapon training. Like everything in her life, she had worked hard to be first in her class.

"Just calm down…" The cowboy lifted his left hand up but moved his right hand down to his zipper.

"Keep your hands where I can see them!" Taylor ordered, her voice clear, firm and calm. "Turn around... do it now!"

The stranger quickly lifted his right hand back up. "Look...unless you want a show, I've gotta zip it up before I face you. All right?"

"Do it quick." Taylor told him. "Then turn around."

The man tucked himself in and zipped up quickly, per the lady's orders. His belt buckle still undone, his button-down shirt still completely unbuttoned, the cowboy raised his hands above his head and turned around slowly.

"Why are you following me?" Taylor demanded with her revolver aimed at the man's chest.

"Boss's orders." The man told her, keeping his eye on the flat black barrel of her gun. "Your uncle told me to follow you, make sure you're safe, and that's what I'm doin'."

Taylor stared hard at the unkempt cowboy with her hands steady on the gun. She was only one full day into her trek up to the Continental Divide. It was true that she had forgotten a lot about being in the wilderness over the years, but she had traveled all over the world for business and she had developed a heightened sense of awareness.

Once she was certain she was being followed, she had waited until the first light of morning, made a wide circle back and was able to sneak up on the cowboy much more easily than she had anticipated. The empty liquor bottle she had spotted near the cowboy's gear most likely explained how simple it had been to ambush him—he was a drinker.

"You work at Bent Tree?" she asked him.

The cowboy gave a slight nod of his head. Now that she was getting a better look at him, he did look familiar. She remembered a cowboy who had tipped his hat to her the first day she had arrived at her uncle's ranch. He'd been wearing a sweat-soaked chambray shirt, a black cowboy hat and boots caked with mud and manure. But just because she could place him at Bent Tree didn't mean that he was following her on her uncle's orders. Uncle Hank hadn't mentioned one word of this to her before she had headed out.

"I'm lowerin' my arms, lady. You got that?" the cowboy asked. For a man staring down the barrel of a gun, he seemed to have the mistaken impression that he was in charge of this encounter.

The man's collar-length dark hair was unruly from the night; his face had been unshaven for several days. She wasn't overly impressed with his height or the jailhouse tattoos on his exposed skin, but he was surprisingly fit from the look of his defined chest and shredded abs. His eyes were squinty and bloodshot, and he was obviously hungover. If he had been her employee, she would have fired him on the spot.

"And if you don't plan on shootin' me, you'd best holster that weapon," the cowboy told her.

"I haven't decided not to shoot you." The man's arrogance wasn't unexpected—he was a cowboy.

Clint watched her through sore, narrowed eyes while he buttoned up his shirt. Getting caught with his pants down by Hank's niece had sobered him up quick enough. And he didn't like having that gun pointed at him.

"Lady—do you even know how to shoot that gun?"

Clint unzipped his jeans a little so he could tuck his shirt in.

"I'm a crack shot." she answered him. "Now, get your hands back where I can see them!"

Clint heard the slightest squeak in Taylor's voice when she issued the command. She didn't want him to know it, but she was rattled. And a rattled woman with a gun aimed at his chest didn't sound like a good time.

"Look..." Clint tucked in his shirt. "You need to get on the horn to your uncle. Convince him that you don't need me and you'll be seein' the hind end of my horse before you can say Gucci."

Clint finished tucking in his shirt, zipped up his pants, buckled his belt buckle, and then pointed to the campsite.

"Now—I'm going over there...if you shoot me, you'd better do a good job. If you just graze me, you're gonna regret it..."

"What's your name?" she asked tersely. Clearly she had lost control over this situation. A phone call to her uncle was the next logical step.

"Clint." The cowboy settled his hat on his head and adjusted the brim. "Clint McAllister."

There was a bite in his tone and rigidness in his body she didn't like at all. He was an ill-mannered man, too jagged around the edges for her taste.

"Just stay put until I talk to my uncle," Taylor ordered when Clint started to walk over to where his horse was tethered, his saddle hoisted onto his narrow hip.

"Take it easy." He shook his head in frustration.

This was a rotten beginning to an already lousy day.

"You take it easy." Taylor snapped, but she holstered her weapon.

"Uncle Hank!" The connection was bad on her end. "It's Taylor…can you hear me?"

"I can hear you…"

"I can barely hear you…but, listen… I've got some guy named Clint following me and he says he's under orders from you…is that true, or should I shoot him?"

"I'd rather you not shoot him, Taylor." Hank told her. "He'd be a hard one to replace."

Taylor glanced quickly at Clint's back—he wasn't looking at her, but she knew he was listening to every word.

"Uncle Hank—I told you that I needed to make this trip on my own."

She had taken a leave of absence from her job so she could ride the Continental Divide. Her plan was to ride a section of the divide alone; she'd never imagined it any other way.

"Negative," Hank said in a brusque tone that she had heard many times in her life. Her uncle was a big man, physically as well as in the world of ranching, and he wasn't fond of explaining his decisions.

Clint turned around and they locked eyes for the briefest moment before they both broke the connection.

Taylor lowered her voice. "Uncle Hank—I don't want this. This wasn't part of my plan."

"Plans change." Hank told her in a no-nonsense manner. "Take Clint with you or make a U-turn and come on back to the ranch."

Taylor moved farther away from her cowboy bodyguard. "Did Dad call you? Is that it? Because if he did, let me assure you…"

"Your dad didn't call me—my brother hasn't bothered to call me in years, so I don't expect him to start now."

Hank was her father's older brother. When their father, her grandfather, died, a disagreement about the validity of the will sparked a family feud that had lasted for most of her adult life.

"Uncle Hank." She sounded like a child beseeching a parent. "Please. This is really important to me."

"*You* are really important to *me*, Taylor. I was wrong to go along with your cockamamie idea in the first place. I've come to my senses now, and I'm not changing my mind. So, what's it gonna be?"

"I have to do this," she said quietly. "I can't turn back now."

"Come again?"

More loudly, she repeated. "I can't turn back now."

Not after she had come this far—farther than anyone in her life, including her, thought that she would go.

"It's better this way," her uncle reassured her.

It was pointless to disagree, so she didn't bother to put her energy into a lost cause.

"And Taylor?"

"Yes?" She didn't try to hide the disappointment.

"Clint knows the divide like the back of his hand—and I trust him."

Clint didn't have to hear the conversation to know that it wasn't swinging in Taylor's favor. Her body language—hunched, tense shoulders and lowered head—said it all. Which meant that he was still on the hook to babysit a woman who looked as if she'd be more comfortable getting pampered in a ritzy spa than riding the divide on horseback. She didn't make sense to him, and he wasn't keen on things that didn't make sense.

"Everything squared away?" Clint asked as he swung his saddle onto the back of his sturdily built buckskin quarter horse.

"Looks like we're stuck with each other." Taylor swatted a fly away from her face. "I don't know what possessed my uncle to change his mind at the eleventh hour—I don't need a babysitter."

Clint reached beneath his horse's belly to grab the girth. "I ain't no babysitter."

Taylor cringed at the way in which Clint colorfully put a sentence together. She was an English major in college. Syntax was always her first love and double negatives made her nuts. Even though he'd managed to butcher the English language with a four-word sentence, she couldn't deny one thing: the cowboy didn't want to be here anymore than she wanted him. They were both in the same rotten boat. And by the looks of him, there was a chance he could be persuaded…

"You could wait here for me. No one has to know," she suggested casually. Then, when she had his attention, she sweetened the pot. "I could pay you."

The cowboy fished a pack of unfiltered cigarettes from his front pocket and knocked one out of the pack with his hand. "That's not gonna happen, lady."

He needed this job. He was trying to dig himself out of a mighty deep financial hole and he wasn't about to bite the Hank Brand hand that was currently feeding him. If he took Taylor's money, it would no doubt be short-term gain with long-term negative consequences.

Before he put the cigarette in his mouth to light it, he

offered Taylor a suggestion of his own. "You could head on back to Bent Tree and save us the hassle."

"I'm not going back." Taylor was firm in her response. It was easy for her uncle and this cowboy-for-hire to toss this suggestion around as if it was nothing. To them it *was* nothing. They had no idea what she had gone through or how much she'd given up to get to this leg of her journey. And, to her, this trek to the Continental Divide had become everything.

Clint took a drag off of his cigarette. He shook his head and when he spoke, curls of white smoke streamed out of his nose and mouth.

"Well, then…it looks like we're stuck with each other."

She felt tears of frustration and anger well up behind her eyes. She didn't typically cry when she was sad—she cried when she was mad as hell. She *hated* Clint for not being corruptible. She pushed the tears down; they were useless to her and she needed every ounce of her energy reserve to spend another day in the saddle.

"I'll hang back." Clint put his cigarette out on the tip of the bottom of his boot before he tossed it into the cold fire pit. "That's the best I can do."

Taylor stared at the wrangler for a moment longer. She had already burned too much daylight dealing with an issue that simply wasn't going to resolve in her favor.

"I'm afraid that you're best isn't good enough, Mr. McAllister."

She had been a vice president at a large bank for many years and knew when a negotiation was over. She didn't have anything left to say to the cowboy, so she headed back up the hill to where she had stayed for the night and broke camp as quickly as she could.

Her uncle had provided her with a small, surefooted mare named Honey and an experienced pack mule named Easy Does It. It didn't take her long to break camp, pack up her belongings and get ready for the day's ride.

Prior to leaving Chicago for Montana, she had moved all of the furniture in her formal living room out of the way so she could set up a practice campsite. She read, and then reread, all of the manuals that came with her new camping gear, and she had even slept inside of the tent for several weeks to get used to sleeping on the ground.

All of her practice and preparation had paid off—she could set up and break camp with relative ease. Her uncle had personally shown her how to pack Easy's load properly and refreshed her memory on the correct way to tack a horse. All in all, she was pretty proud of her ability.

But there was one giant fly in her ointment: mounting her horse.

She was short, she had stubby legs and she certainly wasn't as limber as she'd been in her teens. It was a major chore to get her foot into the stirrup, but once that was accomplished she didn't have enough strength to get her bottom-heavy body into the saddle. The only way she could mount up was to find a log or a stump to stand on and even *then* it wasn't a guarantee. She knew that this was a weakness that needed to be overcome, because if she couldn't find a makeshift mounting block one day, she would be stuck on the ground. Not good.

She led Honey over to a fallen tree she had scoped out the night before, tightened the girth and lengthened the stirrup. Honey was surefooted, that couldn't be denied, but she was also horrible to mount. The mare was frisky from the briskness of the morning air and she danced sideways away from the log right when Taylor had managed to leverage her foot into the stirrup.

"Whoa!" Her foot was caught in the stirrup and pulled her leg forward while she wobbled precariously on the log. She ended up in a half-split position, grabbing urgently to unhook her foot from the stirrup.

"Honey, whoa!" Taylor unhooked her foot just in time to stop herself from falling forward.

That could have ended in a serious injury, and she was lucky it hadn't. The muscles on the inside of her right thigh, already tender from a day in the saddle, had been stretched beyond their limit during that failed attempt to mount her steed.

Taylor clutched the inside of her right thigh. *"Ah!"*

She rubbed the muscle to stop it from contracting. But the minute she let go of that part of her body, she noticed that her left hip joint was aching.

Honey was standing quietly, perfectly still, a few feet away.

"Woman to woman, Honey—give a sister a break, okay?"

Taylor walked Honey in a semicircle and halted her right next to the log. Three more attempts and three more semicircles later, Taylor was tempted to just start walking until she found a better place to mount. It was at that moment that Clint rode into the clearing, dismounted and silently stood on Honey's right side to stop her from moving away from the log. The cowboy adjusted her reins so the right rein was shorter, showing Taylor, without verbalizing it, how to keep the horse from moving away from her.

Once she was in the saddle he checked the tightness of her girth and the length of her stirrups. When he was done with his inspection, he led the mule over to her and handed her the lead rope.

Their eyes met for the briefest of moments, for the second time that morning, but this time she could see that his eyes were the color of the blue Montana sky. Satisfied that she was squared away, he mounted his horse and disappeared into the trees beyond her campsite.

It pained her to admit it—it really did. Clint had just gone a long way to prove his value on this trek. She hadn't said thank you, and he hadn't expected it. He'd done what her uncle had told him to do—watch out for her. And, then, as good as his word, he'd disappeared into the thick wall of brush and trees.

With a cluck of her tongue and a tug on the lead rope that was hooked to the mule's harness, Taylor started guiding the mare toward the trail. She was still on her uncle's land—Bent Tree sprawled out across thousands of acres abutting the Continental Divide. She'd make it to one more designated campsite on this trail, a campsite used by the Brand family for generations, and then she'd finally reach the mouth of the Continental Divide trail. Would the moment be exactly as she had dreamed it so many times since she was a teenager? She could hardly wait to find out.

It was simply a fact that riding on horseback all day had been much easier, and much more romantic, in her imagination than in reality. The last time she had ridden, she had been in her twenties. Years later, and now that she was pushing forty, her body wasn't as pliable or cooperative as it once been. She was chaffed in private places, her hip joints ached, her leg muscles ached, her back ached and for some reason, her neck was stiff, too.

She had used every psychological trick and pep talk she could think of to push through the pain, stay in the saddle and make it to the next campsite. When she finally reached a landmark, a steep hill on the trail, that let her know she was nearly there, Taylor tightened her grip on the lead rope and grabbed the saddle horn in order to stop herself from flying backward in the saddle when Honey galloped up the steep hill.

At the top was a grassy plateau perfect for camping. Grateful that she had accomplished her goal, she couldn't stand to be in the saddle for one more minute. She groaned loudly as she swung her shaking leg over her horse's rump. She unhooked her foot from the stirrup and slid, ungracefully, gratefully to solid ground. She winced as she walked—a new blister had formed over the old blister on the back of her right heel. But, she didn't care. She had succeeded! She had triumphed!

Taylor limped her way through the quick camping routine she had established for herself, and then once she was satisfied with her situation she backtracked on foot to go find Clint. It was ridiculous to try to pretend she was alone when she wasn't, in fact, *alone*. She had tried all day long and it hadn't worked. She'd never been good at pretending.

"What's up?" Clint was surprised, and not pleased, to see her come around the corner. He twisted the top back onto the glass bottle he had in his hand before he tucked it back into his saddlebag.

"We may as well make camp together."

Clint hadn't unpacked his gear or unsaddled his horse. "That's what you want?"

It wasn't. But it was practical. She had always been, until recently at least, a very practical woman.

"It's practical," she told him. "It's hard for you to babysit me from way down here."

Clint nodded his head after a bit and then fell in beside her on foot instead of remounting. The silence between them was uncomfortable for Taylor—and when she was uncomfortable, she tended to talk. It was a bad habit she'd never truly been able to break no matter how many times her ex-husband complained about it.

"You must have drawn the short straw to get this gig."

No response.

"My entire family thinks I've gone off the deep end."

"Have you?"

"Gone off the deep end?" Taylor asked with a labored breath. She had exchanged her gym membership for a frequent customer card at the local bakery over a year ago. She had packed on the pounds and her cardio was at an all-time low. This trip was either going to break her or help her snap the heck out of it!

Clint nodded. She could see by the look on his face that the question wasn't sarcastic or rhetorical—he genuinely wanted to know if he was traveling with a loony bird.

Perhaps it wasn't wise to be so forthcoming with the cowboy, but she was tired of living a dishonest life. She'd lived with lies in her marriage—always hiding who she really was in order to fit some impossible standard of the "perfect wife." So she told Clint the truth.

"I'm not sure." Taylor's brow furrowed thoughtfully. "Maybe."

Chapter Two

It was odd. They were strangers, but they worked well as a team. Clint chose a spot on one side of the permanent fire pit, while she found the perfect place on the opposite side to set up her tent.

While she worked, she sneaked quick glances at her cowboy bodyguard. He was unlike any man she had dealt with in her adult life—there was a sharp edge to this cowboy. He had the look of a man who'd fallen on hard times more than once in his life. Years, presumably tough years, were etched on his narrow face and around his deep-set eyes. Everything about the man seemed to be suffering from too much wear; from his cracked leather boots to the hat that had been faded from black to a muddy gray by the sun, everything had seen better days.

Clint went off in search of kindling to start the fire

while Taylor focused on finding a spot in the flat open field for Honey and Easy to graze. After they were settled, she worked on settling herself. She unzipped the black bag containing her tent and pulled it out of the bag. After the olive-green tent was unrolled, she quickly lifted and snapped the four frame braces into place.

She had the tent assembled and staked into place by the time Clint reappeared. The cowboy had a mostly smoked cigarette clutched between his teeth and was carrying an armload of kindling. He dumped the wood into the pit and then knelt down, wincing. She had noticed that he had an odd stiffness in his legs when he walked—it reminded her of how her grandfather moved before he underwent knee replacement surgery.

"I need to hibernate for a minute." Now that they had stopped for the day, the ache in all of her joints and muscles, the fatigue she felt all over her body and the foggy brain that she had been fighting for the last several hours overwhelmed her. She had to lie down.

Clint looked over at her and gave a quick nod to let her know that he heard her. The man wasn't a talker and he seemed determined to stay out of her way. She could appreciate that about him. If she had to have company on this journey of self-discovery, at least her company would be *quiet*.

Taylor zipped herself into her small tent and stretched flat out on her back, palms upward, legs straight, eyes closed. She groaned, low and long, wishing that she could locate a place on her body that didn't hurt. With effort, she pushed her torso upright and reached down for her boot. She had developed a donut belly over the past six months and it was a chore to reach her foot.

With fingers stiffened from holding the reins all day,

Taylor tugged, eyes closed, biting her lip to distract her from the pain she was feeling as the heel of the boot scraped over her blister.

"Ahhhhh!" Taylor yanked the boot off the rest of the way.

Even the simple chore of removing her boots was made harder by the excess weight she had gained.

"Gosh darn it, you're out of shape." Taylor muttered as she pulled off the other boot.

She tossed the boots toward the tent flap; slowly, she peeled off her sweat-soaked socks. Her socks stank, her feet stank, and the bloody blister now covered the entirety of her right heel. Taylor wrinkled her nose while she gently prodded the blister—why hadn't the stupid thing popped already?

After examining it, Taylor struggled out of her jeans, quickly took off her T-shirt and bra, and put on a clean T-shirt that covered a portion of her panties. Once inside of the sleeping bag built for one, she slipped on her standard eye mask to block out the light and sighed the sigh of a woman who had finally found a comfortable spot after a long day of discomfort. She wiggled farther down into the sleeping bag, the top edge tucked under her chin, and prayed for sleep. Ever since the divorce she hadn't slept well. She was hopeful that on this journey, pushing her body to the limit, that exhaustion would force her to sleep.

"Please, God—please let me sleep."

At first, Clint was grateful to have Taylor shut away in her tent. He didn't want this grunt job that his stepbrother Brock, foreman of Bent Tree, had volunteered him for, but with a negative balance in his bank account and creditors trying to track him down, he didn't have a choice. At least while she was in her tent he didn't have to worry about her.

While Taylor was temporarily contained he built a fire, broke into the beef jerky he always took with him when he went on long camping trips, drank some cheap tequila and chain-smoked cigarettes while the sun slowly disappeared behind the taller mountains off in the distance. Dusk was his favorite time to be in the mountains—it was quiet. Peaceful. He'd had a shortage of peace in his life ever since he was a kid. Which made him appreciate moments like this one—a good fire, a full stomach and a little hair of the dog.

But, every once in a while he'd catch the tent out of the corner of his eye and it would remind him that his boss's nutty niece hadn't made an appearance. He couldn't say that he was worried about her—he figured she had to still be breathing—but he was worried about his own neck. As foreman of Bent Tree ranch, Brock, who'd never really had much use for him, didn't need an excuse to give him the boot. If he screwed up with Taylor, he'd be out of luck with Brock. No. He was responsible for Taylor now. He had to make sure she returned to the ranch unharmed. His neck was already on the chopping block, so by default, he had to be worried about *her* neck.

It was nighttime when Taylor awakened. After she pulled off her eye mask, it took her a couple of seconds to make sense of her surroundings. The minute she started to move the reality of her situation came sharply into focus. So very sore everywhere. With another low groan, she pushed herself upright and then toppled forward, her elbows on her thighs and her head in her hands. She stayed in that position, eyes closed, until she could face standing up and getting dressed. In the low light of the flashlight that was hanging from a cord at the highest point of the tent's ceiling, Taylor got dressed. Instead of going through the trauma of getting back into her boots, she opted for rubber-soled slip-ons. Her stomach growled loudly at the same time she was unzipping the tent flap. When she stepped outside her eyes searched for, and found, Clint leaning back against his saddle next to a healthy fire.

Clint had been just about to get up and check on Taylor when he heard the tent flap being unzipped. He hadn't really expected it, but he felt something that could be interpreted as relief when Hank's niece reappeared. They stared at each other for a split second, neither of them speaking, before Taylor grabbed something out of a nearby bag and disappeared into the woods.

The yellow light of a flashlight confirmed what she was going to do—and yet, he found his entire focus turned to the dark edge of the woods. When he saw the light grow brighter, signaling Taylor's return to the campsite, the muscles in his arms, legs and jawline relaxed simultaneously. It was at that exact moment that his body connected with his mind and he realized how important this stranger's safety was to him. He didn't want the job of protector—he had a reputation of putting his own hide above everyone else's. A well-deserved reputation.

What were Brock and Hank *thinking*?

At the edge of the woods, Taylor considered her options. She could go back to the tent or she could join the cowboy. It seemed a little ridiculous to avoid him—for better or worse, they were joined together on this journey for the next several weeks. No time like the present to start making the best of it. Taylor walked slowly over to the campfire, allowing herself to take her time. Even in the slide-on shoes, every step was a miserable one. Once she reached the fire, she switched off the flashlight and carefully lowered her body to the ground. Beneath the brim of his black cowboy hat, Clint's darkened eyes watched her.

"You've got a limp." His voice was a little raspier now.

Yes, Captain Obvious! She stifled her sarcasm for a more congenial "Nasty blister."

Clint stood up and tossed his cigarette into the fire. On his way upright Taylor noticed that he paused with a noticeable wince. The cowboy walked over to her side of the fire to kneel down beside her.

"Let me take a look."

Caught off guard, Taylor pulled her foot back. "What?"

"Let me take a look—see how bad it is."

"No, thank you."

Clint grabbed her by the ankle, pulled her shoe off and bent her leg backward so he could get a closer look at her right heel in the firelight.

"Hey!" Taylor tugged against him. "Hey!"

"Hold still." The cowboy issued an order.

Clint pulled a knife out of a small sheath on his belt. When Taylor caught a glimpse of the silver blade, she yanked her ankle out of Clint's hand and pushed backward away from him.

"Don't even *think* about it!" she snapped at him.

He had *touched* her smelly, sweaty foot! She didn't *like* people touching her feet. She didn't get pedicures because she didn't want anyone touching her feet. She left her socks on during a massage because she didn't want anyone touching her feet!

"It needs to be popped." Clint waved the blade quickly over the flames of the fire.

"No it doesn't. Everyone knows you aren't supposed to pop a blister."

"We need to pop this one." Clint rested his forearm on his bended knee. "It looks like it's on its way to being infected. We'll pop it, drain it—I don't doubt you've got all manner of first aid in that mountain of stuff you packed…" He nodded toward her supplies. "Pour a little alcohol on it, let it dry out overnight—you'll feel a heck of a lot better."

The man looked as though he'd spent most of his life healing something—she was inclined to believe him.

"Are you sure?" Taylor asked.

He nodded his response, so she said, "Go ahead then—but do it quick, please."

"It's done." The cowboy wiped the blade of his knife onto the leg of his jeans.

Taylor opened her eyes and craned her neck to the side to get a look at her heel. "Huh—that didn't even hurt."

She told Clint where he could find her first-aid kit. Popping the blister hadn't hurt, but draining it and then dousing it with alcohol hurt like all get-out. The cowboy was clinical and unsympathetic. He expected her to sit there, quietly—take it like a woman. It was a silent challenge that she decided to accept. She could only imagine what this man thought of her—a soft, socialite city girl without the faintest clue about how to make it in the Montana wilderness. She was a city girl, and proud of it, but she wasn't soft.

The procedure was done and the cowboy returned to his side of the fire. He began to play a harmonica that he had retrieved from his saddlebag. He wasn't just producing random sounds—he really knew how to play. He filled the cool night air with a slow string of pretty notes and those notes blended with the crackling of the fire and the sound of an owl in the distance.

It was at that moment when Taylor felt as if she had really arrived in Montana. No, she wasn't alone on the journey. But it didn't seem to matter anymore. The experience she was having now, sitting by a campfire, beneath a blackened sky dotted with a smattering of white stars, listening to a real cowboy play the harmonica, made her feel like woman of the wilderness. An adventurer in her own right.

Taylor stared into the fire, watching one particular piece of wood glow bright orange right before it broke apart and crumbled into smaller bits of red embers. She didn't have the need to fill the silence with aimless talk as she normally would, which was helpful, because it took energy to talk and she didn't have much of that to spare. Clint would take a break every now and again from playing the harmonica and she would catch the flash of something out of the corner of her eye. Curious, she glanced up to see Clint take a quick swig of something from a bottle. He was leaning down, his head turned away from her. He didn't want her to see him drinking, but she already had.

"What's in the bottle?"

Clint twisted the cap down and tucked the nearly empty bottle back into his saddlebag.

"Tequila," he told her reluctantly.

"Enough to share?"

Those weren't the next words he had expected to hear. Taylor Brand didn't strike him as the type of woman who would drink anything straight from a bottle, much less cheap tequila. Clint tilted his chin up enough so he could see her face beneath the brim of his hat. In the firelight, the natural prettiness of Taylor's oval face caught his attention for the first time. She wasn't model pretty, but she had the kind of face that a man could look at for the rest of his life. And, he was a man, so he had noticed that Taylor had a curvy body, on the thicker side, with round hips, a smaller waist and larger than average breasts. He preferred women who looked as though they wouldn't blow over in a windstorm. Other than the fact that she was as city as a person could be, Taylor Brand was his type of woman.

Clint pulled the bottle out of his saddlebag, twisted off the cap and stretched his arm to bridge the space between them. When Taylor took the bottle from his hand, he saw the flash of a large, round diamond and a platinum band on the ring finger of her left hand. Now, what was a married woman like Taylor doing trying to ride the Continental Divide by herself? When Brock had assigned him to this task, he'd been too angry and too hungover to think, much less consider anything from Taylor's point of view. But even though there was part of him that was curious, he'd discovered early on in life that it was best to mind his own business.

Taylor moved the bottle farther away from her face, then a little closer, so she could read the label. She really needed to get her eyes checked when she got back to Chicago. She could read the larger letters on the bottle, but the smaller letters were a chore to decipher.

"Corazon Blanco…white heart." She read the label aloud. Christopher had always insisted on using Gran Patron on the rare occasion they had hosted a margarita party together.

She enjoyed a frozen margarita, light on the alcohol, but she had never taken a shot before. All of her friends would be shocked to see her drinking straight tequila from the bottle. But wasn't that exactly what this trip was about? Getting out of her rut?

Taylor used the tail of her shirt to thoroughly clean the outside and inside lip of the bottle. Then she brought it up to her lips and tried to pour the clear liquid into her mouth without touching the glass. She titled the bottle a bit too far and a large swig of the clear liquid spilled onto her tongue and slipped down her throat. Taylor started to cough and her body lurched forward, chin tucked, eyes watering as if she were crying. She waved the bottle at Clint so he would take it from her. Her tongue, her gums, her lips, her throat—they all burned. The bitter taste of the tequila made her want to gag. She wiped her eyes on her sleeve and shook her head several times after she managed to get the coughing under control.

"Yuck!" Taylor finally managed to get one word out.

Clint took a mouthful of the tequila, sat back and watched the show. Taylor's face was scrunched up into a sourpuss and she was wiping her eyes every couple of seconds. The woman clearly could not handle her tequila. When she gave her critique of his drink of choice, it made him smile.

"I'm sorry. I don't mean to be rude," Taylor said apologetically in a raspy voice. "But that's repulsive."

Clint held the bottle up to the firelight so he could see how much of the tequila was left in the bottle. He swirled the liquid around for a moment before he decided that there wasn't enough to leave for later. In one long tug on the bottle, he drank the rest of it as though it was water. He'd drunk tequila for most of his life—his father had given him his first taste when he was nine. It used to burn going down; these days he didn't feel the burn until it hit his stomach. That burn in his stomach reminded him that he was alive and it was the sensation he craved. It was a sensation he'd grown to need.

"I admit—" the cowboy stuck the empty bottle into his saddlebag "—it takes some gettin' used to…"

"I don't know why anyone would want to get used to *that*." Taylor wiped her tongue on her sleeve.

Clint smiled a quick smile before he went back to playing the harmonica.

"Well…" Taylor rolled to the side a bit in order to lever herself into a squatting position and then to a standing position. "I'm going to try to get some sleep. So…I'll see you in the morning…"

Clint waited for Taylor to zip herself back into her tent before he exchanged the harmonica for a cigarette. He took his hat off, slid downward and used the seat of his saddle as a pillow. He stared up at the stars scattered across the blue-black night sky. They would reach the peak tomorrow. He wasn't certain, but he imagined Taylor would see what she had come to see and then they'd head back to the ranch. He hadn't packed enough tequila and cigarettes for a long trip. Tomorrow he needed to do what he should have done in the very beginning—find out the particulars of the trip. Better late than never, he supposed. Clint flicked his cigarette into the fire, closed his eyes and covered his face with his hat. Taylor was greener than he had originally thought. And he had a feeling that she could turn out to be a wild card. He was going to have to keep a real close eye on her, which meant he needed to sober up a bit. Damn rotten luck.

Taylor awakened with the feeling of a sharp rock digging into her right shoulder blade. She winced and let out a low groan when she sat upright. How was it possible that this was the sorest day thus far? Shouldn't her body be acclimating? She forced herself to stand up without giving the pain too much thought and tended to the blister on her foot, glad to see that Clint had been right about draining it. She pulled on her jeans and boots, and then rolled up her sleeping bag tightly. When she emerged from her tent she was pleased to see that Clint was already awake and kneeling in front of a small fire.

"Is that coffee?" she asked hopefully. Taylor had decided not to pack coffee. She had only packed items that she had thought were essential in order to keep her load light for her journey. How could she have ever thought that coffee wasn't an *essential*?

Clint had made enough coffee for both of them—he'd already had a cup laced with a small shot of tequila. Yes, he needed to sober up, but Rome wasn't built in a day. Taylor grabbed her multipurpose cup and brought it over to the fire. Clint poured coffee into it.

"You'll get some grounds," he warned her.

She didn't care. The piping hot liquid had already

heated the thin tin of her cup and started to warm her cold hands. The smell of strong, black coffee filled her nose as she blew on it to cool it down enough to drink. When she took that first, grateful swallow, she ignored the bitter taste. Less than a month ago she would have turned her nose up at any coffee that wasn't a custom blend—and it made her feel good that she could notice some change in herself, no matter how small.

Taylor took several more sips, warming her body from the inside out. She opened her eyes with a small smile.

"Thank you."

The closer she got to the bottom of her cup, the more grounds she encountered. Oddly, it didn't deter her. She simply picked the grounds off her tongue as they came along, and then kept on drinking until there wasn't a drop left in the bottom of her cup. She gave herself a little extra time to enjoy the coffee—then she quickly ate a protein bar and started to break camp. It would have gone a lot faster if she had allowed the cowboy to help her. But she wanted to do it on her own. That was the whole point of this journey—to build self-reliance and self-confidence. And, to his credit, Clint didn't interfere. He put out the fire and then smoked a cigarette downwind from her.

The entire time she was packing, she tried to figure out how she was going to get onto her horse. She looked all around the camp, but there wasn't a good makeshift mounting block in sight. Maybe—just maybe—this would be the morning that she could manage it without standing on a large boulder or a fallen tree. She signaled to Clint that it was time to move out. He swung into his saddle with ease. She did not. After several valiant attempts at trying to get her foot in the stirrup while Honey walked in circles around her, Taylor wasn't surprised when the cowboy appeared at her side.

Her noncompliant horse became obedient with Clint in charge—the sturdy mare stood stock-still, and the cowboy used his hands to create a step for her. She needed the help, so she took it. She put her foot into the cowboy's hands and let him boost her up. Once she was situated in the saddle she turned to thank Clint, but he was already walking away from her toward his horse. For the second time, he swung into his saddle and waited for her to lead the way.

She steered her horse onto the narrow trail leading toward the junction where her uncle's property met public land. There, she would finally reach the Continental Divide Trail.

Chapter Three

The morning light cast a gray hue across the dark-green needles of the tall fir trees lining the trail. White fog floated over the trail ahead and dimmed the vibrant yellow and purple of the wildflowers growing sporadically in the wild grass on either side of the narrow path. There was beauty everywhere she looked. And there was beauty in the sound of the horses' hooves—one, two, three, four—hitting the gravel on the trail.

Why had she waited so many years to come? This was the peace that she had been missing. Would she ever be satisfied by her rat-race life after experiencing this? It was difficult for her to imagine.

Midmorning, around the time that the sun had burned away the last remnants of the white fog, they reached the section of the trail that took them above the tree line. Taylor felt her spirit swell at her first glimpse of the peaks of mountains in the distance. At this height the views were unobstructed, and she could see for miles ahead. A wave of emotion—a mixture of awe and joy and even sorrow that Christopher wasn't here to share this moment with her—overwhelmed her. She didn't stop moving forward, but there were tears streaming down her face when she first saw the white and black metal marker sign bolted to a post that let her know she had successfully reached the Continental Divide Trail.

"Will you take my picture?" Taylor asked Clint when he rode up beside her.

She dismounted and handed him her phone. The cowboy saw the tears, because she hadn't wiped them from her cheeks, but he didn't question them. How had she known that he wouldn't?

"Please take a couple so I get one with my eyes open." Taylor stood proudly next to the sign.

After the quick photo shoot, they decided to take a break on a knoll that had knee-high green grass for the horses to graze. Clint watched the horses and smoked a cigarette while she explored on foot. Reaching the CDT was one for the bucket list, but it wasn't the finish line for her.

On the other side of the trail was a sharp drop and then a rocky slope; the slope led down to the banks of an aqua-blue lake, which was full of freshly melted snow from the winter season.

"That's it." Taylor stared down at the lake. "That's the spot."

She turned back, surprised at how far away from Clint and the horses she had walked. Winded, with her cheeks flushed from exertion and excitement, Taylor rounded a corner that would lead her to the spot where she had left her traveling companions. When the grassy knoll came into view, it felt as if she were stepping into a scene from a movie. Clint looked like a throwback from the old West standing in the tall grass with his cowboy hat, chaps and boots, with a revolver strapped to his hip. There was something about the man that seemed more suited for a rougher, less civilized era. He was a real cowboy. The genuine article.

"Ready?" The man certainly liked his one-word utterances.

She gathered her horse's reins with a nod. "There's a lake up ahead. That's my next target."

He didn't ask her why, just quietly helped her mount, swung into his saddle and followed the packhorse as she once again led the way. Around the bend, the lake below came into view. From horseback, it seemed a much steeper descent to the edge of the lake.

"Tricky gettin' back," Clint told her.

At work, she was the queen of handling tricky deals. Montana, she was learning, wasn't much different than back home. When it came to tricky spots, you needed a good strategy and determination.

"I'll manage," she said, not deterred.

They secured the horses in a place where they were still visible from below and then started the twisty, rocky trip down to the lake. She lost her footing several times, slipping on loose rocks. She had to break her fall with her hand on one occasion, so her wrist was throbbing and the palm of her hand was scraped, but reaching the edge of the pristine lake was worth the mild damage to her body.

Clint stood away from her, his thoughts a complete

enigma behind the dark lenses of his sunglasses. Taylor stood at the lake's edge, the ice-blue water lapping close to the toes of her barely used boots. She closed her eyes and listened. She listened to her own breath. She listened to a bird's call in the distance. She listened to her heart. The day she had thought would never come had, indeed, arrived.

She opened her eyes to look down at the engagement ring and matching wedding band she still wore on her left ring finger. Christopher had planned such a romantic proposal the night he had given her this nearly flawless, colorless two-carat round stone. It had been everything a pragmatic, yet still romantic twenty-two-year-old could wish for in a proposal. He had arranged for private dining at her favorite restaurant. He'd had her serenaded by a classical guitarist. They danced and laughed and then he got down on one knee, took the shaking fingers of her left hand and asked her to marry him.

She couldn't wait for him to slide that ring onto her finger. It was, of course, a very large stone set in platinum and purchased from Tiffany. It was bigger than she had wanted—more than she had needed—but the appearance of success had always been more important to Christopher than it had been to her. And she knew that her mom, who often didn't approve of her choice in clothing or hairstyle, approved of Christopher, and she would definitely approve of the engagement ring.

In her mind, without vocalizing the word, she said, *Okay.*

She tugged on the rings, but her fingers were swollen and they wouldn't budge.

Clint wanted to give Taylor her privacy—he wasn't

the sharpest crayon in the box at times, but even he could tell she was trying to have some sort of moment. When he saw her fighting to get the rings off her finger without any success, and wanting to begin the trek back to the ranch as soon as possible, he intervened.

"Put your hand in the water."

That was a great idea. She had been so fixated on trying to pry the rings free, she hadn't considered that simple and pretty obvious solution. After she submerged her hand in the frigid water for a few minutes, the rings slipped right off.

"Hey!" Taylor smiled spontaneously at Clint. "It worked."

Clint was struck by that smile. Taylor's face, which he had once dismissed as pretty-ish, was transformed when she smiled. She had charming dimples on each creamy, plump cheek, her teeth were white and straight, and the smile drew attention to the fullness of her light pink lips. Clint tipped his hat to her as a way of saying "you're welcome." She had married Christopher soon after graduate school, so she had worn these rings for most of her adult life. She had wondered if her finger would feel naked without them. It did.

Taylor gave the rings, cupped in the palm of her hand, one last look before she curled her fingers tightly around them, drew back her arm as if she was about to throw a baseball and prepared to hurl them as hard and as far as she could into the lake.

"Hey, now! Whoa, little lady!" she heard Clint exclaim as he grabbed her wrist to stop her. "I ain't no jewelry expert, but those look like they could be worth a pretty penny."

Taylor tugged her wrist out of his fingers with a

frown. “My marriage is over, so they aren’t worth anything to me anymore.”

“If they’re real, they could be worth a whole heck of a lot to somebody,” the cowboy told her in a sharp voice. “There’s some folks who could live off them rings for a year or two, I bet.”

“Those rings…” Taylor muttered the correction to his English. She opened the palm of her hand and stared at the rings that she had worn with such pride for so many years. They only made her feel sad now and she wanted to be done with them. Yet, Clint was right—they were worth a lot of money. She was a spoiled woman, yes, that was true, but she had never been a wasteful one. Why couldn’t she pawn them and give the proceeds to charity?

Taylor stared for a second longer at the rings before she made her decision. Wordlessly, she tucked them into her pocket for safekeeping.

Taylor met Clint’s eyes. “I’m ready to go back.”

The cowboy squinted at her through a thin veil of white cigarette smoke. She waved the smoke away from her face as she walked by him. Out of the corner of her eye, she saw Clint put the partially smoked cigarette out on the bottom of his boot, and then clench the butt between his teeth.

Instead of taking the lead, as she expected, Clint followed her. It was ridiculous for vanity to rear its head on a rocky hike up a steep hill, but the entire time, she couldn’t stop fixating on the fact that her derriere, which had expanded considerably over the last year, was right at Clint’s eye level. He couldn’t avoid staring at it if he tried. Poor man.

“Careful, now.”

She hadn't been concentrating on her foot placement.She stumbled, slipped backward, and the cowboy caught her with his hands on her rear end—one hand for each butt cheek.

Taylor brushed his hands away, jerked the tail of her shirt downward and pressed on.

"Sorry," she said without looking at him.

Humiliating. She hated her middle-aged spread, especially the widening and dropping of her hind end. She had never been a stick-thin person, not even as a teen, but she had always liked her backside. Now—it looked so big and *old.*

The last part of the climb, the steepest part, where she had to climb with her hands supporting her weight, Clint took the lead. He bullied his way up the steep incline until he reached flat ground. He waited for her—he watched out for her. But he let her navigate the last part of the climb on her own terms. Right at the top, and right when she thought that she was about to beat the hill, she lost her footing again; she fell forward and started to slide downward as though she was on a kiddie slide. She felt Clint's hand on her wrist. Their eyes met and she gave him the nod to let go so she could finish the climb on her own.

Once on safe footing, she looked back at the lake. She hadn't thrown the rings into the lake with dramatic flare as she had envisioned, but it really felt like the divorce was final. Truthfully, Christopher had let her go long before the marriage had ended. And now, finally, she was moving on, too.

"If we start back right away, we can camp in the same spot." Clint took his position on Honey's right side to stop her from moving while Taylor used a boulder as a mounting block.

"I'm not going back to the ranch."

Clint mounted his horse and took it upon himself, without her objection, to lead Easy. Once he was settled in the saddle, he rode up beside her. "No?"

"No."

Clint rested his arm across the saddle horn, his mouth frowning. "Just how far are you planning on goin'?"

"Two weeks in, two weeks out."

"A month."

Honey danced to the side, away from his horse. Taylor circled back around so she could face him and finish the conversation.

"My uncle didn't tell you."

It took all of his self-control not to say something he would regret. Hank hadn't bothered to tell him, and neither had his stepbrother. Just like Brock. Why had Clint thought that anything would be different between them after a five-year break? If he didn't need the money so badly, he'd let Taylor have her way and send her packing on her own. But he was buried in debt, his truck needed an engine rebuild, creditors were hounding him and his cell phone was shut off. He couldn't get back to the rodeo without money for the entry fees. He was flat broke and flat stuck.

"No matter." Clint told her. "Let's ride."

Taylor's pace for the rest of the day was slow and steady. It didn't matter to Clint where they stopped for the night; it mattered to him that he wasn't heading back to the ranch. He'd still been drunk from the night before when Brock gave him the order, but not drunk enough to have forgotten a major piece of information like the fact that he'd be babysitting for a *month*. No. Brock had left that little detail out. It was lucky that his stepfather, a full-time drunk and part-time rodeo clown, had managed to teach him how to survive in the wilderness with limited supplies. He hadn't, however, managed to teach Clint how to survive without a steady supply of cigarettes and tequila.

That night, after they made camp, he taught Taylor to build a small mound fire. Admittedly, she had surprised him—she had actually researched riding the divide and had brought a fire blanket for building mound fires in order to have the least environmental impact. He loved this land and her desire to preserve it impressed him.

Taylor sat down near the fire to catch as much warmth from the low flames as she could. The temperature changed so quickly on the divide—one minute she was boiling in the sun and the next she was freezing at sundown. At least she was starting to adjust to the sore muscles and aching joints and the drastic change in her diet. She really wanted to drop some weight on this trip. It was time for her to shed the extra pounds and claim the next phase of her life with a renewed sense of vigor and excitement.

"You're not much of a talker, are you, Clint?" Taylor broke the long silence.

"I'm in the business of mindin' my own business." Clint flicked his cigarette into the fire.

He reached into his saddlebag and pulled out the harmonica. She smiled a little—she had enjoyed listening to his playing the night before and hoped that he would play again. Taylor breathed in deeply, let it out slowly and tuned her ears to the notes streaming out from the little instrument. She hadn't counted on company, but Clint's role in her adventure had started to solidify in her mind. He was her protector. Her unwilling cowboy bodyguard.

"Who taught you to play?"

"David."

He read the next question in her eyes and answered without her having to ask it.

"My stepfather." After a moment, he added. "He adopted me when I was eight or nine—gave me his last name. That's a heck of a lot more than I can say for my real father, that's for damn sure."

There wasn't any emotion in Clint's voice when he talked about his father—not negative, not positive. But after he answered her question Clint put away the harmonica, stood up and walked a few feet away from the fire. From the light given off by the fire, she could see the cowboy in silhouette and a flash of red as he lit a cigarette. She had unintentionally hit a nerve. His father was a topic she would avoid in the future—in her mind, Clint wasn't a three-dimensional person. He was a cowboy, and he was hired to ensure her safe return to Bent Tree Ranch. She didn't really need to know any more about him than that.

Taylor stood up, brushed the debris from the seat of her jeans.

"Well—good night."

She thought that she saw him tip his hat to her, but she didn't wait around to make sure. She quickly went through her nightly routine, changed into her cotton pajamas and crawled into her sleeping bag. Taylor swatted the flashlight overhead with her hand. She watched the light, letting it shine into her eyes for a brief moment as it passed over her face—up and back, up and back. She reached up and grabbed the flashlight, turned it off.

In the dark, she stared up at the ceiling of the tent. All night she had caught herself unconsciously rubbing her thumb over the unembellished skin of her left ring finger. Would there ever be a man who wanted to place a ring on that finger again? Did she want there to be? It was debatable. But children… Taylor moved her hands down to her abdomen. Oh, how she had wanted there to be children.

It was a week of lessons for Taylor. Clint seemed to resign himself to his chore of watching out for her and focused his energy on teaching her how to ride the divide. She learned how to spot fresh grizzly bear markings on nearby trees and create a high line to tether the horses so that the ropes didn't cause ring damage to the trees. She now knew how to tie a trucker's knot, stake a horse in a field and avoid stepping on rattlesnakes.

Now she knew why Uncle Hank had trusted Clint to be her bodyguard—the Continental Divide was home to this cowboy. He was a walking encyclopedia—there wasn't an indigenous bird or wildflower or tree that he couldn't name. She had actually started to make a game of testing his knowledge. Her first impression of Clint had been that he was uneducated and uncomplicated. He was neither. As far as she knew, he wasn't formally educated past tenth grade, but he wasn't ignorant. The wild Montana mountains had provided his education—and she had a feeling that her cowboy wasn't uncomplicated, either.

"Everything here is…so beautiful." Taylor admired a field of wildflowers that stretched as far as her eyes could see. The rolling hills were dotted with canary yellow and violet-blue purple.

"What are they?" she asked Clint once he reached her side.

"The blue flowers are Camassia Quamash—Blue Camas—edible. But not the yellow—those are Death Camas..."

"Let me guess...*not* edible." Taylor smiled, her eyes drinking in the brightly colored field of flowers. "What do they taste like?"

"Sweet—local tribes have used them for generations as a sweetener." Clint repositioned his hat on his head. "If you want to taste one, I'll dig up a bulb for you."

"No—that's okay. Conservation."

Clint dismounted. "One ain't gonna make the difference."

He returned to her side with a single Blue Camas bulb. He washed the dirt off the bulb before he handed it to her. She smelled it and then nibbled on the side.

The odd sweetness hit her tongue, and for some reason, it made her laugh.

"It's sweet." She held out the remainder of the bulb to him.

Clint ate the rest. He didn't hesitate to put his mouth where hers had been. Christopher had never drunk after her or shared a straw—he'd always wiped off her fork if he used it after her and that had always bothered her. And here, a near stranger, a man she had only known for a few days, had eaten after her as if it were nothing. It was an intimacy that she hadn't shared with her husband in all of their years of marriage.

"Is there a place where I could wash?"

She felt gritty from days of sponge bathing and dry

shampoo. She had packed water purification pills and filters for found water, as well as some potable water to drink, and tried to use as little as possible of her supply on washing. She needed to submerge her body in water, no matter how cold, and rinse the grimy feeling off her skin.

"I've got a place in mind." He swung into the saddle. "I'm tired of jerky. How 'bout fish for dinner?"

She was tired of instant soup and protein bars. Washing the grease out of her hair and chowing down on freshly caught fish seemed like luxuries now.

"I would love fish for dinner."

"Let's ride about another hour and a quarter." Clint tugged on Easy's rope. "We'll make camp a little early tonight."

The promise of a real dinner made the last hour in the saddle tolerable. But, even after a full week in the saddle, she was still raw and sore by the time she dismounted at the spot Clint selected for their campsite. They had fallen into a campsite routine—Clint had his duties and she had hers. Part of her job at the bank was putting together teams that could complete a project efficiently and effectively. She had a knack for putting two unlikely people together to create a winning team. It was like that with Clint—they were very different, but somehow they worked together to accomplish a common goal as if they had worked together for years.

"We've got some storm clouds formin' quick." Clint took his hat off, wiped his forehead on his sleeve. "You'd best wait on that bath."

"Is dinner a no-go, too?"

"I gotta be quick." Clint eyed the darkening sky in the distance. "You got the fire?"

"Absolutely."

Clint headed off on foot toward the freshwater lake he had fished from over the years.

"Hey—Clint."

He turned to look at his companion.

"What happens if it rains?"

It was an odd question.

"We get wet."

Taylor laughed. "No. I mean—you don't have a tent."

"Don't need one." Clint shrugged off her concern. "Go on and get that fire started and I'll cook you the best damn tastin' fish you've ever had in your life."

Chapter Four

Good as his word, Clint had caught, cleaned and cooked the best trout she had ever eaten. And, even though the menacing promise of the storm clouds cut their dinner short and canceled her plans to bath in the stream, she went to bed feeling completely full for the first time since she had started her journey up to the CDT.

When the rain started, she tried to convince Clint to join her in the tent, but he flat-out refused. She had peeked out of the tent while there was still a little light to see by and spotted him hunkered down away from the trees, covered by a small tarp. She didn't ask him to join her a second time—she had made the offer once, and that was enough. Clint had grown up in high country and she could surmise that this wouldn't be the last time he'd weather a Montana storm with his saddle as a pillow and a rain tarp as a shelter.

The next morning she awakened to a clear sky and the welcome scents of fire and coffee. She didn't see Clint, but the first thing on her mind was taking a quick rinse-off in the stream. She slung a bag of supplies over her shoulder and walked through the small cluster of trees that led to the stream below the campsite. At the edge of the tree line she spotted Clint kneeling by the stream. He was stripped down to the waist; the word "Rodeo" was tattooed across his shoulders with a bull rider riding a bucking bull down the middle of his long back. There was a large, jagged scar that cut across his low back, just above the waist of his jeans.

Taylor stopped for a moment, not sure if she should return to camp or join him. Clint stood up, and she was sure he sensed that he was being watched because he turned his head a bit and caught sight of her. He waved her over.

"Good morning." Taylor called to him.

The closer she came to the cowboy, the more her suspicion was confirmed that he'd had the same thought she'd had, to clean up before their next ride. His hair was slicked straight back from his forehead, his thickening beard was wet and the jeans were different. He was twisting the water from the shirt he had been wearing for the past several days, and a fresh T-shirt was slung over his shoulder.

"That was quite a storm," she said to make conversation.

Standing next to a half-naked Clint was uncomfortable for her, even though he didn't seem bothered. He wasn't extraordinarily tall and he was on the thin side, but every muscle on his body was defined. The muscles were hard and long, and he had the type of veins that were close to the surface of the skin—you could trace each vein with a finger from the inside of his elbow down to his wrist. She tried to keep her eyes on his face, yet they were drawn time and again to the array of tattoos and scars that made the landscape of his naked torso inherently interesting to her.

"I was worried about you," she added.

Clint shook out his shirt. "Don't waste your time."

He slipped on his clean shirt and brushed loose hairs back off his face before putting his cowboy hat on. "I'll keep watch—make sure you have your privacy."

"Thank you." Taylor knelt down to feel the temperature of the water. It was icy cold.

Clint smoked a cigarette several yards away, his back turned to her. She didn't question that he would keep his back turned—he'd had a rough life and his manners were not civilized at times, but he wasn't a pervert. Wearing only underwear and a bra, a pair of rubber shower shoes to protect her feet, Taylor braved the frigid, clear water of the stream. As fast as she could, she waded to the deeper part of the stream. She couldn't wait to try to acclimate to the temperature—that wasn't a viable option. Instead, she took in a deep breath and forced herself to sit down.

"Cold, cold, cold…" She muttered the word over and over again.

She dunked her head back, scrubbed the roots of her hair with soap and stood up so she could quickly soap her body. She spent extra time on her armpits because the odor had been too tough even for her clinical-strength deodorant to combat, and then she sank back into the water, waist deep, and put her hand inside her underwear to clean thoroughly between her thighs.

It was one of the quickest baths she'd ever taken, and that was more than okay with her. She hurried to the shore and to her awaiting towel. Even as rapidly as she had gone through her routine, she was shivering from the cold, her arms and legs were covered with goose bumps and she was clenching her teeth to keep them from chattering. One swipe of the towel across her face and then the rest of her body was all she could stand. She had to get dressed. But she wasn't about to change her underwear out in the open. Instead, she wrapped the towel around her body and raced up to where Clint was waiting.

Clint heard Taylor's approach and turned to greet her. He wasn't expecting her to be wrapped in a towel with her creamy, rounded shoulders and shapely legs exposed. She smelled like orange peels and honey, and even though she was noticeably cold, the way her wet hair framed her freshly scrubbed face held a sexy, natural appeal.

"Ready?" He knew he had been caught looking at the rounded tops of her breasts.

She nodded, not wanting to speak—only wanting to get back so she could get into dry clothing. Once inside her tent, she stripped out of her wet undergarments and slipped into her sleeping bag to warm her body. She closed her eyes and willed her body to warm up and quit shivering.

"Taylor?" Clint was outside of her tent. "Here's coffee."

She opened the flap enough to take the cup of hot coffee. With a word of thanks, Taylor wrapped her hands around the warm tin mug; the minute the hot liquid hit her stomach she started to feel warmer. It was the perfect remedy, and it touched her that Clint had been thinking of her in that way.

As soon as she could, she dressed and joined Clint in breaking camp. Packed up and mounted on her mare, Taylor didn't like the look of the sky in their direct path.

"I'd rather not ride in the rain," she told Clint.

He rode up beside her with Easy trailing behind him. "Your call."

"How long do you estimate we have before the storm hits?"

"Two hours—three tops."

They agreed to get two hours of riding in and make camp ahead of the looming storm. She had built in several nontraveling days to enjoy the scenery and give the animals a rest. Perhaps it was time to take an early break to let the weather front move through.

They made camp just before the rain came. She hadn't expected it, but she managed to talk Clint into joining her in the tent under the guise of not wanting to be lonely. He didn't know that she loved her alone time, and she didn't intend to share that fact with him.

The inside of her tent seemed much smaller now that Clint had joined her. He had to hunch his shoulders forward so there was some room for the top of his head.

"Make yourself at home," she teased him.

His hunched shoulders were tense, his legs were half bent, half stretched out, and he seemed to be completely uncomfortable in her little temporary world. He smiled at her and she actually thought that she saw a hint of teeth.

"You mind if I play?" He took his harmonica out of his pocket.

"No." She lay back. "I like it."

Clint played a soft, haunting tune while the rain tapped out a rhythm of its own on the canvas roof of her tent. She closed her eyes and unintentionally fell asleep.

When the rain stopped, Clint stopped playing the harmonica. Taylor was asleep—he didn't see any reason to awaken her to help him finish setting up camp. He unzipped the tent flap and stepped out onto the wet ground. Before he zipped the flap shut, he stared at Taylor. She had slowly started to gain his respect; she had prepared herself for this trip, and other than attempting to make the trip alone, she was a woman who made smart decisions. He was a man—he glanced at the generous curve of her breasts beneath the material of her shirt before he closed the flap of the tent behind him.

Taylor rolled onto her back, her eyes opened slowly. It took her a little bit to get her bearings—she was alone in the tent and her bladder was full. When she emerged from the tent, she saw that Clint had already set up the rest of the camp, tended to the horses and Easy, built a fire.

"Sorry." She joined him at the fire after relieving herself. "I fell asleep."

Clint shook his head and handed her a plate with fish reheated from the night before.

He waited for her to finish before he smoked a cigarette.

"Do you mind?" She pointed to the tequila bottle next to his leg. He didn't bother to hide his nightly routine of drinking a healthy portion of the alcohol.

He looked surprised but untwisted the cap and handed her the half-empty bottle. Taylor didn't bother to wipe off the lip of the bottle before she took a swig, coughing in spite of her best attempts not to when the clear liquid burned her throat. He took the bottle back from her and she watched him, through watering eyes, take several consecutive swallows of the tequila.

"How do you do that?" she asked him thoughtlessly.

He put the bottle away. He was running low and he needed to conserve the rest. After one last draw on his cigarette he flicked the butt into the fire and blew smoke out of his nose.

"Practice."

She laughed. The sound of her own laughter sounded good to her ears. There was a time that she loved to laugh—she used to laugh frequently. Years of trying to get pregnant without success, years of passing Christopher in the hallways of their childless house, years of meeting with attorneys and divorce proceedings and dividing property had taken a toll on her spirit—eroded her confidence.

"Do you mind a personal question?"

His hand moved upward in a gesture of consent.

"What happened to your back?"

His brow furrowed in thought, then it occurred to him that she was asking about his scar.

"I was gored by a bull in Boise, Idaho."

He smiled a little at the shock that registered on her face.

"I'd been riding bulls since I was a kid, so I should've been able to get out of his way. But that one got the better of me."

"How did you even survive something like that?"

"I almost bled out by the time they got me to the hospital," Clint recounted. "I didn't get back on a bull for six months."

"*Six months?* I can't believe you ever got back on one." She shook her head in wonder. "Are you retired? Or just on a break?"

"I got some money things I gotta clear up first—then I'll be back at it. I think my knees got a couple more goes left in 'em."

"It must be nice to know exactly what you want to do," she said aloud, even though she really meant to only speak the words in her head.

"I'd think someone like you had it all figured out."

"Someone like me?" she scoffed. "On that note!" She stood up. "Do you think we'll get more of the same tomorrow?"

"Naw." Clint tipped his hat back on his head so she could see his eyes. "Should be blue skies."

"Then we'll make up some time. I had a spot picked out to spend a couple of days, but we'll have to push it a little tomorrow to make it, I think."

She had already figured out the little movements he used to respond. A slight nod of his head was a confirmation for her plan.

"Okay—good night, Clint."

"Night, Taylor."

There was a roughness in the way Clint said her name—it was unlike anything she had heard before. It was so compelling that she almost stopped and turned toward him to see the look on his face. The way he said it, like silk against sandpaper, made the hairs stand up on the back of her neck. She liked it—probably more than she should have.

Two days later, they reached the spot where she planned on staying for several days and truly taking in the beauty of the Rocky Mountains—the wildlife, the foliage, the majesty. She wanted to be able to take it all in without feeling as if she was on a schedule. Would she be able to find the answer for the next phase of her life hidden in the mountain peaks? She had resigned from her position at the bank, walked away from the only career she had known for over a decade. For the first time since she was a young woman, she was functioning without a net.

"I'm going for a hike."

Taylor had awakened feeling refreshed and ready to explore the area surrounding their new campsite on foot.

Clint was checking his horse's hoof. He let the horse's leg go and gave the buckskin a pat on the haunches.

"You planning on goin' off alone?"

"Yes."

She had become accustomed to having Clint around. She had been able to embrace the good of having a man on the journey with her. But her increased comfort with the man didn't change the fact that this journey was about rediscovering herself—self-reliance, rebuilding self-confidence. There had to be some time that the only person to rely on was the one she looked at in the mirror.

"Do you know how to use that gun or is it just for show?"

There was a decidedly chauvinistic tone in his question. The challenge had been issued.

"I'll make you a wager that I'm a better shot than you."

The look on Clint's face was better than she could have predicted. He tipped the brim of his hat up so he could get a better look at her face. In his deeply set grayish-blue eyes, she saw a mixture of disbelief and admiration.

"Lady—I ain't got nothin' to bet but two cigarettes and my last bottle of liquor."

"Loser—i.e., *you* cook dinner. I like how you cook freshly caught fish."

Clint laughed—a deep, hearty laugh that made her smile in response. "You don't have to give me nothin' when you lose—I'm shootin' for my honor."

They set up targets.

"Ladies first." Clint tipped his hat to her.

"Don't mind if I do."

Clint made a big show of backing away from her when she pulled her gun out of the holster.

"Worried?" She unlocked the safety with a small smile.

"Always, when a woman has a gun."

Clint watched closely while Taylor took her shots. He was looking for comfort with the firearm, safety and skill. He had to admit that he saw all three. She might be a city, socialite kind of woman, but she knew her way around a revolver.

"Five out of five," Taylor announced proudly.

"Not bad."

"Not *bad*?" She reloaded her weapon, turned on the safety and holstered it. "Please."

Clint took his turn and scored four out of five.

Taylor clapped her hands together and gave a little jump. "I won! Wait—did you lose on purpose?"

Clint holstered his gun. "I never lose on purpose."

The cowboy took losing to her more graciously than she had expected.

"Looks like I'll be catching that dinner I owe you while you go on your hike."

It made her feel empowered. Underneath it all, Clint had been worried about her hiking alone and now that he'd seen her shoot, that he'd been beaten at his own game, he had confidence in her. And his confidence boosted her confidence in herself. It was a win-win.

"Wow!" Taylor put her hands on her full stomach. "You are an amazing cook! What did you cook the fish in?"

"Blue Camas."

"*That* was the sweetness!"

"I'm glad you enjoyed your winnings." Clint dug into his pack of cigarettes and pulled his very last one out of the pack.

"I did." Taylor smiled happily.

Clint lit his cigarette and took a long, hard drag from it. He'd been without cigarettes before, so he wouldn't like it, but he could handle it. When times were tough, like now, things like cigarettes and tequila gave way to gasoline for his truck and food.

"How old are you?" Taylor asked her cowboy. "If you don't mind me asking."

"I'll be thirty-two next month."

"*Thirty-two*? You're younger than me?"

"Guess so." Clint flicked the cigarette butt into the fire. "Don't know how old you are."

"Thirty-nine." Taylor frowned. "And a half."

Clint crumpled the empty cigarette pack tightly in his fist and threw it into the fire, as well.

"Was that your last one?"

She got a nod.

Taylor wanted to say something—had *wanted* to say something—for a couple of days now. "I'll be right back."

Taylor went into her tent and searched for a small box that was deliberately packed on the very bottom of her backpack. She unlocked the box, opened it carefully—inside of the box was a long, thin piece of rolled tinfoil. She removed the tinfoil and put the box back in its place.

After she left Chicago, she had driven to Denver to visit some friends from college before heading to Montana. Her friends had given her a parting gift and she had driven all the way from Denver to Bent Tree Ranch with the contraband in her glove box. Basically, it was her first real stint as lawbreaker—crossing state lines with an illegal substance while driving exactly five miles over the speed limit. Until tonight, she hadn't really been certain that she would ever unlock that box. But she felt safe with Clint. In truth, she felt safer in Clint's company than she'd ever felt in Christopher's. Her cowboy wouldn't judge her.

When Taylor returned to her spot by the fire, she almost lost her nerve.

"Clint?"

"Hmm?" His head was back and the brim of his hat was pulled down low over his eyes.

"I have an activity penciled in for this leg of the trip, but I may need your help."

Clint didn't move his hat off his face. "Uh-huh."

Taylor carefully unwrapped the joint from the tinfoil. She picked it up, handling it as if it were breakable. The sweet, pungent smell of her friend's favorite specialty marijuana was distinctive and strong. This was her first time personally handling a joint. She wasn't even sure if there was a correct end to light. Clint, on the other hand, seemed like the type of person who may have had some experience with the Mary Jane.

"Do you know which end is the right end?"

Clint had been so close to sleeping—he had a full belly and had drunk more than his fair share of tequila. Usually Taylor was quiet when they sat together by the fire. She wasn't a yappy female, which he had grown to appreciate about her. Tonight, for some reason, she was chatty. Was she more comfortable with him now? Was that the difference?

Clint readjusted his hat so he could look at his traveling companion with only one eye open. When he saw what she was holding between thumb and index finger as if it were going to bite her, he realized that the option of sleep was no longer in his immediate future.

Chapter Five

"I'd like to believe that's tobacco."

"Sorry." She didn't sound sorry. "It's not tobacco."

"What're you doin' with weed, Taylor?" He sat up all the way. "That ain't legal in Montana."

"I didn't get it in Montana. I got it in Colorado. It's perfectly legal there." She examined the joint. "Which end do I light?"

"Neither."

"Oh, I'm gonna smoke it—trust me. I've played by the rules my whole entire life and I'm not exactly thrilled with where it's gotten me. No—it's time for me to start breaking a few rules."

"I can't stop you, but I ain't gonna help you neither."

He didn't want to have anything to do with Taylor's plan to experiment with marijuana. That's the last thing he needed for her to report back to Brock or Hank.

"Fine. I'll figure it out on my own." She said. "Let me see your lighter for a minute."

When Clint hesitated, Taylor held out her hand for the lighter. "Just let me see it! Geez Louise! With all of those tattoos—who would've thought that out of the two of us *you* would be the square?"

"I'm not a square—I'm a man who needs to keep a job." He handed her the lighter.

She took the lighter. "Do you really think that I'm going to run back to my uncle and tell him that I was smoking pot? Please. I told you—my family already thinks that I'm a few sandwiches shy of a full picnic basket. Why would I add *pothead* to their list of reasons to throw me in the loony bin? I mean—come on. Get real."

She was disappointed in Clint—no doubt about it, but she could understand his concern over his job. They had only known each other for roughly two weeks, but that wasn't long enough to build trust.

Taylor looked at one end of the joint and then the other—they looked exactly the same to her. So she picked one, put the joint in her mouth and tried to operate the lighter. It was a throwaway plastic lighter, the kind that she had seen at the counters of convenience stores over the years, but she'd never actually had one in her hand. She ran her thumb over the wheel one time, two times, and then a third time. Frustrated, she took the joint out of her mouth.

"It's broken." She grumbled.

During her attempts to operate the lighter, Clint had stood up and was pacing a little, his hand on his forehead beneath the brim of his hat. What in the world just happened? He'd been having a nice night—the job babysitting Hank's niece turned out to be not a bad gig—and he couldn't have seen this one coming from a mile away.

Clint pushed the brim of his hat up so he could get a better look at her. "It's not broken."

"Yeah—it is. Watch."

"There's a safety," he explained in a tone reminiscent of their first encounter when she had him at gunpoint. It felt a little like she had him at gunpoint again.

Taylor pressed down on the small red safety tab. But, when she tried to run her thumb down on the striker, it didn't work.

"Come on!" Taylor shook the lighter. "I was in charge of a large team of people, you'd think I could operate a stupid lighter."

"Here." Clint just wanted the whole thing to be over. "Let me have it."

Taylor extended her arm and the cowboy took the lighter from her hand after he broke the invisible line that had separated her side of the fire from his.

"Look—you run your thumb over the striker, let your thumb land on the safety, push it down, hold it down and look at that—*amazing*—you've made fire."

Clint handed the lighter back to his unpredictable companion. He liked her better when she was in a quiet, introspective mood.

"Hey!" Taylor said, pleased. "Look at that. I did it."

"It's a miracle," Clint muttered on his way back to his side of the fire.

"Don't be such a killjoy, Clint."

He rubbed his hand over his face, then took his hat off, dragged his fingers through his hair to push it back and replaced his hat.

"Have you even smoked pot before?" he asked her.

"I haven't even smoked a cigarette before, if you can believe that," she responded with a little shrug. "That's why I'm doing this now. I'm doing all of the things that I've always wanted to do, but have put off, or wouldn't dare do because Taylor Brand *always* puts other people first and *always* does the right thing. I've always wanted to try pot, so I'm trying pot. And, no offense Clint—but this is happening whether you like it or not. In my plan, you weren't here."

"Did your plan include a lighter?"

Taylor took the joint out of her mouth to answer. "Yours was closer. *And* I thought that you would be joining me, so I didn't dig mine out."

Clint put his hands out, palms up. "Why would you think that?"

"Because you smoke like a chimney and drink tequila straight out of the bottle like it's water, that's why."

She had a point, granted.

"I don't do drugs."

"Never?" she asked disbelievingly.

Clint stared at her, his arms crossed. If he lied, she'd know it. "Not since I was a kid."

Her cowboy was trying very hard to stall the inevitable—she'd used stall tactics before in business, so she recognized them for what they were. She operated the lighter like a champ and lit the end of joint. After a couple of seconds of trying to suck in the smoke without any success, Taylor inspected the end of the joint to see what was wrong.

"Darn it! Why'd it go out?"

"*Jesus Christ*, this is gonna take all flippin' night!"

"Why don't you just go to sleep?" Taylor suggested harshly.

"You're in my bedroom!"

"Well—I'm not going to do this in my tent. That's not safe."

Clint threw up his hands, crossed back into her territory, knelt down beside her, took the lighter, took the joint, lit it, puffed on it until the end was cherry red and handed it back to her.

"There. Have at it."

"Thank you." But her tone didn't match the words.

She took a tiny little puff, held it her mouth and then blew it out. She repeated the act several times, with Clint watching her like the fun police.

"I don't know what the big deal is—I don't feel any different."

Clint didn't want any campers that may be nearby to smell the distinctive scent of marijuana. The way Taylor was dragging this out, it could be another hour of this nonsense.

"And…he's back," Taylor said when Clint crossed over to her side of the fire for the third time. This time, however, he sat down next to her on the log she was using as a makeshift bench.

She could tell that he was about to cave and help her. So, she reminded him, "I have as much to lose as you do. Maybe more."

"Not more." Clint looked her right in the eye. "Now watch. You've got to inhale it and hold it in."

He demonstrated before he passed the joint back to her. She tried to follow his example, but just ended up coughing so hard that she started to gag. Her eyes were watering, she couldn't stop coughing and there was an odd, unpleasant aftertaste in her mouth. But she wasn't willing to give up until she had succeeded and she told Clint as much.

"The only way we're gonna get this friggin' thing done is with a shotgun." Clint took charge of the operation. "I'm gonna blow the smoke into your mouth and you're gonna breathe in deep and hold it like you're about to go underwater. You got it?"

She gave him a little salute. Clint took off his hat, put it down next to him, and before she could think about it he had his hand on the back of her head, guiding her face toward him as he put his lips next to her lips.

Taylor closed her eyes to focus on the instructions Clint had given her moments before. Against her face she could feel the softness of his beard that, surprisingly, mirrored the softness of his lips. She wouldn't have thought that his beard would feel so soft. And she wouldn't have ever believed that such a rough man could have incredibly soft lips.

"Hold it, hold it..." Clint told her.

When she couldn't hold the smoke in her lungs for a second longer, she blew it out and started coughing again. But this time she was laughing between coughs. Her eyes were watering again, her lungs were burning, her nose was burning, her throat already felt sore from all of the coughing. But she still felt like laughing. It took some doing, but after a couple of minutes, she managed to get the coughs under control. She found herself chuckling while she wiped the tears from her eyes.

"Oh, my..." Her watery eyes smiled at Clint. "Do it again!"

Clint remembered the first moment he had ever seen Taylor. He'd been coming in from repairing fences in the south pasture and she had just arrived at the ranch driving a VW Bug. She appeared to him, at the time, to be an educated, successful woman. It was more than the haircut, the cut of her clothes or how she accessorized—it was the way she walked, head up, shoulders squared. To him, she appeared to have a confidence not often seen in the women he had known. She seemed to know who she was, to be confident in her position in the world. And, by the way she had looked him directly in the eye when they passed each other, he had the feeling that she was used to dealing with men in business and *winning*. But of all of the impressions he'd had of Taylor Brand, he'd never suspected that she was the type of woman who would get him high as a kite.

Now he was lying flat on his back on a woven blanket next to Taylor, boots off, hat off, staring up at the stars dotting the night sky overhead. He was aware of everything about Taylor, as if all of her womanly assets were being brought to the forefront of his mind. When she brushed his hand with hers, was that purposeful? When her shoulder touched his, was that a signal that she wanted to be close to him? His brain was scrambled and he couldn't figure this woman out. But what he did know was that he really liked how her hair smelled, and out of the corner of his eye he could see the swell of her full breasts. He had the undeniable urge to reach over and fondle them.

"Look at my hand." Taylor was holding up her left hand in front of her eyes. "I've never noticed how weird knuckles are..."

"You've been looking at your hand for five minutes."

"I have?" she asked with a laugh. "That doesn't make a bit of sense."

She started to giggle and pressed her hands into her stomach. "*Ow*—my stomach hurts from laughing."

Her face hurt from smiling, too. It took her a minute to stop giggling, but when she did, she brought up a new topic.

"Do you know what I find surprising?"

"Mmm?"

"You're beard is so very soft, like a little baby bunny," Taylor mused aloud. She ran her fingers over her own lips. "And your lips are really soft, too."

Clint turned his head toward the woman lying beside him. He'd found her attractive from the get-go; he liked her curvy, womanly figure, her large breasts, her full, rounded hips—he liked the fact that she challenged him, didn't give him an inch and often beat him at his own game. She was totally off-limits—he understood that. But she was making it damn difficult not to act on his body's urges and see how far he could get with his sexy companion. And he had to imagine that he might have a pretty good shot to score with Taylor—newly divorced women were usually sexually deprived and looking for a rebound to soothe their wounded pride. At least, that was his experience.

"Are you a married man, Clint?"

"No."

"I'm not a married woman. I was," Taylor said on a sigh. "Eighteen years. Would you believe that?"

Taylor studied her left hand again. "My hand looks weird without my rings. I'm so glad that I never took Christopher's last name. What a pain in the neck it would be to change every single thing back to Brand. My driver's license, credit cards, bank account..."

Taylor's voice trailed off for a moment before another thought popped into her head.

"Do you have any children?"

When Clint didn't respond right away, Taylor kept on talking.

"I don't have any children," Taylor mused. "I want kids, though. I've always wanted three, but I'd settle for just one. Christopher—that's my ex—had unmotivated sperm."

Taylor turned toward Clint. "Do you know that a woman is born with all of the eggs she's ever gonna have?"

The cowboy had his eyes closed, but shook his head no.

"Now that I'm almost forty, I have a pretty limited supply... My doctor says that the best eggs go first and now the ones that are left are the less desirable eggs. I have *slow eggs*! I didn't even know such a thing existed, and here I have it! So even if I *do* find a man to marry in the next year or so, the chances of me getting pregnant with my *slow eggs* is a long shot at best..."

Clint didn't respond—not because he didn't hear her, but because he knew that she wouldn't be sharing any of this personal information with him if she weren't under the influence. It was best just to let the conversation trail off naturally and pretend he'd never heard any of it. Not his business. He closed his eyes; he really wanted to drift off to sleep, but not with Taylor right next to him. He felt her stirring beside him. Clint opened his eyes to find her staring at him.

"Now I know who you remind me of—Sam Elliott!

The actor with the hair and the mustache—remember? He played a bouncer in that movie with Patrick Swayze…"

"Road House."

Taylor propped up on her elbow. "That's it."

"I've heard that before," he told her.

"It's the voice." Taylor looked the cowboy over. "And the hair."

Taylor rolled onto her stomach and rested her head on her arms. A feeling had been growing inside of her for a while and it was getting stronger and stronger, to the point where she couldn't force it to go away.

"Clint…"

Her cowboy didn't open his eyes. She thought she heard him make a sound that sounded suspiciously like a snore. She poked him the arm, hard, with her pointer finger.

"You need to rest." Clint mumbled.

"No." Taylor disagreed emphatically. "I need food. I'm *starving.* I mean, really—where's a McDonald's when you really need one?"

She tucked her head into her arms, frustrated by her rumbling stomach begging to be fed. "Man…why am I so *hungry*?"

Clint groaned loudly and rubbed his hands over his face before he dragged his fingers through his hair. "You have the munchies."

Taylor awakened the next morning with an odd type of hangover. She was exhausted, her lungs hurt and she felt really fuzzyheaded and groggy, as if she hadn't slept at all. She was still dressed, so all she had to do was jam her feet into her boots and crawl her way out of her tent. Honestly, the end of the night was a blur and she didn't even remember going to bed. She emerged from her tent and was immediately met with a sun that was too bright to be tolerated.

"Oh…"

She squinted her eyes and shielded them with her hand until she reached the edge of the fire pit where there was some shade.

"Good morning," she mumbled, then sat down on her makeshift bench and dropped her head into her hands. Her voice was raspy; it hurt to talk.

Clint handed her a cup of black coffee. It was his coffee, so it was strong and chock full of grounds. She didn't care. Taylor thanked him, took her first sip of the bitter brew and said a silent prayer for the caffeine to work its magic on her body as quickly as possible.

"What do you want me to do with this?" Clint held up the remainder of the joint.

"Ugh—get rid of it."

Clint flicked it into the small fire he had built to heat the coffee and to give Taylor a place to warm up a little until the late morning sun took the chill out of the air.

"Done experimenting?" Clint looked as though he had survived the night without much damage done. His eyes were a little puffy underneath, but his eyes always seemed to be chronically bloodshot from the tequila.

Taylor grimaced and karate chopped the air with her free hand. "Completely."

"Not all it was cracked up to be?"

Taylor picked some grounds off her tongue, wiped them on the pant leg of her jeans. "It was interesting, I'll give it that. But, uh…" She made a face. "My lungs are on fire, I woke up surrounded by a graveyard of wrappers—I ate two days' worth of snacks last night. No. Never again."

After three cups of grainy coffee, Taylor forced herself to stick to her schedule and spend another day exploring on foot alone. It was hard to believe, but she was closing in on the halfway mark of her journey and soon it would be time to turn back.

The whole point of this trip to the Continental Divide was to figure out her next move. She had quit the only career she'd ever known, she had sold the house she had called home for most of her adult life, had divorced the only man she had ever loved. Perhaps it was foolish to think that one trip to the mountains would bring about an epiphany—she had never been without a safety net before, but this time, she didn't have a plan B. In truth, other than fulfilling her childhood dream of riding the CDT, she didn't even have a plan A.

After a day of hiking, Taylor returned to camp with a nagging thought in her head. She had thought about so much on the hike, but the one thing that her brain wanted to mull over the most was the fleeting feeling of Clint's lips on hers and the fleeting feeling of the surprising softness of his beard on her skin. At first, she had thought there was nothing to admire about Clint. But she was wrong. Yes, he was rough, and crude at times, and his English was deplorable and he drank too much. On the other hand, he was strong, protective, resourceful, intelligent. He had more positive attributes than she would have ever suspected. And there was a handsome ruggedness about his face—decent bone structure—and he had a trim, but muscular physique. A lot to like there.

"Hungry?" Clint asked her when she joined him by the fire.

He was cooking freshly caught fish again. She hadn't gotten tired of eating fish because Clint cooked the fish with different native plants and the flavors were so unusual that Taylor couldn't wait to taste his next culinary creation.

"Famished."

"Not too long now." Clint was kneeling by the fire.

His hat was sitting back on his head, the sleeves of his long sleeve shirt rolled up to the elbow. His hands were large—she'd never noticed that before.

Clint could feel Taylor's gaze on him. He looked up from the fish he'd just turned over in the pan, directly into her light-blue eyes. She was staring at him, examining him as if she was seeing him for the first time.

"What's up?" he asked her.

"I had an idea last night," she told him. "And the more I've thought about it today, the more I think that it's not…the *craziest* idea I've ever had."

Clint didn't say anything when she paused, so she decided to just keep on talking before she lost her nerve.

"You've mentioned in passing, that you're having some financial difficulties…" Taylor threaded her fingers together on top of her knees and pulled her bent legs closer to her chest. "And I've shared with you that I really want to have a child of my own…"

A flicker of concern—and *fear*—appeared in his dark eyes.

"And it made me wonder…why *couldn't* we help each other out?"

She had the cowboy's attention now.

"Have you ever…" She shook her head a little. "No…let me rephrase that—*would* you ever—consider selling…your sperm?"

Chapter Six

"I'm sorry…" Clint's entire body tensed. "What?"

Once she got out her thoughts, the thoughts that had been nagging her since the night before, she felt calm. In control. It was the same feeling she'd always had after she ran a great meeting or brokered a solid deal for the bank.

"I think the fish is burning." She pointed to the pan on the fire.

It took a second for Clint to take his eyes off her and put them on the fish. He took the pan from the fire. He stood up and, out of habit, fished around in his front shirt pocket for a pack of cigarettes that wasn't there.

She stood up, as well. "I've been thinking about this all day, and I really believe that we can help each other."

"I have something you need—money—and you have…" Her eyes naturally dropped to his groin before meeting his eyes again. "Something *I* need."

Clint didn't know how to respond to Taylor's nutty idea, an idea that was obviously hatched when she was high as a kite the night before. So he said nothing. He was hungry, and the fish he'd caught and cleaned for their dinner was getting cold. He divvied up the fish onto two plates, handed Taylor hers and took his to his usual spot by the fire. Clint sincerely hoped that she would just drop the subject. He'd had some women ask him some strange things over the years, but this was the most bizarre.

They ate in silence. Taylor complimented him on the fish, he nodded his thanks and that was the end of the conversation. He kept the brim of his hat low to save him the trouble of avoiding eye contact with the woman sitting across from him. And he didn't want to avoid looking at Taylor. He *liked* looking at her. She had a pretty face; he liked the way she smiled, he liked her laugh, those wide-set, bright blue eyes. He'd grown accustomed to enjoying the view.

"Just hear me out." Taylor waited until he'd finished eating before she broached the subject again.

Clint was leaning back against his saddle. He had a belly full of fish, had taken a couple of tugs off his last bit of tequila and his harmonica was ready to play.

"I like you, Taylor, but that just ain't gonna happen."

"You like me?" Taylor asked with a pleased smile. "That's nice."

"I do like you. But that don't change right from wrong."

"Hear me out," she repeated. "And then I promise—I'll never bring it up again."

He heard her out. She had to give him credit for that. Of course, he was a captive audience. But she put forward her best pitch for the idea. She would have thought that giving a voice to her idea would have deterred her, yet it only made her feel more strongly that it could be the perfect solution for the both of them. He would be debt free, or close to it, and she would have one last hail-Mary chance to have the child she had always dreamed of having.

Clint listened to Taylor as he'd agreed to do. While she was talking, he rubbed his hand over his beard; his ears were tuned in to her voice, but his eyes were focused on his left boot, which had been duct taped on the bottom to cover a deep crack in the sole. He'd needed new boots for a year now.

There were a lot of things he needed, including making back payments on his truck and fifth-wheel trailer. He'd been living on the edge for so long, barely making it, that his latest injury, broken ribs, had taken him out of the game. He'd burned through what little savings he had paying doctor's bills; he was seriously delinquent on his truck and his fifth wheel. If he lost his fifth wheel, he lost his home.

Taylor's idea was flat-out nuts, but he'd be flat-out lying if he told her he wasn't tempted.

Clint didn't respond for a minute or two; he took his hat off and raked his fingers through his thick, wavy hair several times before he put the hat back on. It was a stalling tactic—she knew it and he knew it.

"Why..." Clint started to formulate his thought into speech. He stopped and then restarted a moment later. "Why would someone like you *ever* want to have a kid by someone like me?"

"Why do you keep saying that? What do you mean someone like me?" Taylor asked defensively.

"Educated, classy—rich," the cowboy clarified.

"Oh." Her tone changed. "I thought...whatever...it doesn't matter what I thought."

The only sound between them was the crackling of the fire. Taylor tried to put words to the comfort she felt with this man sitting across from her. How could she explain to him that she had always been nervous around men, even though her job demanded that she hide those nerves? How could she tell him that she didn't feel nervous around him; that he felt familiar and comfortable, in a way she had rarely experienced before?

When she was brutally honest with herself, she had to admit that she'd married Christopher because she was too uneasy with men to date regularly. Was she ever truly comfortable with Christopher? Had she ever revealed her true self to him? Or had she always held a part of herself separate?

"You're a good man." She finally found the words. "You're intelligent, you're protective...you have kind eyes."

If she was being truthful with him, those were the nicest words anyone had ever said to him. He wasn't used to it, and he didn't trust it. The harsh words were easier to believe.

"I'm not that guy."

"Yes, you are," Taylor said. "You're a better man than you think you are."

He tipped his head down so she couldn't see his eyes and she knew she had lost him. "Well—that's real sweet of you. And I hope you get what you want. But..."

"You can't help me." She saved him the trouble of finishing his sentence.

"No, ma'am. I can't."

* * *

The day they returned to the spot where the boundary of her uncle's ranch intersected the CDT, Taylor had to fight off tears. They were mere days away from the end of the trip and she had yet to figure out what she was going to do with her life next. She had believed that the mountains and time without being connected electronically would have cleared her head enough to decide on a direction, but it hadn't. Her friends wanted her to move to Seattle and her sister wanted her to move back to Chicago, but neither of those options seemed like the right one for her.

"A couple of weeks without service and I have two hundred emails." Taylor sighed. "I'm not ready for real life."

She decided to ignore the emails and listen to her voice mail, instead. Most of the messages were from friends, several were from her mother and one was from her uncle Hank. The message from her uncle wasn't for her—it was a message for Clint. And it wasn't good news.

Taylor walked over to where Clint was staking his horse nearby for grazing. She extended her phone to him.

"There's a message for you on my phone," she explained. "Uncle Hank didn't know how else to get ahold of you."

Clint took the phone and listened to the message. She watched his face, looking for some reaction. She saw the smallest flicker of anger in his eyes, a tensing of his mouth, but he said nothing as he handed the phone back to her.

She had heard, unintentionally, personal information regarding Clint's financial predicament. He had intimated a couple of times that he had some money problems, but he'd never been specific.

"Is there anything I can do?"

Clint had his head down. He didn't look up at her. "Ain't nothin' for you to worry about, Taylor."

Arms crossed over her chest, Taylor walked away from him. He hadn't meant to be so harsh with her—she was just the messenger once removed. Honestly, he was embarrassed that she had heard that his truck and his fifth wheel had been repossessed. If he'd been able to pay his cell phone bill, then Hank wouldn't have had to resort to using his niece as a go-between.

"Damn it," Clint said under his breath. What in the hell was he going to do now?

Taylor didn't join him at the fire that night. He could only surmise that she was giving him space to lick his wounds. The last of the tequila was downed quickly, and his craving for a cigarette was stronger now than it had been since he ran out. A couple of hours mulling by the fire hadn't dredged up a solution to his most urgent problem from the depths of his mind.

His ribs were healed, but now he had lost his only two possessions in the world. Without his truck, without his fifth wheel, he was dead in the water. He'd already tried to take out a loan—his credit was wrecked. The money he was earning now wasn't enough to get him even with his creditors. He'd already exhausted all of his resources and he'd borrowed money from family and friends—as far as he could figure, he had only one avenue open to him: Taylor.

She was inside of her tent scrolling through the pictures on her camera when she heard Clint quietly call her name. Unless it was inclement weather, Clint never came to her tent. It was her private space, and he had always respected that. For a quick second she froze while her heart raced wildly in her chest. She took in a deep, deep breath, let it out slowly and then unzipped the entrance of her tent.

"You got a minute?" Clint asked her.

When she nodded her head, he held out his hand. She took it, and for the first time she felt sweat on his palms. He wasn't showing it on his face, mostly hidden by the shadows of night, but the cowboy was nervous. That made her stomach flip-flop.

Clint waited for her to sit down before he started the conversation. "A smart business woman like you—you probably think I'm a bad risk."

"I'm not one of your creditors."

The cowboy snapped a branch and tossed it onto the fire. "I broke my ribs six months back—no more bulls, no more money."

She nodded, so he knew she was listening to him as he continued.

"My whole life's tied up in that truck." Clint took his hat off, wiped the sweat from his brow while he built the will to say what he needed to say next. "You still want to make a deal?"

Taylor took a sharp intake of breath. He changed direction so quickly, got to the point so quickly, that it took her a moment to catch up with him.

She cleared her throat to make sure that he could hear her when she said, "I do."

"Aren't there places you could buy…?" He stopped short of saying the word.

"Sperm?"

He nodded.

"I could go to a sperm bank. I've thought about it—I even looked into it once. But I want to know the man who fathers my child. I want to respect him. You can be impressed by a donor's profile, but you can't respect it."

"You'd pay me?"

"We'd have to settle on an amount, yes. Either way, I'd have to pay."

"And I wouldn't be on the hook?"

"No." Taylor was quick to assure him. "I'd have my attorney draw up a contract—we could work out all of the details—you would be absolved of all future financial commitments for the child."

Clint gave a nod of his head as if he were seriously considering the deal. "Would you want it in a cup or the natural way?"

The look on his face when he asked that question was comical. Taylor started to laugh, even though Clint didn't join her. The one good thing that had come out of her pot experimentation was that her brain had hatched this plan. They both had something the other needed, so it truly could be a win-win if they played their hand correctly.

"I'd prefer..." She couldn't believe she was about to say this. "Natural."

She was tired of fertility shots and doctors and scheduling and waiting rooms; she was tired of dealing with Christopher's unmotivated sperm and her slow eggs. She just wanted a man to knock her up the old-fashioned way. Was that too much to ask for?

"Would you have any...objection to that?"

"No." Clint's response was direct. "I wanted to take you to bed the first time I saw you."

* * *

Her plan was to leave the next morning and ride to the last campsite before they returned to Bent Tree. But when she awakened the next morning, having hardly slept throughout the night, she couldn't imagine spending the day in the saddle. And she couldn't stomach the idea of being only one day away from the end of her adventure. Particularly after what had happened the night before with Clint. She had tossed and turned all night, only nodding off every now and again, because she couldn't believe that the cowboy had actually agreed to give her the one thing she wanted in this world: a child.

Everything she had done leading up to this moment had been to build a stable life for a child—her career, financial stability, emotional maturity. It had all been for a child that had never arrived. When she left her old life, she had given up the idea of being a mother. But, now, with Clint's help, she might just have a shot at fulfilling another dream. And, it wasn't just a dream—it was the *most important* dream.

"Good morning." She smiled at Clint, feeling a little shy about seeing him after their discussion the night before.

Clint, as was usual, had already started the fire and made coffee. He poured her a cup of the thick, grainy liquid.

"Mornin'."

The hot liquid burned her tongue and the roof of her mouth; she had learned to drink the strong, bitter coffee black over the past couple of weeks, and even picking coffee grounds off her tongue didn't seem unusual.

"You gotta be lookin' forward to a decent cup of coffee." The cowboy said to her.

She laughed. "Nah. I like a cup of coffee you can stand on."

After several weeks of growing more comfortable with Clint, the discussion, the *agreement*, they had made the night before had erased almost all of it. She tried to relax her shoulders and her neck, but the minute she stopped focusing her attention on relaxing, her entire upper body tensed up. And Clint looked just as tight as she felt. Her biggest fear, all night, had been that in the light of day Clint would come to his senses.

"You excited about headin' out today?"

"No." Her single-word response, gloomy in tone, spoke volumes.

Clint looked at her carefully. "No?"

"Uh-uh." She raised her eyes to meet his. "I'd rather stick around here for a day. Or two. Would you be okay with that?"

"I was thinkin' the same thing."

"You were?"

Clint, who was pouring himself more coffee, nodded his response. He held out the pot and offered to pour her more; she put her hand over her cup. Clint put the coffee pot off to the side and sat back.

"I didn't get much sleep last night." Clint told her.

"Neither did I," she admitted. There was an uncomfortable knot in her stomach, much like the knot she'd had the morning Christopher and she had agreed that their marriage was too far gone to salvage.

"I couldn't stop thinkin' about what we talked about…"

She nodded. Their discussion was all she could think about, too. Was she crazy to even be entertaining the idea? What would her family say? What if, what if, what if? So many—*too many*—what-ifs to think about.

"Are you sure about this thing?"

"I'm sure that I want a baby," she said firmly. "And I'm sure I'm running out of time."

"Are you sure you want me to give you that baby?" Clint was staring at her so strangely, as if he'd never really seen her before.

Taylor felt queasy in her stomach; acid from the coffee had shot up to the back of her throat and she swallowed it.

"Look—if you want to back out, I understand. No hard feelings."

"I don't wanna back out," Clint said with odd tension in his voice. "I want to get started."

"Wait…" This man was always tacking left when she thought he was going to tack right. "What?"

"Ever since last night I've been thinkin' about us being together…" Clint told her bluntly. "I can either take care of some things on my own—or I can start giving you what you want now. Do you know what I'm trying to say here, Taylor?"

She knew what he was saying, but she wasn't sure how she should respond. For the past several years she had lived by her ovulation cycle. She knew all of the signs and symptoms of ovulation—a slight headache, breast tenderness, her stomach feeling a little bloated. When she was clearing out her house, packing everything to be put in storage, she had thrown away a stockpile of ovulation kits. She certainly hadn't thought to pack one to ride the CDT. So she couldn't be certain. But she was pretty sure that she was ovulating now.

"We haven't even discussed the terms of the agreement," she reminded him.

"You want a child and I want to be able to get right side up with my creditors." It sounded so simple when he said it so matter-of-factly.

"How do you know I won't change my mind and sue you for child support? Or get what I want before I've paid you and then not pay you a dime?"

Clint didn't hesitate. "You're not that kind of woman."

Taylor wrapped her arms around her bent knees. "How do I know you don't have a disease? I was going to ask you to get tested. And I was going to get tested, too—for your peace of mind."

"I protect myself. And I get tested every year." Clint said. "But you're just gonna have to trust that I wouldn't do somethin' deliberately to hurt you."

Clint had been protecting her since day one, even when he didn't want to have any part of being her bodyguard. Her gut was telling her that she could trust him in this, and her gut was usually on point.

"How do you know I don't have something I could give you?" She was searching for anything to get to the word *no* and they both knew it.

"Do you?"

Taylor shook her head. "No. I got myself tested right after the divorce. Just in case…well…you know…"

She hugged her knees tightly, wishing she could ignore the yellow caution light blinking in her brain.

"How much do you need to get current with your truck and fifth wheel?" she asked, feeling more comfortable with the business side of this transaction.

When he told her the figure, she realized that, even

though it wasn't a small amount, it was a small price to pay for the chance to have a child of her own.

"Should we shake on it?" Taylor finally asked.

Clint stood up and crossed to her side of the fire. He held out his hand; she took it and let him help her to her feet. He moved his hands to her shoulders—he was going to kiss her and she was going to let him. The kiss was light and quick, but it held a promise of things yet to come.

"Sealed with a kiss," she said with a nervous laugh.

Clint's response was to kiss her again; his right hand slid down her arm to her hand. When he ended the kiss, and she didn't *want* him to end the kiss, he took her hand and led her to the tent. She knew that he wasn't planning to wish her goodnight—he was taking her to the tent and he had every intention of following her inside. He wanted to take her to bed, and she wasn't going to object.

She was at her sexual peak, she suspected she was ovulating and she hadn't had sex in so long that she literally couldn't remember the month or year. Christopher had been her only lover since she was in her early twenties, and she *wanted* to know what it felt like to be with a man other than her ex-husband. And, bonus—it wasn't likely, but it was *possible* that she could be pregnant by the time she returned to Bent Tree Ranch.

Chapter Seven

"Damn." Clint rolled onto his back, his right thigh pressed tightly against hers. "Damn."

"It's okay. Don't worry about it."

The cowboy crossed his arms over his face. "What the hell happened?"

Taylor stared up at the roof of her tent. This wasn't what she'd had in mind when she imagined her first postmarital encounter. It had started out like a scene out of a movie—here she was, play-by-the-rules Taylor Brand, sharing a one-person sleeping bag with a *younger* bull-riding cowboy —and it felt *great*.

He kissed her nice and slow and she liked the feel of his lips on hers—she liked the weight of his body pressing her down into the hard ground beneath the tent floor. The cowboy's body was long and lean, his muscles so hard to the touch. She wanted to run her fingers through that thick, wavy hair, but she hadn't had time to build up the nerve. He wanted her, and she didn't want to ruin it.

Not all that many men had wanted her. She had always been too chubby, too serious, too smart. But she'd been able to feel that Clint wanted her as he lay between her thighs and she'd wondered—how different would he feel once he was inside of her? It had only been Christopher for so long.

"This never happens. I swear." He dragged his tensed fingers through his hair then looked over at her. "It doesn't."

"Don't worry about it." Taylor rested her arms on top of the sleeping bag. "I was worried about how prickly my legs are."

"I didn't care about that!"

"I do," she retorted. Worrying about the hair on her legs and the forests in her armpits had made her stiffen up when she should have been enjoying the feel of his lips on her neck.

"I don't know what happened," he repeated.

But that wasn't the truth. He knew exactly what had happened. His libido had been in charge before they got into the tent—when he was really close to making love to a woman without protection for the first time since he was teenager. He'd gotten a girl from high school pregnant, and his mind had started to spit out every possible worst-case scenario and he completely lost his hard-on. The girl he'd gotten pregnant decided to place the baby, a boy, for adoption. That experience had been enough to scare him straight about unprotected sex.

Clint threw his part of the sleeping bag off his torso, noticing that Taylor clutched the material over her naked breasts. Those breasts, everything he'd imagined they'd be, had felt so damn good against his body. He stood up and yanked on his jeans. It was tempting to leave, but this wasn't a hotel—this wasn't a rodeo chick—where would he go? He'd have to face her one way or the other. He'd rather stay and not look like the biggest jerk in a one hundred mile radius.

"We could always just talk," Taylor suggested.

"Talk?"

"Yeah—talk," she said, when he looked at her like she'd lost her last bit of sense. "It isn't unheard of. Don't you talk to women?"

"One of my best friends is a woman." But Dallas was a rodeo junky like he was. They only talked about horses and how they were getting to the next stop on the line.

"Well—I think it would be good for us to talk. Close your eyes so I can get dressed and then you can ask me anything you want."

"Okay." When she was done Taylor sat down opposite him. "You can look now."

Clint opened his eyes and they went straight to her breasts. She hadn't put a bra on beneath the T-shirt. Her nipples, hardened from the friction of the material brushing up against them, made him want to rub his hands over them.

"You've got great tits."

Taylor's shoulders hunched and she glanced down at her chest. "That wasn't a question."

"No," Clint acknowledged. "Just the truth."

"I'm not sure what I'm supposed to say in a situation like this… I'm glad you like them?"

"Your face is redder than a baboon's butt." Clint

smiled at her. His bottom teeth were a little crooked, but the smile was nice, nonetheless.

"Do you have a question or not?" Taylor frowned at him.

"Can't think of one..."

"I have a question for you."

Clint had slipped his shirt back on, but he hadn't buttoned it up.

"What's with all of the tattoos?"

The cowboy looked down, rubbed his hand over the black-and-gray tattoos on his chest. "I was too young to know better with most of 'em."

"Did you...did you get them in prison?"

Clint laughed at the question. "No. They're just scratcher tattoos is all."

"I don't know what a scratcher is."

"A dude who don't know how to tattoo worth a damn. I was too dumb to know not to let 'em touch me with a needle."

Taylor nodded her head. She'd thought about getting a little butterfly on her ankle once, but Christopher had said tattoos were for biker chicks and indie girls. Her hand went to her tattoo-free ankle—there wasn't a reason in the world that she shouldn't get that butterfly now.

She had obviously taken a mental jaunt, because when Clint snapped his fingers it snapped her back to the present.

"I just thought of a question."

She raised her eyebrows and waited.

"Were those rings real? The ones you almost chucked in the lake."

"Yes." Taylor smiled at the expression on his face. "They're real."

"How much did they set your old man back?"

"Well—they were in a platinum setting from Tiffany's..."

He was looking blank, so she elaborated. "It's a really famous jewelry store—anything that has their name on it comes at a premium. So—platinum Tiffany setting, one carat of diamonds on the infinity wedding band, and a two carat, round, nearly colorless diamond engagement ring—today's prices—40 or 50 thousand. Something like that."

Clint looked at her as if she had lost her mind. "Damn, woman! You're lucky I was there to stop you from doin' a fool thing like chuckin' 'em in the lake!"

Clint continued to shake his head at the thought of the price of her wedding rings.

"Damn." He repeated.

"I tried to give them back to my ex—he didn't want them." Taylor frowned, the memories of the last day she saw Christopher at the attorney's office still so vivid. "I don't want them, either."

"With that kinda money, I could pay off my truck, my fifth wheel *and* have money for a year's worth of tequila and cigarettes." Clint told her. "Come to think of it, I could use a cigarette about now."

"Doesn't a person usually smoke a cigarette *after* sex?"

Surprised that she was teasing him, he pretended that he was stabbing himself in the heart with a knife.

"That was cold," he joked back. "And here I was going to offer to cook you an early dinner. Are you hungry?"

"Always."

Usually Clint fished alone. But this time he asked Taylor to join him and she accepted. She followed him down to the creek and found a large, flat boulder she could sit on. She watched Clint cast his line with a new appreciation for the cowboy's physique. In his own way, he was a handsome man. Clint let out a hoot when he caught a fish soon after he cast his line. He reeled it in and held it up for her to see. Taylor clapped her hands and smiled at how genuinely pleased he was with himself. She didn't have the heart to tell him that she was sick to death of fish, fish and more fish. Food was one of the perks of completing her journey. Hot showers, mattresses, indoor plumbing—she had sorely missed those luxuries, as well.

After dinner, Taylor headed down to the stream near Clint's fishing hole to take what would likely be her last cold-water bath. The sun was still out—it wasn't strong, but it was enough to keep the boulders by the creek heated. She thought about shaving her legs—the hair was long enough to pet—and the gorilla patches under her arms, just in case, but it was too flipping cold. She did manage to wash her hair, which smelled strongly of campfire smoke and fried trout.

Wrapped in a towel, she climbed onto the boulder, turned her face to the sun and let the rays warm her face and shoulders. Over the past four weeks she had stopped bathing in her underwear, bathing in the nude, instead. To be out in the wilderness, among the trees and the bugs and the birds and everything living in the water—naked—she imagined that this was how Eve felt in the Garden of Eden.

When Taylor didn't return to camp, Clint went

looking for her. He followed her footsteps back to the stream. At the edge of the trees, before she would be able to see him, he spotted her. And it stopped him in his tracks. Perched on one of the boulders in the middle of the stream, Taylor's beautifully rounded body, with all of its lovely curves, was scantily covered by her towel. Her head was back, hair slicked away from her face, which was upturned to take in the sun.

Over their monthlong trek her body had tightened, was more toned, but she still had that voluptuous figure that he found so appealing. She reminded him of the Renaissance paintings he had seen in one of the few books that his mother had kept in the house. He used to sneak the book off the shelf to look at the naked women when he was a kid. The way Taylor was posed on the boulder, that's what she was—a Renaissance woman.

Taylor opened her eyes and saw Clint walking toward her.

"I was worried." He explained why he had interrupted her alone time.

She nodded her understanding. She had never stayed this long before, so he had a right to be concerned.

"Mind if I borrow that soap?" Clint started to unbutton his shirt.

"Be my guest." Taylor clutched her towel to her chest and climbed off the boulder, being careful not to hurt her feet on the stones lining the creek bed. Her feet had toughened along the way; they were calloused and rough to the touch. It was hard to believe that she actually *liked* the way they felt. It meant that she was tough—tougher than she'd ever given herself credit for.

"I'll see you back at the camp," she told Clint, who had taken off his hat and stripped off his shirt.

Inside her tent she brushed the knots out of her hair—it was long enough now to make a decent ponytail. Maybe she would grow it out; maybe she would cut it super short. Whatever she did, she wasn't going to wear it the way she had for the past several years. It was time to change. The sun was just starting to set when she heard Clint return to camp. After her bath, all she wanted to do was change into a clean T-shirt and underwear, and crawl inside of her sleeping bag.

She was exhausted and thought that she would fall asleep quickly listening to the sound of Clint's harmonica mingled with the familiar night sounds of the wilderness. At first, the howling of coyotes in the distance had kept her awake, but now she knew that one thing she would miss when she returned to civilization was that eerie howling. Yet it wasn't the coyotes keeping her awake tonight—it was the wondering about Clint's intentions. Would he try to join her in the tent? Or would he sleep outside beneath the stars as if nothing had happened between them.

"Taylor?"

The cowboy was outside of her tent. She had wanted him to come to her tonight.

"I'm awake." She had left the flap unzipped, in hopes that he would see it as a subtle invitation.

"You want company?"

"You can come in." He was looking for a "yes" and she had given it to him.

He opened the flap, and the moment she saw him, his features obscured by the night, she knew that he wanted to make love to her. The spot between her thighs, neglected for so long, sent little shocks of anticipation throughout the rest of her body. To get a divorce while entering her sexual peak had felt like a double whammy. She had thought that sex was permanently off the table, unable to imagine the next man that may come into her life, but here was sexy cowboy Clint seeking *her* out. Amazing.

"We gotta do somethin' about that bag of yours." Clint knelt just inside of her tent.

She turned on the flashlight hanging overhead. Clint had his bedroll with him. She knew what he had in mind, so she crawled out of her sleeping bag and unzipped it all the way so it could be spread out flat like a thin mattress for two.

Still in her T-shirt and underwear, Taylor switched off the flashlight before she lay back to wait for Clint. Every sound she heard that brought Clint closer to touching her with his fingers, or his tongue or his lips created a reaction in her body. When he zipped them inside of the tent, her heart started to beat a little bit faster. When she heard him unzip his pants, she started to feel wet between her thighs. Her breathing was more shallow, her nipples so hard.

Clint lay down beside her and covered them with his blanket. They turned toward each other—they both knew what they wanted. He started by only touching her with his hand and his lips. It was such a sweet, sensual tease. How long had it been since she had genuinely been kissed? Her ex didn't like to kiss, but apparently Clint didn't have a similar aversion.

He brushed his fingers across her cheek to thread his strong fingers through her hair so he could cup the back of her head in his hand. Soft, butterfly caresses turned into deeper, more demanding kisses. Clint's were unlike any she had ever known. He was commanding without being aggressive, he took charge without taking away her power. He wasn't sloppy or fumbling—and when he slipped his tongue inside of her mouth, it felt so good and it felt so right that she rested her hand on his bare chest, over his heart, and relaxed into him with a pleasured sigh.

Her brain registered all of the differences between Clint and Christopher—it wasn't intentional, it was unavoidable. Christopher had been stocky, while Clint's legs, arms and torso were long and lean—his body didn't feel as dense or substantial next to hers, but she liked how he had her legs intertwined with his.

How different would it feel to have Clint inside of her? With her ex, the sex had always been good. They had been together for so long that they knew how to get to orgasm quickly and without any deviation from their roles and positions. It had become very routine—very *boring*. Especially when ovulation had ruled their sex schedule. Yet, she worried that she wouldn't be able to achieve orgasm so readily with a penis she didn't know.

"My feet are always cold," she whispered apologetically.

"I'll warm 'em up for you." Clint's breath on her ear sparked a wonderful shiver all over her body.

Clint slid his hand beneath her T-shirt; he filled his hand with her naked breast, the taut nipple pressed into the warm palm. He began to massage her breast, and it was sore, so the squeezing and pressure was a welcome relief. She pushed her breast harder into his hand with a moan.

"Are you okay?"

"Yes," she said urgently. She didn't want him to stop. "They're so tender—I think I'm ovulating."

She knew that revealing that information might end the night, but he had a right to know.

Thankfully, he didn't stop. Instead, he tugged at her T-shirt, asking her to remove it. She sat up and pulled off her top. Now she was nearly naked with the cowboy, the cool night air on her skin and her bared breasts. Instead of having her lie down again, he moved behind her, wrapped his body around hers from behind and encouraged her to lean back against him. He nibbled on her neck while he reached around her body and took her heavy breasts in his large, warm hands. He tweaked her hard nipples with his thumbs; he massaged her breasts while she dropped her head back against his shoulder and uttered moans of pleasure as the soreness that had plagued her for days was released.

"You like this." Clint bit her earlobe gently.

"Yes," she said in a breathy voice.

Her senses were overwhelmed by everything Clint; the softness of his beard on her skin, his breath, his lips—the hardness of his erection pressed into her lower back. Clint trapped her breasts beneath one arm, keeping the pressure steady and using his free hand to explore another area of her body that was desperate for attention. Clint's fingers slipped beneath the waistband of her cotton panties; she let her thighs open so he could touch her, so he could ease that almost painful need that had been building inside of her for far too long.

"Ah…" Clint was pleased with the wetness he found with his fingers. "Yes, Taylor. *Yes*."

He hugged her tightly to him, his teeth grazing her neck, his fingers inside of her. She lost herself and the moment—she couldn't stop herself from moving her hips. She *had* to move.

Why was he waiting? Why was he *waiting*? Clint found her swollen clit with his finger and worried it until she cried out, so loudly, her voice so gravelly with need, that she didn't recognize it. With Clint, she wasn't worried about her bulgy belly or whether her thighs were too big—he made her feel so womanly. So deliciously sexy and desirable.

She was on her back now. Clint took his time to draw her underwear down over her hips, over her thighs and past her ankles. Then he lay between her thighs, the head of his shaft teasing her slick opening. He kept himself propped up with his straight arms, but he bent his head down to kiss her and tease her with his tongue at the same time he teased her down below. Impatient, she reached down between them. She wanted to feel, to begin to learn, the part of his body that was going to be inside of her. His shaft, like the rest of his body, was long and lean and hard—the tip was pointed like a spear.

"Put me inside of you," Clint commanded.

She guided him inside of her body with her hand. Slowly, purposefully, as if he wanted to savor every second of pleasure with her, he slid inside of her. So deep, so deep—until their bodies were mated completely.

Clint was a quiet lover; she listened to his breathing quicken as he seated himself more deeply inside of her body. The cowboy stopped moving, his head buried in her neck. He rested his chest against hers, his fingers intertwined with hers above their heads. She had to move, she *needed* to move. She pushed at his hips so he would slide his shaft in and out of her slick opening harder, faster—she needed to take more and more and more of him. Clint found her nipple with his hot mouth and sucked on it—hard.

"Ahhh!" Taylor arched her back and dug her fingernails into Clint's shoulders. *"Ahhh!"*

In the darkness of the tent, in the arms of the cowboy, Taylor screamed with ecstasy. She screamed louder and longer than she had ever screamed in her life. She screamed with relief, she screamed with release. Clint tugged harder at her nipple with his mouth, suckling until the last waves of her orgasm subsided.

Clint couldn't hold back any longer.

"Do you want it?" he asked gruffly, beads of sweat covering his forehead.

"Yes!" She felt his shaft at the opening of her womb and it drove her wild. "Yes!"

Clint pressed his shaft as deep inside of her as he could and exploded. Knowing that he had just given her his seed, Taylor writhed beneath, pressing back against him as hard as he was pressing into her.

"Ah—ah—*ahhhh*!" It was a primal cry that was wrenched from her body, a mixture of the pleasure and joy that she felt in her body mingled with the sadness and heartbreak that she felt in her soul. It was a release, beyond the physical, that she had needed since the day she left her old life behind.

"Taylor." Clint's body was still connected to hers, his large, capable hands holding her face. "Taylor. Why are you crying? What's wrong?"

"Nothing's wrong. Nothing's wrong." Taylor started to laugh through her tears. "I'm high on endorphins. *Two* orgasms! *That's* never happened before!"

Chapter Eight

They made love again before falling asleep. She wasn't accustomed to sleeping in the spooning position, so after some cuddling time, which Clint seemed to enjoy, she scooted out from beneath his arm and moved onto her back to sleep.

Exhausted from the trip and from the lovemaking, Taylor didn't awaken until midmorning. After she opened her eyes, she started to take a happy inventory of her body: her left nipple was a little bit darker and sensitive from Clint's attention. She ran her hand over her breast with a smile and then continued down to between her legs. With his really-rough-around-the-edges exterior, and being a cowboy and bull rider, a woman wouldn't suspect that Clint McAllister was a passionate, attentive, *thorough* lover who genuinely appreciated a womanly figure. The way he touched her, they way he kissed her—he loved her thick thighs and large, natural breasts and her extra-rounded apple bottom.

Exiting the tent she said, "Good morning," to Clint, who was cooking the rest of the fish for his lunch.

"Mornin'." He smiled at her. "You sick of fish yet?"

"Beyond." She sat down on the log bench by the fire.

"If you'd let me shoot somethin' I could fix that for you."

He kept on asking her if she wanted him to shoot a bird or a rabbit or a deer. She had given up all meat except for seafood and couldn't stomach the idea of him killing something, skinning it and then cooking it in front of her.

"I've got a couple of freeze-dried meals we can share." She wrinkled her nose. "Is there any coffee left?"

Clint poured her a cup and brought it to her.

"Oh—thank you."

Instead of returning to his side of the fire, Clint sat down next to her. He didn't have his hat on and he pushed his hair off his forehead.

"Are you okay?" he asked her.

She took a grateful sip of the coffee, not caring that it was tepid and grainy and bitter.

"No regrets." She smiled at him. It had been a long time since she felt this *alive*. "You?"

"No. Once I decide, I decide." Clint returned to the fire to flip over the fish. "Not much sense in takin' off today."

"Agreed."

"It's hot enough to swim." He knelt down by the fire. "You up for it?"

She was. After she ate one of two remaining protein bars and downed a second cup of thick, cold coffee, they hiked down the mountain a ways until they reached a place in the stream that was wide and deep and surrounded by giant boulders.

Taylor dropped her stuff in a pile; Clint was facing her, pulling his shirt out of the waistband of his jeans.

"You comin'?" He started to unbutton his shirt.

In the dark, her tarantula armpits and hairy legs weren't a major concern. But here? In the bright light of day? That was a whole other situation entirely.

"Come on!" Clint lifted his arms in the air. "Look at this place!"

"I really haven't shaved…"

"I don't care." Clint shrugged out of his shirt. "And neither should you."

When she hesitated, the cowboy walked over to her, the look in his eyes undeniably appreciative. He was free to look at her any way he wished and he was taking advantage of it.

"You know what? You're right. I came here to find out who I am…" She hit her palm with her fist. "And then love the *heck* out of that person."

"I've got no complaints." Clint yanked off his boots and socks.

"But…" She added. "I'm leaving on my top."

Clint, who lacked the usual self-consciousness about his own nudity, pulled off his jeans, balled them up and dropped them next to his boots. He stood in front of her, completely unabashed, and dragged his fingers through his hair to push it off his face. The man had obviously spent quite a bit of time, out in the woods, in nothing but his birthday suit.

Taylor shook her head with a laugh. Clint just stood

there with a pleased grin on his face. The question in his eyes was easy to read: *Do you like the view*?

She did like the view. She had found her Adam in this beautiful Garden of Eden. After she took off her jeans and folded them neatly next to her boots, she tucked her towel under her arm and carefully picked her way over to a flat boulder.

"If you're not careful the rocks will cut you up." Clint stood with his back to her. "Let me carry you out there."

No one had offered her a piggyback ride in years—no doubt they had been afraid that she would have sent them to the chiropractor. But Clint was the kind of man who knew what he could handle; she needed to put her trust in him. Deciding to take a leap of faith, she climbed onto his back. Without a second thought, Clint carried her to one of the giant boulders in the widest part of the creek. From her perch on the warm boulder, she dangled her feet into the cool water.

Clint flipped his body backward, dunked his head back into the water, and then shook his hair like dog. He pushed his hair back and waded out to the deepest part.

"You can swim, can't you?"

"Like a fish," she retorted.

He waded back over to her and held out his arms. He lifted her off the rock and held her hand until she reached a spot that was deep enough for her to tread water. She didn't like the feel of slimy rocks on her toes, but the cold water was refreshing. To a point.

"I'm already cold." She swam over to the boulders where she had left her towel.

Clint watched her climb out of the water onto the boulder. He didn't hide his thoughts—her wet T-shirt was showing off her assets and he enjoyed looking at her.

Even though the sun was strong and the boulder was radiating heat through the towel to her skin, wearing the wet T-shirt and panties was keeping her from feeling warm. When Clint was under the water, she quickly slipped her shirt off and waited for him to break through the water's surface. Playfully, she threw her balled-up shirt at the back of his head.

Surprised, Clint turned around, soaked shirt in his hands. She squealed when he sprang forward to grab her.

"Don't you dare try to pull me in!" She scooted backward as far as she could, holding the towel tightly so it wouldn't slip down from her breasts.

Clint threw the waterlogged shirt and it landed with a splat on the shore. "I'm not gonna pull you in…"

"Then what are you going to do to me?" she asked on a laugh. She hadn't acted this playful for such a long time. There was a devilish twinkle in his eye that let her know he had something very specific in mind.

"Something I've been wanting to do to you ever since I saw you yesterday." Clint slid his hands up her thighs, underneath the towel, and hooked his fingers in the top of her panties.

"Whoa! Not the panties!" Taylor pulled her legs up to her chest. "I thought you wanted to give me a kiss!"

Clint held on to the edge her panties. "I do want to give you a kiss."

It took her a split second to catch his meaning, but once she did, she shook her head and pressed her thighs together to keep her panties in place. "No! No *way*! Not out here!"

"I thought you were brave?"

After spending a month on the CDT with her, he

knew exactly which button to push to get his way. She had a very hard time passing up a dare, as Clint was well aware.

"Nice play, McAllister." She glanced around nervously.

"I play to win." Clint put his hands on her knees. "We're alone out here, Taylor. No one else will know."

Taylor met Clint's eyes. It was so tempting. I seemed like years since someone had wanted to love her that way—she had missed it so much that she'd had fantasies about it.

"It's a jungle down there," she warned Clint.

Clint tugged her knees apart. "You worry about the strangest things."

His fingers hooked back onto her panties, but this time, she didn't put away. "I have gray hair."

Clint pulled her panties down her thighs. "I don't care."

He balled up her panties, threw them, and they landed on the shore near her T-shirt. "Lie back, Taylor."

Holding tight to her towel, Taylor leaned back all the way on the boulder. It was uncomfortable, like lying down on uneven concrete, but the anticipation of what was to come helped her ignore the ridges of stone scratching at her skin.

Given the green light, Clint pushed the towel up to her waist, exposing her sensual flower to the bright light of the sun.

"Beautiful." Clint murmured. Her thighs were creamy alabaster, like a porcelain doll, but the bud between her thighs was the palest pink. Delectable.

Taylor closed her eye tightly, the warmth of the sun flushing the skin of her cheeks and her forehead. The cowboy's hands, strong and calloused, traveled up the inside of her thighs, asking her to open more for him. She bit her lip and let her thighs fall apart. She felt the familiar softness of his beard on the inside of her thigh, the unfamiliar sensation of his breath dancing across the most sensitive center of her body—and then he kissed her. She had to stifle the sound of shock and pleasure and relief that bubbled up inside of her. Now that she had it, she didn't want it to stop.

Please don't stop. Please don't stop.

Clint had no intention of stopping. Taylor tasted sweet, like a delicacy designed with his pleasure in mind. When he heard his lover gasp, it only made Clint want to have more of her. Taylor arched her back, her thighs fell further apart, and the towel that she had been clutching so tightly fell away. She felt the sun on her naked breasts, on her stomach and the top of her thighs; she knew that she was completely unclothed for anyone to see. But she didn't care. In that moment, with Clint's searching tongue buried deep inside of her body, she didn't care. All she could do was enjoy the gift of pleasure Clint was giving to her. He was relentless with his love; he was taking her on a different kind of journey—a new journey that her body had never known but so desperately needed.

"Don't hold back," Clint ordered in a husky voice. "Give me what I want, Taylor."

He stayed with her, loved her, caressed her until her muscles began to tighten and her breathing became shallow and it seemed that the only sensation that mattered was the incredible pleasure that Clint was creating with his mouth. Without planning to do it—she was running on instinct alone—she reached between her legs, dug her fingers into Clint's hair and pressed him down into her body with a passionate scream.

Breathing heavily, leg muscles as weak as a rag doll, eyes closed, Taylor drifted down from the orgasmic cloud while Clint dropped little lover's kisses on the insides of both her thighs. She opened her eyes when she felt him take her hands.

"So sweet," he said before he kissed her.

She didn't have any words to explain to Clint what he had just given to her.

Clint reached down and squeezed his erection to stop it from hurting.

"We need to go back to camp."

Taylor nodded her understanding. He needed relief, too.

Clint took her in his arms and carried her to shore. They gathered their clothing, putting on only what was necessary, and returned to camp as quickly as they could. Inside of the tent, Clint stripped off his jeans, his erection gone. She had never been sexually aggressive, but with Clint she was empowered to be someone else—to take more control.

"Sit down." She dropped her towel.

Clint had made it very clear that he loved her body—he loved her hips and her breasts and her backside. She was more comfortable being nude in front of Clint than she had been with her ex-husband.

The cowboy smiled at her as she knelt between his legs. She took him into her mouth until his shaft was thick and hard.

Clint, who had been reveling in her attentions, opened his eyes and reached for her. "Come here."

Taylor straddled his thighs and slowly slid down his shaft making Clint groan loudly; fully impaled, Taylor wrapped her legs around his back and they wrapped their arms tightly around each other.

"God *damn*, lady—you feel like you were made for me." Clint grabbed her backside and pulled her tighter into his body.

Taylor buried her face in his neck and held him as tightly as he was holding her. "You feel so good. You feel so good. You feel so good."

They rocked together, giving pleasure, taking pleasure, and making love hard and long and deep and rough. Sweaty, panting—their bodies slick and wet—Clint cupped her breast in his hand, took her nipple into his hot mouth and sent her over the edge.

"Ah! Ah! Ah! Ah!" Taylor dropped her head back, her hands gripping Clint's shoulders.

"Ahhhhh!" Clint found his release, pumping her full of his seed.

They collapsed into each other's arms to catch their breaths, to come down from their orgasmic highs. Taylor was the first to move; she slid off Clint's lap and rolled onto her back. With Clint, she had taken charge of her sexuality—she *owned* it.

"Wooo…" He rolled onto his back and lay down next to her. *"Damn."*

She started laughing—she couldn't help it. Had she ever been this happy before? Had anything *ever* felt better than making love with Clint McAllister?

Clint looked over at her and smiled, reaching for her hand to stay connected to her while he closed his eyes again. Their fingers intertwined, she closed her eyes, as well. Soon after she heard his breathing become slow and steady, until he was lightly snoring. She thought about getting up, rinsing off, but then she changed her mind and just let her body *be*.

Several hours later, Clint awakened with a raging erection. Taylor was still asleep. She had turned on her side, her curvaceous, sexy backside facing him. He curled his body around hers and ran his hand down her arm to her hip and down her leg. It had been while since he'd been with a woman, so it made sense that he was horny as hell, yet this unparalleled desire he felt for Taylor was beyond his experience. He was a pretty sexual guy, but this craving to connect his body to hers *again* was blowing his mind. He pulled her back into his body and kissed the back of her neck.

"Taylor..."

"Hmm?"

Clint rubbed the head of his shaft along her soft, tight opening, filled his hand with her breast and gently bit her shoulder.

"More?" she asked groggily.

"More," he growled into her neck.

Taylor smiled sleepily, pressed his hand hard into her breast and let out a sexy little sigh of pleasure when he entered her from behind. He wanted this time to be slow, controlled—he wanted to torture their bodies, bring them to the brink of ecstasy and then pull them back until they couldn't stand another second without demanding a release. He loved her with long, slow strokes, plunging deep, plunging deep, plunging deep until her muscles squeezed his shaft, until he felt the wetness of her orgasm. With Taylor shuddering in his arms, Clint took his own release.

* * *

"Damn, woman! What the holy heck did you do to me?"

They'd broken down the tent, eaten a quick breakfast and were getting the horses and Easy ready for the last leg of the journey. They would be back at the ranch by late afternoon.

Taylor zipped the last few items into her pack. "What are you talking about?"

Clint grabbed his crotch and shifted his package inside of his jeans. "The family jewels are *sore*! You drained every last ounce out of 'em."

"Suck it up, cowboy!" Taylor laughed. "You did some damage yourself."

When she first started this trip, she had ached all over her body. In particular, her lady parts had been chafed and raw, which made riding on horseback excruciating. A couple of days into their return, she noticed that her body had adapted. The muscles didn't hurt as much, she was much stronger, and her cardio had improved. Now, after two days of nonstop lovemaking with Clint, she was so sore between her legs she was right back to where she started—but for a much more acceptable reason. She wore her soreness proudly, like a badge of honor.

"You ready to be back today?" Clint tightened his horse's girth a couple of notches.

For days, she had been dreading her return. She didn't feel ready for reality. But now? Today? She was ready.

She nodded her head. "What's the very first thing you're going to do when we get back?"

"Bum a cigarette." Clint adjusted his hat on his head. "You?"

"Hot shower," she didn't hesitate to say. Oh, how she had missed hot water!

Before Clint could make it to her side to help her mount, Taylor got her foot in the stirrup and pulled herself up from the ground without using a boulder or a tree stump as a mounting block.

"Did you see that?" Taylor asked excitedly. "I finally did it!"

Clint swung into his saddle. "You're beautiful."

Surprised, Taylor smiled at him fondly. "Thank you. You make me feel beautiful."

"You ready to head out?"

She looked around the last campsite—it was hard to believe that it had already been a month. She had changed so much on the inside, and even though she hadn't seen herself in a mirror, there was a very good chance she had changed on the outside, as well.

"Ready."

She had no idea where she was heading once she returned to the ranch—would she stay in Montana and get a job working at a local bank? Would she move to Seattle or Chicago? Would Clint go through with their agreement and try to give her a child? Was she pregnant already? And how would she explain *that* to her family? It was rare that she didn't have the answers; she had always been the woman with the planner and a plan. Now she was on the "no plan" plan.

"Hey—isn't this where we met?"

Taylor stopped her mare and waited for Clint to ride up beside her.

"Not my finest hour," he mused. "Half drunk with my pants down."

She looked at his profile. How far they had come from that first moment. She had hated the idea of Clint being with her on this journey, but in the end, she couldn't imagine taking this trip without her cowboy.

"A couple more hours and we'll be back at the ranch," Clint told her.

"I know." She caught his eye. "I'm really going to miss…all of this…"

She was going to say that she was going to miss *him*, but she didn't want to pressure him to return the sentiment. What happened on the CDT would stay on the CDT and the chances that things would stay the same between them were very next to nil.

"Clint—if you change your mind about our agreement when we get back…" She needed to let him off the hook. The closer they got to the ranch, the more it was starting to hit her that the protective bubble they had been living in for nearly a month was about to burst.

"Hey…" He held her gaze to reassure her that he wasn't going to back out. "I could've already hit the bull's-eye, you know."

He wanted to make her laugh and see her smile. It worked. Taylor replied with a laugh. "If you did…it would be a true miracle. And I would be the happiest woman on earth."

Chapter Nine

"Taylor!" Barbara Brand, her aunt and first lady of Bent Tree Ranch, hugged her as though she was surprised that she had made it back alive. "Let me get a good look at you!"

Her aunt Barb was dressed in slim, dark-wash blue jeans, a cranberry button-down shirt that, tucked in and belted, looked polished as always and smelled like vanilla with a hint of light musk.

"You've lost weight." Her aunt put her hands on Taylor's cheeks and smiled at her affectionately.

Taylor looked down at her full figure that felt less *full*. "I thought so—my jeans are looser."

"Are you hungry?"

Taylor wasn't surprised that her aunt wanted to feed her—Barb was an excellent cook and loved to spoil her family with food.

"I am—but I really need to take a shower. A *hot* shower."

Barb nodded her agreement and lowered her voice. "You are a bit ripe."

Taylor laughed at her aunt's attempt at diplomacy. She knew that she stank. She'd given up on trying to fight it a week into the trek—she'd always sweated through her deodorant thirty minutes into her day on the trail.

"Clint—you'll take care of all of this…" Barb turned her attention to the cowboy, who had been quietly standing nearby with the two horses and mule.

"Yes, ma'am." Clint tipped his hat to Barb and then caught Taylor's eye for the briefest moment.

"Thank you, Clint." Barb said. "And thank you for watching out for my niece."

And, just like that, their lives shifted. For a month, they had been alone together and they made the rules. But now they were back at the ranch. Here, Clint was an employee and she was family.

"Go on and get yourself cleaned up." Barb physically turned Taylor around and gave her a gentle push in the direction of her cousin Tyler's log cabin. "The guest room's all set up for you. When you're done, head over to the main house for something to eat. You want breakfast or lunch?"

"Breakfast!" After a month of protein bars, trail mix, and fish, she'd earned a splurge. "Pancakes, please… with a mountain of butter and a boatload of syrup!"

Once inside her cousin's rustic log cabin, which had been built strategically near the main farmhouse, she stripped out of her filthy clothing, turned the hot water on full blast and stood beneath the steaming water until the water started to turn tepid as the hot water began to run out. A hot shower had *never* felt that good. In fact, she couldn't remember a time when a genuinely clean bath towel felt this good on her skin.

Once her body was damp dry, she wrapped the towel around her chest and went to the kitchen to hunt for a step stool. She found one in the pantry and carried it back to the bathroom. Just like a typical man, Tyler didn't have a full-length mirror in the house. When her cousin returned from Virginia, Taylor was confident that his new bride, London, would fix that bachelor design flaw. Until then, she was going to have to be creative in her attempt to get a full view of her post-CDT body.

Back in the bathroom, she used her towel to wipe off the condensation on the mirror hanging above the sink. The mirror wasn't completely clear—but it was clear enough. Naked, in front of a mirror, hadn't happened in years. She usually averted her eyes when she got out of the shower to avoid seeing the shape her body had adopted during the middle and later portions of her thirties. For so long she had hated how she looked in clothing, much less how she looked disrobed.

"Here goes nothing." Taylor dropped the towel to the floor and stepped up onto the sturdy little handmade step stool.

In the still-foggy mirror, she could see her body from the knees upward. She started at her changed body—not as transformed as she would have liked—but it was undeniably different. She turned to the side, her hands skimming the flesh to combine the tactile with the visual. Her breasts still drooped way too much without a bra, this was true, yet her stomach was much flatter than it had been when she left for the CDT.

"Wow." She faced the mirror again.

Her figure, which was still full, had this wonderful hourglass curviness to it now. She had a waist! Her thighs were thinner and the hardened muscles from a month of riding and hiking had shaped her legs beautifully—there was actual space between her thighs now. *Actual space!* It wasn't a tiny, petite, thin-framed naked body, but it was a very sexy, curvy body.

"Not bad." Taylor said to her reflection. "Not perfect—but…better."

The head-to-knee examination of her body made her want to indulge in pancakes less. If she was going to keep her post-CDT body, she was going to have to watch out for her weak spot, *sugar*.

"Seconds?" Her aunt held up the bowl of pancake batter.

Taylor had a mouthful of the last giant bite of pancakes soaked with sweet maple syrup and salted melted butter. She shook her head *no* quickly before her aunt took her silence as a *yes*, as she was known to do. Once the batter hit the griddle, Taylor would be locked into another stack.

"I'll just save the batter for later, then." Barb took a roll of tinfoil out of a drawer.

"It was so good, though, Aunt Barb," Taylor said after she had devoured that last bite. "Thank you."

Her aunt smiled with pleasure. "I'm glad you enjoyed it. Coffee?"

Taylor brought her dirty dishes to the sink. "I'll make it."

"Thank you, sweetheart."

Taylor went to the cabinet where the coffee had been located prior to her trek; it wasn't there.

"Where'd the coffee go?"

"Oh—I moved it." Her aunt closed the refrigerator door. "Look in the last cabinet—first shelf."

Taylor smiled as she retrieved the coffee. She remembered from when she was a kid that her aunt had a reputation in the family for rearranging her kitchen whenever she was upset or stressed. Taylor scooped coffee into the filter and then pressed the On button on the coffeemaker. While she helped her aunt clean up the kitchen, Taylor told Barbara, in animated language, all about her once-in-a-lifetime trip on the CDT.

There were a few details that she didn't reveal—the pregnancy deal she had struck with Clint was a secret she intended to keep until she became pregnant. If her scheme didn't work, then she didn't see any reason to tell anyone in the family beyond her sister, Casey.

"Well..." Barbara sat down at the kitchen table with her coffee. "I'm glad that you made it back safely. You got in touch with your parents, yes? I know your mom has to be sick with worry."

Taylor joined her aunt at the table with her own cup of freshly brewed coffee and shook her head. That was just her aunt Barb being nice. Her mom, a die-hard socialite, wasn't worried—she was angry. Her mother was angry about how the divorce reflected on the family. Her mother hadn't approved of the divorce, particularly since Christopher's family were active members in their country club. And her mother was angry that she had quit her career for any other reason than to raise socialite grandchildren. Vivian Bartlett-Brand and Taylor, although genetically mother and daughter, had rarely seen eye to eye on any topic; she had given up on ever obtaining her mother's approval around the time she turned thirty.

"I'll shoot her an email."

Her aunt looked at her over the rim of her coffee mug—a look that bordered on disapproval. It was a fact that there wasn't any love lost between Barbara and her mother, but her aunt would still expect Taylor to show deference to her.

"Do you know what you're going to do next?" Her aunt pursued a different subject.

"I was hoping it would be okay if I hung out at the ranch a little longer."

"You are welcome to stay here for as long as you want, Taylor. If you like, you can stay in Tyler's guest room until he gets back."

"Thank you." She liked staying in Tyler's guest room. His house was close to the main house, but offered a level of privacy she would need if Clint decided to go through with the handshake deal they had made. "Any word on that?" she asked her aunt.

Tyler's new wife had a child from a previous marriage and was embroiled in a custody battle. Until the situation was resolved, London's son, J.T., had to remain in Virginia. And, until London was free to be with him in Montana, Tyler was dedicated to sticking it out in Virginia.

"No." Barbara sighed. "I'm afraid it's going to drag out much longer than any of us ever suspected."

"I'm sorry."

"Me, too." Her aunt smiled a small, melancholy smile. "I hate that I'm missing so much of Maggie's life. When she was born, I always imagined her here—at the ranch—just across the way."

Soon after Tyler and London's daughter, Maggie, was born, they left Montana for Virginia to fight for the right to raised J.T. at Bent Tree Ranch. They had been gone several months before Taylor had arrived at the ranch.

"Well…no sense dwelling on the negative when you can dwell on the positive." Her aunt put her hand on Taylor's hand. "I'm blessed that you're here after so many years." Barb stood up. "And I'm blessed that Sophia and Luke are back in Montana with me. You haven't met their children yet, have you?"

"No." Taylor joined her aunt at the sink. "I've seen pictures."

"They're joining us for dinner tonight, so you'll get to get to know their three little ones all at once."

Taylor rinsed out her cup and set it, upside down, in the drainer. "Do you need help fixing dinner?"

"Sophia'll be here to help around four, if you still feel like helping out."

Taylor headed back to the cabin after agreeing to meet her cousin-in-law, Sophia, and aunt in the kitchen at four. On the porch, Clint had piled up her belongings from the trip. She couldn't deny the fact that she was disappointed that she had missed him. It was odd not to know his every move now that they were back in civilization. Where was he now? And, when would she see him again?

"Taylor! You look *incredible*!" Casey Brand exclaimed loudly. "Holy cannoli!"

Taylor had moved away from the computer camera

so her younger sister could get the full image of her post-CDT figure.

"Be honest." Taylor sat back down at the breakfast bar. "Can you really tell the difference?"

"I swear, Taylor. You look like you dropped two sizes *at least*. Your clothes must be huge on you now. You're going to need a whole new wardrobe!"

Her jeans were looser in the waist and in the legs, but she still had her birthing hips. And, just maybe, they might actually come in handy.

"I might—but not the kind that you think."

"That was cryptic." Casey's eyebrows lifted suspiciously. "What's up?"

Taylor felt as though she had to tell *someone* about her bargain with Clint. Casey was the only person she knew she could trust a hundred percent.

"You can't tell another living soul, Casey…" Taylor told her sister.

"Spill it!" Her sister leaned into the camera. "Start at the *beginning* and tell me *everything*!"

Spilling the beans was exactly what she needed. For the next hour, she shared all of those juicy CDT experiences that she would never share with the rest of the family. But Casey, who had always been more open about sexuality, would be proud of her for having a hot fling with a Sam Elliott look-alike cowboy.

"Wait. Wait, wait, *wait*!" Casey flipped backward onto her mountain of decorative pillows dramatically and then popped back upright with an amazed expression on her face. "Are you telling me that you could be pregnant *right now*?"

Taylor looked down at her flatter stomach. "It's possible."

On her last visit with the fertility doctor, her blood tests confirmed that she wasn't out of the procreation game just yet. Close, but the door wasn't completely shut.

"And this cowboy..."

"Clint." Taylor filled in the name for her sister.

"So...this cowboy, Clint...he already made his *deposit* before you made *your* deposit?"

Taylor laughed. "Several deposits, actually."

"Holy cannoli." Her sister gave an amazed shake of her head. "I, for one, applaud you."

"You know, Mom and Dad won't be applauding me." Taylor frowned a little.

Casey waved her hand like she was swatting a pesky fly. "Please—Mom's too busy trying to convince Dad that they need a new yacht for their annual migration. She won't even notice you've got a kid until it's old enough to talk."

"True." Taylor couldn't disagree. Their mother had always been obsessed with keeping up with the Joneses.

"Darn it—I've got to get myself ready for work tomorrow. But I want a play-by-play on this new project of yours. Swear! Hi to Uncle Hank and Aunt Barb!"

They ended the video chat with a promise to make time each week to catch up. She was lucky—her sister had always been her best friend, and she would always keep Casey in the loop. If she did succeed in pulling off the nearly impossible and she *did* get pregnant with the cowboy's baby, she would need her sister's unwavering support more than ever.

A week had gone by since she returned from the CDT. In some ways it had gone by so quickly. She loved meeting her three little second cousins, Danny, Abigail and Annabelle; she had enjoyed reconnecting with her cousin, Luke, and his wife, Sophia. But, there was a noticeable hole in her daily life that Clint used to fill, and it worried her that she hadn't seen him since they had returned. She had watched out for him, and she would be lying to herself if she didn't acknowledge that it bothered her that he hadn't sought her out since their return.

"Look how handsome you are," Taylor greeted the gangly colt vying for her attention. "I've heard so much about you, Rising Star..."

The young colt whickered softly, his ears perked forward, eyes wide at the prospect of getting one of the small apples she had in her hand.

"Here you go, handsome boy." Taylor fed the horse one of the apples and took the opportunity to rub the young colt's neck.

"I knew I recognized that voice."

Taylor spun around. She recognized *that* voice. That deep, sexy, rough-around-the edges voice that could only belong to her cowboy sent shivers skipping down the middle of her spine, from the nape of her neck to her lower back.

"Where have you been?" Her question was much more honest and much more raw than she had intended.

"Brock had me moving the herd. I got back late last night."

He was a sight for sore eyes, as the saying went. His beard had been clipped back, and his long hair was pulled back into a ponytail at the nape of his neck.

"I've been looking for you." He stared hard into her eyes.

"I was afraid I'd never see you again."

Clint's eyes narrowed a little, then he grabbed her hand and started walking toward a small office at the far end of the barn. Taylor knew that Clint wanted to take her to a private place—she could read it in his eyes. He wanted the same thing she wanted: a stolen moment alone.

Clint closed the office door behind them and locked it. Wordlessly, he took her into his arms and kissed her. He broke the kiss, spun her around so her back was pressed into his body. He wrapped his arms around her, filling one hand with her breast while the other hand slipped behind the elastic waistband of her bohemian skirt and down into her panties.

"Oh..." Taylor's head dropped back onto his shoulder, her eyes closed.

"You missed me," Clint murmured into her neck.

The minute her ears had heard his voice again her body had started revving up—when he slipped his hand into her panties, she couldn't pretend to be aloof.

The cowboy pulled her tighter into his body, his teeth grazing the skin of her neck. "My body's been hurting for you."

She moved her hand in between them and covered the bulge in his jeans. He wanted her as badly as she wanted him.

Clint left her for a moment to stack up some bales of sweet-smelling alfalfa. At first, she didn't know why he'd stopped their lover's moment to do that, but then Clint led her over to the bales of hay stacked waist high against the wall and she understood exactly what he intended to do.

The cowboy lifted her up onto the top bale, slid his hands under her skirt, hooked his fingers onto the waistband of her panties, and then pulled them down her legs and over her boots. With a look that could only be described as devilish, Clint tucked her panties into the front pocket of his jeans before he unbuttoned and unzipped his jeans.

"Are you sure nobody can come in?" she asked urgently.

Clint gently pushed her knees apart, stepped between her open thighs and guided his shaft to the center of her body with his hand. And, then, just like that, so quick and so quiet, Clint was inside of her.

"God...*damn*." The cowboy pressed himself as deep inside of Taylor as he could get.

Taylor tried to stifle the sounds of pleasure that were in her throat. She hugged Clint tightly and kissed him.

"Hold on to me." Clint ordered in a gravelly voice as he braced his body by pressing his palms against the wall behind them.

A second after he growled his command, Clint began to love her with fervor and an intensity that was beyond her experience. It was hard and fast and demanding and urgent; all she could do was hold on to his body and let him take her for the ride of her life. The sensation of his hard, thick shaft sliding in and out of her slick center, again and again and again, brought her to a quick peak.

"Ah...ah...*ah*!"

When Clint heard Taylor start her sweet whimpering, he pounded into her body harder, deeper and faster until he was ready to join her. He grabbed her round bottom, pulled her into his groin and exploded. Breathless and stunned by what had just happened, Taylor could feel each shudder of Clint's body as he found his release.

Clint reached back to the wall and held himself up until he could catch his breath.

"I suppose this means the deal's still on?" Taylor asked with a breathy laugh.

Clint pulled up his pants with an odd look on his face that she couldn't quite read. Instead of trying to decode the cowboy, she held out her hand.

"Panties, please."

They both finished dressing—Clint zipped up his pants and buckled his belt buckle while she pulled her panties back on.

"I've got to get back before someone notices I've gone missin'." He unlocked the door.

"Wait—don't you think we should talk?"

"Leave your door unlocked." The cowboy said before he opened the door. "We'll talk tonight."

Chapter Ten

"A bed beats the ground, hands down." Taylor was on her back, naked, with only a sheet covering the lower half of her body.

"Lady—you've got some strong-ass thigh muscles." Clint had one arm behind his head; his free hand was on one of the thighs to which he was referring. "I felt like I was being squeezed by an incredibly sexy nutcracker."

She laughed again and curled her body toward him; she was happy that he was with her, next to her. She had waited for hours for their rendezvous. Near midnight she had finally given up and gotten into bed. Right before she nodded off, she heard the front door open. Clint had locked the door behind him and found her in the hall. Neither one of them wanted to talk about the details of their agreement. Both of them, without discussing it, wanted to find out what it would be like to make love in a bed for the first time.

Clint, who had taken the edge off when they had their lover's tryst in the barn, let her have her way with him. She wanted to be on top, and she wanted her pleasure slow and sensual, and she wanted multiple orgasms. And she got them. She reached one fabulous peak after another until Clint couldn't hold off any longer. It was, for her, the most incredible, empowering lovemaking of her life.

"I stayed on longer than eight seconds." Taylor moved her fingers through the hair on Clint's chest.

"Hell, yeah, you did."

She could feel Clint's laughter beneath her fingers.

"What do you want, Clint? For what you are doing for me—or trying to do for me—what do you want?"

"So—that's how you're gonna do me?"

Taylor lifted her head a little. "What do you mean by that?"

"You get me into bed, ride me like a stud and then *boom*, right down to business."

When she didn't respond right away, he added. "That was a joke."

"It was *really* funny," she retorted dryly.

Clint hugged her affectionately. "You're gonna get me yet, Taylor."

The cowboy kissed her one last time on the lips before he untangled himself from the sheets and got out of bed.

"You're leaving?"

He pulled his T-shirt on over his head. "Got to."

Taylor sat up. "But we haven't talked yet."

"Don't worry. We'll get to it."

"That's what you said last time about this time," she reminded him. Wasn't it in *his* best interest to hammer out the details?

Taylor watched him in silhouette as he tugged his jeans on. He sat down on the bed so he could pull on his boots.

"At least tell me what you want," she pressed.

Clint pushed his hair out of his face before he put his hat on. He leaned over and kissed her again on the lips.

"I want my truck and fifth wheel out of hock and enough money to hold me until I start winning again."

"That's it?"

"Well..." he added after a second or two of thought. "I suppose I could do with a new pair of boots."

How many months of her life had she watched the calendar, praying that she wouldn't start to feel those telltale signs that her period was a few days away? This time was different. For the first time in her life, she *felt* different. She wasn't bloated, she hadn't gotten her obligatory period pimple on her chin, she hadn't craved chocolate, and her breasts were not sore. And, more important, she was a week overdue. True—as she had approached forty, her period was shorter and less regular, but still. It was possible that the cowboy's super sperm had managed to do in one month what Christopher's unambitious sperm had failed to accomplish—hit the target!

Exactly one day past the one-week mark, Taylor awakened early, sprang out of bed and raced to the bathroom. She had two early-detection pregnancy tests out of their boxes, out of the wrapping, and ready to rock and roll. Up with the toilet seat, down with the panties, Taylor sat down on the seat and grabbed the first test.

"Please, please, *please* be pregnant," she said aloud.

One test down, she grabbed the second test and peed on the stick.

"Please, please, *please* be pregnant!"

She forced herself not to look at the results until she had finished her business in the bathroom. If she was pregnant, she didn't want the story to her child to be that she found out about him or her next to the commode in her cousin's guest bathroom.

Without looking at the result window for that coveted plus sign, she moved the event into the living room. The living room had a beautiful vaulted ceiling with large, rough-hewn beams and a wall of glass with a view out to a pond in the forefront and majestic mountain peaks capped with white in the distant background. It was the perfect place to find out if she had gotten the one gift that had eluded her for most of her adult life—a child.

Taylor sat down on the edge of the couch and held the two tests clutched in her hands with her eyes closed.

"Dear God—I love you and I accept your plan for me."

Taylor opened her eyes to face the results. She stared at the one test that was facing upward with the results window visible. After a second of staring, she turned the second test over and read that. Tears started to flow from her eyes, down her cheeks—a couple fell onto the tests, dropping with a little splash onto the clear plastic window of the results screens. Crying had always been an infrequent indulgence, but today, after getting the results from not one, but *two* pregnancy tests, she felt that she had *earned* those tears.

Compared to the two years, hours of mediation, and thousands of dollars it had taken to split assets and dissolve her marriage with Christopher, it had been ridiculously easy to strike a baby bargain with Clint. He was a simple man with simple needs, the complete opposite of her ex-husband. And that wasn't to say that Clint was simple-minded—she had grown to understand and appreciate the cowboy's intelligence on their journey on the CDT. He required less to live—he valued his time, his freedom and his cowboy lifestyle. Accumulating *stuff* wasn't on his radar. And it occurred to her that she had quite a bit to learn from a person who could live a happy, full life that was stripped down to the necessities.

Taylor knocked on the door of Clint's fifth-wheel trailer that, as part of their deal, had been paid off and brought back to the ranch along with the cowboy's truck. As it turned out, the proceeds from the sale of her wedding rings had gone to a good cause—hers. She sold them and used part of the money to get Clint's trailer and truck out of hock.

"Hey..." Clint answered the door shirtless with his wet hair slicked back from his face.

The cowboy looked over her head toward the farmhouse.

"I know." She read his mind. "It's broad daylight. Anyone can see me."

"That's about the size of it."

"If you're okay with it, I'm okay with it."

"I was only thinkin' 'bout you."

He was someone in her life, up to date, who had consistently watched out for her. She trusted his sincerity.

"Thank you."

He understood her concern, but she was the mistress of her own life. She hadn't shared her baby bargain with her family, beyond her sister, because it was personal and really none of their business. When it was the right time to tell them, she wouldn't hesitate to do it. Good or bad, she had always stood by her decisions.

"You're my friend and I want to see your home."

He met her eyes, took a second to think and then backed away from the door so she could come in. Taylor stepped up into the trailer and was met with a compact, fully functional kitchen with an island and black granite countertops.

"I'm surprised." Her eyes wanted to look everywhere. "It's a lot bigger than I thought it would be."

"Grab a seat anywhere." Clint pointed to the living area to the left of the kitchen. "I'll get back with you in a minute."

Clint headed to the other end of the trailer where Taylor assumed the bedroom was housed, while she headed to the living room and dining area. The inside of the trailer was clean and updated and organized. Clint had always presented as a ragtag cowboy—this was unexpected. In the carpeted living area were two reclining chairs, a big-screen TV, a small desk and a couch next to a dining set that seated four. Taylor looked around and finally decided to take a seat at the table.

Clint reappeared wearing a fresh white T-shirt. His hair was pulled back into a ponytail.

"You want somethin' to drink? A beer?"

"I wouldn't mind some water." Her mouth felt dry.

He joined her at the table with a bottle of water for her and a bottle of beer for himself.

"You okay?" Clint asked her after he took a swig of his beer.

She nodded her head and gestured to his trailer with her finger. "I like your place."

"Thank you." His eyes moved around his home. "It would've been auctioned if it weren't for you."

"Well…I'm glad that you got your home back."

"I got my life back because I met you," Clint told her plainly. "I thought I'd flat run outta luck."

Their eyes met. "Me, too."

There was a break in the conversation. Clint drank his beer while she mustered the nerve to say what she had come to say.

"I know you want to get back on the rodeo circuit as soon as you can."

Clint went to the kitchen to get another beer. "Maybe next year. I'm not leavin' until we see our deal through."

"Well…" Taylor pulled a check out of her pocket and slid it across the table to him. "I think you're going to get back to it a lot sooner than that."

He picked up the check and looked at it before he put it upside down on the table.

"I'm pregnant."

She smiled shyly at him—she didn't really know how he would take the news.

"I'm pregnant." She repeated the words more strongly. "I thought you should be the first to know."

Nothing could prepare him for this moment. He'd made a deal with Taylor—he would give her a life, a child, so he could get his life back. And he didn't regret it. He'd wondered if he would—he didn't. Biologically he was the father of her unborn child—but he had been contractually absolved of any financial responsibility, so he wouldn't play the role of dad. It was strange for him to think that this would be the *second* biological child he had out in the world.

"Congratulations, Taylor." He finally felt ready to speak.

He stood up and held out his hand to her. They had made love many times, but they hadn't hugged very often. Yet being held tightly in this cowboy's arms felt like home.

"Thank you, Clint." Her head was resting on his chest. "You can't possibly know what you've given me."

After the embrace, Taylor didn't sit back down at the table. "I have to get going. I promised Aunt Barb I'd help her with dinner tonight."

Clint walked her to the door. Before she opened the door, she paused and turned her head to look at him.

"I'll leave the door unlocked for you." There was a question mark in her statement.

Clint smiled at her with his eyes. "Then I'll see you later."

After dinner Taylor headed back to her temporary home for a video date with her sister. It had been a quiet meal with her aunt and uncle, but inside she was bursting. She couldn't *wait* to tell Casey the news.

"I've got the most incredible news!" Casey's face was lit up with happy excitement.

"Do you?" Taylor leaned back against her pillows with a smile. "I have some pretty incredible news to share of my own."

"Probably not as good as mine, but you go ahead…"

"No." Taylor kept on smiling at her little sister. "You go first."

"That was the right choice, my friend." Casey bent to the side and disappeared from the view of the camera.

When her sister popped back upright, she was holding a black half boot in her hands and she had the wide grin of a Cheshire cat on her face.

"After *months* of saving—look what came in the mail today!" Casey spoke in a singsong voice and held the boot closer to the camera so Taylor could only see the boot and her sister's fingernails, lacquered a deep plum color.

"A boot?"

Casey lowered the boot a little with a horrified expression on her pixy face. "A boot? This is *clearly* not just any boot. You do see that?"

"Not really."

Casey groaned dramatically. "This is the Jimmy Choo crushed leather Burke boot."

When her sister didn't get the response she was after, she repeated with emphasis. "Jimmy Choo. *Burke boot.*"

"You know I don't follow fashion. But it's nice."

"Nice?" Casey took the boot away. "*Nice?* How could we have possibly been raised in the same house? It's like you were raised on a hippy commune."

"Sorry." Taylor laughed. "I really do like them..."

"You obviously do not understand the significance of owning these boots. So I can't talk to you about them anymore," Casey said teasingly. "So—what's your news?"

In Taylor's hand, she held the two positive pregnancy tests in front of the camera for her sister to see.

After a second of silence, Casey screamed. "You're pregnant?"

"I'm pregnant."

"Oh, Taylor..." Casey had her hand up near her mouth; her eyes were wide with wonder and surprise. "You're going to have a baby."

"Are you crying?" Taylor asked her sister. "If you start, I'm going to start!"

"I'm so happy for you." Casey wiped the tears off her cheeks. "I'm just so happy for you. You're going to be a mom, Tay. I'm going to be an *aunt*!"

"It means a lot that you support me." There were tears in Taylor's eyes.

"Of course I support you! What else? I mean—just look at you. I've never seen you this happy before."

"I never have been this happy." Taylor wiped her eyes. "I'm happier right now than I've ever been in my whole entire life."

That night, Clint came to her. They had been lovers with a purpose, and now that they had completed that purpose, Taylor didn't know if they would ever make love again. She waited for him in the living room. When he arrived, he took her hand and led her to the bedroom. This time, when he made love to her—and it felt more like making love than anything she had experienced before—it was slow and sweet, and careful. His lovemaking was different this time. It felt like he was saying goodbye.

Afterward, they lay together, naked, in the dark, holding hands.

"When will you leave?" she asked him quietly.

He squeezed her fingers. "I told Brock that I'd be leaving at the end of the week."

She knew he would be going, but she hadn't known he would leave so soon.

"Are you okay?"

"Yes." She turned into his body and put her free hand on his chest. "You're worried about me, aren't you?"

"I feel like I'm doin' somethin' wrong by leavin' you."

"You're *not* leaving me, Clint. You're going back to your life." She wanted to reassure him. "I'm happy for you."

When he didn't answer her, she continued.

"You're worried about doing the right thing by me… because I'm pregnant with your child."

"I suppose that's right."

Taylor sat up so she could make sure she got her point across. "I don't want you to feel that way, Clint. I'm great. I'm better than great. You don't have to do right by me—that wasn't part of our deal. I'm going to be a single mother and I'm prepared for it. If I could have had what other women had with the husband and the children and the picket fence, I would have taken it in a heartbeat. But those weren't the cards I was dealt. So I'm making my own family, my own way. And honestly—I feel like I just won the jackpot. Go live your life, Clint. Because I promise you, I'm gonna be living the heck out of mine."

At the end of the week, Clint was up at the crack of dawn to get ready to leave Bent Tree Ranch. He could pick up the circuit in Colorado, and if he could keep from getting injured too badly, he'd put some winnings in his pocket. No doubt about it, the older he got, the harder it was to bounce back from his injuries. Staying out of the emergency room was priority number one. But he couldn't wait to get back on the bulls.

"Good morning." Taylor found Clint kneeling down at the back of his truck hooking up the taillights for the fifth wheel.

"Mornin'. I didn't expect you to get up this early to see me off."

"I know you didn't. I wanted to say one last goodbye."

The cowboy finished his chore, stood up, and walked over to where she was standing. He fixed the collar of her coat so it was protecting her neck from the early morning chill.

"I'm glad you did."

They put their arms around each other, not bothering to worry about any potential raised eyebrows. Clint had become a friend. He would always be the biological father of her child.

"When are you set to leave?"

"Right now."

Her chest clenched a little. She would miss her cowboy. They walked together to the driver's side of his truck.

"Did you say goodbye to your stepbrother?"

"No." Clint stopped walking. "That's not how we work."

In the low morning light, they hugged each other tight. Then her cowboy kissed her one last time.

"You'll take good care of yourself." Clint tucked a strand of her hair behind her ear.

She nodded. "You've given me the best reason in the world."

He let her go then and opened the driver's door.

"You know, Clint—I hated you when I first met you. I really did."

That made him laugh.

"But now—I'm grateful that we met."

Before he got into the truck, he took off his cowboy hat and put it on her head.

"It suits you." He climbed into the cab of the truck and rolled down the window. "Is it all right if I call you every now and again to see how you're doin'?"

"If that's what you want." Taylor stepped back when he started the engine.

She stood in the spot where his rig had been parked. She waved until the bright red taillights of his trailer disappeared from view. Perhaps he would call or perhaps he was simply being nice. It was okay with Taylor either way. Every ounce of her physical energy, every ounce of her mental energy, had to be spent bringing a healthy baby into the world.

Chapter Eleven

"So…what do you think?" Sophia Lee Brand, the wife of her cousin Luke, asked her.

They were walking through the neighborhood in Helena where Luke and Sophia had purchased a cozy Craftsman bungalow for their family of five.

"I really like it here." Taylor told her cousin-in-law. "I think this could work for me. At least, for the short term."

It was a perfectly clear day—cloudless periwinkle-blue skies stretched as far as the eye could see. There was a panoramic view of the mountain peaks off in the far distance. The houses in the neighborhood were new construction, built around a central park, and Taylor understood why Sophia and Luke had chosen to buy there. There were many houses still under construction, and many more lots for sale, but already there was a sense of community. The voices of the children playing in the park carried to the surrounding houses; families waved or stopped to chat as they walked to and from the park. It seemed like a lovely, wholesome, safe place to raise children.

Sophia, who was carrying her daughter Abigail, stopped and waited for her son to catch up with them on his bicycle.

“You’re doing great, Danny!” Sophia encouraged her tow-headed son.

Taylor was holding Abigail’s twin sister, Annabelle, in her arms. The little toddler had fine blond hair pulled up into pigtails, her legs were soft and chubby, and her eyes were that signature Brand-family bluest, sapphire blue. Taylor hugged her sweet-tempered second cousin. Holding this little girl in her arms made her fantasize about the day she would hold her own daughter or son. She had always wanted a little girl. Always. But watching Danny, so determined and daring on his brand-new training-wheel bike, made her think that a son would make her just as happy.

Now that she was pregnant, she’d discovered that the wish for a *healthy* baby overshadowed any gender preference she had ever had. At her age, she was acutely aware of her status as a high-risk pregnancy. She was also acutely aware of the fact that her unborn child was at a higher risk for being born with a genetic condition like Down syndrome. She was concerned—she was cautious—she was doing everything she could to make sure she had the healthiest pregnancy possible. But, ultimately, she was prepared to love her child no matter what.

"Mommy—watch me!" Danny pedaled by them, his legs churning furiously.

"I'm watching!" Sophia called out to her son with a smile. To Taylor she said, "Will you look at that tongue? Just like Luke—whenever he's concentrating really hard he sticks his tongue out. I swear one day we're going to have to take him to the hospital to get the tip of his tongue stitched. I've tried to get him to stop, but he does it unconsciously."

Now that Danny was in front of them, they started walking again.

"I'd really love it if you decided to live here, too," Sophia said. "It would be great to have you as a neighbor."

"You said there were a couple of rentals available?"

Sophia pointed with a nod. "This house coming up here on the left and one more on the other side of the park."

She was roughly six weeks into her pregnancy and it was very tempting to move into town. Her OB/GYN wanted to see her every two weeks. Bent Tree Ranch was an hour outside of Helena and that trek wouldn't be fun to make when she was further along. It would be so much easier to be near her doctor and the hospital. She hadn't decided whether or not she would stay in Montana permanently, but she had decided to stay in Montana until her baby was born. She had been spending a lot of time with Sophia, and she liked the idea of building a friendship with a woman who was already a mother three times over.

"How do you like living in Montana? It must be culture shock after living in Boston."

Sophia shrugged and gave a little shake of her head, sending her thick, honey-blond ponytail flipping back and forth. "I'm having a hard time of it. I'm not used to being a stay-at-home mom—that's an adjustment—I'm not used to so much quiet and fresh air—that's an adjustment. Even with neighbors, sometimes I feel like I'm living smack dab in the middle of nowhere. But Luke seems to be doing…better. He likes working with other veterans who served in Iraq and Afghanistan."

Sophia crossed her fingers and held them up in the air. "And, fingers crossed, he seems to like his therapist at the VA—Luke was diagnosed with PTSD—I'm not sure you knew that. But, anyway, living in the city was just too much for him. He was always freaked out and guarded—it got to the point where even going to the grocery store was hard for him—so we moved back to Montana hoping that it would be easier for him to be back somewhere familiar without so much *stimulation* all over the place."

Sophia sent her a self-conscious smile. "Please don't get the impression that I'm not happy here. I'm happy to be anywhere my husband can feel better. And Danny loves his preschool. In time, I'll adjust and I'll love it, too. I hope."

"Do you think that you'll go back to work anytime soon?" Sophia was a licensed psychologist. "Maybe open a new practice?"

"I want to, for sure. I've already seen a couple of spots in town where I'd love to set up shop. But I'm going to hold off until I get the girls in school and then I'll look into it. Can you stay for lunch?"

Annabelle had wiggled out of her arms and was running, on chubby legs, after her older brother. Taylor took the opportunity to snap a picture of the for-rent sign posted in the lawn of a cornflower-blue bungalow that was cattycorner from Sophia and Luke's house.

"Sure."

Abigail wanted to join her sister—she started wiggling and protesting until Sophia put her down.

"Are you hungry, Danny?" Sophia called out to her son, who had reached the driveway of their house.

"Chicken fingers!" Danny got off his bike and ran up the sidewalk toward the front door.

"Of course," Sophia said to Taylor with a frustrated sigh. "That's all he wants to eat. It drives me crazy."

Sophia scooped up Abigail as she cut across the front lawn of their house.

"Will you bring Annabelle?" Sophia nodded to her second toddler, who was squatting in the lawn, digging in the grass with a stick. "She'd stay out here all day trying to dig to China if we'd let her."

Taylor was happy to bring Annabelle into the house, just as she was happy to help Sophia prepare lunch for all of them. Danny, as his mother had warned her, had a major meltdown when chicken fingers weren't on the menu. But once he realized that the tantrum wasn't working, he settled down and ate his sandwich. After lunch Danny had computer time and the twins were put down for a nap.

"I need some coffee." Sophia came back to the kitchen. "Want a cup?"

"Do you have decaf?"

"Decaf?" Her cousin's wife laughed. "No. Luke thinks decaf is the work of the devil."

Taylor smiled. Her cousin Luke, Hank and Barbara's eldest son, had spent twenty years on active duty in the Marines and he liked his coffee high octane.

"I'll pass then." Taylor took a seat at the breakfast bar so she could still interact with Sophia while she was in the kitchen.

Sophia filled the coffee pot with water from the sink. "I get it. I wish I could give it up. I've tried before, but I get headaches. And, honestly, I'm worthless in the morning until I have my first cup of coffee. Are you trying to quit just because?"

Taylor didn't like lying. She'd never been particularly adroit at it, so she avoided telling even white lies when she could. She liked Sophia. Sophia was smart and sweet, and had the makings of a really good friend. And, more than that, they were family. Taylor didn't want to start their budding friendship telling lies.

"No. I have a reason," Taylor told her new friend. "I'm pregnant."

Sophia stopped what she was doing to look up at her.

"Did you just say you were pregnant?"

Taylor nodded.

Sophia, who had the reputation in the family for being a sweetheart, immediately came around to her side of the counter and gave her a hug.

"I had no idea! Barb never said a word!"

"She doesn't know yet.

Sophia looked at her strangely. "Is it a secret?"

"No. Not really." Taylor shook her head. "It's just really new."

"It must be." Sophia looked down at her stomach. "You can't be more than a month or two..."

"Six weeks—roughly."

"And the father...? It's not your ex-husband..."

This was the tricky part—fielding questions about the father and her relationship with the father. She knew they were going to come; it was natural for people to ask questions about paternity. And Clint, who was beholden to no one, had given his consent for her to reveal the paternity of the child or keep it private. It was totally up to her.

"I'm prying." Sophia must have read the conflict on her face. "Forget I asked."

What she immediately respected and liked about her cousin's wife was Sophia's complete lack of judgment. Luke's wife felt a child was a blessing no matter how it came to be and she didn't have to know all of the details in order to celebrate with her.

"Do you already have an OB/GYN? The doctor I had here when I gave birth to Danny was amazing. I think I still have one of her cards in my wallet."

"I actually overheard you talking about your doctor to Aunt Barb and I called her."

Sophia put her hand on her arm with a genuine smile. "Perfect. Have you already had your first appointment?"

Taylor nodded. "Next week I'm scheduled for my first ultrasound. I hope I can hear the baby's heartbeat by then."

"It might be a little too soon. But maybe." Sophia poured herself a cup of coffee. "Well—now I understand why you want to move closer to town. Bent Tree is too much of a hike when you're pregnant. Why don't we call about the rentals and see if we can get in to see them today? We could go right after the girls get up from their nap."

Clint rested his forearms on the wall of the shower, bent his head down and let the hot water run down his aching shoulders and lower back. He'd had some luck back on the bull-riding circuit—he'd had some good rides and he'd had some really good times catching up with his buddies—but, today, his luck had run out. When he'd drawn the name of one of the biggest, meanest bulls on the circuit, he knew he was about to have a bad day.

He'd managed to hold on for six seconds, but that old bull twisted and turned and bucked until Clint lost his grip and flew off backward. Instead of landing on the ground, which at least had some give, he'd been thrown into the fence and broken one of the wooden slats with his back. From the nape of his neck, all the way down to his hips, he was covered in bruises.

"God damn, God damn, God damn..." Clint cringed when the water hit sections of chewed-up skin. "What the hell are you doin' to yourself, Clint?"

He'd be out for a few days, for sure, and making the drive to the next stop in Texas was going to be a bear. But this was the life. And he was glad to be back at it. The only thing that had nagged him ever since he'd left Montana was Taylor.

It didn't matter what she'd said to him or how many contracts they had signed or bargains they had struck—he still felt like a giant jackass for leaving her back at the ranch. She had wanted him to go—*hell*, she basically *told* him to go and backed him financially so he *could* go—and, yet, he couldn't get it out of his mind that it was just plain wrong. He wasn't perfect and he'd led a rough life, but he'd like to believe that he wasn't without honor.

Clint shut off the water and dried off as best he could. He'd been gone from the ranch for two weeks, and in that time he hadn't called Taylor. He'd wanted to—he'd missed talking to her. But he also didn't want to overstep his place. She was the kind of woman who had a mind to do things her way—and her way of having this baby was on her own without interference from him. Not that he *wanted* to interfere…he just wanted to hear her voice every now and again. He just wanted to see her pretty face and that pretty smile of hers.

Once he was dressed, Clint dialed Taylor's number. He couldn't believe that his stomach actually felt nervous at the thought of talking with her, felt nervous about the possibility that Taylor may not *want* to talk to him.

"Hey!" Taylor sounded happy to see his number come up on her phone. "I was just thinking about you! Where are you?"

God, it was good to hear her voice.

"Colorado. I'm heading out for Texas tomorrow." Clint's shoulders relaxed when he realized that his phone call was welcomed. "How are you?"

"I'm great. I looked at houses in Helena today. I'm thinking about renting for a while until I figure out my next move."

Taylor filled Clint in on her visit with Sophia, which blended into her sharing her experience with the first visit to her OB/GYN.

"I'm sorry…" Taylor scrunched her face. "I didn't even ask you if you wanted to know about the nitty-gritty details like that."

"You tell me whatever you want to tell me, Taylor. I want to know about you. I want to know that you're doin' okay."

After a pause when Taylor didn't fill the silence,

Clint decided to keep on talking. "I got somethin' I need to say to you…"

"Okay…"

"I'm real glad to hear your voice."

He paused again and this time he waited until she responded.

"I'm glad to hear your voice, too, Clint."

"Well, that's good then. We're on the same track here." He pushed his hair back out of his eyes. "Now I know that we made a deal for you to have this baby on your own. But that don't mean we can't…"

"…be friends?" She filled in the rest of the sentence for him.

"Yeah…" he agreed a moment later. "You know—talk, catch up, I tell you about my day, you tell me about yours…if you went to the doctor, that's a part of your day—I want you to tell me about it if you want to…"

Taylor smiled a pleased smile. She had become accustomed to talking to Clint—she was happy that he seemed to miss speaking with her as she had with him. In fact, he actually seemed a little nervous talking to her. It showed a vulnerable side of the tough, bull-riding cowboy—it was endearing.

"If I could, I'd talk 24/7 about my baby—so if you don't mind me talking about it, I am more than happy to share."

"You know I have this iPhone deal now, right?"

"That was an odd segue, but yes—I was there—I told you to join the twenty-first century and get a smartphone, yes."

"It's got this video dealio…"

"You want to learn how to use video chat?"

"Yeah—why not? I've got it—why not use it?"

"Hang up, then."

"Hang up?"

"Hang up, then press the video icon, select my number and voilà! You will be officially video chatting. Trust me. Hang up."

The next week she was at her first ultrasound appointment. If she couldn't hear the heartbeat, she could wait. But what she had to know—what she had been up all night worrying about—was would the doctor *see* a heartbeat? Was it a viable pregnancy? The only time she had conceived with Christopher, they couldn't detect a heartbeat at the eight week mark. After years of trying, after years of disappointment and thousands of dollars down the drain, they had lost the child.

After that, Christopher wasn't willing to spend one more penny on IVF. She didn't know it at the time—how could she have known?—but that was the end of their marriage. For her, it was the end of her chance to have a child and she never quite forgave him for making the decision for both of them. For him, as he was quick to tell her any time they had a disagreement, she had wasted the money for the Porsche he wanted, the boat he wanted, the vacation to Tahiti he never got to take…

"Okay…" The technician, who had been completely quiet during the first few minutes of the intravaginal ultrasound, turned the screen toward her and pointed to a little flicker on the screen. "There is the heartbeat."

The technician had no idea how much those four words meant to her. She left the ultrasound appointment feeling better and happier than she could remember ever feeling. This was, to date, one of the best days of her life. And, the first person she wanted to tell about it? Clint.

But first things first. She stopped by the agent who was in charge of the rental house catty-corner to Luke and Sophia's house, filled out the paperwork and signed a one-year lease. It was unfurnished, which wasn't ideal. All of her furniture was in storage and she didn't want to spend the money to replace everything. She would have to work out the furniture situation—there was time.

If she had to buy some pieces to make the rental livable, then that's what she would have to do. It didn't have to be perfect. And even though she'd like to be out of her cousin's cabin and into her own place sooner rather than later, there was no rush. At the very latest, she wanted to be moved into the rental during her second trimester.

"Hey! There's my pretty lady." Clint was now a regular user of the video-chat feature on his smartphone.

"Hi." She smiled more broadly. He said the same thing every time they video chatted, but it never got old. "You look tired."

"I am all the way worn out. I keep drivin' but I can't seem to get the heck outta Texas."

Clint shifted and she saw him wince.

"How's the shoulder?" she asked him, concerned. The last time Clint had climbed onto the back of a bull, he'd held on for eight "incredible" seconds and then he jumped off and executed what would have been a perfect tuck and roll—if his right arm had been in the right position. But, since the right arm wasn't in the right position, he had twisted his shoulder out of joint.

"I'll live." Clint winked at her. "I didn't call you to

hear myself complain—I want to hear about you. How are you?"

"Wonderful." She beamed. "I had an *amazing* day."

"Oh, yeah?" he asked before he lit a cigarette.

"Oh, yeah, I did! I had my six-week ultrasound today."

She was so glad that they were using video—the expression on Clint's face was the cherry on top of her ice-cream sundae of a day.

"I saw my baby's heartbeat today. I couldn't hear it yet, but I saw it."

The cowboy appeared to be stumped for something to say. It took him a moment to formulate the words. "That's good news, Taylor. I'm really happy for you."

"Thank you. I'm happy for me, too," she said to him. "But do you know what's better than seeing one heartbeat on the monitor?"

Clint blew out a stream of smoke before he asked. "No. What?"

"Seeing two."

Chapter Twelve

Thirty weeks into the pregnancy Taylor was settled in her bungalow—she had relented and bought new furniture for the house. It was a fresh start, after all. No sense dragging all of the furniture she had purchased for a house she had shared with her ex-husband all the way to Montana. Down the road, she would figure out what to do with everything she had in storage. It was too late for a yard sale.

"Oh, babies—you are going to be so happy in this room." Taylor rested her hands on her round belly.

She knew that she looked more pregnant than her seven months because she was carrying two beautiful angels instead of one, and she *loved* it. Yes, she had chronic hemorrhoids and indigestion and had to pee every five minutes. She didn't care. She loved being pregnant. None of the bad, or the uncomfortable, outweighed the miracle of her unborn twins.

Somewhere in her cozy bungalow her phone rang. Taylor walked quickly down the hall toward the kitchen. Halfway there she felt a wave of dizziness hit her. She stopped, leaned against the wall and closed her eyes. This wasn't the first time this week that she had gotten dizzy, but then again, she had been having so much fun decorating the nursery that she must have overdone it. Now that she was happy with every square inch of her beautifully appointed nursery, she would force herself to take it easy.

By the time she reached the phone, the caller had been sent to voice mail.

"Casey."

Taylor redialed her sister. Even though Casey was in another state, her sister had been with her every step of the pregnancy.

"Hey—I was just leaving you a message." Casey smiled and waved.

"I'll listen to it later." Taylor smiled tiredly at her sister. "I want to show you the progress on the nursery."

When she reached the end of the hall, Taylor turned the camera toward the interior of the baby room.

"Can you see it?"

"Oh, Tay—I *love* it!"

Taylor took her sister on the virtual tour—she started with the brand-new identical cribs, moved to the new changing table and the refinished rocking chair she had found in an antique store, and ended with the handmade quilts that their aunt Barb had gifted to the unborn babies.

"I don't think I've ever seen a more beautiful room. It's the happiest nursery *ever*."

Taylor sat down in the rocking chair. "I think so, too!

I couldn't have done it without the family. Sophia and Luke and Aunt Barb—they've all been so supportive. Six months ago I couldn't even begin to comprehend how much help I was going to need…."

"I'm glad Aunt Barb's been able to smooth things over with Uncle Hank."

"I know. I love him so much, but the man is permanently stuck in the '50s."

Taylor had to admit that she hadn't exactly handled the situation with as much diplomacy as she could have. Once she found out that the pregnancy was viable and decided to rent the house, and after confirming with Clint that she could rip the Band-Aid off and reveal the pregnancy and the paternity in one fell swoop, that's what she did.

Her mother, in typical fashion, drowned her disappointment with Xanax and zinfandel. Her father quietly supported her decision and went back to working at the law firm from early in the morning to later and later in the evening. Uncle Hank went into his icy mode, refusing to talk about it or acknowledge it—Taylor was actually glad that Clint was out of the state. And Aunt Barb—dear Aunt Barb, had the most motherly response—she balanced lecturing with nurturing and quiet disapproval with very vocal joy.

"So, what else has been going on with you?" Casey asked.

"You know what? Why don't you talk for a while and I'll listen?" Taylor rocked gently in the chair and closed her eyes.

"Are you okay?"

"I think I am. Just really tired. I may have overdone

it a little. I'll take it easy all day tomorrow. But I'm not ready to get off the phone yet. You talk, I'll listen."

For the next fifteen or so minutes, Casey talked while Taylor listened. She was about to doze off when Casey asked her about her second favorite subject behind her babies—Clint.

"Have you talked to Clint lately?"

Taylor's eyes opened up with a smile. "We talk all the time."

"All the time, huh?"

"He calls to check on me every day," Taylor said. "Sometimes we talk for a few minutes and then other times we talk for hours. I feel bad for saying this, but when I first met Clint, I didn't think he was all that smart. But he loves history and astronomy…he reads…"

"Literacy is always a bonus."

Taylor laughed. "You know what I mean. He's different than I expected. He's really rough on the outside—even a little intimidating—but on the inside… I don't know…he has a very kind heart."

"Huh…"

The look on Casey's face reflected her sister's thoughts perfectly.

"I know what you're thinking, Casey…and you're absolutely right." Taylor rubbed her hand over her belly. "I think I may have fallen for my baby daddy."

After she ended the video chat with her sister, she went to her bedroom to lie down. Just talking had worn her out. If she couldn't shake this feeling of exhaustion, she would have to call her OB/GYN. Her doctor monitored her carefully and wanted her to report any unusual symptoms as they developed in real time.

It was still daylight when she crawled into bed, but

it was dark outside when she finally awakened. She didn't sit up. The nap hadn't really helped—she could gauge that right away. Her head was killing her, and she wasn't prone to headaches, so that set off alarm bells. Her full bladder finally drove her out of bed and into the bathroom. She turned on the light in the bathroom and the glare hurt her eyes so much that she shut it off and used the bathroom by the light of the night-light she had plugged into the wall.

She got back into bed and curled up onto her side. Walking the short distance to and from the bathroom had made her feel out of breath—she felt hot and there was an odd pain under her right ribs.

Okay...okay...keep calm...just keep calm. Think.

It took her several minutes to process, and then accept, the fact that something was wrong. She reached for her phone on the nightstand and dialed Sophia's number.

"Hello?"

"Luke? Is that you?"

"Yes," her cousin confirmed.

"I was…looking for Sophia."

"She's giving Danny a bath. I'll have her call you back when she's done."

"No…wait…"

She could hear the distress in her own voice—she knew that Luke heard it, too.

"What's wrong?" Luke asked her.

"I'm not feeling very well. Horrible headache, a lot of pain right under my right rib—I feel sick to my stomach…" Taylor told him. "I need to go to the hospital."

Oh, the joys of the emergency room. It was never any fun, but an emergency room while pregnant with twins—the worst. Checking in, waiting, hard chairs, cold rooms that smelled faintly of isopropyl alcohol and disinfectant—even in a small-town hospital, nothing moved quickly. Then came the vital signs—her blood pressure was too high—and the wristband and then she was taken back to an exam room. Soon after she put on her gown, the nurses were in to insert a catheter.

Luke, who had been a silent Rock of Gibraltar, waited just outside of her room while the nurses collected a clean urine sample. Because she was pregnant, and had presented with high blood pressure, they expedited the lab results. Taylor was savvy enough to know they were looking for protein in her urine. The diagnosis, when it came back, wasn't a shock. Preeclampsia—gestational high blood pressure.

The diagnosis wasn't a shock, and neither was the fact that her OB/GYN, through the emergency room staff, had determined that she needed to be admitted to the hospital. Luke stayed with her until she was situated in her hospital room, then he went home to watch the kids so Sophia could come to the hospital. While she waited for Sophia to arrive, Taylor left a message for Casey. Casey would make sure that their parents were informed and play the buffer, if need be, with their mother.

"Hi…" Sophia knocked quietly on the hospital room door.

Taylor waved her hand for Sophia to come in. "Thank you for coming."

Sophia came over to the bed and gave her a solid, reassuring hug before she pulled the visitor's chair over to the side of the bed.

"How are you doing?" her friend asked her.

"This isn't unexpected. I'm almost forty, this is my first pregnancy, I'm pregnant with twins—let's face it—I check a lot of 'high risk' boxes. But I'm in the hospital now and I have to believe that it's going to be okay. I have to believe that my babies are going to be okay."

She heard herself speaking the words, but who was she trying to convince? Sophia or herself? Her twins had been her job for the past six or so months. They were her whole, entire focus. She knew how serious a preeclampsia diagnosis was—she knew that the only treatment for preeclampsia was delivery. She was a long seven weeks away from that magical thirty-seven week mark when the lungs were developed.

Her OB/GYN would be at the hospital to discuss the course of treatment, but she already had a general idea of what needed to be done. She needed to stay in the hospital, have the babies' growth and status monitored, keep her high blood pressure managed and keep her twins in the womb for as long as possible.

"They have an excellent neonatal intensive care unit here," Taylor added.

"They do..." Sophia put her hand on her arm and gave it a reassuring squeeze. "Is there anyone you need me to call? Your parents? Have you called Barb and Hank?"

"My sister will take care of my parents. I'll call Aunt Barb tomorrow—I don't want her to drive into Helena at this late hour and you know she will..."

"True..." Sophia agreed. "What about Clint?"

Sophia had gotten to know Clint during the time she lived at the ranch when they first moved back to Montana, and she liked him. So Taylor always felt comfortable talking about Clint with Sophia.

"He's on a long haul—he wants to pick up a couple of events in Ohio. He called earlier and left a message. If he doesn't call back, I'll wait to tell him in the morning."

"Don't you think he'll want to be here with you?" her friend asked.

"He's been talking about coming back for a visit for a while now." Taylor's eyes drooped closed. "But..."

"If he wants to come, you should let him." Sophia stood up and kissed her friend on the forehead.

Exhausted, Taylor fell asleep without noticing that Sophia had left the room. But for the rest of the night she could only catch small stretches of sleep because of the steady flow of nurses and technicians and phlebotomists. She was monitored, the babies were monitored, the machines were beeping, and carts rolled by. Her body wanted to sleep, her brain was onboard, but the routine of the hospital simply wouldn't allow it. That's why she was still awake when Clint called again just before midnight. If she didn't answer it, he would worry. They hadn't said the words "I love you," but as an outcrop of their long-distance friendship, a deeper understanding, a deeper relationship, had blossomed.

"Hi, cowboy." She answered the phone with an honest attempt at sounding normal.

"Hey, sunshine—did I wake you?"

"No. I was already awake. Where are you?"

"Casper, Wyoming. Today's been a real crap day. Construction everywhere. The fifth wheel caught a nail in one of the back tires. Broke the lug nut tryin' to change the flippin' thing."

Taylor heard Clint light a cigarette.

"You should probably go try to get some rest." Taylor didn't want to pile on any more bad news onto his already lousy day when there wasn't a thing he could do for her.

"Why're you tryin' to rush me off the phone? Is your boyfriend over?"

"Ha! Not hardly."

"Talk to me then—I've been looking forward to hearing your voice all day—but if you're too tired, just let me know…"

"No, Clint…it's not that." Taylor closed her eyes with a sigh. "I wanted to wait until the morning to tell you this, especially since you've already had such a crappy day…"

Clint didn't say anything, but she could feel his energy shift on the other end of the phone. She could feel him listening to her more closely while he waited for her to finish her sentence.

"My doctor had to admit me to the hospital."

She hadn't had the energy to talk Clint out of making a U-turn in Casper after he got the tire on the fifth wheel fixed. He was not going to be dissuaded from coming to Helena. Once he found out that she was in the hospital—and that there was a real possibility that she could be hospitalized for the duration of her pregnancy—it was decided.

She had been worried about seeing Clint in person again. Yes, they had spent hours talking on the phone and video chatting since he went back on the road, but the distance between them had always been a safety wall, a barrier that had kept them just far enough away from each other that they never said anything *too* serious. Their relationship, whatever it was, was unlike anything she had ever known. They were friends, yes. They had deeper feelings, yes. They had conceived twins together, yes. But they weren't a couple.

"Is it too early for a visitor?"

Two days later, Clint showed up at her hospital door with a small bundle of daisies, her favorite flower.

"Howdy, cowboy."

"Howdy, sunshine." Clint loitered in the doorway.

"You didn't come all the way from Wyoming to stand in the door, did you?" she teased him lightly. "They haven't changed out the water yet—I think there's a whole pitcher over there just waiting for daisies."

She could tell that Clint had cleaned himself up to come see her. His clothes were new and clean. His hair was freshly washed and slicked back into a ponytail, and the beard was clipped close to the skin.

"I'm glad you came, Clint."

Clint put the flowers in the pitcher and brought it over to her crowded nightstand.

"Is that the truth?" He stood next to her bed.

"It is." She reached out to take his hand. "I just didn't want you to feel like you had to change your plans."

"Plans change." Clint liked the feel of her hand in his. But he didn't like to see her looking so flushed in the face with dark circles beneath her eyes. "I'd much rather be hangin' out with you then getting my butt bucked off a bull."

"You could sit down and stay for a while, you know."

Clint looked behind him, saw the chair and brought it closer to the bed.

"What happened to your wrist?" Taylor asked about the bandage on Clint's left wrist. He looked at it as if he had forgotten all about it being injured.

"Sprained it back in Washington."

"I don't mean to tell you how to do your job. But, you might want to try to get hurt less."

Clint smiled for the first time since he arrived. "I'm the one who's supposed to be cheering you up—not the other way around."

"You cheered me up when you walked through the door." What was the sense in hiding her feelings? "Thank you for the flowers. Daisies are happy flowers."

"So you've said." Clint's eyes shifted to her belly. The last time he had seen her, she didn't look pregnant at all. Now…she looked *very* pregnant. And, no matter how many ways he tried to parse it out—she was pregnant with *his* children.

"I feel like we're talkin' about everything but what we should be talkin' about." He leaned forward, his eyes on her face. "I want to know that you're going to be okay."

"I'm going to be okay," she said in as strong a voice as she could manage. "My babies are going to be okay. The doctors are making sure my blood pressure stays as low as they can keep it, and they're making sure that the babies are growing like they should and that they aren't in distress." Her hands immediately went to her stomach. "I can't think about any other outcome than my babies being born healthy and ready to face the world. And neither should you."

Clint stayed by her side until she was too tired to talk anymore. He walked out of her room and down the hallway in a bit of a daze. Taylor didn't look so good. She tried real hard to put lipstick on a pig, but he could see right through her act.

"Clint!"

Clint looked up and saw Sophia Brand walking toward him.

"Taylor told me you were heading back to Montana." Sophia held out her hand for Clint to shake. "Good to see you again."

Clint tipped his hat to her. "Ma'am."

"How's she doing today?"

"She got tired out real quick." Clint looked over his shoulder to Taylor's room.

Sophia looked up at him thoughtfully.

"Do you want to grab a cup of coffee with me?"

Sophia was a woman with inside information. He also got the sense that Sophia was on his side.

"Yes, ma'am."

Sophia wrinkled her nose distastefully. "Look—I know it's your upbringing to call me ma'am, but please don't. It makes me feel like I'm ninety-two. Sophia is fine."

They found their way to a small family waiting room with vending machines. Clint got them both a cup of coffee, with cream and sugar for Sophia.

The coffee burned the roof of his mouth, his tongue and his throat, but he felt numb to it. His gut had been twisted since the minute he saw Taylor lying in that bed, hooked up to every machine the hospital could cram into her room.

"Taylor was workin' mighty hard to convince me that everything's under control in there." Clint looked down at the black liquid in his foam cup. "What's the real story?"

"You don't mind if I'm blunt with you, do you, Clint?" Sophia asked the cowboy she only knew in passing. "I mean—you seem like the type who appreciates hearing things straight without a chaser."

"Blunt's better." Clint looked up at his companion. "What's worse-case scenario?"

"Worst-case scenario?" Sophia looked away with a little shake of her head. "Taylor loses the babies."

Sophia looked back at Clint and held his gaze. "Worst, *worst* case scenario? We could lose Taylor."

Chapter Thirteen

After his conversation with Sophia, Clint found himself sitting in the front pew of the hospital chapel. It had been a long time since he felt lost. Not since he was a kid. Not since his mom left for the third, and last, time when he was eleven.

That summer, the summer he turned eleven, his father gave him a secondhand Swiss Army pocketknife. No card, no cake—the knife wasn't wrapped. That was the first time he'd gone up to the Continental Divide by himself. He took some camping gear and that pocketknife and he left.

Somewhere along the way he'd eventually lost that knife, but he'd never lost the skills he learned on that first solitary trip up to the Divide. He'd always been with his father or with his older brother, Brock, or with one of the Brands—never alone. Not only did he survive—he thrived. He had watched and learned since he was a boy, and he was better than all of the men he'd ever followed. That's why Brock and Hank had picked him to watch out for Taylor on the CDT.

They hadn't picked him because he was a good man. He hadn't always been a good man. He drank too much. He smoked too much. He gambled. He slept with too many women and forgot their names. They'd picked him because when it came to the CDT he was the best. And a woman like Taylor—she was the kind of woman who deserved the best.

Did he deserve a woman like Taylor? Smart, sweet, funny, educated—such a pretty smile. When she looked at him, she looked at him as though she could really see him. As if she could see all of his warts and she liked him anyway.

Did he *really* deserve a woman like Taylor? Did he?

"No." Clint opened his eyes.

No. He didn't.

But, dear Lord, he *wanted* to deserve a woman like her.

He hadn't set foot in a church in over two decades, but when he left the hospital chapel after an hour of sitting in the silence, watching the flames of the candles that loved ones had lit for their family members, Clint had gained some clarity. It made him wonder if he shouldn't stop by a church more than once every couple of decades.

"Hi, sunshine..." Later that afternoon, Clint was back to see Taylor.

"Hey there, cowboy." Taylor attempted one of her chipper smiles but fell short. "I'm glad I didn't scare you away."

Clint hooked his hat on the back of the door. "You should know by now—I don't scare so much."

She looked at him in that way she did—as if she saw him for who he was and accepted him. When had he ever had that?

"Did you see my aunt Barb? She just left…"

"I did—but we didn't talk for long. I wanted to get to you and she had to get back to the ranch."

"I'm glad to see you." Her smile reached her eyes that time. "Keep me company. Tell me about your day…"

"Nothin' exciting to tell—I got some work done on the fifth wheel—got some rest." Clint leaned back in the chair, crossed his leg and rested his ankle on his knee.

"I like your new boots there, cowboy." Taylor said. "Better than the ones with duct tape."

"I don't know—I kind of miss the old ones. They were all broke in…"

Taylor laughed. That was what she loved about spending time with Clint—in person, on the phone or video chat—he always made her laugh.

"I was thinking about our days on the CDT." Clint told her. "We had some good times up there, didn't we?"

"It was the most amazing trip I've ever taken."

After visiting hours, he went back to the campground where he'd parked his fifth wheel and gotten some sleep so he could be rested for Taylor the next day. She needed him—she did. She needed him more than she knew, and certainly more than she was willing to admit to herself or to him. And, for once in his life, he was going to be there for her.

He arrived back at the hospital soon after the staff was clearing away the breakfast trays. Right away he noticed that there was something off about the look in her blue eyes. There was dullness to the blue, when normally they were bright. Her skin was still flushed; she seemed so tired. As though she hadn't gotten any sleep at all.

"Come here... I want you to feel the babies move." When she waved him over, her fingers were slack and her hand limp, as if it was almost too much energy to hold it up.

He let her guide his palm to her round belly. There was a band around her abdomen, used to monitor the twins.

"They're busy right now." Taylor smiled so sweetly at him. When she talked about the twins he caught a fleeting glimpse of the fire and gumption he was used to seeing in her eyes. "I couldn't feel them move yesterday. I couldn't... I was so worried."

Her skin was warm to the touch—maybe too warm. But her skin was still so soft. Softer than any woman he had ever known before. Like silk. He loved her skin—the way it smelled and the way it felt against his own scarred-up, rough hide. He wanted to hold her again. If she wasn't hooked up to so many damn wires he would crawl into bed with her and hold her right now.

"Did you feel them?" she asked him urgently.

He slid his hand away. He had—something moved under his hand—to him it felt alien. But he didn't say that to Taylor. To her, *everything* about the pregnancy and the babies was beautiful and magical. Who was he to disagree with her, even if he couldn't agree?

He didn't think this preeclampsia—the gestational high blood pressure—was so magical. He'd listened to Sophia and read one of the pamphlets he found in the family waiting room, and he'd grilled one of the nurses on duty at the nurse's station. If this thing got out of control, Taylor could have a stroke—she could have a seizure—she could die. And the only way to fix it was for her to deliver the babies. Right now, the babies were hurting Taylor and he was a part of it, too. He was the one who agreed to her pregnancy plan in the first place.

Clint sat down next to the bed. He didn't feel a connection to the babies. Even though he knew they were his, he just didn't feel connected to them in his heart. But he did feel very connected to Taylor.

"They can't seem to get my blood pressure under control." Taylor looked at him, her eyes locking and holding his gaze.

"If things don't turn around soon, I'll have to deliver."

"When?"

"I don't know—but it will be by C section." Taylor turned her head away from him. "She doesn't want to risk trying to induce me—she's worried that will put too much stress on my babies. They've already started giving me steroids to help their lungs develop, so I know they're prepping me to deliver. The longer we can wait, the better it will be for these angels."

"But it's not necessarily better for you." The second he blurted out those words, he wished he could have taken them back.

"What's good for them *is* good for me." Taylor had a noticeable catch in her voice.

It took Clint a minute to realize that the glistening he saw on Taylor's cheeks wasn't from the reflection of light coming in through the window—it was tears—a steady, stream of tears slipping down her cheeks into her hair and onto the pillow.

Clint looked everywhere in the room for some tissue and finally settled on toilet paper from the bathroom. He tried to dab, as gently as he could, the tears from her face and where they had rolled down her neck.

"I don't know if you're girls or boys or maybe one of each..." Taylor spoke to her belly. "But I love you both so much."

She looked at him with blue eyes bright with tears. "I wanted it to be a surprise. The gender."

"That's okay." He kissed the hand he was holding. "Surprises can be good."

She reached up and put her hand on his face. "You were a surprise."

It was a moment that couldn't be planned—it was a stripped-down, honest, bare your soul to someone you trust kind of moment. He leaned down and kissed her hand.

"You were a surprise for me, too, Taylor."

"Clint...?"

He raised his eyebrows and waited for her to continue.

"Tell me that everything's going to be okay."

"Everything's going to be okay, Taylor."

Her eyelids lowered a little, her head moved back and forth and she licked her dry lips. "No. Say it like you mean it."

"I do mean it," Clint repeated with more conviction. "Everything *is* going to be okay."

The next morning, Clint stopped by the florist to pick up a fresh arrangement of daisies and then headed to the hospital. He was expecting to find Taylor alone in her room eating breakfast. When he got there, flowers in hand, he walked into an empty room. Taylor's bed was gone.

"Clint! Oh thank goodness you came early." Sophia arrived. "I didn't have your number, Hank didn't have your number..."

"Where is she?"

Sophia had a look on her face that could only be described as "stricken." Her eyelids were puffy from crying and her shoulders slumped forward.

"They had to perform an emergency C section late last night." Sophia wiped fresh tears from her lower lids. "Her blood pressure shot up...she started to get blurred vision. The nurse told me that her brain was starting to swell...."

Clint looked everywhere in the room, other than at Sophia. He couldn't take her tears right now. He had his own tears to fight. He walked over to where Taylor's bed had been; he walked in a small circle, thinking, thinking, thinking...

"Clint..."

He laid the flowers on the rolling table before he turned to face Taylor's friend.

"Last night—right before the doctor made the call to deliver—they couldn't detect the heartbeat of one of the babies."

The room started to spin for a split second—Clint reached out and put his hand on the wall to get his equilibrium back.

"The little girl..." Sophia said quietly. "She's in the NICU..."

He had been staring at the speckled pattern on the

polished linoleum, but for her next words, he looked up into her eyes.

"But the little boy. The little boy…he didn't make it, Clint."

How many hours did he sit in that chapel praying for Taylor? He'd rarely prayed for anything that wasn't selfish—like an eight-second ride so he could win cash and rank higher. Clint wasn't in the business of praying to God for someone else's good. But, for Taylor, he prayed harder and longer and more selflessly than he'd ever prayed at any other time in his life. Down on his knees, hands clasped, head bowed, his mind begged God over and over to make Taylor well…to make Taylor whole.

Sophia had told him more than he knew how to handle. Taylor had lost one baby, her daughter was fighting to breathe in the NICU, and Taylor was in ICU while the doctors and nurses struggled to get her blood pressure under control. Taylor had named him as the father of the children and if he wanted to see the little girl, as the father, he could.

Do you want to see your daughter? Sophia had asked him that question.

He hadn't answered her, because he knew she would think the worse of him for it. But, no—*no*—he didn't want to see the baby. What he wanted was for Taylor, the woman he loved, to recover. *That* was what he wanted.

After he lit a candle for Taylor in the chapel, Clint went to the visitor's waiting room. It was a small room and that small room was crowded with Taylor's family. He hadn't seen Hank or Barb since he'd left Bent Tree months ago—under the circumstances, he wouldn't disagree with them if they laid a lion's share of the blame for their niece's critical condition at his doorstep.

Barbara Brand saw him standing in the door. She looked at her husband, who was sitting in the chair next to her. Barbara put her hand on Hank's leg and gave it a little pat before she stood up and walked over to him.

With any woman other than a class act like Barbara Brand, he could imagine a slap as easily as he could imagine a hug. Without needing to say a word, Barbara hugged him. Over Barbara's head, Clint caught Hank's eye. The man who had once trusted him to watch out for Taylor had lost faith in him. They wouldn't have *words*—Hank didn't need to say anything. Everything the rancher felt was right there to be read in his eyes.

"We are so sorry, Clint." Barbara kept her hand on his arm. "We're all here to support you and Taylor and your precious daughter. You must be so worried."

He couldn't get any words out, so he just nodded. Barbara had always been kind to him. Even when he was just a scrawny, wild kid who was left to his own devices most of the time—Barbara Brand always took the time to speak with him—to teach him some manners, to give him some encouragement or praise.

"Have you seen your daughter?" Barbara asked him.

Again—no words—he shook his head.

"I'll take you," Barbara said to him. To her husband she said, "I'll be back in a bit."

Barbara Brand wasn't someone you refused. She was just *that* woman on the ranch. He walked with her toward the NICU, toward a daughter who didn't seem like his at all.

"You care for Taylor, don't you, Clint?" Barbara had her arm linked with his.

"Yes, ma'am." Clint finally found his voice. "I love her."

"I thought so. I saw you together—you didn't know I could see you. The way you looked at her—the way she looked at you. I thought—that's what love looks like."

He listened while she talked to him quietly as they walked toward the NICU—toward his daughter.

"What you can do for Taylor, right now, is to take care of her daughter. That's all any mother would want."

The doctor in charge of baby girl Brand filled him in on the medical status of the twin who had survived. Immaturity of the lungs and respiratory distress syndrome were the two diagnoses that stuck in his mind as he stared at the little girl hooked up to a ventilator and warmed by an incubator. The little girl, only two pounds ten ounces and thirteen inches long, was attached to all manner of medical machines: cardiac monitors, IV lines, electrodes stuck to her tiny pink foot. Her eyes were covered and when she cried she sounded more like a kitten than a human baby.

"Her name is Penelope." Clint stared at his daughter, wishing that he could feel some sort of attachment to her. "That's her mom's top pick for a girl."

"You can touch her hand—let her know you're there." The doctor told him. "We find that all of the baby's vital signs improve when they're touched by their moms. Or their dads."

Clint hesitated for a moment before he made the decision to cowboy up. In some respects he was helpless, surrounded by a team of people quietly going about their business—a controlled chaos—but he could comfort this little girl. If holding her hand would help her feel better, perhaps it would make him feel better, as well.

Through the armholes, Clint reached into the incubator and ran his finger over Penelope's tiny clenched hand.

"Hi, Penelope." He was the first to call her by her name.

He rubbed his finger across the back of Penelope's hand; she surprised him by wrapping her fingers around his pinky. Clint didn't move—he didn't want the moment to stop.

It was surreal. Standing in the NICU with the beeping and the people and the monitors and the wires—he had a moment. That one simple move, his daughter holding on to his pinky as if she knew that he was there to protect her—touched his heart. So fragile and innocent—no one in his life had ever needed him in the same way as this little girl needed him. He had wondered how he could earn his way into a life with Taylor. Now he knew that he needed to begin by earning his way into the life of his daughter.

Chapter Fourteen

One week later—a week that seemed more like a month to Clint—Taylor was moved from ICU to a regular hospital room. Baby Penelope was stable in the NICU and the entire NICU staff was amazed by her resilience. She was gaining weight and had transitioned from the respirator to nasal oxygen delivery. The steroids she had been given prior to her birth had worked their magic and her lungs were in much better shape than originally thought. She was a fighter, like her mother, and she was determined to forge her own path.

When Clint arrived at the hospital and didn't find Taylor in her room, he knew where to look for her. If she wasn't in her room, she had to be with Penelope. He was a familiar face to staff in the NICU; he tipped his hat and smiled at the nurses who were quietly and quickly moving around the room. By Penelope's incubator, her temporary home to keep her warm, Taylor was sitting in a small rocking chair with the baby sleeping on her chest. She looked surprisingly well for a woman who had gone through so much. Taylor had her eyes closed and she was rocking slowly, humming softly to the sleeping baby. The hospital gown Taylor was wearing had been lowered enough at the neckline to allow Penelope to have skin-to-skin contact with her mother. A blanket was tucked around the baby's body and she was wearing a tiny beanie cap with Penny written on the front.

Clint watched the two—mother and child—for several minutes, not wanting to disturb the moment. He had spent a month on the CDT with Taylor, so he knew that she was a force to be reckoned with. She was what his mother used to call a steel magnolia—pretty and sweet on the outside, but a spine of steel on the inside. But even knowing that about her, he hadn't been prepared for how gracefully she would handle the loss of her son and the complications of the premature birth of her daughter. Perhaps focusing on her daughter, and putting all of her energy toward her welfare, had allowed her to refocus her sorrow. She had cried for her son—a son she'd named Michael—but she had a single-minded focus on making sure that her living child survived and thrived.

Taylor opened her eyes and saw him standing nearby. She smiled at him, as she always did. "Come see her—she's wearing her preemie hat for the first time."

He stood next to mother and daughter—he couldn't resist reaching out and touching Penelope's hand, which was balled up into a tiny fist. Her fist was the size of his thumbnail. He still couldn't believe how little she was.

In a whisper, Taylor said. "The staff love you here—

especially the nurses," she teased him. "They've all told me how much time you spent with her those first couple of days when I couldn't be with her. Thank you for that."

"It was the only thing I could think to do for you..."

"It was the best thing you could have done for me, Clint. You didn't sign on for any of this, but you really came through for me. And for Penny."

When Taylor referred, in a roundabout way, to the deal they had struck, it made his gut hurt. He had signed his parental rights away—even though Taylor had listed him as the father on the hospital documents, legally, Penelope wasn't his daughter. It bothered him. He didn't want that to be the reality of his situation.

"Have you held her?" she asked him.

He shook his head. The staff had tried to get him to hold her, but he'd been too intimidated to do it. All of those wires and electrodes and how delicate she was—he couldn't muster the nerve to do it. And part of him wondered if he had the right.

"I think you should hold her, Clint," Taylor said quietly. "But only if you want to."

"I'd like to," he explained, "but she scares the heck out of me."

With the help of the staff, a still sleeping Penelope was transferred from her mother's arms to his. He unbuttoned his shirt so she could benefit from the warmth of his skin, and then the blanket was draped over Penelope's back and legs.

Her abdomen was so sore, Taylor stayed sitting in the rocking chair—but she asked the nurse to take a picture of Penelope and Clint with her phone so she could hold on to this moment. She had quickly learned to lean on the NICU staff—she was still recovering from the

C-section physically, and the loss of her son, emotionally. In order to do her best for her daughter, her angel blessing, she had to give up some control, some of her autonomy, and let others help her. One of the people she had learned to lean on was Clint. She couldn't have known how much it would mean to have him watch over Penelope for her—but it had meant more than words. She had loved him before, as a friend, as a lover—now she took him into her heart as the father of her child. It was a love she didn't know existed.

"She looks content with you," Taylor said quietly.

"She just yawned," Clint said in amazement, as if Penelope had just invented the act of yawning.

They stayed with the baby in the NICU for a while longer and then Clint wheeled Taylor back to her room. The nurse helped transfer Taylor back into her bed—the exertion of the day had drained the color out of her face.

"I should let you rest." Clint stood at the end of her bed, his eyes concerned.

"No—don't go just yet. I want to talk to you."

Taylor gestured to the chair next to her bed.

"I am so grateful to you Clint—the way you looked after Penny—you didn't have to do that, but you did," she said. "And I will always love you for what you've done for the both of us. But I don't want you to feel like you have to hang in there to the bitter end. I know you've already missed several rodeos—you're not going to win a championship hanging out here with me..."

Clint ran his fingers through his hair a couple of times as he considered what Taylor was saying to him. He was worried about his chances at winning a championship—if he was gone from the circuit too long, he'd have to give up on this year and shoot for next. He knew he had a championship win in him—he just needed to take his career seriously for once.

Winning a championship meant more than prestige—it meant endorsements. And endorsements meant money. He didn't have that many more years left in him—the sport was brutal on the body. If he won a championship, he could retire with a sweet little nest egg. But what about Penelope and Taylor? How could he just walk away from them now when they needed him the most?

"Are you giving me my walkin' papers?" he asked jokingly.

Taylor shook her head. "No. No. I love having you here. But you and I both know that this wasn't part of the deal. *I* made the decision to bring these children into the world. You shouldn't have to give up what you want because of a misplaced sense of obligation."

"Look—I appreciate you letting me off the hook and all. But I haven't been thinking too much about leaving. I've been worried about you. I've been worried about Penelope."

He stopped short of saying that he was worried about the arrangements for the funeral service for Michael. There was no way he was going to leave before they put his son in the ground. There was no way.

"I just want you to know that I support any decision you make. If you need to go—I understand. That's your career. That's how you make your living."

"Well—thank you." Clint nodded his head. "But I ain't goin' nowhere just yet."

Taylor had thought that the worst day of her life was the day her divorce was final. Looking back, she couldn't imagine why she had ever thought that could be the worst that ever happened to her. The worst day of her life was the day that she watched her son's small casket being lowered into the ground. Family surrounded her at the graveyard, and she was glad for them, but she had never felt more alone.

Michael McAllister Brand, so named by her to honor both sides of his lineage, was laid to rest beside Hank and Barbara's second eldest son, Daniel, who had been killed in the Iraq War. Side by side, these two Brand males had been taken too young. Daniel died in his thirties and never had the chance to meet his unborn son. Her angel, Michael, was gone before he could have any life at all.

How could God be so cruel? How could God be so *cruel*?

She had stood beside Clint, holding on to his hand through the entire ceremony for support. Taylor was so grateful that her cowboy had refused to leave. How would she have ever gotten through the day without his quiet, strong, reassuring presence?

"You need to eat something." Aunt Barb came into the study where Taylor had retreated to be by herself after the wake.

"I'm not hungry." Taylor shook her head.

Barbara looked at her niece with compassionate eyes; she had lost a child. She understood the pain. It just wasn't right for a mother to lose a child.

"Scooch over…" Barbara said. Her niece was sitting in the coveted chair-and-a-half with matching ottoman. It was, undeniably, the most comfy chair in the study.

Taylor scooted over for her aunt to join her. She could take the comfort from Barbara—she had been a mother figure to Taylor all of her life. And she had lost Daniel. It was a club that nobody wanted to join, but once you did, only the other members of the club could possibly understand what it was like to be the mother of a lost child.

"I love you." Aunt Barbara put her arms around Taylor's shoulders. "And it doesn't feel like it now, but the pain will become tolerable."

"I know I can't lose myself in it, Aunt Barb—I have to be strong for Penny. But it hurts—it hurts so much."

Aunt Barb reached over and wiped Taylor's fresh tears away. "I know, baby. I know."

Her immediate family—her father, mother, sister and brother—hadn't been able to attend the funeral. Casey, a special education teacher, wanted to take off from work, but Taylor convinced her to save her money for a visit during the summer break. It was such a long trip for her sister to make for such a sad event. And Aunt Barb and Sophia went a long way to fill the void.

"If the offer is still open, Aunt Barb—I'd like to take you up on your offer and bring Penelope back to the ranch when she's discharged. I don't think I can face that nursery…just yet."

There was two of everything in that nursery. Two cribs, two blankets, two mobiles—it made her feel sick to her stomach just thinking about removing *one* of everything.

"You can take the rooms upstairs—the crib Sophia used for Danny is in the attic. Or you're welcome to use Tyler's cabin. Tyler, London and the kids are all going to be here for Thanksgiving, but it will be vacant until then."

"I think I'll go back to the cabin, if that's okay with you," Taylor said. "I want Clint to be able to visit Penelope without running into Hank too much. Hank won't even acknowledge him when they're in the same room."

"I know—I've talked to him. But the man is stubborn. And old-fashioned, God love him. Just be patient and he'll come around. He always does…in his own time."

Spending time with Penelope, loving on Penelope and learning about how to take care of Penelope was Taylor's saving grace during the week directly following Michael's funeral. Clint was with her every step of the way. He had been by her side, quietly and solidly, at the funeral and at the wake. He had been there when she was too tired to take a shift with Penelope and to remind her to eat.

In their own way, they had "dates" in the hospital cafeteria and took walks around the hospital grounds while Penelope was sleeping. A friendship that had started by accident, when they were thrown together on that memorable trip on the CDT, had turned into so much more. And even though there had never been a right time to talk about "us," she knew that she was more of a team with Clint than she had ever been in her marriage.

And, no, they had never had a conventional relationship—but why did it have to be? The only thing that mattered was that they *loved* each other, that they *respected* each other, that they supported each other's dreams and that they enjoyed being together. All of that, and much more, was true about her relationship with Clint. She never would have seen it coming, but her perfect match was rough-around-the-edges, professional bull rider Clint McAllister of Montana.

* * *

"Look what we made." Taylor was on one side of the incubator and Clint was on the other.

Penelope had her right hand wrapped around Clint's pinky and her left hand wrapped around Taylor's pointer finger. That was the moment when Clint knew exactly what he needed to do for the rest of his life. Yes, he knew he loved Taylor. Yes, he knew that he wanted to be a father in every sense of the word to Penny. But not every piece of the puzzle had fit into place until right this moment. When he looked at Taylor, he saw the beautiful woman he loved. When he looked at Penelope, he saw the tiny little girl, his daughter, who needed him more than anyone ever had. They were a family—unofficially. He needed to make it official. If Taylor would have him, he would be honored to call her his wife.

"I got to get going." Clint slipped his finger out of his daughter's grasp.

Penelope began to protest, wrinkling her forehead, kicking her legs and crying a couple of times.

"I know, sweetheart—I don't think he should leave, either," Taylor said to Penny. "Where are you going?"

Clint picked his hat up off the nearby chair, put it on and then gave Taylor a kiss on the lips. "Don't you worry about it—I've got some errands to run."

"What errands?" she asked.

"You're on a need-to-know basis and you don't need to know," Clint said with a conspiratorial wink to the nurse who walked by and heard the exchange.

"I'll see you at the cabin later on—around five, do you think?"

"I was going to spend the night here," Taylor said.

"She's in good hands, Taylor. You gotta take a break every once in a while so you don't burn yourself out."

She agreed to meet him at the cabin for dinner. When she arrived, Clint led her out to the deck overlooking the lake where he had lit the fire in the fire pit.

"I'm cooking my famous CDT fish tonight." Clint held her chair for her.

"Out here?"

"Right here." Clint handed her a glass of nonalcoholic sparkling cider. He picked up his half-empty beer bottle for a toast. "Here's to unusual beginnings."

"Unusual beginnings." She touched her glass to his.

"This reminds me of our dinners when we first met. You made the best fish, you really did, but holy moly did I get *sick* of it."

"Fish is on the menu," Clint said wryly. "It's the only thing I really know how to cook."

"And I will enjoy every bite," Taylor said. "Promise."

Clint had saved some herbs from the CDT and he used them that night. The smell took her back to all of those nights they had spent talking around the campfire. No matter how much talking they did, they always seemed to have more to say.

"Hey—you aren't smoking!"

"Gave it up." Clint cut the fish in half with a spatula and put half of the cooked fish on her plate and half on his.

"You gave it up? Just like that?"

"Just like that."

Taylor picked up her fork, but let it hover for a minute above the plate. "Okay—I'm amazed. What made you do that?"

"I figured it was time," Clint said before he took a

bite of the fish. "My pop had emphysema, was sick with it for years—that's not my road."

Taylor took a bite of her fish. "Mmm. So good." After another bite, she added, "And I'm glad, by the way—about the smoking. Penny needs you healthy."

The fish was delicious; and the notes of Clint's harmonica, along with the view of the three-quarter moon casting a light on the mountain peaks in the distance made her feel calm and tranquil.

"Thank you for this," Taylor said to her cowboy. "I had no idea how much I needed this break."

"You're welcome." Clint tucked his harmonica in his shirt pocket before he stood up. "I've fed you and serenaded you and now I need to talk to you."

Clint moved his chair so it was facing hers, sat down and took her hands in his.

"You know, before I got back out on the road, all I could think about was getting' back out there. I woke up in the morning and thought about the road. I put in a day's work and the whole day long I thought about the road. But when I finally got out there again…"

He paused, wishing he knew how his next words were going to be received. "When I finally got what I wanted and got back out there…all I could think about was you."

"Oh, Clint…thank you."

"I don't want you to thank me—God, don't *thank* me—that's what you say right before you give a guy the 'let's be friends' heave-ho."

That got the first genuine smile out of Taylor. "No. I didn't mean it that way. I meant—thank you for thinking about me. I thought about you too—all of the time."

"Good." The cowboy nodded. "That's good."

Clint pulled a ring out of his front pocket and looked at it. "I couldn't get you one like the last one you had… this one don't even come with a pretty box."

Taylor stared at the ring that Clint held between his thumb and forefinger. It had a thin white-gold band, antique filigree and tiny white diamonds surrounding a small, round yellow stone.

"Clint…" She said his name so he would look up at her. "I don't want another ring like my last one. I didn't want *that* one. I like simple and classic. You should know that about me by now."

"I do. I do know that. I looked at a lot of rings on my errand today…" He looked at her with a smirk. "This is the one that looked like you…to me."

It was such a pretty, sweet little ring. "It looks like a daisy."

He stared at this woman who had changed his life so completely. She'd given him his old life back—and he'd discovered that he didn't want it anymore. He wanted something completely different. He wanted a new life, a different kind of life, with Taylor.

"I wanted you to know that all of those months I was out on the road, our talks meant a lot to me. It didn't start out this way between you and me, but I love you, Taylor. I love you like I've never loved anyone in my life. And I love that little girl. I want to be her dad—I want to be your husband. I want us to be a family."

Amazed, Taylor could only listen to the wonderful words Clint was saying to her. They had grown close, but she hadn't had an inkling that he was thinking of proposing.

"I love you, Taylor," Clint said in a husky voice. "I want you to be my wife."

"And I love you." Those words were so easy for Taylor to say. There was a time that she thought she'd never say it to another man, ever again. But saying it to Clint was as natural as taking a breath.

"And—I think that Penelope deserves to have a mommy and a daddy. She deserves to have a family."

"Is there a yes in there somewhere?"

Taylor laughed. "Yes—there's a yes."

Clint slipped the ring onto her finger and she held up her hand so the fire from the light would catch the facets of the stones. "It's the most beautiful ring I've ever had, Clint. Thank you."

Clint responded by putting his hands on either side of her face and kissing her, long and deep and sweet.

"We had a child, now we're getting married." She wrapped her arms around him and rested her head on his shoulder. "We're doing everything backwards, you and me."

"I don't care which way we do it, sunshine," the cowboy said. "Just as long as I get to do it with you."

Chapter Fifteen

"Why can't you just be happy for me?" Taylor was back at the rental house.

She had finally decided that it was time to face it and get on with life. All of her clothes were at that house, and everything she needed for Penelope was in the nursery. It was time to go home.

She moved in front of the computer camera. "Here… how does this look?"

"I really like that one." Casey gave her a thumb's up. "And, I *am* happy for you, by the way… I just don't understand why you can't put the ceremony off until I can get off work."

Taylor was kneeling in front of her closet looking for a specific pair of shoes. "Because the world doesn't revolve around you, Casey. That's why. Clint and I don't want to wait. We have the license, we have the rings and we have Penny. That's all we need."

"Not one person from our family is going to be there," Casey grumbled. "I should be at your wedding."

"We're going to have a reception down the road after Penny's home. You can come to that." Taylor held up two pairs of heels. "Which ones? These or these?"

Casey leaned into the camera to study the two shoe options. "Those, I guess. But then again, what should one wear to a NICU wedding?"

"Quit being bitter." Taylor threw the rejected pair of shoes toward the closet and slipped on the pumps that her sister had selected. "Okay—here's the best I'm gonna do on short notice. What's the verdict?"

Casey watched her sister spin in a circle wearing a figure-flattering cobalt-blue wrap dress and a pretty pair of embellished heels.

"It's a little dressy for day, I know…" Taylor frowned down at her shoes.

"It's perfect, Tay." Casey finally relented to the reality that her sister had chosen to have a simple ceremony that she wouldn't be able to attend. "You look beautiful. Really happy."

"I am happy." Taylor sat down on the bed next to the computer. "I don't want to wait anymore, Casey. After losing…" Taylor had to stop talking, quiet her emotions and then restart. "After losing Michael, I understood—I mean genuinely understood what it meant to not take one moment of life for granted. I love Clint. Clint loves me. And we both want to give Penny the family she deserves."

"I know… I know. I just wish I could be there to celebrate with you. That's all."

"I wish you could, too. But, you have to work. Nick has to work. Dad has to work. Mom doesn't have to work, but you know she would be passive-aggressive, she would find a way to make me feel badly about my weight and drink too much before noon."

Casey laughed. "All right—you win. Probably better just the two of you."

"I rest my case." Taylor blew her sister a kiss goodbye and then ended the video chat.

It was her wedding day. Unbelievable. She was getting married to her cowboy. They could shred their baby bargain and make an entirely new bargain—to love each other, and Penny, for as long as they both shall live.

"There you are." Clint was waiting for her in the hallway just outside of the NICU double doors. "I was startin' to think that you changed your mind."

"I'm sorry—my sister was upset that we're going ahead with the wedding without her. I had to smooth things over."

Taylor hugged her cowboy and then kissed him on the lips. "Hi, cowboy."

"Hi, sunshine."

"Are you ready?" she asked him. Her skin was starting to feel hot and flushed from nerves, and from excitement and adrenaline shooting through her body.

"I've been waitin' on you," he teased her with a wink. The cowboy seemed nervous, too—he was fidgeting in his white shirt and blue blazer.

"You look mighty fine in that dress…" Clint's eyes made an appreciative tour of the curves of his bride-to-be's body. "Mighty fine."

She made a little curtsy. "Thank you kindly, cowboy. May I say that you are looking very handsome yourself?"

"All day long and twice on Sunday."

They were in the middle of another kiss when the hospital chaplain arrived to perform the ceremony. The NICU staff, who had started to feel like family, would serve as their witnesses and, of course, Penelope would be with them.

The nurses who had been so instrumental in stabilizing and caring for Penelope in those crucial first days of her life had scheduled their breaks together so they could witness the ceremony. Clint held Penelope and proudly stood next to Taylor, who looked more beautiful today than any other day before. How could a poor kid who had barely made it out of high school end up with a classy woman like Taylor? It didn't compute and he didn't care. He was the luckiest bastard he knew—that was all that really mattered.

"And now—the bride and the groom have written their own vows."

Taylor faced her unlikely husband-to-be and hoped that she could remember everything she had planned to say. She wished now that she had written it down instead of trying to keep it "romantic" by memorizing.

"Clint—I love you. You're smart and funny…you make me laugh all of the time and you always try to make me feel good about myself. Thank you for giving me the most amazing gift I have ever been given—our daughter Penelope Melissa McAllister. Thanks to you, I am going to be what I've always wanted to be most—a wife and a mother. I promise to love you and take care of you for the rest of my life. I promise to be faithful and kind and honest. Thank you for being my best friend. I love you."

Clint kissed her hand and she could tell that her vows

had touched him. There were tears in his eyes; those tears only made her love him more.

"Taylor—I have never met another woman like you in my life. You are so beautiful and so loving—you are kind to everyone who meets you. I will never know how I ended up deservin' a woman like you. I'm still not sure that I do. But I promise you that I will spend every day of the rest of our lives workin' to deserve you." He stared into her eyes when he said the next words. "Thank you for Penelope. Thank you for agreeing to be my wife. I love you so much, Taylor. That's all I can really say… I love you so much. I'm gonna do my very best to do right by you and our daughter."

"And now we will exchange the rings," the chaplain said.

Clint slipped a simple white band of white gold onto her finger and she placed a matching white-gold band on his. They stood together, the three of them, mother, father and baby, while the chaplain pronounced them husband and wife.

"You may now kiss the bride…"

For the first time, they kissed each other as husband and wife. Then Taylor said with a happy laugh, "You may now kiss the baby."

They decided to spend their first night as a married couple in Taylor's rented bungalow. It was inevitable that Clint would return to the rodeo circuit once Penelope was given the green light to go home. Bent Tree Ranch was an option as a place for them to live, and one that Taylor had decided to take before Clint had proposed. But now that didn't seem realistic. How could she live in a house where Clint was persona non grata?

Hank refused, to date, to forgive Clint for what he considered to be a betrayal of trust. Right, wrong, good, bad or indifferent, the ranch had to be taken off the table. The rental house was the best available option. She had returned to it, and even though she hadn't yet opened the door to the nursery, she had discovered that it actually felt good to be back in her own space.

For dinner they ordered takeout, and their first night as a married couple involved a hot shower, pajamas and an early night. Truthfully, they hadn't spent that many nights sleeping in the same bed. She had grown accustomed to sprawling out, on her stomach, arms and legs spread-eagled from one side of the queen-size bed to the other. Sharing the bed might prove to be problematic.

After kicking the sheets loose so her toes weren't scrunched up at the bottom of the bed, Taylor gently turned onto her stomach, careful not to pull on the stitches still in place after her surgery. She had to sleep on her stomach or she wouldn't fall asleep.

"I can't spoon. Remember?" she explained. "I get too hot."

Clint was on his back, one leg on top of the sheet, his hands resting on his stomach. "That's okay."

Several minutes of silence passed before Taylor spoke again. "Are you upset that we can't make love?"

He reached over and put his hand on her arm to reassure her. "I want you to be okay. Your doctor said six weeks—we'll wait six weeks. If it's longer, it's longer.

"Don't keep yourself awake worrying about it, sunshine." Clint turned onto his side so he could kiss her on the lips. "We have the rest of our lives to make love. Go to sleep. It's been a long day."

"Good night," Taylor said. "I love you."

"I love you."

Not too soon after her new husband spoke those three words, his breathing steadied and she knew that he had already fallen asleep. It was true that her suggested recovery time post C-section had put the brakes on their wedding night, but it was still kind of a bummer to spend their first night as a married couple in bed and—in Clint's case—asleep before nine. Perhaps it wouldn't feel that way if she weren't the only one awake. But she was. And she was still awake an hour later. Frustrated, she wrestled the sheet and the blanket off of her body and sat up on the edge of the bed. She needed to get up for a while and try again later.

Taylor slipped on a robe, closed the bedroom door behind her and went into the kitchen to raid the refrigerator. Luke and Sophia had left a congratulatory basket filled with all sorts of goodies on their doorstep. Taylor picked through the basket and found a small box of Godiva chocolates.

"Come to mama." Taylor pulled at the cellophane wrapping.

She leaned against the kitchen counter and one by one ate all of the chocolates in the box. Sadly, when she was done, she only wanted more. Another couple of minutes rummaging through the basket turned up some chocolate-covered mints, and Taylor took them to the couch. She couldn't find anything to watch on TV, soon the chocolate-covered mints were gone and she still didn't feel the least bit tired. What was keeping her awake? Why couldn't she sleep when her body felt so unbelievably tired?

There was simply no use avoiding it any longer—the nursery was the last place in the bungalow that she hadn't been able to enter. It bothered her to have a hang-up like that; it didn't matter that she had a legitimate reason. Of course she did. But if she continued to avoid that room—a room that would be a beautiful place for Penny to spend her first year—would it lessen the sorrow she felt for Michael? The pain of losing her son was like a burning pain deep in her tissue that throbbed and ached all of the time. It was always there. It was hard to imagine that it would ever completely go away.

It took some self-talk to motivate her to get off the couch and tackle the elephant in the room that was the nursery. In her mind, it had to be done, and since it was obviously keeping her awake she might as well deal with it right now. At the door of the nursery Taylor stopped, her hand on the doorknob that was cold from the AC vent blowing in the narrow hallway. She closed her eyes in order to stiffen her resolve. She needed to break the stigma of the nursery that she had created in her mind.

"Just do it, Taylor," she whispered aloud.

The door, a door that had seemed like such a heavy weight, swung open as if it weighed nothing. Why was she surprised that everything was as neat as a pin, exactly as she had left it? She had undergone a dramatic shift on the inside, so it was hard to compute that everything else and everyone else hadn't shifted with her.

Taylor walked over to the side-by-side cribs. Which one would have been Michael's? She couldn't know. At the time she had set up the room, she didn't know she was carrying fraternal twins—a girl and a boy. She had only known how much she loved them; she had only known how she was counting the days until she could kiss them and sing to them and hold them in her arms.

Taylor picked up a quilt from one of the cribs and held it up to her face. She breathed in the clean scent and rubbed the soft material over her cheek. With the quilt still in hand, Taylor sat down in the rocking chair. She wrapped her arms around the quilt, hugged it tight and started to rock slowly back and forth. Tears, tears that she had pushed down and pushed back in order to get on with things for Penelope, slid down her cheeks and dropped, one after another, onto the quilt.

"Hey." Clint had awakened to go to the bathroom and discovered that his wife of only a few hours was missing from their bed. "Couldn't sleep?"

When Taylor's only answer to him was a sniff, he knew she was crying and went to her side. He knelt down in front of the rocking chair and put his hand on her knee.

"Taylor…?"

She lifted her head and looked at him. Her cheeks were shiny and wet with tears. When she spoke, her voice sounded off because her nose was completely stuffed from crying.

"Why did God take Michael?" she asked him. *"Why?"*

Clint gently pulled the quilt from her arms and pulled her into his arms for a tight hug. "I don't know, baby. I wish I did, but I don't."

He petted her hair with his hand to soothe her and murmured, "I've got you, sunshine."

Taylor cried in his arms while he held her close. This was the first time she had let him comfort her the way he had wanted to comfort her all along. She was a strong, independent woman—and he loved that about her—but it wasn't always easy to be the man standing next to such a determined, accomplished woman.

"Come on." He kissed the top of her head. "Let's go back to bed."

She nodded. She had achieved her goal and now she believed that sleep would come much easier for her. Now that she had shed her tears, she was able to pay attention to Clint's sleeping attire—or lack thereof…

"You're naked," she said to her husband who was walking beside her in his altogether.

Clint looked down at his naked body, then looked at her with a pleased smile. "I like to let it all hang out at night. Let the cool air get to all of my cracks and crevices."

"I didn't know you liked to sleep in the nude."

"Sunshine…that's not usually the horse I like to race right out of the gate…" Clint winked at her.

After her bout with insomnia, not only did Taylor fall asleep, she slept through the night and late into the next morning. The master bedroom was flooded with light that was flowing through the wooden shutters. Clint's side of the bed was empty and she could hear suspicious noises coming from the general direction of the kitchen. She was more of a consumer of food than a cook—but she was fanatical about kitchen cleanliness. She would rather *never* cook in the kitchen then see a random crumb left on the counter. It was a phobia—she admitted it—and she still liked her kitchen to be spotless. Several more clanks of pots and pans being pulled out of her cabinets and Taylor was out of the bed and into her robe.

"Good morning, sunshine!" Clint greeted her in a booming voice.

Wearing only his jeans and a kitchen towel slung over his shoulder, Clint reminded her of a mad scientist who had just detonated a food bomb in her kitchen. Dirty pots and pans were piled in her sink, and on the counter were egg shells, abandoned pieces of burned toast and balled-up wet paper towels that had been used to clean up spills.

"Hi…" Her eyebrows lifted in horror as Taylor stopped on the other side of the kitchen island. "What's happening in here?"

"I was trying to make you breakfast in bed," he confessed. "But I encountered a couple of minor problems…"

Do not go off on him and ruin this very sweet gesture. Do not go off on him and ruin this very sweet gesture.

"It's the thought that counts."

Clint came around to her side of the island, gave her a good morning hug and kissed her. "This is drivin' you nuts, isn't it?"

"Did you have to use absolutely *every* pot and pan?" she asked him in a half-serious, half-joking tone.

He looked over his shoulder at the kitchen. "I probably could've scaled it back a little, huh?"

She held up her thumb and pointer finger with a half-inch space between them.

"How 'bout this…" He turned her around and hugged her from behind with his chin resting on her shoulder. "I'll clean the kitchen—you go get ready—and I'll take you out for breakfast before we go see Penny. How's that sound, Mrs. McAllister?"

Her hands on his hands, she leaned her head back and smiled. "I think that's a very good idea, Mr. McAllister."

Clint took her to his favorite breakfast spot, the No Sweat Café in downtown Helena. The wait was long, but once they got their booth inside of the homey greasy spoon, the smell of the made-from-scratch breakfast food made her think that their time spent in line was worth it.

"How hungry are you?" Clint asked her.

It hit her—this was the first time in a long time that she felt really hungry. "I am, actually. What's good?"

"Pretty much everything."

Clint ordered the Rocky Montana and she ordered the Tibetan Toad. The service was slow, but their waitress was a sweetheart, the coffee was strong and she kept it coming, and when the food arrived Taylor couldn't remember having scrambled eggs that delicious in her life.

She had eaten her way through the golden hash browns and eggs with green onions, and she was busy buttering her sourdough toast when she sensed Clint's eyes on her. She looked up to find her new husband watching her with a pleased expression on his face.

"What?"

"Nothing." He gave her a small smile. "I just can't believe I'm sitting in the No Sweat Café with my *wife*."

She smiled back at him before she took a bite of her toast.

"You're starting to look like a rodeo wife, you know that?"

She nodded. Her clothing choices had definitely

changed since she moved to Montana. She had swapped her power business suits and heels for jeans and boots.

"Have you thought about when you might go back out on the road?" She covered her plate with her napkin.

"We've been married for less than twenty-four hours and you're already trying to boot me out the door?"

She laughed; it sounded worse than she meant it. "No… I'm just trying to establish a timeline."

"Let's get Penny home and then we'll take it from there." Clint took one last sip of his coffee. "Speaking of Penny—are you ready to go see her?"

That was a no-brainer.

"Always."

Chapter Sixteen

Six weeks after Penelope was born, she was healthy enough to be discharged from the NICU, and Clint and Taylor brought their daughter home to the bungalow. They'd kept one crib for the nursery and donated the second crib to a women's shelter. Michael's crib would help a woman start a new life with her child, and that eased the pain just a little for Taylor. His life had mattered—his life would continue to matter, even if she was the only person who knew it.

"Five minutes!" Taylor called to Clint from the nursery.

Taylor leaned over the changing table and kissed her daughter's bare feet. "It makes Mommy crazy when Daddy makes us late…yes it does…"

It had only been two weeks since they had brought their daughter home from the hospital, but Penny was thriving. She had gained weight, her cheeks and legs were actually starting to look a little chubby and her skin was peaches and cream, just as it should be. Penelope was a happy baby. So easy to love.

"Look at you in your christening gown." Taylor sat her daughter upright after she put on her lacy white socks and her first pair of patent leather shoes.

"Two minutes!" she called out after she checked her watch.

"Why are you yelling?" Clint asked from the doorway. "I'm right here—on time and ready to go."

Holding Penny in her arms, Taylor turned around to see a version of her cowboy that she had never seen before.

"Well? What's the verdict?" Clint turned a little to the right and then the left to show off his new dark-blue suit. She stared at him, shocked, and that shock left her momentarily at a loss for words.

"Clint..." she finally said, "you look so...*different*."

"Different good or different bad?" He glanced down at his suit. This was the first time he'd ever owned or worn a suit.

"Different good... I think." She was thrown by his dramatically changed appearance. He hadn't given her any indication that he was going to shave his beard and cut his hair for the christening.

Clint ran his hand over his new short hair and laughed. "I went for it."

Taylor shook off her surprise, walked over to her husband with their daughter in her arms and kissed him.

"I kind of miss your old look, but you look very handsome like this, too. I just hope you didn't do it for me."

Clint smiled at Penelope, who had wrapped her finger around his thumb.

"I wanted to clean myself up for the pictures. I don't expect I'll stay like this for too long," he confessed while he admired her with his eyes. "You look incredible in that dress, sunshine."

She handed Penelope off to him and self-consciously ran her hand over her abdomen. "I was thinking about changing—this dress is still too tight right through here."

"No. Don't change a thing. You look perfect."

They had scheduled the christening for late morning, to be held at the one-hundred-year-old chapel at Bent Tree Ranch. The pastor at the church the Brand family attended had officiated at both weddings and funerals there, and agreed to come to the ranch to christen Penelope *and* Michael.

When she was planning the christening with Barbara and Sophia, Taylor couldn't bear the idea that Michael would be left out of the ceremony entirely. They all agreed, after a suggestion from Hank, that at the conclusion of the ceremony the family would plant an oak tree outside the chapel in Michael's honor. Taylor loved her extended family for wanting to memorialize her son on the ranch in that way; it made her feel more connected to the ranch and it made her feel more at home in Montana. She had married a cowboy, so chances were very good that she was in Big Sky Country to stay.

The ceremony in the little whitewashed chapel on the hill was simple and poignant. The chapel, with the original thick pieces of stained glass in the windows and the hand-carved pews, was the perfect backdrop. However, Penelope did not appreciate being awakened by the water that was used to baptize her and she cried for the remainder of the ceremony. Barbara and Hank hired a photographer to come out to the ranch; the professional photographs taken that day were one of the christening gifts to their new grandniece.

"Thank you for today, Aunt Barb. The ceremony for Penny and the tree for Michael." Taylor stood next to her aunt while the men in the party, their jackets removed and sleeves rolled up to the elbow, began to dig the hole where the oak tree would be planted. The Brand chapel, built by Hank's grandfather, was positioned on a small hill overlooking the main ranch homestead below. There was a flat, grassy area in front of the chapel and that was where Michael's tree would be planted. The oak tree, for centuries to come, would grow and expand, and create shade and beauty. From many different angles, from the mountains above and the main farmhouse below, Michael's tree was visible.

"We love you, Taylor." Aunt Barb put one arm around her back and hugged her. "We love sweet Penelope. And we love Michael. He's one of our angels now."

"Thank you," Taylor said again.

Sophia joined them with a freshly changed Penelope in her arms. "What a gorgeous day for a christening. That's the perfect spot for Michael's tree."

Sophia handed Penelope to Barb, who had been impatiently waiting her turn to get her hands on the tiny little girl.

In a lowered voice, Sophia said. "I was floored when I saw Brock at the ceremony."

"Clint invited him, but he didn't think Brock would come," Taylor said quietly. "I wasn't sure who he was until after the ceremony."

It wasn't a secret that Clint and his stepbrother hadn't ever gotten along. Brock's dad had adopted Clint, given him his last name and treated him like his own. But Brock and Clint had never taken to each other. They embodied the phrase *oil and water*; the two of them did not mix.

"Is that Hannah?" Taylor nodded discreetly to a young girl sitting away from the rest of the group with Ilsa, the family German shepherd, and Ranger, the family cat.

Sophia's forehead wrinkled in surprise. "You haven't met Hannah yet?"

"Uh-uh."

"Hannah!" Sophia called out to Brock's daughter. "Come meet your cousin!"

Brock stopped digging for a moment to watch his daughter walk over to them.

"Hannah has autism, so she may have some trouble making eye contact…"

Taylor nodded. "Clint told me. He's crazy about her. I think it's sad he doesn't get to spend much time with her."

Brock's daughter was tall and lanky; she had long, wild, curly brown hair that looked as if it could use some untangling and her skin was tanned golden brown from time spent outside.

"Hannah—this is Uncle Clint's wife, so she's your aunt Taylor," Sophia started the introduction. "And this is your new cousin, Penelope."

"Hi, Hannah." Taylor smiled at the girl. "It's good to meet you. I've heard so much about you from your uncle Clint."

Hannah smiled a little, her eyes flitting to Taylor's

face for a second and then flitting away. She gravitated toward Penelope—she leaned forward to look at Penelope's face.

"You can touch her hand, Hannah," Barb said to Brock's daughter. "Feel how soft her skin is..."

Hannah took her pointer finger and ran it quickly over the back of Penelope's hand. Then she turned away from them and headed back to her spot next to Ilsa.

"Don't forget to say goodbye, Hannah," Brock told his daughter.

"Goodbye," Hannah said with a wave of her hand.

"I feel so bad for her," Sophia said with a sad shake of her head. "She used to talk so much more before her parents separated. Her mom lives in LA now—it's been a really hard transition for her."

"My sister is a special education teacher..."

"Is she?" Sophia asked.

Taylor nodded. "She works with a lot of students who have autism and they all have such a hard time with change."

"Would you look at my grandson?" Barb nodded to Sophia's oldest child and her first grandchild. "He's just another one of the fellas now, isn't he?"

Luke had let Danny use his small collapsible Marine-issue shovel to help the men dig the hole. Danny had taken off his little suit jacket, just like the men, and his father had rolled up the boy's sleeves, just like the men. When his father stopped to wipe the sweat off his brow, Danny did the exact same thing.

"We're ready, ladies." Hank had helped dig, but since his mild heart attack the year before, he was opting to let the younger men handle getting the tree into position.

They planted Michael's tree, and there was a spontaneous moment of prayer once it was in the ground. The family encircled the sapling and held hands, forming a complete circle around it, and then they all bent their heads while the pastor said a blessing for Michael. Afterward, everyone was hungry and they went down to the main house for a family luncheon.

It was an emotional, exhausting, incredible day. A day Taylor would never forget.

"Is she asleep?" Clint asked.

Taylor nodded her head instead of answering with her voice. Penny was fussy and tired, but she'd cried every time Taylor tried to put her to bed for the night. Finally, after an hour of rocking, their daughter fell asleep and stayed asleep when Taylor put her back into her crib.

"I've got a spot saved just for you."

Her husband was waiting for her on the couch. While she was putting Penny down, Clint had lit candles and opened her favorite bottle of zinfandel. The doctors had diagnosed her with lactation failure, which meant that even though she had desperately wanted to breastfeed Penny, her milk never came in. The only upside to that disappointment was that she could enjoy a couple of glasses of her favorite wine.

Taylor sat down on the couch next to her husband with a loud sigh. Clint handed her a glass of wine and then held out his bottle of beer for a toast.

"Here's to us," Clint said before he took a swig of his beer.

"To us," she agreed.

"We had an amazing day," Clint said. So many people had come together to honor their daughter and their son. Even Brock had been there with Hannah. Clint had extended the invitation on Taylor's suggestion, but he hadn't figured that his stepbrother would accept.

"I am sorry that your sister wasn't here for the christenings," he said to his wife. He hadn't met Taylor's sister Casey in person—he had video chatted with her before—and he knew how close the two of them were.

"I know—that was hard…for both of us. But she's coming for the whole summer. So that's something for us to look forward to."

Taylor put her empty glass on the table—her free hand holding Clint's hand. The candles, the romantic music—Taylor knew what Clint had in mind. She had gotten the green light for sex from her OB/GYN, but she had avoided any of Clint's advances. To his credit, he hadn't pushed the issue. He wanted it to be right for both of them.

"I want to try tonight."

She had healed, for the most part, physically. She still had quite a bit of baby weight to lose and her stomach had a lot more padding than she wished, but Clint had done his best to make her feel good about her post-baby body. It was her mental state that was the problem. She didn't *feel* sexy in her mind and she was scared. She was scared to be sexual again—she was scared of being in pain—she was scared that things just wouldn't work they way they did before. But, the truth was, they had been married for several months and hadn't consummated their marriage. It was time.

"Are you sure?" Clint had his arm around her shoulders.

Taylor looked into his eyes and saw so much love there. More love and acceptance than she had ever experienced with a man. How unlikely that she had found unconditional love from her high country cowboy.

"I think I'm ready."

Clint tucked her hair behind her ear and then his warm hand rested on her neck. "I want to make love to you, Taylor. But I can wait—as long as it takes."

She leaned into him, put her hand on his clean-shaven face and kissed him. He had turned out to be such a good man, with such a good heart.

"I'm ready," she reassured him.

Clint polished off the rest of his beer, took her hand in his and blew out all of the candles, except for one that he took with them. Instead of taking her to bed, he took her to the bathroom. With the candle as the only light, Clint turned on the shower, adjusting the water to her liking. They both stripped out of their clothing and Taylor was relieved that Clint had thought to bring the candle. Candlelight was so much more forgiving than light bulbs.

Taylor stepped into the shower, letting the warm water rain down over her body. She dipped her head back to wet her hair.

"You're a beautiful woman, Taylor." Clint poured his wife's favorite liquid soap into his hand.

Taylor opened her eyes. "I'm glad you think so."

Clint stepped into her body so he could begin to wash her. His soapy fingers slipped down her shoulders and over her breasts. He was careful to avoid her C-section scar as he ran his hands along the wide flare of her hips and down her thighs.

Clint's strong fingers on her naked, wet skin ignited the smallest flame of desire—she hadn't felt aroused since before their daughter was born. She had begun to wonder if her libido had disappeared for good. But Clint's mouth on her breast, tantalizing her nipple with his tongue, and his cupped hand between her thighs sent pleasure impulses from her erotic core fanning out all over her body.

Taylor closed her eyes with a barely audible gasp of pleasure as her body began to relax. Her husband sucked on her nipple one last time and then moved his mouth to her neck. He licked the water off her neck, nibbling her skin until he gently bit her earlobe.

Clint kissed his wife's mouth, tasting the sweetness from the wine on her tongue. They stood together, their slick bodies pressed together beneath the water, their tongues intertwined in a deep kiss. Clint's hard erection slipped between her thighs and it would be so easy for him to slip inside of her body.

"Oh..." Taylor moaned against his lips.

"I want to make love to you right here, right now..." Clint curled his body into hers and tightened his arms around her.

He wanted to keep going but knew they couldn't. They had agreed to not try for any more children. After Taylor'd had such a rough time giving birth to Penelope, coupled with the loss of their son, neither one of them wanted to risk putting her through another pregnancy. Until he scheduled a vasectomy, they had decided to use condoms.

"Let's go to bed," she whispered.

They dried off quickly and raced to their bed, laughing like teenagers about to have sex for the first time. Clint put on a condom and met her under the covers.

Taylor was on her back and Clint had pulled the blankets over their shoulders. He lay on top of her, careful not to give her too much weight. He kissed her lightly on the lips.

"Are you okay?" he asked.

"Yes."

Clint reached between them and guided himself into her opening. He dropped his head and buried his face in her neck as he slowly, so very slowly slipped into her body. He held himself back, not wanting to hurt her.

"Are you okay?" Their bodies connected again, after such a long time. Clint had to focus his mind to keep his body in check.

She wrapped her arms around him, breathed in the familiar scent of his skin and nodded her head.

"Just go slow," she whispered into his neck. "Just go slow."

Clint moved slowly and sweetly, kissing her, massaging her breasts, whispering words of desire and coaxing her body, moment by sensual moment, to relax and revel in their lovemaking.

"I love you, Taylor," her husband murmured in her ear. "I love you so much."

Taylor wound her legs around her cowboy's thighs and held on to him tightly. She arched her back as he lifted her arms over her head and threaded their fingers together.

"I feel you coming…" Clint groaned into her neck. "God, you feel so damn good, baby. So damn *good*."

"I love you, Clint…" Taylor dug her fingernails into his back as the wave of her climax crested and rolled over her body.

He had held back for as long as he could. It had been

months since he'd had been able to release the sexual tension building inside of him.

Clint's orgasm co-occurred with a loud, *"Ahhhh..."*

"Shhh!" Taylor laughed happily. "You'll wake Penny!"

Clint dropped his head with his own laugh. He pressed little kisses all over her face that ended with a long kiss on the lips. After a quick run to the bathroom to get cleaned up, they jumped back under the covers. Taylor snuggled into Clint's body, her hand resting over his heart. Clint was like his heartbeat—strong and steady.

"We are officially man and wife now," she informed him.

Clint brushed her hair out of the way and kissed her forehead. "Any regrets?"

"No." She lifted her head a bit so she could look at his face. "Why do you always ask me that?"

"I suppose—" Clint pulled her in closer "—this life still don't quite seem like it's meant for me."

"You deserve a great life, Clint. You deserve to be loved and cared for. You always have."

Her cowboy hugged her a little tighter. "I'm not exactly what you would've picked out of a catalogue, now, am I?"

"No," Taylor admitted with a laugh. "That's true. But it just shows you how wrong I was about what I needed in my life."

She turned to her other side and Clint turned with her and wrapped her up in his arms. She was starting to get overheated, the way she always did, but she forced herself to ignore it so she could prolong the embrace. Soon Clint would return to the rodeo circuit and she would miss moments like this. He must have been thinking along the same lines, because he brought up his impending departure a few moments later.

"You know…the rodeo is my business—you and Penny—you're my heart." Clint hesitated before he added. "You know you can trust me when I'm out there, right?"

"Yes. You let me know how much you love me every day," she reassured him. "Do you know how much I love you?"

"Yes. I do," Clint murmured sleepily. "Are you hot yet?"

"Burning up…"

"Do you want me to let you go?" he asked on a yawn.

"Never…" She held on to his arm. "Go to sleep, cowboy."

Penelope wasn't sleeping through the night yet; grabbing a couple of hours of uninterrupted sleep was a luxury.

"Good night, sunshine. I love you."

"I love you more…" Taylor blew out the waning candle on the nightstand and then closed her eyes with a satisfied sigh of happiness.

The past year of her life had been filled with an incredible mixture of joy and pain and love and loss. She had come to Montana to ride the Continental Divide and write the first page of the next chapter of her life. How could she have known that she was about to meet the man who would give her the child of her dreams? How could she have known that she was about to meet the man who would show her what unconditional love was all about? Taylor knew that her life would never be perfect, but finally, her life was perfect for her. Her beautiful daughter was asleep, safe in her crib, right down the hall, and she was safe, right here in the arms of her high country cowboy.

* * * * *

Lynne Graham has sold 35 million books!

To settle a debt, she'll have to become his mistress...

Nikolai Drakos is determined to have his revenge against the man who destroyed his sister. So stealing his enemy's intended fiancé seems like the perfect solution! Until Nikolai discovers that woman is Ella Davies...

Read on for a tantalising excerpt from Lynne Graham's 100th book,

BOUGHT FOR THE GREEK'S REVENGE

'Mistress,' Nikolai slotted in cool as ice.

Shock had welded Ella's tongue to the roof of her mouth because he was sexually propositioning her and nothing could have prepared her for that. She wasn't drop-dead gorgeous... *he* was! Male heads didn't swivel when Ella walked down the street because she had neither the length of leg nor the curves usually deemed necessary to attract such attention. Why on earth could he be making *her* such an offer?

'But we don't even know each other,' she framed dazedly. 'You're a stranger...'

'If you live with me I won't be a stranger for long,' Nikolai pointed out with monumental calm. And the very sound of that inhuman calm and cool forced her to flip round and settle distraught eyes on his lean darkly handsome face.

'You can't be serious about this!'

'I assure you that I am deadly serious. Move in and I'll forget your family's debts.'

'But it's a *crazy* idea!' she gasped.

'It's not crazy to me,' Nikolai asserted. 'When I want anything, I go after it hard and fast.'

Her lashes dipped. Did he want her like that? Enough to track her down, buy up her father's debts, and try and buy rights to her and her body along with those debts? The very idea of that made her dizzy and plunged her brain into even greater turmoil. 'It's immoral... it's blackmail.'

'It's definitely *not* blackmail. I'm giving you the benefit of a choice you didn't have before I came through that door,' Nikolai Drakos fielded with a glittering cool. 'That choice is yours to make.'

'Like hell it is!' Ella fired back. 'It's a complete cheat of a supposed offer!'

Nikolai sent her a gleaming sideways glance. 'No the real cheat was you kissing me the way you did last year and then saying no and acting as if I had grossly insulted you,' he murmured with lethal quietness.

'You *did* insult me!' Ella flung back, her cheeks hot as fire while she wondered if her refusal that night had started off his whole chain reaction. What else could possibly be driving him?

Nikolai straightened lazily as he opened the door. 'If you take offence that easily, maybe it's just as well that the answer is no.'